Nan's Arsonist

A Six Sigma Mystery

Also Available from ASQ Quality Press:

Nan: A Six Sigma Mystery
Robert Barry

The Six Sigma Book for Healthcare: Improving Outcomes by Reducing Errors
Robert Barry, Ph.D.; Amy Murcko, APRN; and Clifford Brubaker, Ph.D.

The Six Sigma Journey from Art to Science
Larry Walters

Six Sigma for the Office: A Pocket Guide
Roderick Munro

Six Sigma for the Shop Floor: A Pocket Guide
Roderick Munro

Six Sigma Project Management: A Pocket Guide
Jeffrey N. Lowenthall

Defining and Analyzing a Business Process: A Six Sigma Pocket Guide
Jeffrey N. Lowenthall

Customer Centered Six Sigma: Linking Customers, Process Improvement, and Financial Results
Earl Naumann and Steven H. Hoisington

Office Kaizen: Transforming Office Operations Into a Strategic Competitive Advantage
William Lareau

Improving Healthcare with Control Charts: Basic and Advanced SPC Methods and Case Studies
Raymond G. Carey

Measuring Quality Improvement in Healthcare: A Guide to Statistical Process Control Applications
Raymond G. Carey, Ph.D., and Robert C. Lloyd, Ph.D.

To request a complimentary catalog of ASQ Quality Press publications, call 800-248-1946, or visit our website at http://qualitypress.asq.org.

Nan's Arsonist

A Six Sigma Mystery

Robert Barry

ASQ Quality Press
Milwaukee, Wisconsin

American Society for Quality, Quality Press, Milwaukee 53203
© 2004 by ASQ
All rights reserved. Published 2004
Printed in the United States of America

12 11 10 09 08 07 06 05 04 03   5 4 3 2 1

Library of Congress Cataloging-in-Publication Data

Barry, Robert, 1938 Dec. 29–
   Nan's arsonist : a Six Sigma mystery / Robert Barry.
     p. cm.
   ISBN 0-87389-626-2 (soft cover, perfect bound : alk. paper)
   1. Six Sigma (Quality control standard)—Fiction. 2. Hospitals—
Administration—Fiction. 3. Quality control—Fiction. I. Title.

PS3602.A7776N367 2004
813'.6—dc22   2004003920

ISBN 0-87389-626-2

This is a work of fiction. Any similarity to places, events, or persons living or dead is purely coincidental.

Publisher: William A. Tony
Acquisitions Editor: Annemieke Hytinen
Project Editor: Paul O'Mara
Production Administrator: Randall Benson
Special Marketing Representative: David Luth

ASQ Mission: The American Society for Quality advances individual, organizational, and community excellence worldwide through learning, quality improvement, and knowledge exchange.

Attention Bookstores, Wholesalers, Schools, and Corporations: ASQ Quality Press books, videotapes, audiotapes, and software are available at quantity discounts with bulk purchases for business, educational, or instructional use. For information, please contact ASQ Quality Press at 800-248-1946, or write to ASQ Quality Press, P.O. Box 3005, Milwaukee, WI 53201-3005.

Quality Press
600 N. Plankinton Avenue
Milwaukee, Wisconsin 53203
Call toll free 800-248-1946
Fax 414-272-1734
www.asq.org
http://qualitypress.asq.org
http://standardsgroup.asq.org
E-mail: authors@asq.org

AMERICAN SOCIETY
FOR QUALITY

To place orders or to request a free copy of the ASQ Quality Press Publications Catalog, including ASQ membership information, call 800-248-1946. Visit our Web site at www.asq.org or http://qualitypress.asq.org.

∞ Printed on acid-free paper

To three nurses in the family, with love:
Paternal aunt Kathleen Barry Todd, BSN
Lieutenant, U.S. Navy Nursing Corps, 1944–1945.
Maternal aunt Amy Flanagan Stockman, RN.
Daughter Amy Barry Murcko, MSN APRN CNAA BC.

Table of Contents

Dramatis Personae

Character	Role
Nan Mills	Chief Nursing Officer and Vice President, General Hospital
Jack Mills	Nan's husband, self-employed software consultant
Jake and Bake Mills	Their twin sons, now college freshmen
Max Lemieux	EMT technician
Norah Washington	Supervisor of EMT service bureau
Rafael (Ralph) Lopez	Chief of EMT service bureau
Heather Jamison	Emergency department nurse supervisor
Marcy Rosen	Nan's administrative assistant, or secretary
Sanjar Subramaniam	Project manager in the IT department and protégé of Nan
Maggie Kelly	Nurse manager of freestanding clinics
Cash Szyvczyk	Husband of Maggie Kelly
Carl Burke	Senior accountant
Vivian Smith	Nurse manager of pediatrics
Josey Walberg	Public relations intern
Tanya Hunt	Nurse manager of burn unit
Sam Collins	Burn victim
Wilma Collins	Burn victim, wife of Sam
Sam Collins, Jr.	Son of burn victims
Marge Collins	Wife of Sam Collins, Jr.
Dr. Alex Sanderson	Burn specialist
Dr. Esther Emanuel	Burn specialist
Claudia Benedict	Nurse manager
Annie Rostow	Nurse manager, third floor post-op unit
Lu & Ray Morgani	Future nurses
Alice Newcomb	Chief counsel
Maddy Nordquist	Nurse, needle-stick project
Dr. Robert Anderson	Chief Medical Officer

This book is a sequel to *Nan: A Six Sigma Mystery* by the same author and publisher.

In the previous book, Nan Mills solved the mysterious death of the Chairman of the Board and town celebrity known as Mr. Bill, some six months before the setting of the present story. Mr. Bill's sizeable estate was bequeathed to the hospital.

While many of the characters are common to the two books, the present book stands on its own; no knowledge of the prior book is required to follow the story.

1

Emergency!

Ambulance sirens. Nan's nurses and the rest of the emergency room crew were trotting to the ambulance entry with gurneys and equipment carts. The ambulance crew had radioed in their assessment of the patients' conditions, which were serious. Burns. Trauma. Not good at all.

Nan felt the professional pull to jump in and get her own hands on these patients, but she knew the crew was trained and ready for this emergency, and she herself more than a little rusty. Nan hadn't worked in the emergency room for at least 15 years. She was there, at four in the morning, doing a routine but unannounced visit to see how things worked in the middle of the night. As head nurse, she was responsible for all the nurses on all the shifts, and she disciplined herself to get out of bed from time to time and go see what was going on. Weekends, too, so this Sunday night visit was part of the game.

Nan had been in the building for an hour, dropping in on each of the units. Each of the night supervisors knew her, and they were used to her showing up. They had their own grapevine, so they all were alerted the moment Nan came into the building. Nan accepted that; when she had worked on the back shifts earlier in her own career, she had had her own grapevine for the same purpose.

Nan's last stop was the emergency room, and things started to happen just as she walked into the unit.

Nan stood back, keeping out of the road of people doing important work. She scanned the area. The burn kits had been drawn from inventory. Fluid bottles were ready. The physician on duty had just hung up after placing a call to the chief of the emergency service to report serious burn cases coming in. Two beds were ready, curtains open. Everything looked clean, prepped, and ready to go.

The ambulances were now at the door, and the patients were being unloaded. The patients were kept on the gurneys they had been strapped to for their ambulance rides, saving a transfer and saving time. The emergency room physician took charge, issuing crisp orders that were repeated back by the nurse or by the orderly at the nurse's side. Or, by both of them. No time to risk misunderstood orders.

Now the patients, accompanied by the emergency room crew, were being rolled rapidly back to the beds. Brisk. Crisp. Competent. Intense. Cool. No, not cool, despite the appearances, clearly heated and full of adrenaline, but under control. Nan was impressed.

A second doctor appeared, and Nan wondered if the second one had been on shift or had been called in. If so, it was quick response, because the accident, from what she had heard, had been only half a mile away. The second doctor got instructions from the first doctor and took over one of the patients.

Nan decided to go in the other direction to see what she might learn from the ambulance crew. She wasn't interested in gossip, but she wanted to know of any gaps in the service or problems or blunders. The best time to find out was before people had time to smooth out their stories and recollections.

Nan did not know the ambulance emergency medical technicians, although they were easy enough to pick out in the throng by the door. They were not hospital employees, being part of the city's emergency service department. She spoke to the first one she came to, a muscular young man with a lot of red-gold hair. "Hello, I'm Nan Mills, head nurse for the hospital." She extended her hand.

"Mrs. Mills, I'm Max Lemieux. I've heard of you, and I'm pleased to meet you, even under these trying circumstances." Max smiled and shook Nan's hand gently, showing that he was aware that he could easily crush her hand.

"Max, tell me please if everything worked the way it should have. I need to hear about operational things that don't go smoothly so that they can be attended to." Nan added a professional sort of a smile and looked Max in the eye to convey that her interest was professional and administrative, not idle curiosity.

"The pickup went by the book. The call-in went by the book. Your folks were ready when we got here. So I guess the operation was the way it should have been."

Max continued, "The accident scene was a mess. I didn't know that manholes caught on fire. Never saw one of those before. The car these two people were in must have been crossing that intersection at the worst possible moment, because they wound up with the back left wheel caught in the manhole opening with the fire going full blast. Their gas tank didn't explode or anything, but the car interior burned pretty much. I don't know why they didn't get out of their seat belts; maybe it all happened in a flash.

"We got there only a minute or two after the fire truck, and the fire in the car was already being doused when we got there. We pried the doors open, cut the two people out, got them in the wagon, started them on IVs, and called it in. Since this was a short run to the hospital, we didn't do much in the way of cutting them out of their clothes, figuring that would be done more easily here. Their faces are covered with soot, so I didn't try to guess whether they were burned all over or just scorched."

"Max, did you find that you had the right tools and supplies with you?"

"Yes, ma'am, we do a lot of car fires, maybe one serious one a week. This was a bad one, but it wasn't the worst I have seen. We do a follow-up report to our supervisor on every one, and then we review comparable cases maybe once a quarter to see if our tools and supplies are proving out."

"That sounds like a good system. Maybe we could learn something from how you do that. Is your supervisor the one to talk to?"

"Yes, ma'am. My supervisor is Norah Washington, and the big boss is Ralph Lopez. I think it's really Rafael, but he goes by Ralph. Either one of them, although I suppose you should start with Ralph so that he doesn't get bent out of shape. They're both good folks, and both of them can tell you how we do things, although Norah Washington is a little closer to the action, if you know what I mean. The switchboard can direct you if you call this number." Max handed Nan his business card, which had his switchboard, direct, and pager numbers as well as his e-mail address. "Why don't you give me a day to tell them that we talked so that when you call they won't immediately think you are calling to make a complaint about me?" Max gave Nan his best grin.

Nan found herself returning the grin, wondering how many of the calls to the emergency service were complaints about Max Lemieux. Not very many, if she didn't miss her guess.

"Of course. I'll wait a day or so and call Ralph Lopez's office and make sure that everybody understands I am just calling to see what we here at the hospital can learn from the way you deal with field planning and evaluations. We try to learn from the experience of others, every chance we get. Pretty foolish not to."

"Amen. I look forward to hearing from both sides how your meeting comes out."

Nan decided to ask another question. "Max, I suppose you've made many deliveries to this hospital emergency room. Is there anything you notice in particular about how our people function? Maybe you notice something better or worse that we do that other hospitals don't do."

Max looked at Nan for a moment, and then he replied with a smile.

"Yes, there is one thing. It takes me back to my days in the Navy. Your people do it, and I don't see it most anywhere else. Your people repeat back every order given to them. That's the way we did it in the Navy, but I don't see it much anywhere else. So, I'm not saying it's better or worse, it's just something I notice."

"We do that throughout the hospital now, because we figure that we have a better chance of avoiding errors in verbal communications in tense situations. We think it helps, and in fact we got the idea from the Navy. It works for you, so we figured it might work for us."

Parting on friendly terms, Max went back to his ambulance and Nan returned to the patient treatment area. She found that the level of controlled frenzy was still the same in both booths. More fluids were being hung. She guessed that the burns were extensive. There was nothing for her to do, but she didn't want to leave without saying at least a word to her unit supervisor, who was herself busy at the bedside of one of the victims. So Nan waited. A few minutes went by, then the supervisor, Heather Jamison, stepped away and crossed the floor in the direction of her desk. Nan matched foot speed and said, "Heather, is there anything you need?"

"No, Nan, we've done this before. I am sorry I'm occupied with a patient when you're here. Is there anything you wanted to see me about? Any complaints?"

"I just dropped in to see how things are going on the night shift. I seem to have caught you in a real emergency. You and your crew seem to be on top of things, and I'm just going to be in the way, so I'll leave. If there is anything you would have wanted to talk about, call me later or send me an e-mail. And no, there are no complaints. Not from me. I'm impressed by how you're handling things here."

Heather Jamison smiled at Nan. "Let's do this another time. You're always welcome, even at four in the morning, and even when we have burn victims. With or without complaints. I'll take a rain check on the call invitation, if you don't mind. Something I'm thinking about but not ready to put into words yet."

"Anytime. The door is always open, and the e-mail always gets through."

2

Breakfast and TV News

It was five in the morning when Nan got home. It was too early to stay up, too late to get much sleep, so she stretched out in her reclining chair in a robe and closed her eyes, hoping for the best. She was soon fast asleep and stayed that way until she was awakened by Jack, rummaging in the kitchen. Nan stretched, pressed her eyes shut for a moment, and arose to face the brave new day.

Having worked enough long nights in his years of software development to know what Nan was going through, Jack tried to maintain a perfectly normal morning routine, not making any unnecessary noise, and not tiptoeing, either. He turned the small kitchen TV set on to the local news channel.

"Good morning, Jack, my love," said Nan, with one eye open.

"Good morning, Nan, bright morning star."

"No poetry, if you please, at least not until I am awake." She smiled the best smile she could muster.

They got breakfast onto the table and sat down to eat, one eye on the television screen. The lead news item was a story about the fiery car accident.

"Jack, I thought manholes were for water and sewer pipes. I didn't know they could burn like that."

"Cities have everything running under the streets. Water. Gas lines. Sewer lines. Telephone cables. Fiber-optic cables. Electric lines. Everything that hangs on a pole out here in the suburbs is run under the streets downtown. Sometimes in separate tunnels, sometimes in one big tunnel. That's in addition to old railway tunnels and mine tunnels and other things long forgotten."

"So, what do you think? Gas line explosion?"

"We'll probably hear the facts later on, once they can get a fire inspector down into that manhole. Or else people will start calling

"Marcy, I know the hospital has its own water tower on top of the main wing, but I don't know how long that would last or even if they keep it full. That's something to ask later on, I guess. You told me you're getting telephone calls, so the telephones must be working."

"I've only had calls from inside the hospital. I don't know if the city lines or long-distance lines are working. I guess we could call somebody and ask if the phone rang or not.

"If anything is out, I'm sure they are working on it, so let's not do anything just for curiosity's sake.

"Is there any report on those burn victims who came in last night?"

"They were both transferred to the burn unit after being stabilized in the emergency room. One is in very bad shape with lung damage from breathing in the hot air or whatever it was, and the other is not good but not that badly off. They don't expect the one patient to survive the day."

"Okay, Marcy, that happens in lots of fires. The victims can die from inhaling superheated air even if they are not burned at all. I'd like to go see them later in the morning. Let the unit know that it is just a courtesy call, because I was here when they came in on the ambulance last night, just a follow-up. Nothing special or formal. No red carpet.

"Also, here's the card of a technician from the city ambulance service I met here at the door last night. Please wait a day and then call that switchboard number to ask for a get-acquainted meeting with their boss man, Rafael Lopez, who goes by Ralph. You can mention Max's name there, on the card, but the important thing to get across is that it's not a complaint. I just want to get acquainted and learn how they do things."

"Yes, ma'am."

Nan thought for a moment. Nan knew that Marcy had a network of informal family members that seemed to extend to the reaches of the city, as well as every department in the hospital. "Marcy, do you have any cousins who work there?"

"My husband knows some people there through the Rotary or one of those service organizations. He belongs to all of them. They usually have city administration people as guests or speakers, so he knows a lot of them. If not, I'll ask around. There's always somebody who knows somebody."

"I don't recall seeing too much about the city's emergency service in the newspapers."

"They get some notoriety every year when it's salary time, because they don't get paid the same as the firemen. But they seem to settle every year, and then nothing gets said until the next contract negotiating time."

"What else for today?"

"The executive staff meeting is canceled because too many of the executives are out of town, so that saves a couple of hours right there.

"Sanjar Subramaniam asked for a meeting, and Maggie Kelly asked for a meeting. So I booked them both, subject to your being available."

"Sanjar has certainly done well, hasn't he? It was, what, seven months ago that he talked his way into being our computer geek, as he called himself, and now he's manager of special projects for the information technology department."

"Mrs. Mills, Sanjar was always very good, and then when he was in the spotlight that first week you were here, he was bound to get some attention from his senior management."

"My husband, Jack, thinks the world of Sanjar. Jack got Sanjar onto some technical society committee so that he can become better known in those circles. They stay in touch on some topics that I don't understand but they seem to.

"So, I'll be happy to see Sanjar. Did he say what topic he has in mind?"

"He said it was to update you on his projects that involve your department, but no particulars.'

"Okay. What does Maggie Kelly want?"

"She said the topic is career planning. No details."

"Well, that sounds managerial as opposed to social, but she is welcome in either case. We'll find out what career planning she has in mind. And whose.

"Anything of great import in the mail log today, Marcy?"

"No ma'am. The usual. I took care of the bumf—isn't that your word for paperwork?—and logged each item so you'll know what I did in case somebody asks."

"Fine. That gives me some time to think about career planning before Maggie gets here, and I didn't get as much sleep as one ought to at my age, so let's keep the activity level a little on the low side today."

"Yes, ma'am."

Marcy turned and left the office. Nan indulged herself with a cup of tea, leisurely scanning through the mail log and observing that Marcy had indeed cleared away the day's bumf. What a precious person she was! She brewed a good cup of tea, too.

Nan tried her Internet browser to check on the nursing association committee she was on, but the browser couldn't make the connection. She tried a news site, and got the same thing. Maybe the Internet was fouled up by that manhole fire. Well, it wasn't anything urgent, so she would wait and see.

4

Maggie Kelly's News

Marcy brought in Maggie Kelly, who was manager under Nan in charge of the four freestanding clinics in the city and the project leader on some of the department's Six Sigma projects.

"Hello, Maggie. Tell me what's on your mind," said Nan, with a friendly smile to the most promising of her direct reports.

"Nan, I've got a career decision to make, and I'd like your advice."

"Tell me all."

"Well, this started the first week you were here. We were talking about how to get ideas for the clinics, and we decided I should contact the head of the nearest big-city clinic group and see if we could do home-and-home visits. That eventually led to their sending a couple of people here, and then I went there, and we traded some ideas, and we got to be acquainted on a personal as well as a professional level."

"Yes, I recall having lunch with the visitors once when they were here."

"They told me they were very impressed with you and the way you run the nursing service. I suppose they were just being nice, but then they didn't have to say anything and besides they were right. Still are right."

"Well, knowing them has led to the career decision I mentioned a moment ago. They were contacted by a headhunter looking for a body to run a string of clinics belonging to a group of physicians, and they gave him my name. He contacted me, and after some interviews and visits, they have made me an offer to be the operations manager and head nurse for their clinics.

"The clinics are a lot like the ones we run here, but there are more of them, and they are willing to pay me a lot of money. It would

"We now have the receptionists booking the patients who call in or who need follow-up appointments. That's better than the first-come, first-served system we had before, which had lots of people waiting in the waiting room for hours. I don't think we have figured out very well how to mix the scheduled and non-scheduled patients, but I think it's better than it was before. Maybe the new manager can figure that one out better than I have, so far. We have computerized records of appointments and wait times, so maybe a computer jockey could figure it out, now that we have some data."

"Maggie, one of the first things you told me when I first went to visit you at a clinic was that you had rounded up some retired general practitioners and persuaded them to give your young physicians a little backup. Is that still going on?"

"Yes, they still come in. They see themselves as the coaches of the next generation of general practitioners, and they don't mind getting out of the house or away from the shuffleboard court for half a day a week. That's what most of them contribute. The young physicians who work these clinics like them and put up with them and pay a little attention to what they say, and so it all works out. The patients seem to like to see the older doctors sitting there nodding their heads while the young doctors are waving their stethoscopes around, so it calms the patients down, too."

"Do you think they will continue to contribute their time if you leave?"

"I am going to make a point of telling them that they owe it to me to continue what they have been doing for six months. By that time, they will have forgotten I was ever here, and they will keep it up indefinitely."

"Your nurses are following the practice of repeating verbal orders back to the physicians?"

"Yes, and nobody seems to mind at all. I thought maybe the older physicians might think it rude, but they tell me it helps them remember what they just ordered so they can write it down. That's a benefit I hadn't thought of when we started. The younger physicians say it makes them feel more important, hearing their orders said back to them. I suppose it all goes back to those John Wayne submarine movies, but our female physicians seem to like it, too."

"What else were you leading for us?"

"For a couple of days, I was the leader on the needle-stick reduction project, but I passed that along to Vivian Smith in the pediatrics unit, both because they have more needle-stick incidents than we do in the clinics and because at the time, as you will recall, they needed something to put their energies into. I have followed their work, but

I don't suppose I know any more about it than you do from the reports you are getting on the project."

"Yes, Maggie, I have been getting favorable reports.

"Well, Maggie, is there anything else?"

"Nan, I've always been a little on the independent side, which I suppose is how I wound up running the clinics. I don't think I was ever anti-organization, but I always felt that I was bumping up against the organization. That is, until you came here. You have given me the confidence to do what I think I would have done anyway, but with you I feel that the organization is on my side, maybe for the first time. I treasure that, which brings me back to feeling that I am not repaying your leadership very well by leaving the hospital."

"No, Maggie, that's the best payment you can give me. It makes it that much easier for me to recruit and retain good nurse managers, because they see career paths that don't stop at my door. Opening doors, opening career doors, that's part of my job. You are the first to leave, but I know there will be others.

"Let's just make sure we stay in touch, because you will eventually have nurses working for you who need a career move to a large hospital, and I will have nurses and supervisors and others who need a career move in your direction. If we get a network covering our region, we can do better career development for more people together than we could ever do alone. Let's see if we can get that to work over the next few years."

Maggie reached forward and put her hand on Nan's. "Yes, Nan, I want that very much.

"Now, it may seem churlish to ask for a favor at this particular moment, but I don't have many moments left. Do you think I could get Sanjar to tell the telecommunications people for my new employer how to set up the video stations the way he set yours up? Yours was the first, and now all the nursing managers have that setup, and I see some of the other departments are doing the same thing. The vanity lights around the PC screen, the dimming of the room lights, and the microphone and camera setup are all just great. It does a lot to promote video conversations, and with my new clinics spread out all over the state, I am going to need all the help I can get to promote video over airplane and windshield time."

"Sanjar doesn't work for me, and I can't speak for his management. As for the general idea of helping out, I can tell you that Sanjar spent a Saturday afternoon at our house, helping Jack do the same kind of setup for his home office stations. It works fine, too. Then Jack got our sons to do the same thing in their college room so we can do video family conferencing, and they were able to do it themselves after being instructed. So my guess is that Sanjar will help you informally. If you need something more formal, you can hire Jack, and I will make sure he gives you clergy rates."

"Maybe I can hire your sons during their next vacation break. We will have a number of these to set up, and the group is buying up clinics at a steady pace."

"Well, they're old enough to take on some responsibility, so maybe that would be the right solution. In any case, why don't you start with the real guru, Sanjar, and see what he says."

"Okay. Nan, I have butterflies about taking this new job, but you have lightened the load, more than you can possibly know.

"I do very much want to stay in touch. I'd like to keep up with your Six Sigma projects, and I'd like to contribute back to you any projects that turn out well for my new clinics. So it won't be a one-way street."

"We can certainly do that through the nursing society. That way there is no possible conflict of interest or collusion between competitors. We can set up a special interest group on Six Sigma projects, if there is not one already in existence. Then our results will be available to everybody on an open basis. That's good for the whole community, and besides, I don't think our competitors are awake anyway and won't pick up on this for years to come."

Maggie responded with a big smile. "Yes, you're right. Not all organizations are ready for change, even in the positive direction.

"Nan, you've been wonderful. I will ask Marcy about resignation forms and send you an official notice and a termination date this afternoon."

Maggie rose and extended her hand. Nan took the hand in friendship, and then the handshake became a warm hug with just the hint of a tear in every eye.

Maggie turned and left.

Nan sat at her desk and reviewed the bidding. The fact that Maggie had been sought out by a headhunter did not surprise Nan, given the overall shortage in the supply of nurses and nursing managers all over the country. Headhunters had become as common in nursing as in high-tech. Nan repeated to herself the positive message she had given Maggie just moments before, that Maggie's leaving would free up slots for rotating and promoting promising new people, and Maggie's landing a good job would make it that much easier for Nan to attract high-potential people to her department. So there were positives.

There were also negatives. Maggie had been the first name on Nan's own replacement table, the one immediately qualified to fill

Nan's position. That had been a little bit of a stretch, but Nan had figured she would have a year or two to round out Maggie's professional
experience before she herself got the boot or got run over by a bus.
Even then, you never know how somebody is going to respond to a
big, new job. It had been enough of a shock to her own system, the first
couple of weeks in this job, and she had all the support in the world to
fall back on. Which had been a good thing, because it turned out she
had needed all that and more that wild first week. Maybe it would
have been the same for Maggie.

So, Nan made a mental note to update her replacement table.
The table itself didn't matter, but the thought process did, because
succession planning was a part of her job she couldn't delegate or
ignore.

Then Nan addressed the practical aspects of replacing Maggie at
the clinics. That job required more independence of thought and
action than any of the other services, which was why it was a great
stepping-stone to higher management. Not everybody likes that
kind of a job, even if they think they do. Independence means a certain degree of loneliness, uncertainty, and professional risk taking. It
was good experience for anyone aspiring to higher ranks, but it was
not easy duty.

Nan could use the hospital's job posting system and leave the
whole thing to those who chose to apply. Or, she could name somebody to the position and ignore the job posting system. Or, she could
post the job and twist some arms.

Maggie's leaving triggered another thought. If the best of her
managers were going to be picked off by headhunters, Nan would
have to make sure that she herself picked off the worst of her managers and supervisors and regular employees. Nan would need to
cull the flock. Otherwise, the whole roster would be filled up by the
lowest performers, which would not be good for the hospital and
would cause the better people to flee all the faster. Nan admitted to
herself that she didn't know how to do that, and what's more, if she
waited for some inspiration on how to do it, she would never do it.
So, she'd have to do it without any inspiration.

The hospital had a reputation for being a paternalistic, or perhaps maternalistic, employer, rarely firing anybody, and then only
for blatant cause. Not for weak performance.

How would the Japanese do this? Nan guessed that they knew
how to shame people into resigning with just the slightest hint. That
didn't seem promising for an American crowd.

At the very least, she ought to balance the top and bottom
actions, thought Nan. I'll take care of my lowest-performing manager

this week. Nan knew the name immediately, and she didn't like the thought of having to do it. It was a rotten thing to have to do, which is probably, she thought, why so many managers never get around to doing it.

Well, she had given herself a week, so at least she could talk it over with Jack before she pulled the trigger. She would also have to tell the personnel veep, who would very likely give Nan several dozen reasons why the person needed another chance.

Nan hit the intercom and asked Marcy to come in. She did, steno book in hand. Marcy had a new pot of tea in the other hand.

"Marcy, Maggie Kelly is giving notice this afternoon that she will resign. I suppose she told you that when she left my office a few moments ago. Had you heard any rumor to this effect before this morning?"

"No, ma'am. No word on any grapevine. She did tell me on the way out just now, when she stopped to ask if there is any hospital form to use for resignation. I told her there is no form, a regular letter will do, addressed to you and to the vice president of human relations, and to give a final date but no discussion of reasons for leaving. What she told me is that she had a great job offer and couldn't afford to pass it up. I have not heard any word that she was unhappy here, so I think she is telling it straight."

"Did she say when she would have the letter back to us?"

"I told her to have it here by noon. I figured if I said three o'clock, she'd just spend three more hours composing the perfect letter."

"Noon will be fine. Call my managers together for a stand-up staff meeting at one o'clock. Principals only, no substitutes. Call Maggie and tell her she is not to attend. That will hurt, but that's the way it has to be.

"Then let nature take its course on going-away parties for Maggie. I know she is popular with everybody, so there will be lots of parties. Just put the word out to make sure any and all parties are over with inside of a week.

"Marcy, I want you to know that I am happy for Maggie. We have more good people at her rank than we will ever have openings above her rank, so we have to lose some of them to the outside world, even to our competitors. Pyramids get skinny at the top.

"At the same time, I am feeling as sorry as can be for myself, losing the best manager we have and a great person to boot. So, this is a happy professional moment and a sorry personal moment. I hope I can keep the two separate for the next week or so.

"Maggie's is a key management position, so I will need to have a courtesy meeting with our human resources veep early on."

"I booked that for four o'clock this afternoon."

"Good. We'll need to make some public announcement, and I think I mean not just to our own troops, although they need to get the word immediately from us, or else they will believe what they hear on the grapevine, and who knows what the grapevine version is going to be. I think I also mean we should put out some statement to the public or the press, making the case that this is good for the hospital and therefore for the community at large. Any ideas on how to do that?"

"There is a young person working in the public liaison office who has something of a name for that kind of writing. An intern named Jocelyn Walberg. Josey. She's my niece, once removed. If you give her the bullets of what you want to convey and let her draft something, maybe you'll like it. Or maybe she will give you some ideas that you can use."

"Okay, that might be helpful. Will you set something up?"

"Josey is out here by my desk, waiting to be called in."

"Let it be now. Also, on a related topic, I am going to be doing the replacement table over, and I am going to be taking some action this week to make sure that in losing our best people we don't wind up with nothing but slugs. Well, you know we don't have any slugs, but we do have some who are more sluglike than others. I don't know yet what I am going to do. Do you have any cousins in that line of work?"

"Better you shouldn't ask. That's a hard thing to do in a large organization. It's easier to shuffle people around than it is to put them out on the street."

"Okay, Marcy, tell our new young friend Josey Walberg to come talk with me.

"Before that, though, did you tell the burn unit that I want to pay a call?"

"Yes, they are on notice. I'll give you 15 minutes with Josey and then that will be a good time to go to the burn unit. I will line everything up."

After Marcy left, Nan sat quietly and thought about how to handle the personnel matters. It was something she would have to teach herself to do. Something worth learning.

5

Josey Walberg
Introduces Herself

"**M**rs. Mills, this is Josey Walberg," said Marcy, bringing in a thin young woman with a guiding grip on the elbow.

"Hello, Josey. Please call me Nan."

"Yes, ma'am," replied Josey Walberg, who looked as ready to call Nan anything other than Mrs. Mills as she was to walk on the ceiling. "Marcy called me to say that you would like a little help writing a press release. I'm the intern press flack, so that's right up my alley, although I have never done the kind of executive statement that I think you have in mind. Of course, I don't know what you have in mind, but whatever it is, I will put heart and soul into it."

Josey produced a nervous smile, revealing butterflies in great profusion.

Nan smiled. How long had it been since she herself had been thrown into a situation that was both alluring and yet dreadful? Josey seemed to be harmless, at least, and thinking through the matter with her might help Nan frame the issues in her own mind a little better. Not the same as talking things over with Jack, but that was something special.

"Josey, I want to say to the world out there that one of our very best nursing managers is leaving our service to take a responsible senior position with a clinical group. It's a promotion for her, without doubt. Those are the cold, cold facts. I also want to say that while we are sorry to lose her on a personal level because we all like her so much, we are happy for her professionally. We are also happy to see that other organizations think that we have good people worth poaching. The message is that this is a good place to work because you'll be noticed by lots of potential employers."

"I get the idea. You're like the head coach who is pleased to see his assistant coaches get head coaching jobs on other teams, because that makes it all the easier for him to hire new assistant coaches."

"That's it exactly. You surprise me with the sports metaphor."

"Simile. Excuse me, that was reflexive, I didn't mean to be correcting your grammar, especially with something everybody gets mixed up." Josey blushed just a little around the edges. "I have five older brothers, so I know more football than anything else in the whole world. I even took courses in sports journalism and thought of that as a major for quite a while. So with me, you get football."

"Do you have enough to get started?"

"Yes. I'll get name, rank, and serial number from Marcy. I'll draft something by two o'clock. This isn't the sort of thing that will interest the television news shows, so all we have to do is to get it out in time for the morning papers. That could be midnight if you want to do it that late. Five o'clock this afternoon will probably be more convenient for everybody. Any press statement has to be vetted by my boss, the press liaison, and maybe by the chief counsel. So we should plan on maybe four o'clock this afternoon for final copy from you.

"I'll draft something. If you use some of my draft or none of my draft, I will do the legwork on it either way. Lot of legwork in this game. Keeps me trim."

Nan tried to recall the last time anyone had corrected her grammar. Eighth grade? Fourth grade? She thought for a moment of explaining the bathtub curve of effectiveness to Josey, and then she decided that was just defensive blather. Josey had nailed her on her grammar, so score one for Josey.

"Okay, Josey. Tell Marcy the timeline you just set out so that she can set my calendar up to match. I look forward to seeing what you have to say."

6

Nan Visits the Burn Unit

Nan walked to the burn unit to check on the status of the two patients admitted as a result of the manhole fire, the patients she had seen in the emergency room several hours earlier. Nan went to the unit desk to make sure her staff knew she was there, and she asked for a status report on the patients.

Tanya Hunt was the supervisor in charge of the unit for the day shift. Tanya welcomed Nan to the unit and stood ready to answer questions.

"Tanya, please tell me the status of the two patients admitted overnight. I was there when they came in, and I'm curious to know how they are coming along."

"Nan, the two were admitted as John and Jane Doe, because they didn't have any identification that we could find in any legible form. Since then, the police have identified them by working backward from the automobile they were driving. So we now identify them as Sam and Wilma Collins, mid-forties, Caucasian. Local address. What I am told is they were simply driving home after visiting friends out of town, and they were on the shortest route, right through town, which makes sense in the middle of the night when there is no city traffic.

"The situation is not good. Mrs. Collins was driving. She inhaled a lot of superheated air and has suffered extensive lung damage. She is on the watch list, and her doctor does not expect her to survive the day. The family has been told. In fact, the family is in with her now. The family consists of one son, also named Sam, and young Sam's wife. They are both in the room with Mrs. Collins.

"Mr. Collins is a little better off, but he has a lot of lung damage, too. His doctor expects him to survive the day, but if he gets a touch of pneumonia or any other lung problem over the next few days, he's not going to make it. Even if he does survive the week, he is going to be severely incapacitated for the rest of his life. The doctor has talked with the family about marking him 'Do Not Resuscitate.' No decision yet. I don't know how a family can ever make that decision, particularly when they are looking at the loss of Mrs. Collins almost for sure."

"Tanya, that's rough. Is either doctor here? I don't want to intrude on anything the doctors are doing."

"Mrs. Collins's doctor is Dr. Sanderson, who is just down the hall. I can get him for you. Mr. Collins's doctor is Dr. Emanuel. She is not here presently. I haven't seen her for an hour or so, and I don't think she is signed in. She may have gone to get some sleep."

"I will speak to Dr. Sanderson if that is convenient for him. Thank you."

Tanya Hunt stepped quickly down the hall to fetch Dr. Sanderson. Alex Sanderson, a trauma and burn specialist, was well known to Nan as a highly skilled and dedicated physician specializing in a very difficult field. He was established in his field and added a lot to the prestige of the hospital's burn unit. Esther Emanuel was Alex Sanderson's star pupil and protégée, so the Collinses were getting the best physician care that the hospital could offer.

Dr. Alex Sanderson approached with a shuffle that revealed a level of fatigue. He had his rumpled look, wearing a smock that was long on wrinkles.

"Nan, I am happy to see you, even in trying circumstances. I suppose you want to know about Mrs. Collins. All I can tell you is that she is beyond what medicine can deal with today. Lungs are burned. She also has extensive skin burns that would put her in jeopardy even if the lungs were okay, which they aren't. I have her heavily sedated, and I regret to say that I don't think she will wake up.

"Her son and daughter-in-law have been in with her. I've been down the hall with another patient, so I don't know who's in with her now. I marked her family-only, given her condition.

"Esther Emanuel is treating Mr. Collins. She went over to the bunkroom to take a nap, which I prescribed for her myself. We can get her back if you think it necessary. I don't know the particulars about Mr. Collins, since Esther has been treating him and not me, but from what I heard Esther tell the family, he's in serious condition but not anywhere near as bad as Mrs. Collins. You'll see as much on the chart, I think.

"So, what can I do for you?"

"Alex, I happened to be here last night when the Collins couple were brought in, so I just came by to see how they stand. I can say a few words to the family if you think it would help, or if not, I will stay away. They are not people I know, so I might just be seen as meddling."

"Tanya has handled the situation very well, from what I can see. Sad to say, the nurses in this unit get some practice in dealing with awful situations. Even so, if you would just say a word or two to the family, I don't think they would take it amiss. If you have anything perfect to say, write it down so I can use it myself next time."

"All right. I'll go in with Tanya and say what little I can say."

Nan went to the unit desk, where Tanya Hunt was doing some paperwork. "Tanya, I'd like to speak with the Collins family, and I'd like you to go in with me so they won't get confused about who's in charge."

"Yes, ma'am," replied Tanya Hunt, who put down her ballpoint pen and led Nan to the room of Mrs. Collins. Tanya opened the door gently and stepped inside, leaving room for Nan to follow her in and close the door.

Tanya Hunt introduced Nan to the family as head nurse for the hospital. Nan extended her hand to the younger Mr. Collins.

"Mr. Collins, I would like to express my deepest feelings of concern for you in these difficult moments. I have just spoken to Dr. Sanderson, who told me that the situation with your mother is very grave. I want you to know that Dr. Sanderson is a most wonderful doctor who has spent his entire career dealing with such difficult cases, and he is the most famous of the doctors for this unit. He is known all over the world. Your mother is in the best hands that she can be in."

"Well, can you tell me that my mother got the best emergency room care in those vital few minutes when she first got here to the hospital?"

"In this case, I can tell you that myself, because it happens that I was at the emergency room door when your mother and father were brought in. They both got prompt and intense care from the moment they left the ambulance. If you would like to bring in another doctor to review the record, I will make sure that you have full access to all information. Dr. Sanderson will give you some names of specialists in the field if you like. Or, the medical society can do it if you don't want to ask Dr. Sanderson. I can get you the phone number."

"I suppose my question sounded to you like a threat of a lawsuit. I'm not on my best behavior, I guess, what with Mom and Dad both at death's door. I don't have any basis for a complaint, and from what I have seen since I've been here, which is a couple of hours now, everybody has been just super with Marge and me. It's not your fault my folks got in a car fire. I can't imagine it was their fault either. I can't even imagine that this is all happening. So, I am sorry about what I just said. I didn't mean it that way."

"The offer stands. You have an awful situation to deal with right now. I can't do much about any of that, other than to tell you that your

you have been doing this past month since you were promoted to project manager. Congratulations again on your well-deserved promotion. Now that I don't see you every day, I wonder what you're up to. When I did see you every day, I didn't know what you were doing either, but I knew it was something good."

"Mrs. Mills, those few months when I was working under your direction were the most satisfying of my professional life. Now that I have this management position, I have to supply that direction myself, and I am not so sure that I am putting each foot properly. When you were directing things, that was never, ever a question in my mind. So, I am pleased with my promotion, but I am finding it to be a little bit lonely."

"I understand that feeling, Sanjar. I understand that feeling. It's all right to feel isolated, but please understand that you are not alone. Not here. You are surrounded by friends and admirers. That includes me. It even includes my husband, Jack, who thinks the world of you. Maybe that's because you and Jack have software interests in common while our sons think software is old hat. They are into nanotechnology, whatever that is."

"Youth must deal with the future, and perhaps nanotechnology for their generation will be what software and computing have been for the past one or two generations. And thank you for your kind words.

"You asked what I have been doing. There are a couple of ongoing IT projects that I have picked up, and that indeed I was working on before. Wishing to follow your lead on professional development, I found a web-based Six Sigma course for healthcare, and I have been pursuing it as time has permitted me to do so. I now have reached the Green Belt rank and I have hopes of reaching the Black Belt rank in the next few weeks. This has been quite easy to do, having seen you apply the fundamental principles of Six Sigma before my own eyes. The course is more formal and has some statistics in it, but I have learned statistics in my formal education. The interesting aspects are not mathematical statistics but rather how to get some good out of very little data. That has triggered some thinking, and that's always welcome to someone like me.

"Part of that course has dealt with the reliability one should expect from the infrastructure of an institution such as a hospital. The electric supply, the heating-ventilating-air-conditioning, or HVAC in shorthand, the computer data networks, the communications systems. Other than perhaps the HVAC, these infrastructure systems connect the hospital to the outside world, and it is not enough to have a reliable system inside the hospital, although that is certainly a necessary ingredient. It is necessary to consider all the things that might go wrong outside the hospital.

"So, I took it upon myself to investigate the electric supply and the communications networks outside our own building. You may recall that a study was started for the systems inside the building, and that that was caught up in the unfortunate business with the demise of Mr. Bill."

"Yes, Sanjar, I remember that all too well."

"After that Mr. Bill business, the IT department hired a consultant to complete the study and to include the wireless and radio networks as well as the wired networks in the hospital. So, I started with that, and I have continued the engagement of that consultant, who, I must say, did not think very much of the idea of studying the public networks. His opinion was that they were much more robust that anything inside the hospital, and that I was wasting his time and my own.

"That was a cautionary moment for me, I must tell you. I came very near to agreeing with him and conceding the point. However, it was a rather small study project, and I had the time to do it, so I have continued."

"Last week, I wrote a small memo to document the first thing I had learned. It had been my intention when I made this appointment with you, that was last Friday, to give you a copy of the memo and ask you to consider it from a Six Sigma viewpoint.

"Now, however, we have been overtaken by events."

Sanjar paused and seemed to be drawing from deep within himself the courage to go on. Nan tried to find the right intensity of smile to encourage him onward.

"Mrs. Mills. I started with the part of the infrastructure I know best, which is the data networking part. The hospital has two separate and distinct suppliers of network services to the outside world, to connect to the backup site across town where we archive the databases, and to connect us to the Internet. The consultant had studied these as far as the hospital wall and had declared the system to be quite satisfactory because there are no common elements between the two.

"What I had done was to get the two network service vendors to come in with their route maps, both together, and then we got in a car and we drove each of the routes. This took a great deal of preparation on the part of the two vendors, because they do not own their own physical copper and fiber over the entire length; they rent capacity from others. Now the first thing we established is that they do have two distinct sets of subcontractors, so there was no obvious weak spot. However, the subcontractors have their own subcontractors, and it took a good bit of digging by each of them to come up with the physical routings.

"We drove the routes, all in one car so that nobody could complain later. We found that the physical copper and optical fiber are distinct, all the way. However, both vendors have their networks running through the same conduit and tunnels under the city streets for approximately one mile. For that length, one exogenous event might wipe out both networks, and the hospital would be without data communications to the backup site and to the outside world.

"The unhappy proof of this was that overnight fire. While our loss was trivial in comparison to the loss of those unfortunate ones who were caught in the fire, that same fire was precisely where the two vendors had underground facilities in common. That fire knocked out both data networks. That was perhaps six hours ago, and the data networks are still out of service. We have been promised a solution, probably some temporary work-around patch, within 24 hours. Our business computer systems are thus at risk for these 24 hours, and if anything goes wrong here with those computer systems during this blackout period, we could have a serious business mess on our hands."

Nan thought for a moment. Here was her protégé, who had applied her own principles and discovered a flaw in the data networking, who has a memo recording his findings and necessarily giving a black eye to the people who had been in charge before, and the same to their consultant. He has a memo with a date on it, a date several days before the fire. Will that mean he will be blamed for failing to take action in those few days, even though others had not taken action over a period of years?

"Sanjar, what has that consultant done in the light of your discovery?"

"On that point, I am pleased to respond that he has made a complete change in view. One hundred eighty degrees. What you might call an epiphany, if I may use that cultural term. He is now most vociferous that we look at all the outside networks to seek common failure elements and hidden flaws. On that small point, I am gratified."

"What has he had to say today, in the light of this fire?"

"I have not been in contact with him directly today, although he did leave a voice message saying that the fire vindicates our position. You see that he now says it is 'our' position, even though some few days ago his position was the opposite."

"Well, having the consultant on your side is better than having him oppose you," she said. "Who has seen your memo inside our organization?"

"I had discussed the topic with my boss, the vice president in charge of information technology, when I first took up this matter. I did not pitch it as a big deal, but rather as a logical continuation of the in-building study he had started himself. I did not make a big deal out of it, and it was not given any serious management review. Just one additional small study to go on the stack of other small studies. Since the day we discovered the commonality and weakness of the routing through the tunnels and conduit, I have not had meetings on the subject with anyone, that is until this very meeting with you. I did circulate my memo to my boss and to the other managers on my level with a big DRAFT stamp across the face. It had been my intention to bring the topic up at our next staff meeting and to invite others to review the matter as a sort of peer review. This is a new finding for our organization, and I did not want to be seen as tilting at windmills."

"How long did you think you would have to circulate and review the memo before taking any action?"

"On a logical basis, there was no hurry. We have had the common tunnel condition for years without deleterious effect. The likelihood of anything happening in a few weeks or even a few months was exceedingly small, based on the record. So I did not see a reason to rush this through. After all, there was a significant chance that I had missed some important fact and that I was wrong. I wanted to be wrong, if I was wrong, on a quiet basis if I could do so.

"Looking back on things, I can see that that was a management error even though it was not a mathematical error. You would not have been so timid as I proved to be."

Sanjar sat with his hands in his lap, looking at his knees. He was clearly disappointed with himself. Did he have any cause to be? Nan didn't think so, but she agreed with him that she herself would not have been timid. It was not in her makeup to be timid. But then she had a husband with a prosperous business to fall back on if she made some blunder that got her fired. It suddenly occurred to her that she had never met Sanjar's wife or even heard mention of her. That's something to rectify, but not at this moment.

"Sanjar, you found the facts, you drafted a memo and circulated it for review. You did not hide the facts or bury the memo. You did a rational calculation and concluded that the time scale for action was weeks, not seconds, and acted accordingly. I think you have a defensible position. That doesn't seem to be timidity to me. I don't think others will think so, either."

"You are kind to say so. Let me complete my story by telling you that this morning, when I learned of the fire and of the knockout of our two data networks, I wrote a letter of resignation and put it in the in basket of my boss. I have heard no response from him."

"If he has any sense, Sanjar, he will tear it up.

"All right," Nan said, "let's see what to do next. Have you been mapping the other networks, too?"

"Yes, ma'am, at least we have the telephone and cell phone vendors organized for a routing trip this evening. I don't know what to expect, since I didn't expect to find common conduit on the previous ride. The electric supply we are doing tomorrow morning. I accelerated the schedule on that just now.

"Of course, I may not be the one carrying out these studies, if my resignation is accepted. Even so, it seemed to me that these studies are worth doing, particularly in the light of that fire last night."

"Yes, that fire certainly says that the other studies need to be completed quickly.

"What have you done with the HVAC?"

"I have done only one thing, applying one of your rules of complexity. I looked at the building engineer's drawings for the HVAC system, and even though I have some technical training in engineering and have looked at some large number of drawings in my time, I found them too complex for the kind of study I had in mind. They are so complex that only an expert can understand them. But the point of the study is to discover things the experts themselves missed, and so we need drawings that a non-expert can understand. Using what I think you call the NASA rule, if a civilian can understand it, then the expert will understand it without error.

"I am not saying that as well as you say it. I will try again, if you permit me. The expert will make a rare error in reading a complex display or diagram, but he will never make an error reading a simple display. And the standard for simplicity is that a civilian can understand the display. So, to reduce the likelihood that the expert will make an error, require the expert to provide civilian-level displays. Now, did I say it rightly that time?"

"Yes, that's it. A display is simple enough when a civilian can understand it. And experts make fewer errors with simple displays than they do with complex displays, and the experts themselves are always the last to ask for such simplicity because they think they don't need it. Yes, that's it."

"So, I directed the building engineering group to produce three-dimensional views of the air ducts with color coding, showing how they run through the building. That is not so difficult for them to do, because they have all the information in their computer records. These will be schematics, which is to say cartoons, not precise drawings, but they should show how the ducts are connected, where the dampers and cutoffs are, and where there are common elements, particularly when there should be no common elements. And the same for the electric circuits that control the dampers and fans. They finally decided that they might find such drawings to be of some use in explaining their work to civilians, and so they said they would do it as time permits."

"They may feel a little more urgency today."

"Perhaps, but I thought it wise to let them discover that for themselves so they can take credit for having been on top of this issue, at least as far as it falls within their scope of responsibility."

"Sanjar, there is never any difficulty in getting things done if you don't mind letting others take the credit. That's the iron law of organizational theory."

"Mrs. Mills, that law seems to apply in all cultures."

"Okay, Sanjar. What's next?"

"I have called the data network vendors and told them that they will need to eliminate common elements when they repair their networks and have given them 30 days for a complete solution. I have notified our purchasing department that suitable changes will be needed in those contracts. And I just told you about the actions on the HVAC, the electric supply, and the voice communications networks."

"You didn't mention our radio links to ambulances and helicopters and, I guess, to the police department. Is that part of your study?"

"I had it in mind to do the telephone networks first and the radio networks thereafter. That may have been an error. In any case, I planned to do the radio links later on."

"Okay, Sanjar. I understand."

Nan sat there for a moment, looking at Sanjar. "You realize that if I make a phone call to your boss to make an argument for you, that might work against you in the long run."

"Yes, I realize that."

"Therefore, let's not start there. Please consider asking for an immediate appointment with your boss to tell him that you have already taken corrective action on the data networking and that you have accelerated the other parts of the project. In other words, get in there and tell him your story before he hears other versions from other parties. You're the one who put your finger on the problem, and you need to be the one who identifies the solutions. This is not a time for timidity. Manners, yes, timidity, no.

"Just remember, it's only a job. You can get another job in two minutes. It's not your life. Do the job the best you can, and bag the rest.

"If I know your boss at all well," Nan continued, "he will want to see something on paper. Do you have a project file or some such?"

"Yes, ma'am. I have a Gantt chart and milestones and schedule dates. We are actually a little ahead of the scheduled dates. I will print out that chart in color, using your simplicity/complexity theory, and I will make the point, if I can do so, that we are following the plan he had previously approved. And that he was right to authorize this program, because it puts him in the driver's seat as events have proven him to be right."

"Sanjar, you may have learned a little too much about managing your boss in so few weeks. You're right. That should do it. Get in there and tell you boss how smart he was and still is."

"Yes, well, he is a good person with many responsibilities. The question he will need to ask himself is whether he was wise to put this particular matter in my hands and whether I have let him down.

"So, I will brace him, and we shall see what we shall see. As you rightly say, it's only a job, it's not my life. Perhaps your husband will put in a word for me somewhere if I find myself pounding the pavement."

"Sanjar, you are going to outgrow your job with the hospital, and someday you may need to look outside in order for you to fulfill your career. When that day comes, Jack and I will both do what we can to get you introduced in the right places. When that day comes. Right now, let's straighten out this networking mess and make sure we smoke out any difficulties in the other networks.

"Let me know how you come out."

"Yes, ma'am." Sanjar stood and bowed, walking out backward while continuing the bow. Nan, having seen this many times over the months, still wondered how he could do that without falling over or walking into the door frame.

8

Maggie Tenders
Her Resignation

At noon, Maggie Kelly arrived at Marcy's desk and delivered her letter of resignation. Maggie gave Marcy a big smile and thanked her for her many kindnesses over the preceding months.

Marcy checked the letter against what she thought the hospital would require, found it in conformance, and carried the letter into Nan.

Nan read it at a glance, since it was only one short paragraph, and found that it was all business. No flowery prose on the thrill of having worked here. No recriminations over slights felt. Just I resign and thank you very much. The letter was addressed to Nan and to the vice president of human relations. That was good.

Okay. Given that it had to be done, it was well done, and quickly, too.

experience to be a positive for anyone contemplating higher positions within the hospital or elsewhere in life.

Again, no response. Nan hadn't expected any.

Vivian Smith then asked if it would be okay if they had a dinner or something for Maggie Kelly. Nan responded in the affirmative.

Claudia Benedict chimed in with the information that the people in the four neighborhoods where Maggie had clinics were already organizing parties for her starting Thursday night and running through Sunday, so anything they wanted to do would have to be at lunchtime or one of the next couple of evenings. That triggered animated discussions about one date versus another. Nan broke it up by asking them to let her know what was decided and to tell her if contributions for a small gift were to be taken up. And would someone please get some snapshots for her scrapbook.

The meeting was over. It had been brief. The lack of chairs helped.

Before anyone actually got as far as the door, Annie Rostow, manager of the third floor unit, asked, "Nan, can I say two words about the staph infections project? I think it is of interest to everybody."

Nan, replied, "Okay."

The march toward the door ceased. Everybody's ears perked up at the mention of staph infection, which kills thousands of Americans in 6,000 hospitals every year, an average of perhaps one fatality per month per hospital.

Annie said, "Most of you know, I think, that I have been sponsoring a little project with the North High Future Nurses Club, who have sent two volunteers to us after school hours and on school vacation days for the past couple of months. We gave them clipboards and told them to follow our nurses around to keep track of whether the nurses were changing gloves, sterilizing stethoscopes, and so on between patient contacts. Since we get the post-op patients, a lot of them are in delicate condition and more susceptible to staph infection and other kinds of bad things than healthy people are. For the first couple of weeks, our nurses were all on good behavior because these two kids were following them around, but after they got used to them, the nurses went back to their habitual behavior, and we started to get some data. "

A voice from the crowd by the door asked, "Who are the kids?"

Annie replied, "The Morgani twins, Lu and Ray."

The same voice asked, "Did they walk around together or did they follow different nurses?"

"When they were both with us at the same time, they went around together, but sometimes we had one of them, sometimes the other."

Nan felt bound to ask the sort of twin-question that people had been asking her all her life, "How did you know if you had the one or the other?"

Annie knew the answer to this one, "Well, Nan, they are brother and sister. Their real names are Lucrecia and Cesare Morgani."

That same voice from the crowd asked, "You mean to tell us that some parents were weird enough, or should I say cruel enough, to name their own kids Lucrecia and Cesare? Is the middle name Borgia?"

Another voice from the throng helped out: "The Borgia family was Spanish. They would say *loo-cra-THEE-a* and *they-ZA-ray*.

First voice, with hand gestures: "Morgani isn't Spanish, it's Italian. So they are *loo-CREE-chi-a* and *CHAY-zah-ray*. "

Annie looked like she was worried that this was getting away from her, and she hadn't made her point yet, so she jumped back in. "Lu and Ray are American kids, that's why they call themselves Lu and Ray. Let me just say what I wanted to say, and Nan, I'm sorry this is taking a little more time than I thought it would.

"Lu and Ray have gotten enough data to show that we need to do something, so I told them to think of some other organization that does this better than we do, so we can learn from others and not have to invent everything ourselves."

Nan nodded enthusiastically and said, "That's good thinking."

Annie showed a visible measure of relief with that positive response, and continued. "Lu and Ray did so, and now they want to make a recommendation. They told me what they want to do, and I would like to ask you, Nan, and you the managers of the nursing service to give them half an hour to make their pitch."

Nan scanned the room and found most of the eyes on herself. That was to be expected, so she said, "Yes, I'm game. I will ask Marcy to set up a time convenient to you, the Morgani twins, and as many of the rest of you as we can corral at any one time. We'll tape it or something for those who can't make it, the way we usually do."

Annie said, with a smile a little warmer now, "Thank you, Nan. I will work with Marcy to find the time that suits your schedule."

Nan smiled in return, asking herself why any experienced member of her little team such as Annie Rostow would be nervous about bringing up a topic such as this in a staff meeting. Do I frighten my own people? Do I bite heads off people who make the slightest upset in the routine? I hope not.

Nan had been vaguely aware of the future nurses project but had not paid it any mind since it was started a few months before. She had had no expectations, and she was pleasantly surprised that anything at all, let alone a recommendation for reducing staph infections, had come from it. She needed to make a note in Annie Rostow's file.

"I look forward to hearing what these young people have to say, Annie, and I am pleased that you gave them a chance to do something creative. We need all the future nurses we can get. I don't know what the protocol is with North High, but if there is a faculty sponsor or something, please see if an invitation to attend the presentation would be in order, or maybe I should say you might ask the Morgani twins if they would object if you invite the faculty sponsor."

Annie nodded. "I'll check with Lu and Ray. The subject came up when we first started the project, but I don't know how they would feel about bringing in their faculty sponsor. I'll ask. They did ask if they could videotape it."

"That's a sensible request, but having outsiders tape meetings inside the hospital might raise eyebrows with the legal beagles. Why don't I have the public relations department get involved and have them have somebody tape it? That way our lawyers can see it before it is released. The public relations office may want to use this to get a little favorable publicity with the high school and the community at large and maybe help us recruit future and present nurses."

Annie looked intently at Nan for a few seconds and then said, "Maybe we should think this through before we publicize the fact that our nurses are not perfect in their adherence to our own anti-infection guidelines."

Nan considered this carefully and replied, with a serious look, "Annie, you have an important point. Hospital fallibility is a common enough topic in our newspapers, but here we will be talking not about hospitals in the abstract but about this hospital in particular, the place where our community brings their family to be treated. We would not fool anybody if we said we never make a mistake, but do we want to go to the other extreme and tell people that we *do* make mistakes? I guess I would tell everybody the truth, that we do the best we can and try to learn something every day so that we can do it better.

"But I can't speak for the hospital on this, so I will notify Alice Newcomb, the chief counsel, and let her decide if we release a tape of the meeting or if we have any publicity at all.

"We can have the twins do their presentation anyway, so go ahead and set that up. I'll tell Alice what the schedule is and ask her to give us a ruling with enough lead time that we can set up the taping and the high school faculty contact, and all the rest."

Annie said, "Thank you, Nan" and left with the throng, all of whom seemed to be interested in getting a preview of the Morgani report from Annie on the way out the door. Annie didn't appear to be giving anything away.

Nan went to Marcy's desk and gave her instructions to set up the meeting and make the other contacts. Marcy's steno pencil flew across the pad.

10

Josey Writes a Draft

Marcy brought Josey Walberg into Nan's office on the stroke of two. Marcy had a good hold on Josey's elbow, and Josey was carrying several sheets of paper in long uncut format. "Welcome back, Josey. What have you got so far?"

"Well, Mrs. Mills, please consider this the first draft. You may want to can all this and do your own. But, you asked for it, so here it is.

"The first thing is a blurb for the business page. Short and to the point. We'll make a stock photo of Maggie Kelly available to them, too. You know how they put in little head shots of the new bank vice presidents and that sort of thing. This will be one paragraph. You will see that it is written from the perspective of the new employer, Clinical Care. I have been in touch with them, and they are willing to let us draft. That's not unusual. They will probably follow up with some kind of a longer release in a day or two. They don't want to get too far ahead of when they will actually have Maggie on their premises so that they don't look dumb if Maggie gets run over by a bus between now and then."

Nan read the short paragraph at a glance. Clinical Care announces the appointment of Ms. Margaret Kelly-Szyvczyk as vice president of clinical services and nursing, blah, blah, blah. Ms. Kelly-Szyvczyk was formerly manager of clinical services for the city's General Hospital. Blah, blah, blah. That looked to be harmless enough, and she guessed that Josey had spelled Kelly-Szyvczyk right, but that was only a guess. There was a black-and-white thumbnail photo of Maggie in which she looked pleasant and professional.

Josey handed over a longer sheet to Nan. "This is a story we'll plant on the business page, which will probably get about two inches on the front page of the section and a jump inside. They may run it on the health page if they are doing a health feature page tomorrow. That's their call, and it will look about the same anyway."

Nan read this one more carefully.

Key Personnel Move at General Hospital. (date) Mrs. Nan Mills, Vice President of Patient Services and Head Nurse for General Hospital in our fair city, announced today that her manager of clinical services will be leaving the hospital to take a promotion to head of clinical care and nursing for Clinical Care, a fast-growing chain of clinics now spreading across this and neighboring states. That person is Mrs. Margaret Mary Kelly-Szyvczyk, known to one and all as Maggie Kelly, who is a graduate of North High and of the State University School of Nursing. Maggie Kelly holds a master's degree in nursing and is a board-certified advanced practice registered nurse. Maggie Kelly is married to Casmir "Cash" Szyvczyk, who is also a product of our city and a graduate of North High and State University.

Maggie Kelly's selection for this important post is no surprise to those who have followed her success with General Hospital's neighborhood clinics, which Maggie has been running for the four years they have been operating in their present mode. These clinics serve a vital need in our poorer neighborhoods, where medical services can be few and far between. Maggie Kelly has won over the people of these neighborhoods, many of them immigrants with scant English and the same ills and cuts and bruises that all of us are heir to. These clinics have become more than a place to get iodine and tummy medicine, they are a key element in the assimilation of new immigrants. At these clinics, people find receptionists from their own neighborhood who can, among them, cope with almost any language. They get friendly advice on organizing their family healthcare, on getting their papers straightened out, and advice on dealing with family issues in the American way. No more back-of-the-hand from hubby.

If Maggie Kelly brings that same gift to her new, expanded role with Clinical Care, then the state's gain is more than our city's loss.

"Replacing Maggie Kelly," says Mrs. Mills, "is both a burden and a joy. Maggie Kelly did such a good job organizing these clinics and leading our service in a number of special projects that, while we will miss her terribly as a friend, it will be now much easier for her replacement to continue and to expand what Maggie has started for us. While no one in our department is a replacement for Maggie Kelly, we have a number of bright and

energetic nurses who are ready for challenges that come their way, and this is an opportunity for some changes in assignment. Maggie Kelly is a friend as well as a colleague, and I wish her well in her new position. I think the neighborhoods where Maggie's clinics are located will miss her, and I think they will also wish her well."

Clinical Care is privately held, although according to statements made (see link) by Clinical Care management, an initial public offering (IPO) of stock is anticipated within the year. Developments will be chronicled on our business pages.

Nan put this sheet down on the table and looked at Josey Walberg with a quizzical smile. "What next?"

Josey handed over another uncut sheet. "Here's something we will place on the local Internet sports site. We have some access there."

Knowing something of Marcy's reach when it comes to access, Nan thought it best not to ask what kind of access that might be. She took the new sheet and started to read.

Coach Makes First Move.

Nan Mills, who lit up the wires six months ago by solving the crime of the year, the murder of Mr. Bill, well-known car dealer, sports aficionado, and Chairman of the Board of General Hospital, and doing it so well that General Hospital gained a contribution of more than a hundred million dollars, is back in the news.

This time, Nan Mills is playing the head coach game. She has placed one of her assistant coaches as head coach for another team. That's the way the best of the best do it, because they know that helps them recruit new assistant coaches from the best talent available. Nan has placed Maggie Kelly as head coach, which is to say head nurse, with a rival team, Clinical Care, a multistate chain of clinics.

This gives us two birds for us game watchers to watch, Nan and Maggie both. Will friendship abide, or will we see the start of a new team rivalry? If football is any guide, look for rivalry, and soon.

Meanwhile, chalk one up in the win column for Nan Mills."

Nan put this last sheet down on the table and looked at Josey to see what else might be in store.

"Mrs. Mills, the local television gab show will want you on Wednesday or Thursday, probably Wednesday. I don't know if you see that show, since you are at work when they are on the tube. It runs for an hour at eleven o'clock in the morning. They have four women as hosts, of whom usually two or three are present on any particular day. They gab about current events of interest to women. It's pretty popular, and what they cover gets follow-up attention in the newspapers and on the radio talk shows."

"I have seen that show a few times, Josey, but I don't follow it regularly. They seem to be fairly responsible in how they treat topics. Would they really want me, if this topic catches their eye, or would they want Maggie?"

"If they thought there was a rift, they'd try to get you both on at once so you could pull each other's hair. If there is no rift, then they will want you because you are staying in the city and Maggie is leaving. That's my guess, anyway."

"How do I prepare to be on a television show like that? They ask questions that would never occur to me."

"You don't want to overprepare. A professional politician can do that and look polished. An amateur only looks wooden. So don't prepare by memorizing bullets. The only important thing to do is to make sure you have your own makeup person there and the right wardrobe. I can take care of both of those for you. I know some people. You know if you are dressed right and made up right, you'll feel right. As for answering questions, just say what comes out of your mouth. If you're boring, they won't ask you back. If you say something outrageous, they will want you back the next day."

"Tell me about wardrobe and makeup."

"I'll arrange a fitting for tomorrow morning, here. The makeup just takes time, so we should figure on your being available from seven o'clock Wednesday morning on. Four hours will go fast, you'll be surprised. This takes some getting used to, because they will make you up in shades of green and orange that you won't believe, but you will look great under the lights. You'll see the hosts are made up in the same shades, once you are on the set."

"Josey. I approve all your copy. I approve of your plan. I trust you to get internal clearances on everything. Call Marcy or me if you get stuck anywhere. Now tell me how you are dealing with Maggie Kelly. She's the key ingredient here, and I don't want her to feel victimized by our publicity campaign."

"I showed her all this copy and said it was early draft stuff. She read it through, looked a little overwhelmed, and said it was okay with her. She was pleased that I had been in touch with her new employer."

"Have you shown this material to the chief counsel and the head of personnel?"

"They are on my list. What they will see is the press release from Clinical Care. We are not actually making any press release in our own name at all. I will tell them that we expect to be contacted by the local press and will give them background information and spellings of names and so on. Public record stuff, no inside skinny. Since our executives don't have any say-so on Clinical Care's press release, these will be courtesy calls only."

"Okay, I see that logic. Now tell me that you are doing this with the knowledge and direction of your superior in the liaison office."

"Yes. She is tickled pink. We don't get to play these press games very often, and everybody in our line of work salivates at every prospect for doing do.

"There is nothing illicit, naughty, or fattening in any of this. We are feeding stories to the press, and that's a lot of what press liaison is. This one has a little more human drama and human interest, so the press will jump at it. Anyway, that's what I figure to happen. It might go some other way, or there might be another big story tonight that blows this off the radar screen. That's out of our control, although we will try to fight back in a few days in that happens."

"Okay, Josey. I am pleased with your work. Keep me or Marcy posted. Let me know if you hit any snags. Thank you for your work."

For the first time in the few hours Nan had known her, Josey Walberg lit up her face with a bright smile. "You're welcome. We are here to serve. I will keep Marcy posted. Look for this in your morning paper."

They shook hands. Josey nearly ran out of the office.

Nan thought to herself that she would have to find out if Marcy had engineered this, or if Josey had earned herself an internship in the hospital's press liaison office on her own merits. Either way, Nan was impressed with Josey's prose and her grasp of how to do her job. Josey was hardly any older than her two twin boys, which got Nan to wondering how they strike outsiders. Her sons impressed Nan, but she was hardly an impartial judge.

11

Needle-sticks

Just before three o'clock, Marcy came in to Nan's office to remind her of her scheduled meeting with the manager of the pediatrics unit, Vivian Smith. Marcy told Nan that Vivian was bringing along one of her nurses, Madelyn Nordquist, called Maddy.

At the stroke of three, Marcy ushered in Vivian Smith and Maddy Nordquist, both of whom greeted Nan and took places at the small conference table in Nan's office.

"Welcome, Vivian. Welcome, Maddy. I don't think you have been to this office before, Maddy."

"No, Nan, this is my first visit. I like your décor."

"Everybody says that, but I had nothing to do with it. It has something to do with the video conferencing cameras, or so people tell me."

Vivian chimed in with, "Nan, we know you have to say things like that, but we're on your team. We can live with the truth that you have a better decorator than the suits do.

"We're here to talk about the needle-stick project that was started by Maggie Kelly for her clinics and was then transferred to us because we have more action in the needle-stick line. Maddy has been our lead on this, and there are some developments. Will it be all right if Maddy reviews what's been going on for the past few months and then tells you the news?"

Nan replied, "Sure. Proceed as you see fit. I have the whole hour reserved for this topic if you need that much time."

Vivian said, "I don't think we need half that much time, but let's get started so we don't run out. Maddy?"

Maddy began. "Nan, I was amazed to find out, even with all the OSHA rules and all the new syringe designs out there today, that needle-sticks and other kinds of sharps are still a big deal. Maybe we do it better than we used to, but I found one government website that says there are 600,000 needle-sticks a year. And, I found another one that says 800,000. Everybody keeps a log like we do, so maybe those are real numbers. They say about a third of those are during the disposal phase, even though we have disposal boxes in every room and on practically every cart, right near anyplace that we do injections. I went there to find out what the real rules are, and I found one place that says syringes cannot be recapped at all, and another place that says that if they are recapped, you can't use two hands. That's so you don't jab yourself if you miss the cap, so I can see that part. So, that's where I started. Then, I tried to figure out how we stand here.

"We have needle-sticks, but not in great numbers, so I didn't think it would make any sense to try to do a statistical analysis. So rather than looking at the instances that went wrong, I looked at the standard way we are supposed to use these protected needles to see if those poka-yoke rules were being followed.

"The way I heard it, poka-yoke has three rules. The first is that the task should be designed so it is more apt to come out right than wrong, the second is that the person should be able to tell right away if they did it wrong, and then the third rule is that the person should be able to fix it on the spot. So if we hit on all three of those, then we have a well-designed way of doing the task."

Maddy paused. Nan thought about what she had just heard. Then, in best John Wayne submariner style, she said it back to Maddy.

"Maddy, you have the poka-yoke part right. Now, let me see if I captured your point on the statistics. You are telling me, I think, that you simplified and accelerated your study by looking at the normal task and not just at the errors. You increased the denominator, if I can hearken back to my statistics classes in college."

"I don't know much about statistics, Nan," replied Maddy, "but I think we are increasing both the numerator and the denominator. I think we can stay out of the statistics altogether if we stay with the poka-yoke model."

"Okay," said Nan. "I think I understand the point, so let's go on. Tell me what you did next."

Vivian spoke up, "Nan, you caught on quickly. Let me inject here, if I may use that term, that it took me awhile, and I think it took Maggie awhile, to understand this. Maybe you and I are more used to doing post-hoc reviews than Maddy was, so we were stuck in thinking about error investigations. The way Maddy saw this is extremely useful, because we can think about the normal operations and then, when appropriate, look at the exceptions as exceptions. I never would have gotten to this line of thinking myself. So, I think

Maddy's study has served an important purpose already. It's like doing statistics without bothering with any data."

Nan thought for a moment. "It is, isn't it? I think I would have started where you did, Vivian, and I don't know if I would have gotten to Maddy's position or not. So, tell me what happened next, Maddy."

"I can't very well watch myself when I give injections, so I made a point of watching other nurses give injections. All kinds. Big syringes, little syringes, arm, leg, buttocks, the works. Injections, and also extractions of blood and blood gases.

"Then I dug out the training videos that the vendors had sent us back when. They are mostly marketing fluff, but they finally get around to the point of saying 'Hold the syringe this way. Fix the patient's position that way. Approach the site thus and so. Inject, withdraw, and so on, until the patient is released.' Of course in the training video, the patient is always docile and cooperative.

"Then I went back and watched real nurses giving real injections again.

"You realize, I hope, that I was doing my regular nursing duties over this period. I am only talking about those opportunities I could find to watch another nurse give an injection when I had a moment free to watch. That was maybe a few percentage points of all the pediatric injections over the past few months. Still, I saw a few, every shift.

"Now, we started by applying poka-yoke to the syringes with caps over the needle. We looked at three different times in their use, carrying the syringe to where the patient is, doing the injection, and afterwards.

"The cap certainly reduces the number of sticks during the first phase, because with the cap on, the chances are zip that anybody is going to get stuck while the syringe is being carried around. No nurses sticking themselves, no passers-by getting stuck. So, that's good. This follows the first poka-yoke rule because it is easier to do it right than to do it wrong, because to do it right, you just have to leave the cap on.

"During the injection phase, the cap is off and the situation is the same as it would be if there never had been a cap. If the nurse is distracted or if the patient lurches at the wrong moment, somebody gets stuck. So, there is nothing in the cap design that helps at this point. That's bad, but on the other hand this is the phase where the nurse is paying the most attention, particularly in pediatrics because the kids buck and jump and flail around when they see that needle.

"During the post-injection phase, the nurse has to use one hand to press gauze on the site to promote coagulation. If this was an injection and the syringe is going to go into the disposal box, then the nurse does that if the box is close enough. I found that a lot of times it isn't—there just isn't any way to get a disposal box next to the bed or where the work is being done because the nurse's arms are only so long. If the cap were in a holder of some kind so the nurse could line the syringe up with the cap and recap it with one hand, and I have seen holders like those in other departments, that would work, maybe. But, from what I see, that is just as awkward in real situations as reaching for the disposal box.

"So we thought about this last phase and wondered if there isn't some other way to get the needle out of the way without using a hand. We didn't have any good ideas, but we had some mediocre ideas. For instance, suppose the nurse stuck the needle into a big cork after the injection, which she could do without having to try very hard if the cork were on the tray. Then, the syringe can't do any harm to anybody until the nurse can reach over to the disposal box. Do you see?"

Nan nodded in the affirmative.

"We don't think that that is the right long-range solution, but we thought if we talked that up and maybe tried it out, then somebody who knows something would get interested and come up with a good solution."

Maddy paused, looking for feedback from Nan.

Nan provided feedback on cue, "That's very clever. Did you try it out?"

"Yes. It works. Or I should say, it works when the nurse remembers to jab the needle into the cork after the injection. It's one more thing to think about at an instant when there's a lot going on. Maybe if nurses got into the habit, they would remember to jab the cork."

Nan asked, "You surely thought through the cleanliness questions here. Are there any sterilization questions here?"

"We don't think so. We gave that a lot of thought. The cork deal comes in only after the needle is already contaminated, We toss the cork after every use, which we probably wouldn't need to do."

"I understand cork, Maddy. Did you try other materials?"

"We fiddled around with Styrofoam, but we didn't try a lot of different materials. The corks we use are easy to jab, and it's practically impossible to push a needle all the way through, which would defeat the whole thing if the needle point got through the cork and stuck out the other side. And the needle sticks to the cork. The Styrofoam didn't adhere very well.

"Anyway, we thought that if we could find one solution, people who know about this stuff would find lots of others. We just wanted to get the thought planted that we could do better at least in the third phase, after the injection."

Nan said, nodding and presenting a supportive smile, "Yes, you showed that there is at least one solution. Finding more solutions is going to be simpler.

"Vivian, what's the next step?"

"One of the factory reps for one of the syringe companies was in the unit a couple of weeks ago and saw what we were doing. He caught on in a hurry and called back to the factory to see if he could get anybody interested in following up. He came in Friday and said that they would like to field test some designs of their own that have some of the characteristics of our cork, and could they field test them in our unit?

"I told him that he could save himself a lot of time by asking if their new design, or designs, make it more likely that the nurse will do the right thing than the wrong thing, that any goof will be obvious, and that the nurse can correct a problem if something goes wrong. Simple as that.

"He said that they knew all about that, blah, blah, blah, which I don't believe for a moment or they wouldn't be making them the way they are. But at least he now understands what questions we will ask if they bring something for us to test."

Nan said, "Vivian, I think you did him a big favor. If they bring something to test, I believe this has to go to the hospital's internal review board, since patients would be involved in a development project. Also, to the extent that trying out new devices takes time and effort, we will have some costs. I don't know that they would ever be found, but it seems to me that that's so."

Vivian answered, speaking a little more slowly now. "I took a minute last week to tell Dr. Anderson, the chief medical officer, about what we were doing. He told me he had heard about it from one of the pediatricians and was pleased that people were looking for better ways of doing things. He told me that he would convene the internal review board any time we had anything for them to look at. I think he meant it.

"The vendor rep said he is used to putting information packages together for review boards, and he will take responsibility for that. He said they would free-issue any syringes used in the field test, and they would pay a cash fee to cover our incremental costs. He said they always do that, so it's not an issue at his headquarters."

Nan responded, "Well, it would be hard to complain about that.

"Okay, it sounds like that particular ball is with the vendor and then it goes to the internal review board. Meanwhile, are you going to continue with the cork?"

Vivian replied, "I think the simplest thing to do for the interim is to let nurses who like the cork use it, and let nurses who don't like the cork not use it. I don't think we will get enough data to do any statistics, but we might."

Nan smiled at Maddy and said, "This is progress. What else have you been looking at?"

Maddy's face revealed a certain satisfaction with Nan's response.

She replied, "There are a lot of syringes that still don't have any protection at all, or not much. For instance, the vacuum draw syringes that are used to take blood samples for lab work are still the old-fashioned kind. Considering how many of those we use, you'd think somebody would be making protected ones by now. For our pediatric patients, those are big, scary syringes, which means the kid is all the more apt to flinch just at the wrong moment, and then somebody gets stuck. Maybe if this factory rep gets his engineers paying attention to corks, maybe they can get serious about improving the rest of the syringes we use a lot."

Nan nodded and said, "Yes, once they get the simple poka-yoke rules in mind and see that progress is possible, they will be moving a lot faster than we can on our small-scale basis.

"Well, Vivian and Maddy, I am happy to hear of your progress. Let me know if you need anything. I am sure I will be involved when the internal review board takes this up, but I mean if you need anything before then. . . .

"I don't mean just on needle-sticks. If you have something else to talk about, come and see me or invite me to your unit."

Vivian picked up on that point. "Nan, I think the only time you visit our unit is when you make those midnight rides through the hospital to find out who's sleeping on the job or hiring a dance band to while away the hours."

Vivian was suppressing a laugh, so Nan couldn't quite decide if this was a serious complaint or not.

Nan tried a middle ground. "Vivian, I will be pleased to visit your unit three times during the day shift in the next two weeks. Besides, I know you make your own midnight rides through your unit."

"Yes, of course I do. If anybody is sleeping on the job or hiring a dance band, I want to know about it. That's part of my job."

At that point, both Vivian and Nan were having a good laugh. Maddy decided that she didn't understand upper management and stayed with a polite smile.

Nan moved around in her chair to indicate that the meeting was about over and said, "Vivian, would you bring one of your corks to the next nursing department staff meeting? I think that you have an idea that will sell itself to anybody who has ever gotten a good jab with a needle, and that must include every nurse in the whole department."

"Sure, I don't mind taking credit for Maddy's work. Meanwhile, Willie is editing a short video piece that shows the cork in action, which we'll have up on the website in a day or so. So most people will have figured it out before the nursing staff meeting, which will keep the meeting moving along."

Nan stood up, offered her hand, and said, "Thanks for filling me in on this. I am pleased with your work.

"You will notice," she added, "that I didn't ask about all the things you tried that didn't work."

Nan and Vivian were laughing again, and Maddy decided it was a good time to leave.

12

Nan Meets the HR Veep

Nan kept her four o'clock appointment with Susan Gunn, the vice president of human relations, arriving two minutes ahead of time at Susan's office, just to be ornery. Susan was shooing a gaggle of her staff out of her office to make room for Nan.

"Nan, it's very good of you to come here. I would have been pleased to go to your office, I hope you know."

"Oh, I needed a little walk to keep my system working. I did a little drop-in visit to the late shift last night, and that catches up with me late in the day."

"I heard you were here. That sort of thing gets around when a vice president deigns to visit a back shift. I need to do more of that myself.

"Well," Susan added, "is this a business call or can we just gab for a while?"

"Business, sorry to say. Maggie Kelly has given notice. I think you got her letter of resignation. She addressed it to both of us."

"Yes, I got the word this morning, and I got the letter around noon. She has always seemed to be a top performer to me. Do you want to offer her something to change her mind?"

"No, Susan. I am sorry to lose her on a personal basis, because she is a friend. But on a professional level, this is just part of the game. The best ones find other opportunities, and we can't pretend we have more executive positions to promote the good ones to than we really have. So, Maggie goes."

"Okay. I commend you for your clear thinking on such things. Normally I have to spend an hour cooling off a distraught department manager when somebody resigns.

"Maggie set Friday for her last day. That's short notice, and we can require a longer notice period if you want."

"No. If t'were done, t'were well t'were done quickly."

"*Macbeth*, right? 'Out, out, damned spot' is the only line I remember, and I can't remember what that had to do with the play. I do remember that that was racy stuff back in tenth grade.

"So, I will write the stock letter to Maggie Kelly accepting her resignation and her termination date, settling her vacation days not yet taken and all the usual stuff.

"What do you have in mind to replace Maggie at the clinics? That's a pretty big job."

"I am thinking of rotating some people and promoting somebody into one of the less daunting jobs at that level. The job posting mechanism should work for that, don't you think?"

"It works best at the lowest levels," Susan said. "You might want to twist some arms to make sure the right people come forward. The process itself works well enough, but it can only work with the applicants who apply. You retain the right to reject the survivor at the end of the day, although that gets everybody torqued out of shape when it happens. You can also do some reorganizing and shifting of responsibilities at the same time, that's a way of dealing with other problems if you have any. I mean with a department as big as yours, there are always problems of one kind or another. I don't mean to say that I know anything you don't know, I am just saying that the opportunity presents itself if you want to take advantage of it."

Nan sat pensively for a full minute. Susan waited, displaying a smile that might have meant she knew some deep secret or might have meant that she had seen it all and would not be troubled by any wild thing that Nan might bring up next.

Nan said, calmly and quietly, "Susan, since I am losing my best manager, I want to balance the team by losing the worst manager, too. Doing that now, while other changes are being made, may take some of the sting out of that for the person in question."

"Tell me the name, please."

"Shewan Lincoln."

"Are you talking about termination for cause, or termination because she is the weakest performer on a strong team? And do you mean termination, or do you offer her up for disposition?"

"She is not a bad person nor a bad nurse. She is in over her head as a manager, and she doesn't show any signs of progress, in spite of the help I have given her, or maybe because of the help I have given her. If there were a way to get her back into the nursing ranks and out of her management position, that would be fine. I don't hate her. I just don't think she can cut the mustard as manager. If I think that way, my guess is that everybody in the department thinks the same. You'd know that better than I would."

"Everybody feels the same way. Shewan feels the same way. I won't reveal any confidences, but I will say that she has approached our department and made oblique enquiries about a career change."

"Can you place her somewhere that looks like a lateral? I don't want the troops to think that she got a promotion by performing poorly."

"Let me just check my understanding, Nan. I hear you saying that you want Shewan Lincoln out, and out is what counts. Terminated. Transferred laterally. Demoted a little. Demoted a lot. Not promoted. And you want to do it now."

"Yes, you understand me correctly."

"Okay. I'll take care of it. We will do this in three steps. One, you and I meet with her together to give her the word. That way she can't play one of us off against the other. Two, we will give her a job as an assistant director in community relations, which is a respectable job but not one that anyone, including herself, will think a promotion. Three, we will turn our outplacement service loose to get her a job elsewhere within three months. Shewan qualifies as a minority, she has a college degree and a nursing license, so I don't think outplacement is going to be much of a chore.

"I'll explain this to the suits. Let me handle that part. They will jump up and down about beneficiating a minority, and if you are present they may issue you an order to hire her back. That would make you mad, and you'd quit. Then they would have to do a big fandango to hire you back, and that would all be a lot of bother for me. So, I handle that part. I've done it before. That's what I do here. I am even pretty good at it, as you will see.

"Now there's a chance this will all blow up in our faces, particularly if certain community activists get fired up. That's not likely, but you never know. I'll handle that, too, but who knows how that will come out. They can get activated whether Ms. Lincoln wants them activated or not. No matter what happens along those lines, though, I absolutely guarantee that Shewan Lincoln will not be dumped back in your lap."

"Susan, you have made this absolutely painless. I wish I had come to you before about Shewan."

"Nan, I know a lot about what's going on, and the fact that the person you want to move is Shewan Lincoln doesn't surprise me. Nor am I surprised that you have come to this conclusion. I am not surprised, but I am pleased, that you have gotten it straight in your head that the right thing for all concerned, and even for Shewan Lincoln, is to get her out of that management job and into something she can handle better. Too many managers, and I specifically include executives, can't face the music when it comes to getting rid of somebody. I didn't figure you to be lily-livered, and you're not.

"This one is pretty easy. The next one might not be, so this is a good one to practice on. It's going to work out for everybody."

"What was the word you used, Susan? Beneficiation? I've never seen you in your beneficiation mode before. I've learned something about personnel management today, and maybe I've learned something about you."

"Well, Nan, I play the soft-hearted, soft-headed personnel sob sister a lot, because somebody has to. Everybody else on the executive staff has a hard-driving position to fill. Once in a while, maybe once a quarter, I get to be the real me.

"Let me tell you, Nan. Firing people is often the best thing that you can do for somebody. I have people whom I fired years ago who send me Christmas cards and thank me for firing them, because I got them out of a job they *couldn't* do and helped them into one that they *could* do. So, I can't say it's any fun to fire somebody, but I understand that it's the right thing to do, and somebody has to do it. So, I got to be pretty good at it over the years. Maybe that's why I have this big executive office instead of a cubicle."

"Yes, Susan, maybe it is.

"Well, I want to come back in a few days with some notions of how to rotate some people around. I want your views on things before I get too far along."

"Done," Susan said. "I do that kind of thing, too."

"Now, to finish up with Shewan Lincoln, do I understand that you will write a script for me to follow when we meet with her?"

"Better yet, I'll do the talking. You just sit there and smile your most beatific smile. I want her to be mad at me, if she's mad at anybody, not at you.

"Are you ready to do this right now, today?"

"Yes, I am ready. It can't very well happen today, though, because Shewan is already off shift for the day. Shall we plan on tomorrow?"

"Yes, I will get myself informed when she comes in tomorrow morning, and I will invite her to come see me at, say, nine o'clock. When that falls in place, I will call Marcy to get you over here a few minutes before then."

Nan nodded. "Agreed. I want to get this over with, before the word gets around the way the word always does."

"You're right about that. Why we need an Internet when the grapevine works so well, I don't know."

"Thank you for your help, Susan."

"You're welcome, Nan. Let's make it tea and cookies next time. All this work fills up the day."

"Yes, tea and cookies. Or maybe you'll want to drop in on one of the neighborhood parties that Maggie's patients are giving for her this week. You might get something a little stronger than tea."

"I'm going to all of them, Nan. Somebody has to represent the administration here, you know."

"Yes, Susan, I know. It's a heavy burden, but somebody has to bear it."

Nan returned to her office with a lighter step. Maybe this beneficiation of staff isn't so hard after all. She had discovered a secret drill sergeant living in Susan Gunn's body. Are there more buried treasures in this organization that she hadn't found yet? This was the biggest organizational surprise Nan had had yet.

Nan returned to her office and asked Marcy to join her. Nan closed the office door, mostly to indicate that the next subject was confidential.

"Marcy, I am going to transfer Shewan Lincoln to a position outside the department. She will hear of her good fortune tomorrow morning. I decided to do this change at the same time that Maggie is leaving so that we have another slot to use for rotational and promotional assignments."

"Yes, ma'am."

"The human resources veep will call in the morning to confirm that she has set up a meeting at nine to explain this to Shewan Lincoln. That call will go to you, of course, so I want you to know what's going on. I will need to get over there before the hour."

"Yes, ma'am."

"You know everybody, Marcy. Is this going to cause any backlash?"

"You never know, but I don't think so. Most employees think the top management caters too much to the weaker performers, so to the extent anybody notices, this will be given a favorable view. That's my guess, anyway."

13

IT Head Visits Nan

"**M**rs. Mills, Mr. Rudolf in the IT department asked if he could see you for two minutes before you go home. I took the liberty of telling him yes. I notified him when I saw you coming down the hall. He will be here any minute. If you don't want to see him, I can block him at the door."

"No, that's fine. I don't think he has ever come to visit me before. I usually see him upstairs with the suits. Bring him in when he shows up."

"Yes, ma'am."

No sooner said than done; Rudy Rudolf knocked on the door of Nan's office. Marcy opened the door and invited him in.

"Hello, Rudy. Welcome to our humble quarters. I think this is the first time you have been here."

"Yes, Nan, I think it is. I usually see you upstairs with the suits. Somebody told me that you have the best office decorator in the building, and now I see why."

Rudy smiled at Marcy, who took the hint and stepped out, closing the door behind her.

"Nan, this is not about wall paint. I want to talk to you about Sanjar Subramaniam. Sanjar came in this morning and put a letter of resignation in my in-basket. I just about dropped my teeth when my secretary handed it to me. The letter was about two lines long, saying he resigned and that he took full responsibility for the failure to defend against the common mode data networking failure that occurred last night.

"Nan, if I fired everybody who failed to anticipate a one-in-a-million-years event like that, I'd have a pretty small group. Well, I don't know if it's one in a million years, but it didn't happen in the past five years for sure.

told me he had wanted to bring me up to date on his Six Sigma projects. Infrastructure reliability is a Six Sigma issue for obvious reasons.

"Of course, when he got here, he wanted to tell me about the fire and the tunnels and his letter of resignation.

"I heard him out, heard what he said he was going to do to keep you informed and ahead of the bow-wave. He told me about his Gantt charts, and it sounded to me like he wanted to make sure you had some charts in your hands that you could use to defend yourself. I don't think he was worrying about himself, or he would not have put in his letter of resignation."

"I like that in an employee, Nan. Looking out for the boss."

"Rudy, some of the Six Sigma stuff comes from Japan. One of the Japanese rules is that the purpose for going to work every day is to make the boss look smart. I don't know if Sanjar knows any Japanese, but I think he knew that rule instinctively."

"Huh. If I had some of that in a bottle, Nan, I'd spray my whole department. I like that one. Make the boss look smart. Amen to that, although I suppose that means you and I should be making Philip L. Crawford look smart. Good thing he's pretty smart on his own."

"Yes, he is, Rudy, I like your plan. What can I do to help?"

"Couple things. One, if you see Sanjar wearing a long face, give him a big squeeze and tell him the hospital loves him.

"Two, gather up some information on any impact the data networking outage is having on the nursing service so we can have a pile of claims to assert against the vendors or the insurance companies or somebody.

"Three, come and give a talk to my staff one day soon about this Six Sigma stuff. Some of my gang aren't too old to learn something, and it looks like we have something to learn. They're ornery enough to jump right in and make it work for us the way it works for you, especially if they figure they have to compete against Sanjar for my job the day Crawford gets mad enough at me over computer screw-ups to drop me off the roof."

"Four, I am aware that your husband, Jack, is the famous Jack Mills. At the next hospital party, please introduce us so I can ask Jack for his autograph. It's bound to be worth more one of these days than my Willie Mays rookie year bubblegum card."

"Agreed on all points," she said. "We say things back in our department to make sure that the verbal communication got all the way through, so here's what I heard you say. Buck Sanjar up if he needs bucking up. Document costs and impacts of the data networking outage, talk to your staff about Six Sigma, which I am happy to do at the earliest opportunity, and introduce you to Jack."

"Is that Six Sigma? It reminds me of John Wayne in those submarine movies. Wayne says "Up periscope!" and about six others shout Up periscope!" at each other."

"That's it. Navy method for getting verbal orders delivered correctly. It works for us, so we do it. You may recall that we lost a baby several months ago because of a botched verbal communication between a good doctor and a good nurse."

"I do remember. And I see the point. Feedback for system stability is not a foreign concept to me, in my line of work, and you are applying something you learned from the Navy to your work here. That's always smart. Plagiarize, plagiarize, let nothing good escape your eyes, is the way the old college song goes, if I remember it rightly. Good for you."

"Rudy, I understand that the external data networks were supposed to connect the hospital to the Internet and to connect your computers to your backup site across town. I suppose we can get along without the Internet for a day or so, but what are you doing about the backup function?"

"We have a grunt driving across town with CDs full of data every hour on the hour. We are keeping track of the cost, not only to stick it to our vendors if we can, but to have a crisp cost basis for saying that it is cheaper to have two independent networks than to have couriers on bicycles zipping back and forth."

"So, the most data you have at risk is one hour's worth, with the bicycle method."

"Right. That's worse than one second's worth, but it would be a manageable event if we had to reconstruct one hour's data by hand, if the computer center blew up. A day's worth would put us at the ragged edge. A week's worth would put us out of business for sure. Hell, two days' worth might put us out of business."

"Let's talk about a date for my talking to your staff about Six Sigma. When is your next staff meeting?"

"Tomorrow afternoon. Do you want to do a 10-minute stand-up tomorrow, say 1:30? If you want to do a longer shtick we can book you for next month."

"Rudy, I'd just as soon do a short stand-up tomorrow, because I know how easy it is to bump topics like this off month after month. I'll hit a couple of highlights of Six Sigma, and then I will talk about computer systems and how that fits in."

"Can't beat that. See you at 1:30 tomorrow afternoon, at my conference room. You see, I've already learned how to shout "Up periscope!" when you shout "Up periscope!""

"Rudy, I can see you are both a quick learner and a John Wayne fan."

Rudy stood up, shook Nan's hand, gave her a big smile, and turned to leave. Nan reviewed what she had just learned about Rudy and how he ran his department. He was doing the manly thing, taking the heat for the network screw-up. She liked that in a man. She hoped she would do the same if her time should come. Yes, she thought she would, but you never know until it happens.

14

Jerry Miller

As Rudy was opening the door to leave, Marcy was knocking on the same door. Rudy opened, and Marcy came in one step's worth to say, "Mrs. Mills, Mr. Rudolph, Sanjar is here with a Mr. Miller. Sanjar asked if you would be breaking up soon, and if so he would like to introduce Jerry Miller to you."

Seeing that the meeting was already breaking up, Marcy left without waiting for an answer and returned two seconds later with Sanjar and another young man. Marcy gave a perfunctory smile and left again.

Sanjar bowed to Nan, bowed marginally less in the direction of Rudy, and said, "Mrs. Mills and Mr. Rudolph, I have the honor to present to you Mr. Jerry Miller, who is our outside consultant in the external networks matter. Jerry, I present you Mrs. Mills, head nurse, and Mr. Rudy Rudolph, CIO."

Jerry shook hands with Nan and then with Rudy. Jerry said, "Pleased to meet you both, I'm sure. Sanjar and I are off to make the vendor drive along the telephone lines. I never thought I'd be doing that, but then I didn't know manholes could catch fire, not until Sunday night or Monday morning.

"I want you both to know that I am taking this matter very seriously now. I can see I should have been more serious about it three or four months ago, when Sanjar originally raised the idea with me. That fire was a real grabber."

Rudy nodded at Jerry and said, "Jerry, were you along on the vendor drive that found both our fiber networks running through the same manhole and tunnel?"

"Yes, sir, I was. I was as surprised as anybody in the car, and I think I can say we were all surprised. We have a pile of paper about yea-high that says no common elements are used, and you can see what that pile of paper turned out to be worth. Sanjar was the one who said we had to go see with our own eyeballs. I think I probably stalled things for a while, because this didn't seem very important, and there was a lot of other stuff that called out for my attention. Sanjar eventually wore me down."

Sanjar retained his polite poker face, eyes moving slowly from Nan to Rudy to Jerry.

Nan thought she should say something if only to be polite, so she tried, "Jerry, once you found this tunnel and manhole problem, what did you do? That was a number of days before the fire, wasn't it?"

"Yes, ma'am, it was a few days before the fire, the middle of last week, I think. Well, I wrote a trip report and sent it to my boss, then I went around and told all the other worker bees what had happened to me, and then I pushed my way in to see my boss so he would not miss the story if he happened to ignore my trip report. I'll tell you, most trip reports around our place don't have manhole fires in them, and of course this was before the fire anyway."

Nan nodded with a smile, hinting an understanding of bureaucratic tendencies, then asked, "Did your boss follow up?"

Jerry went through a series of involuntary facial changes, looking for a moment that he was having trouble swallowing his saliva, then looking at his shoes, then looking up, first to Rudy and then to Nan.

"My boss is a pretty good boss. He's done all the work in our department one time or another, and he is a straight shooter. I'll tell you. He didn't do anything. He didn't react one way or the other. He didn't say I had solved the riddle of the Sphinx, and he didn't say I had wasted my time. He just didn't react at all. He didn't even laugh. I think he should have at least laughed about a goofy thing like that happening. He sort of looked like he wasn't paying any attention. That surprised me, because you'd think that just out of curiosity he would have perked up a little. Maybe he was doing budgets or maybe his own boss had just yelled at him, I don't know.

"Anyway, he eventually said that was all very interesting and why didn't I look up the incidence of common mode errors like this on the web someplace and maybe I could write a paper for our engineering conference. That's all.

"Now, this was before the fire, of course, and he could not have known that a fire was going to happen."

Rudy may have been feeling a mote of sympathy for the bureaucrat who was Jerry's boss, judging from the combined smile and frown that Rudy was making for Jerry's benefit. He said, "Did you do a web search, Jerry?"

"Yes, sir, I did. I didn't find anything when I searched for common mode construction errors involving tunnels and manholes, so I tried a search for manhole fires. I didn't know a fire was coming, but it seemed to me that the tunnel couldn't cause a problem by itself; it had to be a tunnel plus a fire or a tunnel plus a flood or something.

"I found a million citations about floods, which is the same as finding none at all. When I searched for fires and manholes, I found out that they happen. They don't happen a lot, but there are some every year in this country. One every few years in every state, more or less. I don't know how many manholes there are in our state, certainly not millions but maybe thousands. Ten thousand, would you say? On that order, I guess. So if you are counting fires per million manholes per year, you'd have to say that there are quite a few per million. Maybe somebody could count them up and do the arithmetic.

"Sanjar told me that you Six Sigma people count failures per million opportunities for error, and that you think the goal ought to be 3.4 per million. So manhole fires are a lot higher risk than what you talk about."

All eyes were on Nan, so she said, "Six Sigma and 3.4 per million do go together. That's the quantitative goal we set for everything. That doesn't mean that we get there in one jump, but it gives us something specific to shoot for. So I suppose that's the number to think about when designing manholes and tunnels and fiber optics routes or anything else. Once everything is as good as 3.4 per million, then we will try to do better than that, too," Nan concluded with a friendly smile.

Jerry responded, "Yes, ma'am, when we get there. Right now we look to be a little short, say about a million miles short."

Rudy asked, "Did you find out whether the manhole fires were accidental or otherwise, Jerry?"

"Well, some were spontaneous combustion on hot days. Some looked to be accidental, some were equipment overheating, and some were set on purpose. Some looked to be pranks. And some, nobody knows what happened."

Rudy answered, "Overloads and overheating don't seem very likely in the middle of the night. It's not Halloween this week, so I don't know if we can take much direction from what you found on the web."

The conversation seemed to be running out of steam, so Sanjar said, "Jerry and I have miles to go before we sleep, and miles to go before we sleep, if I remember that poem correctly."

Nan thought that was the way it went but decided to hold her peace.

Sanjar continued, "We are doing the telephone line routes this evening. We have all the vendors meeting us with their drawings. Then we will have a big discussion about who has the biggest truck," Sanjar smiled at his own whimsy, "and then we will follow the lines to see what we find. I hope we find nothing at all, but by now everybody in the business knows about the manhole fire, and I think we will get very close cooperation this evening. I think we will find that each of our vendors has already run his own route this afternoon just to make sure his maps are correct."

Rudy was by then half-sitting on Nan's conference table, clutching one knee in his hands with the other foot resting on the floor. Nan wondered to herself why men find that pose comfortable.

Rudy spoke. "I think you're right about that one, Sanjar. I'll bet there are a lot of eyeballs eyeballing telephone poles this afternoon, and not just in this precinct. I've had about 20 telephone calls from CIOs I know all over town, asking what had happened to us. I'm thinking of making an inspirational audiotape and selling it on late-night television infomercials. I don't have a sufficiently catchy title for it, though. Not yet, anyway. I'm still working on it."

Jerry took the occasion to thank Rudy and Nan for their time, to wish them well, and to turn and walk out the door. Sanjar followed in his own way, walking backward and bowing at the same time. Even after seeing him do that walk a thousand times, Nan still got a kick out of it.

When they were gone, Rudy stood up and made motions of starting for the door. He said to Nan, "Well, I don't know if our new friend Jerry Miller is nervous by nature, overwhelmed by meeting me, or dazzled by meeting you. Or maybe he is just scared that he is going to get canned because his manhole caught on fire and caught that old couple in the fire. I sort of wanted to ask him if he resigned the way Sanjar did here, but this didn't seem to be the time nor place to ask him.

"His boss sounds like a real winner. Maybe I'll look him up. I guess, formally speaking, I am the contracting officer here, and he must be the contracting officer there for their consulting contract with us, so I have an excuse to check him out. Judging from Jerry's report, he's a complete dud. I'm willing to wait a few days to get more data on the guy, and maybe we got the wrong skinny here, but I want first-class people taking our money. If he's half as dudly as Jerry makes out, he can go work on some other consulting contract for some other hospital."

Rudy nodded, smiled, and went out the door, which was standing open.

Marcy came in with her steno pad and a fresh pot of tea. It was late enough in the afternoon that Nan sort of figured Marcy was bluffing with an empty teapot, but she was not going to call the bluff. Gestures count, and Nan was willing to leave it at that.

Nan gave Marcy the business card Jerry had put on the corner of her desk. Marcy said she had collected one from him directly, having exchanged one chocolate chip cookie for one business card.

15

Monday Supper with Jack, at Home

Usually, Nan and Jack turned the television off at suppertime, preferring each other's company to the news. Not this evening. They ate fitfully as they watched the reporters piece together the story of the manhole fire and the enchained death of Mrs. Collins. There were no witnesses to the fire, other than the Collinses, who had not been in condition to do any talking.

The fire inspectors had gotten to the scene while the fire was still blazing and had taken charge of the investigation. They had started with a presumption of arson, although later in the day they found that such fires happen every few weeks somewhere in the United States because of a worker's mistake, flammable fluids getting into the manhole and not drained, and spontaneous combustion. If they had done their database search first, they might have set arson aside. However, not being burdened with this information, they started out figuring this was arson, and they wanted to get the evidence in hand immediately.

The inspectors found, by noon, that there was substantial evidence of arson. They presently believed that the arsonist had constructed a thermite device, probably on a timer, that set off a hot blaze that would have sustained itself for several minutes. The fire was hot enough that the insulation on the electrical cabling was set on fire, and that kept the fire hot, burning for about half an hour. The fire might have eventually burned right down the tunnel to the next manhole in both directions. This particular manhole also had some electronics equipment in it, something to do with the cables, and that had contributed its mite to the fire.

The thermite bomb, which is what the inspectors were calling it, got hot very fast, which caused an overpressure in the manhole, and that lifted the manhole cover off. They didn't know, since there were no observers, whether the manhole cover popped off and flew up in the air, or if it just bumped up a little and got translated sideways. Either way, the Collins car seems to have come along just as the manhole cover was moving itself out of place. They were guessing that Mrs. Collins saw the fire, hit the brakes, and skidded in such a way that the car came to rest with the left rear wheel stuck in the open manhole. That trapped them right over the fire, and their car caught fire before they could get themselves out. It was probably all over for them in a matter of seconds.

People living in the neighborhood were awakened by the screeching of car brakes and another noise, which they discovered to be the fire itself. They called it in, and the fire and rescue services got into action immediately.

Nan knew the rest of the story and had already told Jack what she knew. That nice young Collins couple, the death of Mrs. Collins, and the expectation that Mr. Collins would be severely incapacitated even if he survived the week.

Nan and Jack had not known about the arson.

"Jack, what's a thermite bomb?"

"Thermite is a mixture of metal shavings and ordinary chemicals that causes a very intense fire. It's what they used to use to weld train rails together, and maybe they still do. It is easy to make. I remember our chemistry teacher in high school doing a demonstration. I remember the recipe was in the chemistry text, so I am sure it's on the Internet today. It's an ordinary thing. Some household drain cleaners actually work that way. I don't recall seeing it in the news very much, but it is the sort of thing an arsonist with a little bit of technical education would think of. Like me, if I were an arsonist."

"Jack, don't even joke about that right now.

"Okay," she continued, "so to the extent we know anything, we suspect that we have a technically astute arsonist. Did you hear anything about motive? And since this was done at four o'clock in the morning rather than at high noon, what do you conclude about that?"

"Motive, I haven't heard yet. Since this was done at four o'clock in the morning and not at noon, my guess is the bad guy wasn't trying to kill people. He or she was trying to get at one of the telecommunications companies, at the company owning the tunnels, or at one of the customers. Maybe even the hospital, but that supposes that the arsonist knew more about the network routing of hospital networks than the hospital knew itself. So that's pretty far out. The fact that the Collins family came along just when it did, that looks like a fluke, don't you think?"

"Yes, Jack, I don't know how the arsonist could have known that the Collins family or any other car would be coming along just at that precise moment. If the fire had started even a minute or two before, then Mrs. Collins would have had sufficient warning time to get the car away from the manhole."

"I think the same, Nan. Cataclysmically bad luck for the Collins family. No murder intention for the arsonist, but a crime against property that turned out to be murder or manslaughter or wrongful death, whatever the law calls it."

They watched the news unfold, nibbling without being conscious of what they were eating. After a few moments, Nan turned again to Jack to fill him in on the day's developments at the hospital.

"Jack, Sanjar resigned this morning, taking the blame upon himself for both data networks being wiped out by one fire. Rudy Rudolph tore up the resignation letter, of course. He's no dummy, although he likes to pose as a bumbler. I am coming to believe that he is not.

"Sanjar is out this evening doing a route trace of the telephone lines, and he is doing the electric lines tomorrow morning. That all got accelerated and compressed from two or three weeks down to two days. I think the hospital is as capable of shooting the messenger as any organization is, but so far I think the top management has kept its thinking straight."

Nan continued, holding her fork idly. "The data network outage was not too big a deal for the hospital. No Internet for a few days. A gopher going back and forth across town to carry data on CDs to the backup site. If it had been one of the other networks or the electric power supply, that would have been a bigger deal. You might even think that the motive of the arsonist might have been to fire a warning shot across the bow of the hospital or some other organization."

"Cutting the data networking is almost as bad as burning the office building down for lots of modern companies, Nan. Banks, insurance companies, communications companies, more than you'd think."

"I am so innocent of all this, Jack. I didn't even know the hospital had a backup site across town to hold a copy of all the hospital computer records. That sounds pretty smart, in the light of the day's events."

"Most companies do that these days. They generally don't use their Internet connection; they lease a private connection so they will have, or think they have, more security from intruders and pranksters. In the long run, they will use the Internet, I think, when they figure out that pranksters can get at their private leased lines, too.

"Some companies keep duplicate computer centers on standby. Some companies who have the same kind of mainframe computers pool their money to buy a spare and keep it on a truck. There are companies whose whole business is operating these backup centers, and they themselves have backups for their backups. You can see that this can get pretty intricate pretty quickly. Still, the front-line organizations need some protection, and this is how the industry has evolved. I don't think there is any going back."

"Rudy Rudolf told me he wants to meet you, and he sort of implied that your picture should be on a baseball bubblegum card."

"I think so, too. I would have gotten there if I had ever figured out how to hit a curve ball, low and away. I can see that this Rudy Rudolf is a clear thinker. Who's he?"

"He's head of IT for the hospital. He's Sanjar's boss now, I mean that Sanjar reports directly to him now that he has that project manager position. I had a long talk with him this afternoon, and it changed my opinion of him completely. He put aside the bumbler mask, just for the moment, and told me how he had already set things up so that if any flack came in about the loss of data networks in that nutty fire, he was going to take the arrows in his own chest and keep the wolves away from the sled."

"Nan, I think you throw babies off the sled to keep the wolves away."

"So, I got that backward. Rudy surprises me by being a stand-up guy. Big surprise."

Jack responded, "Each of us is two different people, one for normal times, and one for high-stress times. This is the first time you have seen this Rudy guy under stress. So you learned something. He may be learning something himself. Anyway, the more stand-up guys you have around, the better. You know me, the first sign of stress and my knees turn to water."

"Jack, I love you even if you are a liar. You couldn't fool anybody with that line. Besides, it's not your knees, it's your heart that matters in times of stress. And yours is cold as ice." Nan finished that line with an impish grin.

"Colder."

"Jack, you know Maggie Kelly is leaving. That will be in the paper in the morning, and we'll need to check the local online sports page to see what coverage they give it, if any."

"The sports line?"

"Yes, Josey Walberg, who is an intern in our press office, said she was going to plant a story there. She is a new one on me, some distant relation of Marcy's. Anyway, she turned up this morning and said she would take care of all the press stuff, and she even corrected my grammar. That's pretty nervy for an intern, or maybe she just doesn't have anything to lose. She was right, as it happens. It just caught me off guard. I like to have go-get-'em people around, and so putting up with the utter lack of timidity in the modern workplace is the price I pay, every hour of every day."

"Nan, I love that. An intern correcting your grammar. You must be getting a little sloppy in your declining years. It's the bathtub curve all over again, a grammar bathtub curve. Why you may have been making grammatical blunders for years and nobody had nerve enough to call you on it. Time for a refresher course."

"That's the cure for all bathtub curves. I'll have to start a new grammar-for-nurses remedial program right away."

"Grammar without tears for nursing executives, yes, I can visualize it now."

"The people in the four neighborhoods where Maggie has been running my clinics are going to have street parties or something for her, starting Thursday night and running through Sunday night. We ought to go to one of them, don't you think?"

"I'm game, Nan. I like ethnic food, and I can stay away from their homemade potables. Too strong for mild mannered round-eyes like me."

"That reminds me. Maggie asked if it would be all right if she got Sanjar to tell the communications people at her new company how to set the PC video stations up so that the video works so much better. Like Sanjar helped you set up your stations here in your home office. My guess is that Sanjar is going to be in a defensive crouch and will plead off on the grounds of fraternizing with the enemy. So Maggie asked if you could do it for her, and then she wondered if she could hire Jake and Bake to set it up for her at a bunch of their clinic sites across the state and some neighboring states. That would give them something productive to do over the summer, if they want to do it. What do you think, Jack?"

"Suits me. Since they have gone ape over nanotechnology, they are not going to want to do software with me. They probably think they don't want to spend the summer with their parents anyway, since they are college men now. Why don't we let them decide?"

"Does anybody own that video setup idea, Jack?"

"If Sanjar takes out a patent on the idea, then the hospital will own the patent and will have the right to license it. They'd settle for a small license fee, which would fall on Maggie's company if the hospital bothered to collect the fee. I doubt if they would, since that's a long ways away from their main business. They might decide to publish it instead so that nobody else could get a patent on it. That's what big companies do."

"Let's ask the boys, then, if they would want to spend the summer earning money and living on the road."

They had booked a Internet video call with their twin sons for that evening. At 8:30, they went to Jack's home office and turned on two of the computer stations, and Jack launched a video session over the Internet. He had a broadband Internet access connection for his office, so the video fidelity was good. As the boys came on stream, little windows popped up on both of their PC screens, and they clicked to open the session up. Their key lights, surrounding the PC screen and illuminating their faces to get rid of shadows, came up, and the room lights went down halfway to reduce background visual clutter for the video cameras.

Their identical twin sons, baptized Jacques and James, had been called Jake and Bake since their earliest days. Jacques was in fact Jack's given name, and James was the Anglicized form of Jacques, so their intentions had been paternal, but the nicknames Jake and Bake had quickly won out.

"Hello, Mom and Dad. We're Jake and Bake or Bake and Jake and we'll never tell who's whom."

"Who's who, my much-loved son. *Whom* is objective case, and this is grammar day for the family. And you're Jake. You can't fool me."

"How do you know if we are fooling you or not?"

"You're right. I can't tell. So which one are you?"

"I'll never tell, and my brother always lies and I always tell the truth and you'll never figure it out."

The other one, probably Bake, helped out by saying, "No, *I* am the one who always tells the truth and he is the one who always lies and you'll never figure it out."

Nan could tell that a year of college had not dulled their sense of humor, and they had had a school year to play identical-twin pranks on their faculty and fellow students. She would have to take pains not to hear any of those stories for at least 10 years. Not that she and her twin sister had ever done anything of that sort, themselves. Nor Jack and his twin brother.

Jack decided that it was time to change the subject, so he began, "Boys, Maggie Kelly, who worked for Nan running the neighborhood clinics, has taken a job with a private company that has clinics over two or three states and is growing like mad. Maggie was wondering out loud if her new company could hire you two for part of the summer to set up video stations for her clinics, like the ones you set up for yourselves there and like the ones Sanjar and I set up here. Maggie had that in Nan's department, and she wants it for her new company so people won't fight using video conferencing for routine business."

"What's the name of the company?" asked one of them.

"Clinical Care," replied Nan.

"I think they are doing an IPO, aren't they? Can we get paid in stock?"

"That's up to the company management, and they probably don't think too much of the idea of giving away their stock to contractors," said Jack.

"Maybe we could set ourselves up as a subsidiary or joint venture and commercialize this as a product. We trade our rights for their stock. Would they go for that?"

"You can always ask," said Nan.

"Okay, tell Maggie Kelly we're game and ready to talk. We've been taking this negotiations course this term, and we need a chance to practice our wares."

Jack said, "If you are negotiators, you know you always need a backup position, a fallback position, that is strong enough that you can be fearless negotiators. If you don't have another fallback position lined up, you can do software with me for this summer."

"Yuck. Software is so medieval. Okay for you mature types. We've been poking around to see if we can get summer internships at the nanotechnology lab here. They told us they only take graduate students, but we didn't let that stop us from getting a nose under the tent. We figured we could fake up some IDs if necessary."

"No fake IDs. Play it straight. And speaking of playing straight, if you agree to do this project for Maggie, then you have to do it. You can't say one thing and do another," said Jack, a little more sternly than he had meant to say it.

"Okay, Dad. We know that much, even if we are only freshmen. Our word is our bond, and what's more the word of either of us is the bond for both of us because otherwise nobody would trust either one of us. We can do nanotechnology next year if this Maggie Kelly deal works out. Particularly if we can get hold of some early stock before the IPO. Then we can be rich and lazy rather than just lazy."

"We love you, boys," said Nan.

"We love you, too, Ma," they said in unison. "Before you click off, tell us about that manhole fire near the hospital. What was that all about? It was on the Internet news."

Nan gave them a quick rundown, soft-pedaling the part about the Collins family getting caught in the fire. Jack told them a little about how networks are constructed in cities, using tunnels and conduit, and how the network operators contract with subtier suppliers and how the hospital, innocently, wound up with two network vendors who inadvertently had a common tunnel subcontractor.

"How would anybody ever figure that out, Dad?"

"You have to do what Sanjar did: get the vendors into one car and drive the routes to see what's really there. And you have to repeat it every so often, because network operators renegotiate with their sub-vendors all the time to keep their costs down. The ultimate customer has to look out for himself."

"You mean take responsibility? Who'd want to do that? I like to have somebody to blame, like my brother here, for instance, and it's always his fault anyway."

"A company can hire a consultant to check it out, which is one way of exercising the responsibility, but the responsibility abides," said Jack.

Nan thought that would be a good place to break things off, so she said, "Good night, boys. I love you. Jack can speak for himself. Don't flunk out, go to class once in a while, and brush your teeth twice a day." She finished that off with a broad smile to show her own well-brushed teeth.

"Good night, Mom and Dad," the boys said in unison.

"Good night, boys, and if you flunk out, I'll save a lot of tuition money," contributed Jack, offering his most mysterious grin.

They all clicked off.

"Jack, we could have done worse than those two."

"Maybe we should have had twin girls, too, Nan. That would have rounded things out."

"It's not too late, Jack."

16

Tuesday Breakfast

J ack and Nan were up and on the move at their usual hour, Tuesday morning. Jack commonly checked the Internet news sites before breakfast, and this day he checked the local sports wire to see if they had the story that Nan had told him to look for. Sure enough, there it was. He called to Nan, who came to read the story over his shoulder.

"It must be a slow sports day, Jack, if they have room for a hospital story."

"It's a human interest story, and we sports fans know that sports are only interesting because they are a metaphor for life. And you're right, Tuesday is not your big sports-news day in most seasons."

"I brought in the morning paper, Jack. It has two Maggie Kelly stories, one being a short announcement on the business page with a stock photo of Maggie, and the other is on the health-feature page, jumping from a short lead-in on the front page, left column, where they run lead-ins to second-tier stories. I didn't know how this press release stuff works, but these stories and those sports stories are very, very close to what Josey was showing me in my office yesterday. She wrote these stories."

"She must be a smooth talker. Or a good looker."

"She's not your type, Jack."

"From what I've seen in business news releases, the first round tends to be pretty much whatever the company is handing out. The papers run that so they won't be scooped by the other newspapers. Then if the story has any more interest than the usual handout, they put their own reporters on it to write the second-day story. So this story may change 180 degrees within a day."

"How do they decide if the story is worth any follow-up?"

"All they have to do is to tune in to the local call-in radio shows and listen to what people want to talk about. You can listen on the car radio on your way to the hospital, and you'll pretty well know."

"Josey told me that the local television gab show for women will want to get me on, maybe as early as tomorrow. I don't know if she knows, and I don't know myself. Do you think I should do it, if asked?"

"No, I don't want anyone in the world to know that you are a beautiful, intelligent, poised, and grammatically challenged mother of twins who happens to be the head nurse at the most important hospital around here."

"Okay, I won't do it."

"Yes, you will. You know you will. You wouldn't turn it down for all the tea in China, and I would kick you out of the house if you did."

"We own the house in common, Jack, so that won't work."

"I knew you would find a loophole. So, do it anyway."

"Okay. I kind of figured I would."

"So did I," Jack concluded with a grin of admiration for his very special wife.

"Don't forget, Jack, we are going to that engineering meeting this evening. You get a free meal, I get to talk to engineers, and they don't get to talk back."

"I'm looking forward to the free meal, and I will hang on every word."

17

Tuesday, First Thing

Nan tuned the car radio to one of the local talk shows on her way to the hospital. She and Maggie were the main topic of conversation, all of which dealt with the sports story. The talk was all over the place, no particular dominant theme, but it was certainly the topic of the day. It had caught the community's fancy, at least for the day.

Nan walked into her office. Marcy followed her, two steps behind, carrying her steno pad and a teapot. Nan's cup and saucer were already in place. Nan thought for a moment of the luxury of a saucer in the hospital, a luxury she was now sure she deserved, what with being a talk-show topic.

"Good morning, Mrs. Mills. You asked yesterday if I could get a line on Ralph or Rafael Lopez, who runs the emergency ambulance service for the city. It turns out my husband knows him from the Chamber of Commerce, I think. He says that Ralph Lopez is a career politician with the city political machine, and he will be mayor next time or the time after that. He's around 40, so there is no rush.

"Ralph Lopez doesn't know anything in particular about running ambulances; he is just there soaking up a paycheck and keeping everything in line. He is considered to be a nice guy, and nobody is particularly mad at him for having that job. It's just the way the city machine does things.

"There is a woman who actually runs the place on a day-to-day basis, taking care of the inside stuff while Ralph Lopez takes care of the politics. Her name is Norah Washington. She is thought to be a competent operations type, not a politician, so that sounds like what I would expect for any city bureau. A politician in the visible role and a competent top sergeant actually running the place. Since she is the inside operator, she is not known as well as Ralph Lopez is.

"My husband can get introductions for you, but then you can pick up the phone and get a meeting with anybody in the city administration you want to talk to. That is to say, I can pick up the phone and drop your name to get any meeting you want."

"Okay, Marcy, let's use the occasion of this manhole fire as a reason to have a get-acquainted meeting. I suppose you have to start with Ralph Lopez's office, but I think I really want to talk to Norah Washington, don't you think?"

"If you want to talk nuts and bolts, yes. If you want to talk politics, you don't have to go to city hall to find politicians."

Nan decided not to pursue that line of thought and told Marcy to set something up in the next couple of weeks. No rush. Low key. Get acquainted. Marcy nodded as her pencil flew across the steno pad.

"This evening you are the featured speaker at that quality engineering society meeting. You agreed to be their speaker the first week you were here, when they saw in the paper that you are a Six Sigma Black Belt. I suppose you remember all that. Do you need any last-minute preparation help?"

"No, Marcy, I know what I am going to say. I am used to talking to engineers, since my husband is one and most of his friends are, too. I'm going to keep it light and just talk. They see slide shows all the time, so that would not be a novelty."

"Okay. Now, there is an e-mail from Shewan Lincoln, responding to your request for input on rotational assignments. You might want to check that before your nine o'clock meeting."

Indeed, Nan did. Nan found a short note saying that she, Shewan, was in favor of rotational assignments and respectfully suggested that the rotations be extended to suitable positions outside the nursing service so that people would develop the broad perspective one needs in more senior assignments.

Nothing wrong with that, thought Nan. Might even fit in.

Nan forwarded the e-mail note to Susan Gunn, the personnel chief, so that she would be warned before the intended nine o'clock meeting with Nan and Shewan. Then Nan turned back to Marcy.

Marcy said, "Josey wants to talk to you as soon as you can see her. I suppose you saw that she got her stories placed in the newspapers and on that sports web page."

"I did. Sure, get her over here if you please, while I eyeball the mail log."

Marcy looked in the direction of the PC on Nan's desk, and said, "Just the usual bumf, although I expect we will see a lot of mail about the press coverage, especially that sports story.

"I'll get Josey," Marcy said.

Nan checked the mail log Marcy had prepared, a short note on each of the mail items and telephone calls and other things that Marcy had taken care for her, acting as always on her own initiative. Nan loved it, since it saved her hours out of her day. It all looked pretty ordinary, just bumf, so far. No other notes yet from her nursing managers about rotational assignments.

Josey knocked and stuck her head in, a head with a bright face and a wide grin this morning. Nan waved her in.

"Mrs. Mills, we're hitting on all cylinders. I am pulling together a longer bio on you and on Maggie Kelly, in case anybody wanting to do a follow-up story is willing to take any handouts. They usually want to do their own digging after the first story.

"I told you yesterday that that television gab show might show some interest? They called already this morning! They want you for tomorrow morning. Are you game?"

"I'm game, Josey, I'm game. I am also completely lacking in television experience. And I don't know, but I'll bet the suits upstairs will have a say-so on whether I do the television show or not."

"My boss is taking care of the suits. I have people lined up, I put them on call yesterday, to get you ready for television. They will be here at ten o'clock for a fitting. You'll be in their hands, and they are they best in town. You'll be amazed."

"Josey, have you ever done this before?"

"Only in college, but we had some big-time people come through, and so I have seen it done. You'll be amazed, and you'll be super on the tube. I just know the camera is going to like you a lot."

"Tell me again, Josey, that you are getting any and all clearances today."

"Yes, ma'am, I am getting all clearances today. That's my job, and I will do it.

"The hospital doesn't get many chances to get people on a popular show like this gab show. We can get people on the Sunday morning cerebral talk shows that nobody watches, and we can get people on the regular news shows when something awful happens, but we don't get many shots at this kind of a show. So it's important that this come off. That's why my boss wants the best preparation you can possibly have."

"And your boss trusts you to take care of this, even though you're an intern?"

"Marcy talked to my boss. I didn't listen in. I did notice later that my boss had a big box of chocolate chip cookies on the desk."

Marcy probably told the boss that the evil eye was not just something from the Middle Ages, thought Nan. That and a box of chocolate chip cookies did get people to see Marcy's view of things.

"Okay, Josey. Will you be here for the fitting session?"

"Yes, ma'am. It's just called a fitting, not a fitting session. I don't know why. I'll bring the fitters in and set them up in your conference room. I have this all arranged with Marcy."

"Very well. I'll see you then. And I suppose you will be with me tomorrow?"

"Yes, ma'am. I wouldn't miss it for the world." Big grin. Josey stood, turned, and left.

18

Nan and Susan Beneficiate Shewan Lincoln

At a quarter to nine, Marcy came in to say, quietly, that the nine o'clock meeting in Susan Gunn's office was on with Shewan Lincoln, that Susan had gotten the e-mail note, and that it was time to get going if Nan wanted to be there before Ms. Lincoln got there.

So, Nan stood up, straightened her clothes, and headed for the personnel department. Susan's secretary met her and led her directly to the small conference room off Susan's private office. Nan was the first one there, and having a few minutes' headway, she fiddled around with the coffee service on a side table to make herself a mug of tea. No saucers, she noticed.

One or two minutes past nine, Susan came in one door and Susan's secretary ushered Shewan in through another. Shewan displayed just the slightest hint of surprise to find Nan there, but she quickly recovered and presented a non-committal, professional sort of a smile. Nan returned her smile.

Susan took charge. "Shewan, we have an opening in the community relations department for an assistant director. We think that that would be a good position for you. The grading scale is different in that department, but your salary will be the same. We think you will find it's a good match with your skills and interests. It's an important job, and we'd like you to do it."

"Ms. Gunn," said Shewan after a moment of reflection, "I think I am happy about this, but it is all quite sudden. I just sent a note to Nan early this morning saying that the nursing service ought to consider rotational assignments outside of just nursing. So this is a lightning response. It's so fast that this must have been in the offing before this morning."

Susan maintained her professional executive smile and said nothing at all.

Shewan continued. "Are you saying take it or leave it, or take it or else?"

Susan replied in a steady voice, not forcefully, but conveying authority. "I am saying we have a good job for you in community relations. We do not have a job for you in the nursing management ranks."

Shewan looked to Nan for the first time since the conversation had started. No smile. No hate or anger either, but no smile. A blank face. No blinking. She said nothing for most of a minute.

Nan said nothing and kept her face absolutely the way it was. Light smile. No expression. Nan had never been in a meeting quite like this one before. She didn't know if it was going well or ill. So, she played her part, which was to sit there and keep her mouth shut.

Shewan Lincoln turned back to Susan Gunn. "Very well. I accept. I don't understand everything that's going on here, but I understand that my choices are to accept this new position or to leave the hospital. I am a registered nurse. I can get a new job before lunch if it comes to that. Maybe it *will* come to that, but I would like to give the community relations job a try first. Maybe I will be better at that than I have been as a nursing manager. Maybe I won't. Either way, it seems to be smarter to give it a try since you are offering it to me, so I can see how I do."

Shewan turned to Nan again.

"Nan, you showed up as head nurse after I was given the nursing management job. Looking back, I can see that I wasn't ready for that level of management then, and it was a mistake by the hospital management to give it to me. Since you have been here, you have been clear in what you have told me, what I needed to get better at, and maybe I got better and maybe I didn't. I knew myself what you told me, before you told me. I had no illusions that I was the world's greatest nursing manager. So I am not mad at you. Not right this minute anyway.

"Ms. Gunn, I think I am mad at you, but I'm not sure. I can't complain about anything you have said to me this morning. I can't complain about the job offer. So I won't. I think this change will do me some good. Maybe it will do the nursing service some good. There are plenty of bright nurses who think they are ready for a shot at the management ranks, and maybe they will be ready where I wasn't."

Shewan paused for a moment. Then she continued, "Nan, while I can see why I have to give up that management position, I want you to know that the nursing service is a better place since you've been here. You have shaken things up, you have addressed long-overdue problems and tried to get the error rate down. So the thing I think I am going to miss most is being part of your organization. Maybe we can be better friends now, since we won't have the performance issues, my performance issues, between us."

Shewan faced Susan again. "When do I start?"

Susan answered, "Your new office is ready right now. I will have somebody pick up your personal things from your old office and bring them to you. What you are wearing is suitable for the new position, so there is no reason to go home to change. Your new boss is anxious to meet you and talk about the new position, right now. My secretary will take you over and introduce you as soon as you are ready, and then you can get right to work."

Shewan thought for a minute. "Okay, I am as ready as I am going to be. Thank you for your time, Ms. Gunn. Thank you, Nan. Let's stay in touch."

With that said, Shewan Lincoln, a tall woman, stood and drew herself up to full height, looked at them each in turn, and then walked out of the door that led to the secretary's station. She closed the door behind herself.

Susan and Nan sat quietly for a moment. Nan could not remember a meeting of any kind in her entire career when she had spoken fewer words.

Susan said, "Okay, deed done. Shewan Lincoln may turn out to be a star performer in community relations. Or she may find it utterly frustrating and resign in a few weeks. I already have our outplacement people feeding her résumé to headhunters. The next time she is offered a management position, I think she will be ready for it."

Nan replied, "Susan, I have gotten myself in hot water with management more than once, and I have been yelled at and dressed down when I deserved it and when I didn't. This was something else. You let Shewan draw her own conclusions. Nothing personal. Just, here's your new job. Take it. Not even take it and be happy. Just, take it.

"I can see that it worked. I don't know if I would have had enough nerve to do it the way you did it."

"Stock in trade, Nan. This is the only way that works.

"Although this is an awkward moment for you, Nan, I think Shewan Lincoln is actually a fan of yours. Maybe your paths will cross again. Who knows, you may wind up working for her some day."

"Stranger things have happened. Who's to say?

"Well, Susan, I want to go back to my office, but I don't want to encounter Shewan Lincoln en route. How am I going to work that?"

"I will scout the territory," said Susan, who rose, went through her private office to the door on the other side, looked around the outer office, spoke to a secretary briefly, and came back to Nan. "The coast is clear. Shewan Lincoln is reported to be in conference with her new boss, who has been a peach about this. You can go out either door."

Nan rose, exchanged fervid smiles with Susan, and walked back to her office.

Marcy was printing something out when Nan approached her office. Nan entered her office, and Marcy came in, two steps behind, carrying the printout.

"Mrs. Mills, here's the internal announcement of Shewan Lincoln's new position. That was quick."

"Shakespearian, Marcy, Shakespearian. I don't know if it's *Macbeth* or *Richard II*. I hope it's *All's Well That Ends Well*. In any case, we now have two management positions to fill immediately. Who's acting manager for Shewan Lincoln's old unit?"

"The regular substitute, the same as they do for vacation schedules. No immediate problems there."

"Okay, Marcy. Did we get any other input from the nursing managers about rotational assignments? Shewan's point about rotating outside the department actually has some merit, if we could figure out how to do that."

"Nothing yet, Mrs. Mills, but I expect we are going to see a lot of e-mails this morning saying that rotational assignments are the very thing. Nobody is going to want to be the last person to jump in. Everybody is going to understand the Shewan Lincoln thing; nobody is going to have to explain it or draw pictures."

"Okay, Marcy. Are we ready for the fitting? Or is there anything I need to do before the fitting?"

"Josey says everything is being done for the fitting, and I will tell you when they are ready. No big news elsewhere. Sanjar left me a voice mail thing that said he had learned interesting things last evening in his telephone network tour, and he is off this morning to check out the electrics."

"Marcy, make sure Sanjar is giving his reports to his own manager, too, not just to me. He doesn't report to me."

"I will remind him. Anything else?"

"You know better than I do, I think, Marcy."

"Very well," Marcy said and then left.

Nan thought over the developments of the morning and concluded that the Shewan Lincoln affair could have been a lot worse.

19

The Fitting

Marcy came in to Nan's office to announce that the fitters were waiting for Nan in her conference room. Nan went through the connecting door and joined them.

She found Josey Walberg and three men of the most peculiar mien. They all had that craftily disorganized look, eyeglasses pushed up into the hair, oddly cut and very, very informal clothes, and a peculiar look in the eye. Speaking of eyes, they were all on Nan.

"You'll do fine, love. The camera is going to love you," said the nearest of the trio, who proceeded to affix Nan with a tailor's measuring tape from every angle. "Just stand there and relax. Don't hold anything in, we want your new clothes to fit loose, since you'll be sitting down on the set. Okay, raise this arm. Okay, now hold both elbows up at shoulder level. Okay. Now sit down so we can get the seated leg dimensions." With every measurement, Number One shouted out some number and Number Two shouted it back and wrote it down in a small notebook.

"Now we check you for lighting," said Number Three, who produced a photographer's rack of floodlights and a collection of light meters. "We need to get chroma here, so we do reflections off your skin with three color filters. That goes into your makeup. Now we are going to get some shots with different cloth colors to see how your skin and your eyes pick up those colors." Number Two tossed monochrome cloth swatches across Nan's front and shoulders like a bib. More numbers read out, read back, and recorded, plus camera snaps by Number Three.

"Okay. That's enough. Now here's the drill," said Number One. "You show up at the television building at seven Wednesday morning. That's tomorrow. Don't bother with any makeup, and just wear a tracksuit or something of that sort. We will dress you from the skin out, do your hair, and do your makeup. If the television people will give us a sole-use makeup room for the morning, we'll do you there. If not, and we will sort that out this afternoon with our counterparts there, then we will do it at our place which is only a block further on, and we will shuttle you back and forth.

"Right now it looks like we will do you up with a mother-of-pearl blouse with an oversized bow and a dark blue business suit with skirt to a little below the knee so that it is the right length when you sit down. We'll tell you how to sit when the time comes. And where to look and how much to smile. We'll take care of that. Now, we'll need a lapel pin. Do you have one you wear a lot that would sort of identify you in a crowd?"

"I wear my nurse's pin most days," replied Nan, pointing out the pin on her jacket.

"That's lovely, but it's too small. The camera will never find it. What's your Zodiac sign?"

"Gemini."

"Okay, we'll do you up an oversized Gemini pin that will be in good taste and will catch the camera without taking over the scene. Nothing gaudy. We're doing you as the lady executive. Mild mannered. Professional. Competent.

"One other thing, love. You can't be thinking about work or what to cook for supper while you're on the set. That means you can't be thinking about anything from seven o'clock on. Mind blank. Space out. No cell phones, no newspapers, no pagers."

"I can't go four hours without a pager or a cell phone. That's asking too much."

"No, it's not. You can do it. You got all these people here to mind the store for half a day. Maybe they'll surprise you.

"Josey can have a cell phone, so if the city catches fire, somebody can call Josey. But Josey can only tell you about it when the fire gets to the second floor of the television studio. That's the way it has to be. You may think this is only a local hen party television deal, but there are no bush leagues in television. Everything has to be ready for the Great White Way from the git-go. That's the way we do it, and we do it that way because it works.

"We don't tell you how to stick needles in backsides, you don't tell us how to dress you up. Got it?"

Nan was beginning to wonder if she knew any timid people any more. A Maggie Kelly remark came to mind; Maggie had said that people thought God gave them a mouth to tell Maggie what to do. Now it looked like they all had a new assignment, to tell Nan what to do. Well, she had to admit they knew more about television than she did, so she had either to can the whole thing or do as she was being told.

"Okay. I'll do it your way. Empty mind from seven o'clock on. I'll show up in my sweat suit, and the rest is up to you."

"That is the voice of sweet reason, Love. Now open up. We need to make a dental impression. That's it. That's a wrap. See you at seven, love."

20

Nan Revisits the Burn Unit

Nan decided she would visit the burn unit to see if there was any new report on the Mr. Collins who had been in that manhole fire Sunday night. Nan knew that Mrs. Collins had passed away the previous day.

Nan checked at the burn unit desk and found Tanya Hunt, the unit manager, on duty. Nan asked for news on Mr. Collins.

"Nan, he's in bad shape. He's comatose, although he had a few minutes when it looked like he was coming around, but then he sank into the coma again. Prognosis is unfavorable. Young Mr. Collins is in with him in Room 427 if you want to step in."

"Has he been here a lot?"

"Yes, he and his wife have been here practically full time. I think she went out to make funeral arrangements for the mother, but he stayed here."

"Okay, Tanya, I will step in and say hello. He may have seen me go by in the hallway, and I don't want him to think I have forgotten about them already."

Nan went to Room 427, knocked gently, and stuck her head in to make sure she wasn't disturbing anything. Young Mr. Collins was there in the bedside chair, and he looked up when Nan appeared. He waved one hand a little, which Nan took to be a sufficient invitation to go in and speak to him.

"Mr. Collins," said Nan in a low voice, "I am so sorry to hear of the loss of your mother. I am sorry there wasn't more we could do for her."

That brought tears to Collins's eyes, tears that were not very far away in any case.

"Thank you, Mrs. Mills. I remember you from yesterday. God, that seems like so long ago.

"My wife has gone to settle the arrangements for Mom. She is being laid out this evening, if that's the term people still use, at Humbert and White over on the west side. The funeral is on Thursday morning. Here's a prayer card with the information on it. They only come in quantities of a thousand, so we have a lot of them."

The card was the usual thing with name of deceased, funeral home, church name, and some vital statistics. The opposite side had a Bible verse and a religious picture. Nan took the card and said a word of thanks.

Nan looked at the elder Mr. Collins in the bed. He appeared to be in a deep sleep, probably a coma.

Nan then realized that when she took the memorial card from the younger Mr. Collins, she had wound up holding his upper arm with her left hand, and she was still holding on to him. Well, no reason to break off now, maybe he needs a little support until his wife gets back.

"Dad just about woke up once. That was last evening. He looked at me, and I think maybe he recognized me. I told him we were here. I couldn't touch him because he has burns everyplace, so I just looked at him and talked to him and hoped he could hear me. My wife was here at that moment, so we both stood by the side of the bed and talked to him.

"Then he sort of smiled and sank back into sleep.

"You know when a baby smiles, and they say that the baby isn't really smiling but is just having gas? Maybe it was the same with Dad. I don't care. When I see a baby smiling, I smile back. I smiled the best smile I could for Dad. I hope he saw the smile, even if he didn't know who was here."

"I am sure he knew it was you," Nan offered.

"The doctors tell me his chances are between slim and none. He looks to be getting weaker. We told the doctors to avoid any Herculean efforts, whatever it is you call it. No point in hooking him up to a machine and keeping him alive as a vegetable. My wife and I talked about that a lot before we decided, but now that it is decided, I am at peace with it.

"I don't know if Dad will find peace or not. He was a mean old cuss. Always ready to cuff me on the ear for the slightest thing. Nothing I did was ever quite good enough.

"People react to that kind of thing in different ways, I guess. The way I reacted was, I wanted to show him up. If he set the bar this high, I wanted to jump that high," said Collins, holding his hand at chest level and then eye level.

"Well, even if he was mean, he didn't deserve to go out this way. And Mom was a wonderful person, and nothing in the world could make me believe she deserved any of this. She deserved better than Dad, too, but that's a decision she made for herself and stuck to it.

"I know one thing. I said this a long time ago, and I have been saying it again ever since it was clear that he wasn't going to be going home with us. I don't want his money. I've got enough, and there isn't any other family, so if it came to me, we'd have to pay a big bunch of it in taxes anyway. So for what would finally come to me net, I would rather have the satisfaction of throwing it back at him. I'd bury it with him if I could."

Nan decided it was a good time to just listen.

"I've been walking around the ward here a little, when I get stiff from sitting in that chair. I never thought about burn units before. I knew people got burned, but I never thought about all the special equipment. I just figured burned people got a regular hospital bed like broken-leg people. Now I see all this specialized equipment.

"And I guess I've seen a few patients, too, besides Dad. I don't mean I went snooping, I just mean I see a few patients out in the hall sometimes, and some patients leave their hallway door open. So I see a few. Boy, some of them look bad. I never thought of that before, either."

Nan decided she should say something, so she tried, "This is a pretty good burn unit. We get patients who transfer into our unit from other hospitals that don't have our specialists and our equipment. So this unit stays full, and some of the patients do have very severe conditions. We can help them, some of them, quite a lot."

"I like the doctors we've had. I guess they get grants to buy all this specialized equipment, huh?"

"They get some grants. The board finds money for some of the equipment. In a fast-moving field, it takes a lot of capital money to keep up to the state of the art, because the state of the art keeps moving ahead."

"Yes, I can see that, Mrs. Mills. I know something about technology myself, and I can see that this kind of equipment can cost a bundle. I suppose there are, what, a hundred hospitals in the whole country that specialize in burn cases?"

"Yes, something like that number. One of the doctors could probably tell you the exact number."

"Well, the exact number doesn't matter. My point is that it's not 10,000 or 100,000 hospitals all buying something new, which would keep the unit price down. It's just a small number, and all the R&D has to be recovered in a small lot of sales."

"Yes, I suppose that's right."

"I see you are building a new wing over on that side. Are you going to have a new burn unit over there?"

"I don't think the board has made a final decision about that, Mr. Collins."

"I was just curious. I suppose if Dad were in here with a broken leg, I'd think the new wing ought to specialize in legs." Mr. Collins produced something of a wry smile. "Well, Mrs. Mills, it was kind of you to stop by. My wife will be back shortly, and then I am going to take a nap so that I can be awake when friends come to the funeral parlor this evening. I'm all off schedule.

"Thanks for coming by. I can tell you the nurses and aides that you have on this floor have been very kind to us and as kind as they can be to Dad and to Mom while she was here. I suppose you hear that all the time, but it's true in this case."

Nan most decidedly did not hear that all the time, and she made a mental note to cite that in Tanya's file.

Nan smiled, squeezed the young Mr. Collins on the tricep, and took her leave. Nan waved to Tanya at her desk to make sure that Tanya knew she was leaving the unit, and went back to her office feeling deeply somber.

21

Nan Talks Six Sigma
to the IT Staff

Marcy reminded Nan of her 1:30 appointment to talk up Six Sigma to the IT staff. As she walked to Rudy Rudolf's office, Nan ran quickly through what she wanted to say. Rudy's secretary greeted her warmly, told her she was expected, and put her head into the conference room to let Rudy know that Nan was there. She turned and told Nan with a polite smile that Rudy and the group were ready for her.

Nan found Rudy at the head of a standard conference table with about a dozen people around the table. They all stood to welcome her. Nan noticed that Sanjar was there, sitting halfway down the table. Sanjar bowed deeply to her. Nan acknowledged to herself that she liked that and wished it would catch on with others, even though she didn't think it likely.

Rudy shook her hand and then told his staff, "Folks, this is the Nan Mills who got the write-up on the sports line this morning. That's why she's here, to give us a little coaching. Nan's going to talk about Six Sigma, for which she has a Black Belt, and how it fits into hospital computing. Nan told me yesterday that there is a lot of Japanese thinking in Six Sigma, and that the primary rule is that the purpose of going to work every day is to make the boss look smart. So, Nan is going to tell you how to make me look smart. Now there's a challenge for you. Go to it, Nan!"

Rudy started a vigorous applause and made way for Nan at the head of the table.

Nan began. "Rudy, thanks for your introduction, and since you already gave away the secret, I can be brief. I am sure you have vital business matters to discuss, and I am a late addition to your program.

"We, and I mean everybody working for the hospital plus all the medical staff, do things right most of the time. But sometimes we make errors. The idea of Six Sigma is to eliminate error. Maybe we can't get to zero errors, but we can get to a low number of errors. We talk about 3.4 errors per million opportunities. I have never met anyone who was against reducing error, so we'll skip over that part and talk about how one actually eliminates an error.

"It's done by changing the way work is done, one task at a time. There are three guidelines, each of which is easy to see. First, make it easier for the worker to do the task right than wrong. Second, make any error obvious, immediately. Third, make it easy to correct the error on the spot.

"Those seem so trivial that anyone would think that we would always do that, every time, and the problem would have been solved before it ever happened.

"We're in a hospital, so we can talk about medical error and medicinal error and x-ray error and every kind of error. But since you are the IT department, let's talk about computer errors and how they impact healthcare right here in this hospital.

"Do we still make billing errors?"

Rudy bobbed his head up and down, and following his cue, all the others bobbed their heads.

"Do we still bill people for drugs after they are discharged?"

More bobbing.

"Do we still bill people for telephone calls after they are discharged?"

Bobbing.

"Some of what goes wrong, it seems to me anyway, happens because the person making the data entry doesn't really see the patient. I think we bill a patient for drugs when the drug leaves the pharmacy, not when the nurse gives the patient the shot. Do we still do it that way?"

Nods.

"Well, that looks to me like a poor information flow design. Doesn't it look that way to you? Maybe I shouldn't say an information error, because the person who does the data input doesn't have any information. Or, not all the information. The pharmacy clerk can't possibly know if the patient was discharged or even if the patient died before the drug got to the bed, and maybe somebody checks all that out and maybe not." Heads were shaking in the negative.

"So maybe the pharmacy clerk is not the one who should be making this entry.

"There's one other thing that I have wondered about, and maybe you can tell me it is in good hands. That's the crosschecking of details that arise in different departments. For instance, as I understand it, the hospital counts on the profit margin on drug sales to patients, which make up a decent fraction of our whole revenue. The purchasing department gets the list price and the list cost and the discount rates by negotiating with the drug manufacturer. Then the insurance department negotiates a discount price for each different insurance carrier and government agency. Then they both separately put down their numbers into some database. And then they do it over again every time there is a change in the drug price, which I suppose must be every day, considering all the different drugs we use.

"What I am wondering is, does anybody check one of those entries against the other to see if both changes get made at the same time and that the discounted selling price is still above the discounted buying price?"

One hand at the far end of the table went up halfway. "Mrs. Mills, the audit department checks those when they do their internal audits. They check back with the outside sources at the same time to make sure nobody is fiddling with the data entries."

Nan nodded in that direction, thinking that that would be perceived as positive reinforcement. "That's good. Do you have any idea how often they do that, or if they check a big fraction of the entries when they do that audit?"

The same person answered. "They do a statistical sample, but I think the sample size is determined by how much time they want to give this particular topic. They only do a handful, I can tell you that for sure. They do audits all the time, but it's not always on this topic. So if drug pricing and costing gets audited as often as once a year, I'd be surprised. And not every drug, every year."

Lots of nods around the table. Nan nodded some more.

"So waiting for the auditor to find a goof in one of our most important business lines sounds like it might not be the best way to do things. Could you build in some internal checks so that really dumb things get caught on the fly? Like a price below cost, say, or an update to costs not matched to an update in prices?"

This triggered several murmured conversations. Nan glanced to Rudy, who had a gleam in his eye. After a full minute of murmurs, Rudy rocked his chair back to the vertical position, put both hands up in a "stop" gesture, and said, "Looks like we have a live one there. Let's table that for the moment and get back to it after Nan finishes up. Okay?"

Lots of gleaming eyes and affirmative gestures.

"Before you all jump up and throw your pocket protectors at me," Nan said, "please let me say that I didn't come here to accuse you of anything. Instead, what I came here to say is that the system we have does not conform to good Six Sigma practice, and maybe if since we have Sanjar as our own in-house guru, we can twist Sanjar's arm to spend some time with task groups to help inculcate this new stuff.

"As for the infrastructure study, you all know, I think, that Sanjar had us headed in the right direction on the data networks, and we had a plan to study fixes and work with vendors before that freak manhole fire caught up with us. Sanjar will be telling us in a few minutes about what he has learned about the electrics and the telephones in his running of those lines in the past 24 hours."

Rudy turned to Nan. "Nan, if you have another 10 minutes and would like to stay to hear what Sanjar has to say about those parts of our infrastructure, you are welcome to stay. I'll kick somebody out so you can have a chair. Hell, you can have my chair."

Nan considered the offer and said she would stay for 10 minutes if Rudy really meant 10 minutes.

"Yes, I mean 10 minutes. Hear that, gang?" His staff all bobbed their heads but didn't display much confidence in the new 10-minutes-means-10-minutes rule.

Nan was offered her choice of three chairs. She took the closest one and paid with a smile. Somebody was then short a chair but made do by standing against the wall.

Rudy said, "Sanjar, you're on, and you have 9.7 minutes."

Sanjar walked to the head of the table. "Rudy, Mrs. Mills, ladies and gentlemen," He bowed, "I will be brief. You will be receiving my trip report by noon tomorrow, so I will just hit the highlights.

"On telephones, we have an internal PBX that is partly duplicated so that a computer failure will not wipe out internal calling to vital parts of the building. That includes the IT department. The PBX has its own battery backup. In addition, each department has a few telephones that are directly wired to the telephone company and bypass the PBX. So, that's pretty good. Externally, we are connected to the telephone company's local office by their cables. Many of us have cell phones and indeed most patients and visitors have cell phones, even though there is a hospital rule against using them inside the building.

"What I am saying is that if we lose out wireline connection to the telephone company, the cell phones are a backup. However, all the cell phone companies use the same tower near here, and they all connect to the rest of the world by cables running from that one tower to their point of presence, which is to say, to a point where they connect with wireline providers. The point of connection happens to be, by inspection, the same local telephone building. So, if that building blows up or if those cable bundles get attacked, we will lose both the wireline phones and the cell phones. Am I being sufficiently clear? I will have some civilian-level drawings made of that shortly.

"As for the electrics, we have a single high-capacity connection to the local electric company running from its substation just at the end of the hospital property. We have two diesel generators, each of which was big enough to carry 100 percent of the vital hospital loads when they were installed, although that is no longer true because of the addition of lots of electrical equipment over the years. This was studied six months ago, and a third diesel is being installed as part of the construction of the new wing, and the old diesels are being refitted presently. In the new scheme, any two of the three diesels will have more than enough capacity for the present vital loads plus a lot of room for load growth. In addition, many of the vital loads have their own battery backup systems, such as the PBX and our main computers do. Not everything, though, and I don't know that we have a solid rule for sizing battery backup systems. There are surely experts on that matter that the hospital may wish to consult in due course.

"That's it in a nutshell. We are not in bad shape, but we are not in perfect shape either. Perhaps these are things to evaluate and consider over the next few planning cycles.

"Rather than answering questions right now, I ask that you look at my memo tomorrow, and we can have a follow-up meeting if there is any interest.

"Thank you, Rudy. Mrs. Mills. Ladies and gentlemen." Sanjar bowed, with an extra bow in Nan's direction.

Rudy took over the head position and said, "Thanks, Sanjar. Right on the money. Given our recent untoward experience with manhole fires, I think we'd look pretty dumb if we studied these other networks for six months and then handed up some recommendation. We are going to hand up a recommendation within 48 hours, and I want everybody here to be signed on. I'll make a couple of phone calls and jack up that HVAC stuff, too. There may be something for us to do with that, maybe not. My guess is that that department has 85 contractors working on those drawings, three shifts. Nothing like a freak manhole fire to adjust priorities in the staff groups.

"That means us, too. Let's get everybody's head into the huddle on this one. Sanjar has done the legwork, and I commend him for it. Now it's up to the rest of you to figure out what this means and to give me something I can take to the suits upstairs and I really mean within 48 hours.

"Nan told you, your job is to make me look smart. Looks like we have a leg up on this one, and you don't have to make me look smart last week, when I was dumb, but only this week, when you still have a shot at it.

"Okay, everybody got their heads screwed on right on this one?"

More heads bobbing. Shouting his instructions back at him might be too much of a culture shock, so Nan didn't think she would recommend that. Yet.

Rudy was at a pause, so Nan stood up to say some parting words.

"Thanks again for your hospitality. Rudy, I think you make your instructions clear, although John Wayne would do it differently if he were running your submarine." She smiled at Rudy Rudolf.

Rudy looked at her quizzically for a few seconds and said, "You're right, Nan. I'll have to think about how to do that 'Up periscope' stuff here."

Nan turned to the group and said, "My nursing department is trying to learn to apply Six Sigma. You may want to invite Suzy Wong over some time to tell you how the anesthesia people have reduced their death rate from hundreds per million down to five per million. Dr. Anderson, the chief medical officer whom many of you know, has had Dr. Gaba from Stanford in recently to talk to the medical staff about his research in medical error reduction, which Suzy can also tell you about. The radiology department is working with vendors on better ways to mark the front and the back of x-rays. So, our hospital, although it is tiny compared to the big research centers, has more than a few things to brag about when it comes to error reduction. I am happy to see that your department, Rudy, is joining in the fun." She smiled at Rudy and backed toward the door to make her escape.

Rudy replied, "Anything that makes me look smart, my whole team is in favor of. So, we have some catching up to do, but I will get out my BB gun and take a few potshots at any laggards. Right, gang?" Big toothy smile in the direction of the staff.

"Right, Rudy," they replied in unison.

"Up periscope!" Rudy shouted.

"Up periscope!" the staff shouted back. Big laughs all around, including Nan's.

Nan made her exit, thinking to herself that working for Rudy would be a mixed blessing, but it would never be dull.

When Nan got back to her office, Marcy told her that Sanjar had called to say that he and his wife would be attending the engineering meeting that evening.

"Marcy, I guess I knew that Sanjar is married, because he wears a wedding ring, but I don't think I have met the wife, and I can't think of a name. Do you know anything?"

"Sanjar is married. His wife's name is Sarita. She's from India, too. She teaches chemistry, I think it is, at the community college. They have two boys, but they are not twins. They are about 8 or 10 years old. I have never actually been introduced, but I have seen them at the shopping mall as a family."

"Sarita. That's a pretty name, and easier to say than Subramaniam. Well, I look forward to meeting her this evening. Is Sanjar a member of this engineering society, or did he get himself invited for this meeting?"

"I don't know, Mrs. Mills. I can find out, but you'll probably see him in person this evening before I can get an answer."

"Yes, you're right. I'll just ask him this evening, if our paths cross. I have no idea how many people are going to be there or how they organize their meetings."

"Their staffer called last week to get confirmation that you were going to show up and then again this afternoon to reconfirm. The word from the staffer is that they are going to have about a hundred of their own members plus a lot of spouses, and they have a handful of other guests who are not speaking, they are just there to hear what you have to say. The staffer said that's normal for them. The other guests are usually connected with the university or some other institution that has an interest in a particular topic."

"Okay, Marcy. A big crowd is easier to talk to than a little one, so we'll see how it comes out. Did they say whether they tape the presentations?"

"Nothing was said, but if they are engineers, they are going to have every gadget in the world there, so you can figure on digital video recording of some experimental kind. You can't count on it working, though."

"Marcy, I can see you know some engineers yourself."

funeral process was for the surviving family, and she had talked twice to the son, so she felt she would not be out of place there.

Nan left Jack to sign the register of visitors and went into the viewing room, whatever they called it these days. She recognized the Collins son, standing at the appropriate place in the room, chatting with some people a good deal older than himself, probably friends of his mother or maybe family. Nan went to the casket, only to find it closed. Then she thought a moment about the probable condition of the body and decided that she would have closed the casket, too. Still, it took something away from the whole thing. Nan shuddered and murmured a prayer for the departed.

Nan headed towards Sam Collins Jr., waiting for the little throng to clear so she could approach. That only took a minute or two. Nan extended her hand and said, "Mr. Collins, I wanted to express my deep sympathy for your loss." Nan wondered for a few seconds if she should give her name, but she saw quickly that Collins recognized her.

"You're from the hospital. Mrs. Mills, I think. It's very thoughtful of you to stop here this evening. I know you didn't know my mother, but I do know that you would have liked her. I think she would have liked you, too."

Collins mustered what he could of a smile for Nan. He had the weight of the world on his shoulders, Nan could see, and he stood there holding her hand in both of his, looking at her with troubled eyes.

"My wife isn't here yet. She is taking a turn at the hospital. I don't suppose you can wait to meet her here. I'll make sure you're introduced at the hospital the next time our paths cross. Well, I know that you were introduced before, but I don't think you had any chance to talk even for a moment.

"You know, wakes are a funny thing. There are people here I haven't seen in 20 years, and they remember it to the day. I mean, I was a little kid, and they say they remember me. I must have been a really rotten kid." He made another attempt at a smile. "Then there are people I know never set eyes on my mother or father, and they are here. Groupies, I guess. Funeral groupies. And then there are some second cousins and so on that I only see at funerals. That's our own fault, but that's the way we are. Maybe other families build closer ties."

"I don't know, Mr. Collins. There are certainly cousins in my family and my husband's family that I only see at funerals. It must be the way Americans do things."

Nan thought she should try to get her hand back. Collins was still holding it, gently, in both of his. It didn't seem to be anything personal, more like a need to connect with somebody at this difficult time. So, she gave it another minute to see if something would break up the séance.

Jack came up. Nan reached out with her available left hand and took him by the upper arm and steered him to face Sam Collins Jr. "Mr. Collins, this is my husband, Jack Mills. Jack, this is Mr. Collins, son of the deceased."

Collins let go of Nan's hand and offered his to Jack. Jack shook it formally and said a few words of condolence. Collins was now holding Jack's hand in both of his own. Nan found herself slightly amused by this but kept a restrained face, fitting for the circumstances, with just a slight twinkle in the eye.

Maybe he steals wristwatches for a living, Nan thought to herself perversely. No, most people wear their wristwatch on the left wrist, so that wouldn't work. Just in case, she checked her own wrist to make sure her watch was still there. Then she checked Jack's wrist, too. Since they were both left-handed, they both wore their watches on the right wrist; easy pickin's for two-handed wristwatch grabbers.

Nan knew that her giddy impulses were out of place here, and she knew it was because of the stress of the situation. She kept her face as straight as she could.

Others were now approaching to express their condolences to Collins, so Jack retrieved his hand, they both said a few more words to Collins, and then they left.

People died in Nan's hospital every day. Nan could go to a wake every evening of the year if she wanted to, but this was the first one she had gone to for somebody outside her family, maybe ever. That car fire and Nan's being at the emergency room door when the unlucky couple were brought in caught her up in the affair much more than any routine case. Well, she was happy she had come, she didn't think she had done any harm, and it was hardly out of the way. So, it's over.

23

The Engineering Society Meeting

Jack drove them the few remaining blocks to the engineering society meeting. They hardly exchanged a word along the way. When they went inside, they found a large room set up with round tables set for eight, with maybe 20 such tables. Places had been reserved for them at a table hosted by the chapter president and his wife. Others at the table included a staffer from national headquarters for the society and, much to Nan's surprise, the dean of the nursing school at the state university where, 20 or so years before, Nan had taken her undergraduate degree in nursing. Dean Winifred Sommerfeld, known to all as Freddy. Nan had stayed in touch with the nursing school over the years and knew and was known by Freddy Sommerfeld.

"Freddy, you'll remember my husband, Jack. I'm so surprised to see you here this evening. I didn't know you went in for engineering society meetings."

"Hello, Nan. When word went around that you were talking about medical error, I wangled an invitation so I can see what you are up to. If it's really radical, we can always strike you off the alumni rolls and return all future contributions to the alumni fund."

"Striking me off, I can believe. Sending back checks, that I will have to see."

Their table filled up with other officers of the society chapter and spouses. The meal turned out to be slightly better than the rubber chicken Nan had figured on, and the time went by quickly.

Nan took the opportunity at each lull in the conversation to scan the room to see if she knew anybody else in the room. She spotted Sanjar sitting with a very pretty woman wearing a dark red sari and traditional Indian makeup with a dark red spot on her forehead. Nan figured that person to be Sarita Subramaniam and reminded herself to get introduced to her before the evening was over. Nan recognized one other staffer from Rudy Rudolf's department and . . . another surprise . . . one of the staffers from the hospital's building and main-tenance department. She couldn't see everybody, the way the room was organized, so there may be others there, too, who might be worth noticing.

Nan nudged Jack and directed his gaze in the direction of Sanjar and Sarita. Jack, being more at home at an engineering meeting than Nan herself, half stood and waved grandly in Sanjar's direction. The wave was returned. That increased the likelihood that they would find each other after the meeting, which pleased Nan.

The food had been served promptly, and while dessert dishes were still on the tables, the chapter president went to the speaker's rostrum and called the meeting to order. He dispensed with ordinary business, to which no one objected, and moved immediately to intro-duce their guests, including Freddy, the headquarters guy, Jack, and a few others who didn't ring bells with Nan. Then he introduced Nan and promised to get everybody out early since it was a midweek meeting. Nan took that as a left-handed way of telling her to keep her talk down to the agreed 20 minutes, and being left-handed herself, she didn't mind. The chapter president made one fleeting remark about the article on the sports website that morning and said Nan was the first Six Sigma Black Belt among area head nurses, and that's why she was invited to speak to the group. True enough, Nan thought.

Nan rose to speak and was greeted by enthusiastic applause. We'll see if they still applaud when I'm finished, she thought. Know-ing something about the psychology of engineers, Nan figured that the secret to success that evening consisted in refusing, politely, to get into any arguments with anybody. And she couldn't call on Jack to bail her out in this situation. Well, the natives looked to be pacified after their meal, so she would give it a fast start and see how it went.

Nan stepped behind the rostrum, smiled at the crowd, and thanked the chapter president. She greeted the officers, guests, members, and spouses, and began her talk.

"Well," Nan began, "let's get acquainted. Let's see the hands of those of you who are Six Sigma Green Belts or higher." She paused, and hands shot up all over the room, maybe a tenth of the whole group had a hand up. Some put up both hands; which she put down to the general nuttiness of engineers.

"How many Six Sigma Black Belts?" Almost as many hands.

"How many Six Sigma Master Black Belts?" Several, but not any-where near as many as before.

"How many of you are registered nurses?" Nan put her own hand up, and she saw that Freddy Sommerfeld had one hand up high. One other hand, off to the side. The hand, Nan saw, was that of a nurse she knew from a group practice in town. Nan made a mental note to find out if that nurse was here on her own or as the spouse of a society member.

"How many of you are involved in important, high-value, production?" Every hand went up.

"How many of you are involved in life or death actions on a daily basis, so involved that if you make an error, somebody right in front of you will die?" Nan raised her own hand and saw that Freddy had raised hers. The other nurse raised hers about halfway. No others.

"How many of you figure to be in a hospital some time during your life?" Lots of hands, not very high.

"How many of you would like the see the medical error rate be as low as the error rate you now have in your factories?" Lots of hands, high. General roar of positive-sounding noise.

"Okay, then we have some observable characteristics. We have a community of interest, and we have all the expertise over on *your* side, and all the need over here on *my* side. Maybe we ought to be pooling our efforts. What do you say to that?"

Loud applause. Some indistinct cheers and cries. Foot stomping. Rhythmic clapping.

Nan raised her hands, palms facing the crowd, and tried to get control of the meeting back.

"Okay, we agree on that already, and I have hardly even started.

"Your publications show that American factories are running at about the four sigma level, which is an error rate of a few hundred per million. American service industries are running at one or two sigma, meaning error rates in the tens of thousands per million opportunities. The healthcare industry is probably in the run of service industries because, after all, we are a service industry.

"There are some great developments I could tell you about, like the reduction of anesthesia deaths from hundreds per million operations to five per million operations. And falling. I'll give your chapter president some websites he can link to from your site to if you want to follow up and check that out.

"But rather than tell you everything is in good shape, I want to highlight the differences between factory work and healthcare in modern America.

"Much of healthcare is craft labor. A great deal of it is manual labor. We nurses put our hands on patients. We put thermometers under tongues using our hands. We give injections by holding the patient with one hand and the syringe with the other. Doctors give verbal orders that are carried out immediately, often because time is of the essence. Many of those orders involve medicine, and if the wrong medicine or the wrong dosage is delivered, then the patient can be in big trouble or even dead.

"In the factory today, your primary interest is in reducing the variability of production. So, you work on the quality of the feedstock materials and the cutting edges of your tools and the feed rates and other process variables. You don't work much on improving manual processes any more because you don't use manual processes. Neither would we, if we knew how to get a machine to do what we do. A hundred years from now, maybe robots will do everything nurses do today. But that's not now. It's not the near future.

"In healthcare, we are not going to reduce process variance until we figure out how to eliminate error, particularly manual error. I really think that in this regard, we are perhaps 50 years behind the general run of industry. What you knew 50 years ago, we need today.

"To eliminate error in manual tasks, we apply the Six Sigma poka-yoke method. You may do this slightly differently than we do it, but we apply these three guidelines when tasks are designed: make it easier to do the right thing than the wrong thing, make errors immediately obvious, and allow the worker to fix the error on the spot.

"I can say that our own hospital is working on several projects that apply poka-yoke to the work we do every day. I'll tell you about two. First, we decided that all verbal orders need to be fed back so that any error in communication gets flagged and fixed immediately. We do it the same way John Wayne did it in all those submarine movies. When John Wayne said, 'Up periscope,' what did the rest of the actors say?"

"Up periscope!" yelled every man in the audience, and some women, too.

"You see, you all knew that, and maybe you practice it in your daily work. If you don't, maybe you should think about it.

"I note for your information that we are not a bit bashful about taking good ideas anywhere we find them, including old movies.

"Here's another one. A serious issue is the needle-stick. That's when a nurse sticks somebody other than the intended patient. Usually it's the nurse who gets stuck, and often it's because the patient lurches at the last moment. In the past few years, vendors have developed better syringes so that the number of needle-sticks is down, but it is not zero. Our pediatrics unit is working with our training group to figure out how to handle these newer syringes to reduce the incidence of needle-sticks even further. Just this week I learned that one of the major vendors wants to join in our development project to speed things along. That's fine. We welcome any help we can find, and our hospital has done research projects in formal ways before, and we have a procedure for handling the formalities. You may think that our interest is only in reducing the pain that comes from an unexpected needle jab, especially when the nurse is the most likely jabee, but there is more to it. With all the blood-borne diseases these days, a needle-stick can be a life-and-death matter.

"Recognize this?" Nan held up an x-ray of a skull.

"Skull," was shouted back by the more playful element in the audience.

"Recognize this?" Nan turned the x-ray so that the reverse side was to the audience.

"Skull," shouted the same people.

"Okay, it's a skull. But is that mark here"—Nan pointed at a mark on the upper part of the skull—"on the human's left side or right side?" Nan held the x-ray up, reversed it, held it still for half a minute, and reversed it again.

"Those of you at the front tables may be able to see this lettering." Nan pointed at some typed letters near the bottom of the x-ray. "Can you?"

Those near the podium squinted and one or two indicated that they thought they could see something. The others said they could not.

"I don't know why x-rays are not made with a red back or a green back so that this question would never arise, but they are not. Perhaps I should say they are not, yet. Our radiology department is working with vendors and their own professional society to see if something better can't be done. Something so obvious that even a civilian, say one of you, would be able to tell the front from the back.

"We try to use the NASA rule, which you may know. That is, make the display so simple that a civilian can understand it so that the expert will not read it wrongly. You see, the point is not to help the civilian; it's to help the expert. Experts make rare errors when reading complex displays but very, very, very rarely make errors in reading simple displays.

"The NASA rule says that it's simple enough when a civilian can understand it.

"The other part of the NASA rule will be obvious to you here. That is that the experts themselves never ask for a simpler display because they understand the complex display. Yes, they do understand it, but they make errors, not every time but often enough for us to be concerned, when reading a complex display. Almost never when reading a simple display.

"So it takes an outside push to get experts to do something that, as in this case, seems obvious to all the nonexperts in the world.

faculty member and a couple of graduate students to visit her and follow up in more detail. Nan said she was interested but would need to get more details because, after all, she was in a hospital and not a research center. Freddy said she understood completely and thought she knew how to work things out. Freddy asked if Nan thought that a course in Six Sigma could be added to the undergraduate or graduate nursing curriculum. Nan said that was a little out of her league but that she thought probably so.

By then, the crowd had gotten on its feet and people were heading for the door. Nan had not heard an adjournment, but then formality didn't seem to bear heavily on this group.

Nan caught Jack's eye and reminded him of her interest in meeting Sarita Subramaniam. Jack took his leave of the group and dove into the crowd to intercept Sanjar and Sarita before they got to the door. That proved to be more difficult than it would have seemed because enough people recognized Jack and wanted to shake hands that he made slow progress through the crowd. As it happened, Sanjar and Sarita were plowing the same furrow from the other end, so they met in the middle. Jack waved to Nan, who took her leave from the table and headed in their direction. Slow progress again, because everybody wanted to shake her hand and present her with a business card. Nan had anticipated this and had brought a wad of her own cards to hand to people in exchange.

"Mr. and Mrs. Mills," Sanjar said when Nan reached their little group, "may I present to you my wife, Sarita. Sarita, this is Mrs. Nan Mills, and this is Mr. Jack Mills."

"I am honored to meet you both," said Sarita Subramaniam with a head bow. Nan was rather hoping for the old-fashioned bow with palms together in front of the forehead, but Sarita was holding onto Sanjar's arm with one of her hands, and any bow at all was more than she would get from the Americans here.

"Thank you, replied Nan. "I am pleased to meet you, especially because I have grown to rely so heavily on Sanjar in everything we do at the hospital. He is a very special person."

"Yes, ma'am," said Sarita. "He is that." She smiled at Sanjar and gripped his arm a little tighter.

"Do I understand that you teach at the community college, Sarita?"

"Yes, Mrs. Mills. I teach a few courses now that our sons are in school all day. I also take a course each semester to complete my doctorate in chemistry, some day."

"Sarita, it took me 10 years just to finish my master's degree, so I know what you are talking about," Nan said.

"I can't help noticing, Sarita, that you wear the traditional Indian dress. It's very pretty. Do you dress that way all the time, here?"

"Oh, I am not a fanatic about it, the way some women from India are. I find it comfortable and suitable for such occasions as this. At home I am more apt to wear blue jeans. Our two boys are 100 percent American and wouldn't wear Indian clothes for anything. I am probably an embarrassment to them when I wear a sari. So they can learn a little tolerance at home, perhaps."

"Yes, I see your point." Nan turned said, "Sanjar, I told Jack a little about your infrastructure study. Perhaps this engineering society would be interested in that, because that is something that applies to all kinds of companies and organizations."

"Yes, Mrs. Mills, I was thinking the same thing myself. Or perhaps a small paper at a technical conference for engineers interested in hospitals, because my interest, naturally, is in helping the healthcare industry. We'll need to complete the study and the remedies to have anything worth presenting to an engineering society."

Jack spoke up. "Sanjar, perhaps the national committee you and I are both on would be a sounding board for your findings. Maybe work up some standard questions for people to ask their network vendors or some testing that might be done."

"That is an interesting idea, Jack. Perhaps we can discuss your idea in a week or so, after we see what we have in hand."

Nan said, "Well, it is so nice to meet you, Sarita. I'll probably see you at the hospital tomorrow, Sanjar. Oh, wait a minute, I am not going to be at the hospital myself tomorrow until the middle of the afternoon because of that television show. Well, if not tomorrow, one day soon." They shook hands all around, and Nan and Jack started for the door on their side closest to where they parked.

As they got to the door, they found Freddy Sommerfeld again, this time in close conversation with Dr. Robert Anderson, the chief medical officer of Nan's hospital. Nan stopped to speak to Freddy and Dr. Anderson.

"Dr. Anderson, I didn't hear you being introduced among the honored guests. I see you know Freddy, and I admit to being surprised to see you here."

"Good evening Nan. Good evening, Jack. That was a great talk, Nan. You know how to talk to these geeks, I see. I already knew you know how to talk to physicians, so I am not surprised. I may have to stay home tomorrow and watch that television talk show to see how you do with that crowd. I'd tape it, but I have never figured out how to set my VCR. "

"How did you come to be here?"

"I heard you were the speaker, so I got my son-in-law to invite me as a guest. He's a member. That way I got to sit with him and my daughter at one of the back tables without telling anybody that I am a doctor, and so I didn't have to listen to a bunch of symptoms from everybody at the table who is too cheap to see their own doctor. Then when I saw Freddy being introduced as a special guest, I figured I should come out of hiding and say hello to her. We go back a long ways, don't we, Freddy?"

"Yes, Doctor Bob, we certainly do. It was good of you to attend, not that I had any doubt that you are a big supporter of anything that might reduce medical error rates."

"I am that," replied Dr. Anderson. "Nan, I was just starting to tell Freddy that we had Professor Gaba in last month to talk to our medical staff about his research in reducing error in anesthesia using pretty much the methods you were talking to the engineers about. Machine design, fatigue, simulator training for routine and emergency conditions, and complexity of displays. That puts a little heat on the other medical specialties to get our socks pulled up. I now see more of the medical societies making noise about this, so I am hopeful. I'm just a GP myself, so I don't know how this is all going to end up, but if our hospital can nudge things along, I am all in favor of it.

"Freddy, I think you and some of your faculty ought to visit Nan's clinics. It's a whole different thing than was talked about this evening, and you'll understand it better if you see it with your own eyes. Nan's nurse manager of clinics just got headhunted by a big private group that owns clinics, which is what the sports line story was about. If you have time for another cup of coffee, I'll tell you all about it, Freddy."

"Yes, Doctor Bob, I am staying overnight, and I can stand one more cup of decaf," Freddy replied with a smile for Dr. Anderson.

They separated, Nan and Jack shook a few more hands and collected a few more business cards, and then they left the hall and headed home. Jack drove.

On the way, Jack said to Nan, "I'd never heard about the camera-resistance movement among patients' rights advocates. Is that for real?"

"Yes, although I don't know that it is insurmountable. I threw that out so that the engineers who work with inanimate products every day would think about our problems from our perspective. That might stifle their creativity, though."

"Maybe, or maybe it will intrigue them all the more. Creativity is finding a novel solution, not finding half a solution or no solution at all, novel or not."

"Nan, were you surprised to find Dr. Anderson and Dean Freddy there this evening?" asked Jack.

"Yes, surprised and pleased. You probably didn't notice, but I spotted a staffer from the building maintenance group and one staffer in addition to Sanjar from Rudy Rudolf's group. I suppose they are members of this engineering society, but I am pleased that they were there. There may have been others; I didn't really get a chance to see everybody.

"What did you think of Sarita Subramaniam, Jack?"

"She looks like a very pretty, devoted, motivated, submissive, wonderful woman."

"She's not your type, Jack. My guess is the submissive act is just that, an act. Indian society is a matriarchy, just in case you were wondering."

24

Wednesday Morning: Makeup!

Nan drove up to the television studio's front door at seven o'clock on the dot. She was greeted by Josey, who was waving her arm in wide arcs to catch Nan's eye. Josey jumped into the passenger seat and directed Nan to drive down one block and park. They left the car with a valet (in the middle of the city?) and went into the office and studio of the artistic trio. All three were there, looking as if they had been up all night. As near as Nan could tell, they were all wearing exactly the same outfits they had worn the day before at her office. Maybe they all had six outfits the same, so they wouldn't get confused by days of the week.

"Okay," said Number One. "Behind the screen you'll find a dressing gown. Strip to the skin and put on that gown. It's your size, and it's going to be your friend for the next four hours. We'll dress you at the last minute over at the television studio so that you can stand up until you go on stage. No wrinkles that way. You'll have a standing stool to lean on, so it won't be like you're standing on your feet, and it will only be a matter of minutes anyway. Now, to work. We've got a lot to do.

"You're a handsome woman, Love, and with a little help from your friends, the camera is going to make you beautiful. You'll be on every executive calendar for the next ten years."

Nan wondered for half a minute if it was time to go home. Then she went behind the screen, dumped her tracksuit on the floor, and put on the dressing gown, which was indeed in her size. She found slippers in her size. She returned and followed stage directions to wind up in a very comfortable reclining chair, better than any beauty parlor chair Nan had ever known.

The three of them went to work. Warm towels on the face. Number One and Number Two washed, trimmed, and highlighted her hair. How they could trim it while she was stretched out in the chair, Nan couldn't imagine, but it was too late to ask questions. Meanwhile,

25

Action on Stage!

Someone wearing a headset gave Nan an arm-chop cue, which Nan took to mean for her to start forward. That must have been right, because the man nodded his head and then gestured for her to stop, just offstage. Then the chop again, and Nan walked out onto the stage.

Her hosts stood to greet her, clapping a little. As she got to the set, the hosts, only two today, extended their hands to be shaken and gave Nan a big smile.

The hosts were Wendy Marcolli and Nancy Herndon. Both were local television celebrities of no particular political persuasion or attachment to any of the movements or causes. Just nice, chatty people, judging by the way they ran the show.

Wendy: Welcome, Nan Mills. It's so nice of you to join us this morning.

Nancy: Welcome.

Nan: Thank you. I am pleased to be here with you.

Wendy: Just sit down and make yourself comfortable. Oh, I love that pin! Eddy, zoom in on Nan Mills' pin if you can. Is that a zodiac sign? Is that Gemini? With the American flag? Oh, that's very clever. And diamonds, I suppose those are for your twin sons.

Nan: My sons are the real thing. These stones, I wouldn't vouch for.

Nancy: But you're a twin yourself, aren't you? And isn't your husband a twin, and so you are wall-to-wall twins in your family?

Nan: Yes, twins all around.

Wendy: And, let me see if I understand this, you are named for your twin sister? How does that work?

Nan: My twin sister is named Ann. I was first called Not-Ann, which came to be Nan. My actual baptismal name is Mary Claire.

Nancy: Oh, that's precious. Not-Ann. Well, I suppose that's easier for people to say than the other way around, calling your sister Not-Mary-Claire.

Wendy: Yes, Nancy, you're a big help this morning. Now, Nan, may I call you Nan? We are quite informal here, as you can see.

Nan: Please do.

Nancy: And you call us Nancy and Wendy. Or you can call me Not-Wendy.

Wendy: Now the reason we asked if you would join us this morning is that you are the first head nurse either of us can think of who was ever given a full column on the sports page. In this case, the online sports page that my husband and, I guess, every sports buff in the area reads before breakfast. The column compared you to a head coach, getting jobs for your assistant coaches. Can you tell us about that?

Nan: I saw that column. My husband, Jack, pointed it out to me yesterday morning. You can decide for yourself whether the comparison is valid. I'll just tell you the facts of the matter.

            One of my nurse managers, Maggie Kelly, was recruited by a private company that runs a chain of medical clinics to be their head nurse. Maggie was manager of our clinics, so she has a wonderful background to take to her new job. It was a promotion for Maggie, and I think she will do that new job very well. I think the world of Maggie, and I am happy for her.

Nancy: But doesn't that mean you have lost a key manager? I don't see how you can be happy about that. You train somebody, and then they run off the first chance they get. That leaves you holding the bag.

Nan: That's certainly one way to look at it. We will have to spend time and effort to find and train a replacement for Maggie in our own organization.

Wendy: Is there some other way to look at it?

Nan: The way I look at it is that I have eight nurse managers reporting to me, all of whom are qualified to take my job, as Maggie was. Well, even if I get run over by a bus on the way back to the hospital, that opens up only one slot. So, realistically, some of those nurse managers are going to want promotions that just can't happen in one organization. They have to look on the outside.

Nancy: We'll continue talking to Head Coach Nan Mills after this commercial break.

(*Pause*)

Wendy: We're back with Nan Mills, head nurse at General Hospital and, according to the sports pages, head coach of her nursing team.

So, from what you were just saying, you do look at yourself as head coach of the nursing team, and you want to find head coaching jobs for all your assistant coaches, just like they do in the professional football league.

Nan: You are being a little more generous than the circumstances warrant. I did not seek an outside job for Maggie Kelly, but when she found one on her own, I didn't try to stop it.

Nancy: So do you have a farm team somewhere so you can call up a second baseman if you need one?

Nan: We run our own farm teams right inside the hospital. We do training programs and rotational assignments, and we provide as much opportunity as we can for people to take on additional responsibility. That means we are training more people for senior jobs than we can provide senior jobs for, and so it is natural that we lose some good people over time, like Maggie.

Wendy: If your best people leave to take other jobs, doesn't that leave you with the worst of the lot?

Nan: The worst of our lot are still very good nurses and supervisors and managers. Of course we have upgrade programs for the best performers, the average performers, and the bottom performers.

Nancy: So do you fire the bottom 10 percent every year like some corporations do?

Nan: No. We don't fire very many people at all. We put our energy into shaping people up and finding jobs for each person that match that person's interests and abilities.

Nancy: That's what they say around here, too, until the ratings go down!

(*General laughter*)

Wendy: Now, Nan, you made headlines six or seven months ago when you solved the murder of Mr. Bill. Do you remember that, audience?

(*Murmur from the studio audience*)

Nancy: I remember that! It was on the front pages for a couple of weeks. I think the bad guys are in jail now, aren't they?

Nan: Yes. They both got indefinite sentences, and they are both in jail right now.

Nancy: You and your husband solved the murder. Isn't that it?

Nan: My husband, Jack, is a computer software consultant, and he did have something to do with figuring out how the crime was done. Jack was assisted by Sanjar Subramaniam of the hospital staff. That was all written up at the time. But, let me make sure to be clear on one point, the murder was solved by Detective Stan Laurel of the county detectives at the same time or even before Jack and I had anything to do with it.

Wendy: Well, maybe. But people expect a detective to solve mysteries; we don't expect a head nurse and her husband to do it. So Nancy and I remain impressed by you and Jack. Aren't you, audience?

    (General applause)

Nancy: Stay with us people. We'll be back after this break. Love our sponsors!

    (Break)

Wendy: We're back with Nan Mills, head nurse, head coach, and sleuth.

    Now the other thing about Mr. Bill's murder is that when it was all said and done, his estate went to the hospital, and that was big bucks. Isn't that so?

Nan: Mr. Bill's estate was mostly a block of stock in a high-tech company of great potential value. They do protein markers, which are important for medical research. That company is now doing an IPO to become a public company. When that's all done, the value of the stock will be clear. Everyone says it will be very valuable, but I don't know myself.

Nancy: Isn't an IPO where a little company sells some stock and then the bankers and insiders and politicians and people with connections get rich in one day? That looks like a scandal to me.

Nan: This one is being done as a Dutch auction on the Internet. Anybody can buy the stock at the IPO price, and the price is set by what people are willing to pay. No insider trading, and, I hope, no scandal. That's the new way to do IPOs so the proceeds go to the company for R&D, not to bankers and hangers-on.

    I am not involved with that, I am just telling you what I read in the business pages.

Wendy: Are you and Jack buying any of the stock?

Nan:	We talked about it, but we decided it might be viewed as a conflict of interest, so we are not buying any.
Nancy:	Now the reason I brought this up . . .
Wendy:	*I* brought it up.
Nancy:	The reason Wendy brought this up is that we hear there is now a power struggle within the hospital over the part of Mr. Bill's estate that goes to you as a slush fund. Tell us about that.
Nan:	I can tell you about the estate, but I assure you there is no slush fund, and if there is a power struggle, nobody has told me about it.
	The executor for Mr. Bill's estate established that a small portion of the bequest to the hospital would be earmarked for small development projects under the control of the line management. That includes me. The final details are supposed to be settled shortly, from what I hear.
	The idea is to have a small fund that can pay for pilot projects that can be started up quickly, without waiting for the annual appropriation cycle that the hospital runs on.
Wendy:	Wait a minute. A small portion of a bequest that will run to one hundred million dollars or maybe two hundred million dollars is still big bucks. And if it's up to you to decide how to spend it, that sounds like a slush fund to me.
Nancy:	We need one of those around here!

(General laughter)

Wendy:	I can see how everybody else in the administration, what we would call the suits around here, I can see how they are all bent out of shape that you have a slush fund, and they don't.
Nancy:	You bet. If Wendy had a slush fund, I'd be her very best friend for life. Or until the slush fund ran out.
Wendy:	So what are you doing with your slush fund?
Nan:	It is not a slush fund, and so far there isn't any money in it at all. There may never be. If there is ever any money, then the money will be used very frugally and under the terms of the bequest, which aren't settled yet.
Nancy:	We're going to have to have you back when you can tell us what you're doing with the slush fund.
Wendy:	Back in a minute with Nan Mills!

(Break)

| Nancy: | We're back, and we have just a few more minutes with Nan Mills, head nurse, sleuth, head coach, and slush-funder. You're a great guest, Nan. We could go on for hours. |

Wendy: Let's go back to Maggie Kelly, the manager who has been running your neighborhood clinics and is leaving to run a chain of clinics for a private company. Your clinics are in some of our poorer neighborhoods, where they are a fine part of those communities. We have a lot of immigrants in those neighborhoods, as everybody knows, and we hear that those neighborhoods and particularly the immigrant groups in those neighborhoods are having big parties all week long for Maggie.

Nan: I have heard the same thing, but they are being organized by the people in the neighborhoods, not by the hospital or me. It is a wonderful thing to see.

Nancy: There will be big parties around here when I leave, but they will be after I'm gone.

Wendy: I don't think we are talking about the same thing here. Maggie must have made a fine impression on her patients. She's going to be a tough act to follow.

Nan: Maggie is a wonderful person as well as a wonderful nurse and manager. And yes, she will be a tough act to follow.

Nancy: One other thing, and this will have to be brief. You are a Six Sigma Black Belt. Tell us about that in one breath.

Nan: Six Sigma is a management method for improving outcomes by reducing error. We practice it at the hospital. It's good stuff, and it works. See our website for more information.

Wendy: That's all for today, folks. We've been talking to the beautiful and charming and multitalented Nan Mills, head nurse at our General Hospital. I promise you we will have Nan back soon. We'll put a web link on our page to what Nan was just talking about, folks. We'll have Nan back soon to tell us more about it. Getting rid of error in medical care would be big news. Nan, thank you so much for being with us today.

Nancy: Come back soon. Goodbye, folks!

(Nancy waves to the camera.)

Half the set lights went down, the microphones were cut off, the cameras dollied away from the little set, and Wendy and Nancy engaged Nan in small talk for five minutes to provide a backdrop during the transfer of the broadcast from their set to other programming. Both hosts seemed to be genuinely interested in Nan and her many-faceted professional life. Both had stories to tell about twins in their own extended families, something that Nan was used to hearing from almost everybody she met.

Then they shook hands all around, and the hosts directed Nan to the stage-left wings, where Josey was waving a cell phone at Nan.

Before Josey could get a word out, Nan asked her, "Josey, did you feed Wendy and Nancy all that material they had about me and what happened six months ago?"

"Sure. That's my job. Otherwise, who knows what they might have dug up on their own?

"Look, Mrs. Mills," Josey said, "there's trouble at the hospital. We need to get there right away. Marcy called with the news. She called from your house because the telephones are out at the hospital, even the cell phones. She went to your house to get you clothes to change into when you get to the hospital so you won't have to stop at home on the way.

"Marcy is very upset about the telephone problem."

"Josey, that could be very serious. Okay, let's hightail it to the hospital."

"I'll come back here later and pick up a copy of the show you just did. I'm sure you videotaped it at home, too, but the studio copy will be at double line density, the way it comes out of the camera. Much better stuff. We can convert that at the hospital to digital format and regular VCR format. Willie does that. Do you know Willie?"

"Yes, I know Willie. It occurs to me I haven't seen him for a while."

"He's working in our group now, mostly doing video editing. He's got the eye for it. He's still working part time, like he was before, while he finishes his schooling. I guess you don't see him because he spends his time in a cubicle editing video files."

"I hope you pay him more than he was making as a gopher in the building maintenance department."

"I don't have any idea, since I am just an intern myself. I know that professional video editors make big bucks if they have the eye."

Nan and Josey reached the van at a trot, where Number One handed Nan a big bouquet of roses with an elaborate bow. They jumped in the van, and Number Two sped them off across town. Number Three handed Nan a warm, damp cloth and suggested she wipe the makeup off her face while they were in transit. More towels followed. When Nan thought she was through, Number Three wiggled out of his seat belt, got up on his knees, and applied new business-day makeup to Nan's face, never missing a beat as they zoomed along. Then he combed her hair and rebelted himself into his seat.

Nan thought to herself that she could get used to this level of pampering if she put her mind to it.

Number One told Nan, "We're going directly to the hospital because Josey says so. Number Three will recover your car from the valet and get it to your parking slot at the hospital within the hour. Number Two has a couple of hundred digital snapshots of your day, which we will cull down and make into a digital scrapbook for you. No copies, so you don't have to worry about seeing yourself in green makeup in the supermarket tabloids, Love. We will ask Josey to pick out one shot that we can have for our own publicity stuff, but I am sure that will be a shot off the video camera files so the makeup will do its magic for the camera. If you don't want us to have one, that's up to you. If you want us to have one with the green makeup, we'll start our own tabloid.

"We did up a little gift for you, but it doesn't fit in with this mad dash to the hospital. It's a new tracksuit for you, something with a little more style than what you wore this morning. It's more suitable for the new you, Love, and think of us when you wear it.

"You've been top drawer, Love. A real trouper. Call us the next time you do anything on the tube. Or, on film. That's different, but we do both. You have set a high standard for yourself, now, and you can't just show up in a Mother Hubbard and baseball cap next time and expect your fans to appreciate it.

"Josey can find us."

Nan made a mental note to get her hands on those snapshots as quickly as possible. She could only imagine how fast snapshots of nurses in green makeup could zoom around the Internet. Nan peeled off the tooth facings and put them in a pocket as a souvenir of the day. That's a technology she would bet even her computer-geek husband hadn't heard of. Maybe she would do one front tooth before supper, just to see if Jack would notice.

There was a moment of quiet as they moved briskly though traffic. Nan found herself to be exhilarated by the experience of the morning. She thought she had produced reasonable answers to a wide range of questions. The hosts had changed topics so quickly that she didn't think she had done justice to any of the topics.

And she didn't know that there was a "power struggle" over her slush fund. No, not a slush fund, her development fund. Even if there were a power struggle, how would television gab-fest hosts know about it when she didn't know about it herself?

She could well imagine that there were suits at the hospital who were as green with envy over the slush fund, correction, development fund, as she had been green with makeup. She might as well try to find out. She should also find out from chief council Alice Newcomb just where the slush fund stood and when there would be any money in it.

She'd better find out before the suits got their hands on it, regardless of what the terms of the bequest might be.

26

The Hospital in Trouble

Nan and Josey trotted into the hospital and made for Nan's office. Josey was carrying Nan's bouquet of roses, and Nan was carrying the rather large box containing her gift from Number One, which she had yet to open.

Nan reached her office and went directly in. Josey stayed with her. Marcy came in, two steps behind, with a large vase for the roses, which she handed over to Josey.

Nan gestured to Marcy to close the office door, and then she zipped open the suit bag holding the clothes Marcy had fetched for her from home and started changing.

"Mrs. Mills," began Marcy, "something has happened to the telephones. We can make internal calls but all calls out to the city and all long-distance calls don't work. Cell phones don't work."

At this, Nan stopped still. "Marcy, how do you know that cell phones won't work?"

"I tried mine. Other people all over the place are trying them."

"Marcy. Do this immediately. Call every one of our units and tell them I demand a bed watch on every patient with a pacemaker. Immediately. Second, tell the units to go to every visitor and ask if any of them have pacemakers. Third, tell our people to use no cell phones. None.

"Got that?"

"Yes, ma'am," Marcy said and left immediately to make those calls. She had never heard Nan give a direct order on anything before, so she knew this was something other than a routine matter.

"Mrs. Mills," asked Josey, "what's with the concern about the cell phones and pacemakers?"

"Cell phones radiate energy to carry their communications, and that energy is in the radio frequency range. Pacemakers use just about those same frequencies for control signals, and there is a risk that cell phones can interfere with the pacemaker controls. The way Marcy explained the situation here, and it seems entirely reasonable to me, when the word went around that the telephones were out of order, everybody grabbed their own cell phone and gave it a try. That put a lot of radio frequency energy into the air here, and that is all a source of interference for the pacemakers.

"The pacemakers are the most important for obvious reasons. Other hospital electronics are sensitive to radio frequency interference, too, and we can get to that when the pacemakers are taken care of."

"So when everybody fired up their cell phones, it might have set off somebody's pacemaker?"

"Yes, Josey. It's a serious matter. I don't have any idea how many of our patients have pacemakers today, but they are very common in the older set. The visitors and even employees are at risk, too, if they have pacemakers.

"That reminds me. I didn't tell Marcy to alert any employees who have pacemakers. They could be in any department, not just nursing. Yipes!"

Nan looked at her telephone station and saw from the lights that Marcy was still making those calls. Nan picked up her handset and called the office of her superior, the chief operating officer for the hospital, Philip L. Crawford. His secretary answered the phone.

"Mary, this is Nan Mills. The outside telephone lines are out, and lots of people are trying to use their cell phones, despite hospital policy against cell phone use. If anybody in your suite has a pacemaker, and that could be an employee or a visitor, that person is at risk and should be under supervision right now. Do you understand me?"

"Yes, ma'am. I will interrupt Mr. Crawford's meeting and tell him immediately. I don't know who has pacemakers and who doesn't, so I will go around myself and tell everybody in this part of the building. What should I do if I find somebody with a pacemaker?"

"Call the cardiac center, identify the person and the location, and take instructions from the cardiac center.

"Thank you for your help, Mary. Go to Mr. Crawford immediately. No delay."

"Yes, ma'am. I am hanging up now." She did.

Nan did, too. She turned to Josey, who was standing there with very large eyes.

"Josey, use this telephone here and call every vice president's office in the building. The list is here by the telephone. Tell the person who answers the phone exactly what I just told Mr. Crawford's secretary. Keep a log of whom you reached and the time you reached them.

"When Marcy is through making her calls, and you can watch this light here to see when Marcy is on the phone, tell her exactly what you have done. If Marcy gives you further instructions, follow them. Got that?"

"I will call the vice presidential offices. I will log every call. I will take further instructions from Marcy."

"You got it, Josey. I am going to the cardiac center on foot. Come and see me there after you take care of all this."

"Yes, ma'am," Josey said, as she dived for the phone.

Nan zipped her last zipper and straightened her clothes as best she could without a dressing mirror, trotted out of her office, and went directly to the cardiac unit. Nan did not stop to explain things to Marcy, figuring that the fact that she did not do so would add a measure of urgency to what Marcy was doing. Josey and Marcy could figure things out between them soon enough.

The cardiac unit would have the highest number of patients with pacemakers, but employees and visitors with pacemakers could be anywhere. Nan didn't know if the telephone outage was unique to the hospital or if other organizations in the neighborhood or the city would be having the same pacemaker risks from the high intensity of radio frequency interference from everybody trying to use their cell phones at once. Maybe the emergency room needed to be put on notice, too.

Nan arrived at the cardiac unit and found her unit manager, Carla du Pont, at the desk, looking very intense.

"Carla, I'm glad you are on duty. I'm worried about all the people using cell phones at once and the possible interference with pacemakers. I put the word out to direct calls here to you. Was that the correct thing for me to do?"

"Nan, I got the call from Marcy, and we have three patients in this unit with pacemakers. I put a bed watch on all three. I just spoke to our chief cardiologist to tell her what's going on. She approved of the bed watch and said she would look in on each of the three. Then I sent an orderly to speak to each of the visitors we could find and ask them if they had pacemakers.

"I have not yet received any calls from other departments, but I do know we have a half-dozen employees in the hospital, at least, who have pacemakers. I don't know how many of them are on shift. It's anybody's guess how many visitors have pacemakers.

"You probably know, Nan, that the newer pacemaker models are not as sensitive to radio frequency interference, which is in our favor. People with older models are definitely at risk.

"This is something we never covered in our disaster drills, Nan. Are we doing everything we should?"

declare a pacemaker. Nan figured that the crisis had passed, but she waited until Carla was off the phone for a few seconds to ask her if it would be of any use for her to remain in the cardiac unit.

"No, Nan. I think the crisis is over. I am getting a lot of calls, but they are nervous people asking for information, not people with pacemakers. No reported pacemaker upset either with patients or with visitors or employees."

"Okay, I am heading back to my office. Call me if you or Dr. Parsons think of anything else we should be doing." Nan gave her a big executive smile and started to walk away. Before she could take two steps, Carla called to her.

"Nan, this may not be the time to mention it, but I like the way you have done your hair today. The cut and highlights are just perfect for you. And I think you changed your makeup, too, didn't you?"

"Yes, everything is a little different today, in more ways than one. I was on that television talk show this morning when all this happened, and I got some help with my makeup. Tomorrow, I'll be back to plain old me."

Carla said, "I heard you were going to be on that show, so I taped it. Did they get you to say anything really outrageous?"

"No, garden-variety stuff. It went by so quickly, I'll have to watch it myself to find out what I said." Nan smiled and headed back to her office.

Nan found Marcy on the phone. Nan went into her office, and Marcy came in two steps behind her, carrying her steno pad and pencil.

"Marcy, things are calm in the cardiac unit. What do you hear from the other units and departments?"

"Mrs. Mills, Josey just called in to say that every last person in the building has been contacted by one of her runners and asked not to make cell phone calls within a block of the hospital."

"That was quick. How did she get that done so quickly?"

"She told me she went to her own department first, since you didn't want to take up the nursing staff with this, and she got four of the people there. She told them they had to find four others each, and that they in turn had to find four others each. Then, those people had to fan out and talk to people.

"Josey said it seemed to her like a multilevel marketing problem, and so she did it that way. She has so many people working on getting others to help that there are not very many targets for each of the ones on the end of the chain, so it goes pretty quickly that way."

"Marcy, that was very clever. Josey seems to be a closer relative of yours than you let on."

"Yes, she's pretty clever. There's one other thing. Josey figured out that the non-nurses and the non-doctors generally feel like second-class citizens here, not because they don't do important work themselves but because they can't really do much with the patients like you nurses can and the doctors do. So, in this emergency, they were suddenly doing something pretty important by helping Josey, and I'll bet they will all be talking for the rest of the year about how they saved the pacemaker patients."

"Yes, Marcy, we have a very bright young person in our Josey. When this is all over, see if you can get a list of the people Josey had in her network so that Mr. Crawford can send them a letter of acknowledgement or something."

"Yes, ma'am. That's a good idea."

"Marcy, does anybody know what caused this simultaneous telephone and cell phone crisis?"

"I haven't heard anything yet. The inside telephones that I guess run off the hospital PBX all seem to be working. The Internet isn't working, but that's because of the fire Sunday night. Outside calls and cell phones, nothing doing."

"Marcy, find out if the dispatch radios are working, will you please? See if you can do it without actually calling the dispatcher, because they may be in the middle of a crisis of their own."

"I'll call somebody down the hall from them and ask them to go look."

"Yes, that's a good idea."

Marcy turned and left the office.

Nan wondered to herself if this telephone crisis had anything to do with the Sunday manhole fire. Nan wondered to herself about what she had heard in Rudy Rudolf's conference room the day before, when Sanjar reported on his trip along the network routes. He had mentioned points of vulnerability, including one, if she remembered rightly, that could knock out both the wireline phones and the cell phones.

Coincidence?

27

Nan Briefs Crawford
and the Others

Nan decided she should report matters to Crawford and maybe to the other suits, since she had taken matters in her own hands and had not followed any of the disaster drill procedures. She made a mental note to review the disaster procedures to see if she had omitted any important step or if those procedures needed a rewrite in the light of today's events. And Sunday's.

Nan went to her desk to make calls to the executive suite, and she noticed for the first time that the bouquet of roses was now arranged in the vase Marcy had produced out of thin air, and the box with the gift from Number One had been opened for her so that the contents were displayed in a way that reminded Nan of a bridal shower gift display. Number One had said they had given her a tracksuit. The gift was indeed a tracksuit, Nan found as she lifted the tracksuit top out of the box. A tracksuit, but not a tracksuit to do any serious workout in. This looked more like après-track, if there were such a thing. The material was very soft and in a dark shade of rose, accented by an even darker color on the order of crimson. The cut was narrow, not the baggy thing one expects in a tracksuit. The knit collar was high, just short of being a turtleneck. The narrow pant legs flared at the bottom. Most intriguing of all was the monogram of the left front side of the top. It was that Gemini sign with flag, duplicating the pin Number One had produced for the lapel of her television business suit. The monogram was about 4 inches across, done in a lighter shade of rose, and it had two brilliant stones sewn in. Diamonds? Fakes? They looked real to Nan, and she wasn't going to have them appraised anyway.

There were no merchant tags in the tracksuit, so Nan figured it had been tailor-made for her. She was sure the size and cut would be perfect, having seen the handiwork of Numbers One, Two, and Three that morning.

Quite a souvenir.

Nan went to her desk, opened the drawer that held her laptop computer and camera, and took out the camera. She snapped shots of the roses and the tracksuit, used the wireless connection between the camera and her desktop computer to transfer the photos, and went back to work. Then she went back to the camera, set the shutter for a 30-second delay, put the camera on top of the PC screen, held the track suit top up to herself, and smiled her best smile at the camera. The flash went off. Nan transferred the photo to her desktop computer and went back to work again.

Nan called Crawford's office and told his secretary, Mary, that she was ready to report on actions taken, which she could do in person or by memo. Mary asked her to hold for a moment, after which she told Nan that Mr. Crawford would be pleased if she could come to his office and brief him. Nan said she would come promptly.

Nan stopped to tell Marcy where she was going, and then she headed up to the office suite of Mr. Philip L. Crawford, the chief operating officer.

Nan was greeted by Crawford's secretary, Mary, and ushered into Crawford's conference room. As Mary opened the door and turned back to face Nan, she whispered that she thought Nan's hair was very pretty the way she had it done today. Nan smiled and went into the conference room. Nan found Crawford there, along with Alice Newcomb, the chief counsel; Rudy Rudolf, the head of information technology; Dr. Anderson, the chief medical officer; and Susan Gunn, the head of personnel.

"Nan, thanks for coming. We are just trying to figure out what's going on and what to do next," said Crawford. "Rudy is going to tell us about the telephone problem."

Rudy looked a little more serious than was his wont. "You all know by now that the cell phone service is wiped out and that the wireline telephone service beyond our PBX is wiped out. The dispatch radios are okay, so we have a means of communicating to the public safety people if we need to. The external data networks are still out, because of that manhole fire Sunday night, so we are pretty well isolated when it comes to voice and data communications.

"I took my car and drove away from the hospital to see how far I would have to drive before my cell phone would work. It's about two blocks from here.

"Pagers work, because they work from the radio broadcast towers, not the cell phone towers. Two-way pagers should work, if anybody has those.

"I am waiting for a report from the police or fire department to tell us what caused the problem. They will radio in a report or send somebody here to explain it.

"I do not know if the telephone problem is ours alone or if this district is out, or what.

"That's what I know right now, folks," concluded Rudy.

Crawford nodded intently in Rudy's direction and said, "Thanks, Rudy. Please keep us informed as the facts materialize.

"Now, Nan, we got your call about pacemakers. Fill us in on that, please, and on anything else we need to know about."

"Yes, sir. When the word went around the building that the telephones were out, people disregarded the rule against cell phones and tried to make calls. The calls did not go through, so they kept trying. I am speaking of employees, visitors, even patients.

"So, I had Marcy and others make calls to all nursing units to put a bed watch on every patient with a pacemaker. Then we sent out word to find employees or visitors with pacemakers and to be ready in the emergency room for people coming in with pacemaker problems. We set up the cardiac care unit as the operations center. Then we sent out people to ask visitors and employees not to use their cell phones within a block of the building. From what Rudy has just said, we might have been more helpful if we had said two blocks from the building.

"I do not know of any pacemaker upsets. I hope there were none. The ICU and neonatal units were called and advised to be careful of any electronics that might be susceptible to radio frequency interference."

Crawford seemed to be even more intense than usual. He asked, "Dr. Anderson, can you tell us if we have a pacemaker problem or not? God knows how many pacemakers there are here what with patients and employees and visitors and contractors and everybody. How worried should I be about this?"

Dr. Anderson looked somber. He looked at each face in the small room before answering. Then he said, "Phil, the reason pacemakers are the focus of our attention this morning is that pacemakers have different settings for such things as faster pulse, slower pulse, and so on. They keep a lot of stored data that are reported out to the cardiologist on demand. They don't have any wires hanging out, so the way they communicate to and from the cardiologist is by tiny radios built in. The radios are tiny with dinky antennas, so they don't pick up broadcast radio or television, and they don't pick up cell phone signals from one cell phone.

"But, if a whole lot of cell phones are all blasting away, then at some point the pacemakers are apt to think they are getting instructions from a cardiologist and change settings or even turn themselves off. Or on. Or off and on.

"Now this is uncharted territory so far as I know. I don't know if the problem threshold is 10 cell phones or a hundred cell phones or a million cell phones.

"I just spoke to Dr. Benedetta Parsons, the cardiologist who was in the unit this morning when this came up, and she couldn't tell me where the threshold is.

"There are other electronics gizmos in the hospital, quite a few of them are life support systems. There is a risk that they might have acted up. The literature has a number of odd things that have happened at other hospitals, including power wheelchairs that have run off on their own as a result of cell phone signals."

Crawford said to him, "If there is this big problem with radio signals and pacemakers, why did we put in that new cell phone system last year?"

Dr. Anderson answered, "That's a special low-power cell phone system with a limited number of stations. The frequency range it uses is very narrow and checked against pacemakers for this very reason. So I don't think that contributed to the problems of today, but I think we will need to follow up on that to be sure."

Crawford turned to the chief counsel. "Alice, do we have any liability in all this?"

Alice did not respond at once, but she applied enough body language to hold the stage while she thought out what to say. "Well, Phil, you never know about liability. Our best defense is saying that we have established emergency procedures and that we followed them."

That vexed Crawford, and it showed. "Well, somebody tell me if we followed our emergency procedures. Did we?"

Nobody answered.

Crawford tried his question again. "Do we have an emergency procedure that applies to this pacemaker matter?"

Nobody answered.

Crawford was getting mad. "Who is in charge of emergency procedures?"

Alice answered this time. "You are, Phil."

That did not cool Crawford off at all. "Hell, I am in charge of everything, so that answer doesn't help me at all. Somebody tell me who is in charge of emergency procedures or I will start firing people in alphabetical order until I get an answer."

Susan Gunn spoke up, just barely. "Phil, the buildings and grounds people report to me. They are in charge of fire emergencies, flood emergencies, tornadoes, airplanes crashing into the buildings, and anything to do with the electrical supply.

"The security detail is also under my department. If we have somebody shooting a gun in the lobby, that's my emergency."

Dr. Anderson spoke up, not overly anxiously. "Phil, a straightforward medical emergency, like an outbreak of Legionnaires' Disease, that comes under me."

Philip L. Crawford cooled down a little, as might be gauged by the redness of his face. He was still pretty hot. "Okay, so now I know who is in charge of emergencies I didn't ask about. There are only so many kinds of emergencies, so eventually I may be able to eliminate all the ones I don't care about and narrow in on the one I asked about. Can anybody sort of leap ahead here and tell me something that has to do with the problem of the day?"

Rudy Rudolf spoke. "Phil, telephone emergencies inside the building are my responsibility. But this was not exactly that. What we have here today is a mass disobedience of hospital rules, hundreds of people including employees, patients, visitors, contractors, and I suppose the mop brigade firing up their cell phones."

Silence. Alice Newcomb waited, then she said, "Phil, it sounds to me like we don't have an emergency procedure that covers mass hysteria."

Crawford looked intently at Alice and said, "Great. That helps a lot. You're telling me that our defense is that we followed our emergency procedure except that we don't have one. So what's our next line of defense?"

Alice spoke a little more firmly this time, probably figuring that somebody had better take charge of the meeting before everything got dumped in her own lap. "Phil, the next line of defense is that this was not a foreseeable event and that the administration dealt with it in an organized and suitable way."

Crawford did not brighten up. "Okay, now I have two unknowns instead of one unknown. Let's take the first one. Was this a foreseeable event? Rudy, I am not going to ask the throng here, I am going to ask you."

Rudy wiped away any glimmer of a smile and replied, "Phil, loss of telephone service is not rare. Brief outages occur pretty often. We would probably calculate that a brief outage every five years or so would be expected. We can probably get those figures from the FCC. The telephone company would know, but they would never tell us.

"The loss of all cell phone service is much more common because it is still a neophyte in the infrastructure game. I'd say a cell phone outage like this one would be expected for a brief period of time every year. So on a combined basis, we would probably calculate that we should expect a brief loss of both services at the same time maybe once in 20 years.

"To say whether we should have an emergency procedure for something that happens once in 20 years, we can look at what we do for other disasters. I think we plan on the basis of the hundred-year fire, the hundred-year flood, and so on. This kind of an emergency is at least as likely as those hundred-year things, so if we got pushed into a corner, we'd probably have to admit that we should have had a procedure in place.

"We don't. It's my fault. I'll fix it."

Crawford had cooled down a little while Rudy was talking. "Okay, Rudy, I think I get the idea. Let me say that I am not looking to tar and feather anybody over this, so I will set aside your assertion that it was your fault. I don't think it was your fault. I appreciate your offering to work up a procedure to cover us the next time. However, maybe we should listen to what Alice has to say about that before we make any new paper."

Crawford looked at Alice Newcomb. "Alice?"

Alice tapped her teeth with her long, unused pencil. "Let's not issue any new policies until we know if anybody is going to sue us over this. No new drafts, no letters to file, no meeting minutes. No paper at all. And I mean no e-mails, either."

Crawford hung his head a little lower and said to the table, "I figured you'd say something like that. What's this world coming to?

"Tell me about the other half. What did you say, Alice? 'Organized and suitable?'"

Alice answered, "Yes, organized and suitable."

Crawford looked at Nan, who had been watching the discussion as she would a tennis match. "Nan?"

Nan sat up a little straighter and spoke in a firm, calm tone. "I recognized the risk to pacemaker patients when I was told upon returning to the hospital that people were trying out their cell phones all over the place. I called your office; I ordered calls to all nursing units to put a bed watch on any patient with a pacemaker and to ask visitors and employees if they had pacemakers. I went to the cardiac unit and told the unit manager to stand by for telephone calls and for patients. I then consulted with the cardiologist who was there, Dr. Parsons. She decided to call those units most likely to have other electronic devices in use on a life-support or near-life-support basis. I waited there to see what might develop."

Crawford listened to Nan with some care. "Anything else?"

"Yes, one other thing. To get people to stop using their cell phones, I had an employee organize a chain of volunteers to speak to everybody on the premises to ask them, quietly, not to use their cell phones within a block of the building."

Cliff thought about that for a moment. "Why didn't you use the loudspeaker system? That would have gotten the word to everybody immediately."

Nan answered with a little more firmness than she really felt, "Dr. Parsons and I talked about that. We decided that using the public address system might make people all the more excited, and they were too excited in the first place. So we did the human chain instead."

Thoughtful silence.

Crawford said, "We are looking for 'organized and suitable.' What you are telling us, Nan, is that you organized something that you thought would be suitable. You did not consult with Dr. Anderson or with me or with Alice; you did all this off your own bat. I'm not saying you were wrong; I don't have any idea. I am just saying that we need to find something that will sound like 'organized and suitable' to the first 10 ambulance chasers who come in the door looking for a quick buck for pain and suffering caused to a patient who didn't get their magazines delivered this afternoon because the nurses aides were doing bed watch for something that didn't happen.

"Am I right, people, in saying that nothing happened? No pacemaker deaths? No visitors treated in the emergency room or cardiac unit?"

Nobody answered.

Crawford continued. "Okay, I am going to look everybody in the eye, and I mean every employee and every reporter and every ambulance chaser, and tell them that this was organized and suitable and that you, Nan, had authority to do it under our charter and limits of authority documents approved by the Board. Alice, I want you to read those limits of authority and other Board resolutions until your eyeballs fall out or until you find what I just said. If you don't find what I just said, keep reading until you find it. And don't give me any legal mumbo-jumbo, just find it.

"Dr. Anderson, I am appointing you as a committee of one to look into this matter and give me an oral report within 72 hours. No notes, no minutes, no dictation, no nothin'. And I don't want you consulting with six other hospitals to find out what they do. I just want you to think this through.

"People, we can get by with one Chinese fire drill when we don't have a fire, but we can't do two or three and have the community stand with us. We need to learn our lesson on this one, and we'd better do the next one a whole lot better."

Nan was getting a definitely cold feeling. "Mr. Crawford, you are well within your authority in assigning Dr. Anderson to do this investigation for you, and if Dr. Anderson wants any help, he will get all I can give him. But I don't like the tone of this meeting. I do not think that I did anything wrong in taking precautions against patient harm from cell phones and pacemakers. I think I would have been wrong and irresponsible to do nothing or to call a meeting of the executives to discuss what class of emergency this might be and whether we should write a procedure to cover it. I think I would have been wrong to call Susan Gunn to ask if her department was in charge or Rudy or Dr. Anderson to get their opinions. I saw the need to do something, and I did it. If you want to fire me for doing my job, go right ahead and fire me."

Crawford's head was hanging even lower, and he was talking directly at the tabletop. "Nan, I already said I don't know what anybody should have done, and I am not second-guessing you. I said that I will face the public and say we did everything right. I told Alice to make it so.

"What you need to understand, Nan, is that organizations have checks and balances so that free-spirited types are not running off in random directions when something comes up. Maybe you do the right thing every time. Most people don't, and most people are apt to run in the wrong direction from time to time. That's why we have checks and balances, to reduce the number of times well-meaning people run in the wrong direction. Believe it or not, that's why we have emergency procedures, so that we will be organized in the face of an emergency, not relying on split-second thinking by mere mortals.

"We tell all our patients to get second opinions before they undergo serious treatments. I wouldn't feel too silly if I told all of you to get a second opinion before taking drastic steps, no matter what the event. An emergency procedure amounts to a canned second opinion.

"Hundreds of people know about this cell phone episode, so it's going to get in the papers. So we need to have a position. It would be cold-blooded of me to say that our position would be stronger if we had had one patient with an overactive pacemaker today, but the cold-hearted fact of the matter is that we would. But we don't, so we are going to have to dress this up a little bit and say that we saw a need to take precautionary measures and we did. And then look 'em in the eye and dare them to say anything to the contrary.

"Look, folks, I don't know any more about medicine than Alice does. When I worked for a living, it was right here negotiating insurance contracts. You all know that. So when something happens, I don't have a medical opinion to offer. I just have a paper shuffler's concerns about things going on that might snap back and bite us in the shorts.

"Maybe you'll have this job one day, Nan, and then you'll be the one worrying about what the public comes to think about what goes on here. Sometimes it's medicine, and a whole lot of the time it's not."

Nan had the feeling that this was not going to turn into a team-building session. She realized perhaps for the first time that since nobody in the executive suite, other than maybe Dr. Anderson, had any idea what a nursing service actually did, they had no basis for knowing whether she did a good job as head nurse or a lousy job, whether she made cool decisions under fire, or if she flew off on a tangent over something that a cooler head would have ignored.

Had she done the right thing? Was the pacemaker risk serious enough to disrupt hospital routine or not? How could she know?

More to the point, what would she do the next time? What would she do if she had no basis at all to make a split-second decision that might put patients at risk?

Was there a real risk, or had she been so wound up emotionally by that television session that she overreacted to a teeny tiny risk? Was there somebody she could have tapped for a second opinion?

What should she do now? Should she keep her trap shut and let the heat in the room diffuse? What was her goal, at this moment, for this meeting? She thought about that with all the concentration she could muster.

Nan spoke, "Mr. Crawford . . ."

Crawford interrupted, "Nan, please call me Phil. I'm not that old."

Nan took that as sufficient reason to try a bit of a smile. "Phil, then. I was completely off base here a minute ago when I said it was my way or I'm hitting the highway. I regret what I said, and I offer apologies to you and to all here present.

"I will try again.

"I admit here in this room, where we are protected by confidentiality, thanks to your being here, Alice," Nan said with a hint of a bow in the counsel's direction, "that I did not look for an authorized emergency procedure before ordering bed watches for pacemaker patients.

It would only have taken me thirty seconds to try to reach Dr. Anderson or Dr. Parsons before ordering the bed watch. Therefore, I have no defense for not getting a second opinion. I think either of them would have agreed with me, but I don't have any evidence of that.

"So, I did indeed act on my own initiative and on the basis of my own counsel. In this instance, I think I did the right thing. I admit here, and I will not admit it anywhere else, that the next time my judgment might be off a little.

"What I will do the next time, I don't know. I hope I will look for a second opinion before taking action. But I cannot promise any of you that I will. I cannot say with any certainty. I just don't know.

"I will be pleased to cooperate with Dr. Anderson," Nan said, bowing slightly in that direction, "on his study, and if Rudy or Susan needs anything from me in bringing emergency procedures up to date, please be assured that I will be at your disposal.

"Phil, you said that you'll put on your game face and deal with the public and any nutty thing that comes up as a result of what I did today. I appreciate that, and I recognize that that's something I don't know how to do at all.

"So, to all of you, I offer my good intentions to handle the next event a little more coolly than I handled this one."

Crawford had raised his head just enough to watch Nan finish her little speech. He responded, "Nan, I didn't call this meeting to beat up on you or on anybody else for that matter. I am not now, nor was I before, mad at you. I don't want to discourage initiative, certainly not in a hospital where lives are in our hands. I don't know how to tell you to figure out when to look for second opinions and when to act on your own. Neither does anybody else in the room." Crawford looked around and found no disagreement. "So, I am not asking you to do anything different the next time, or to have done anything different this time.

"We all got ourselves into uncharted waters today. We're playing a team sport here. We're all on the same team. We each play our position, and we each count on the others to play theirs. I think we have a good team, and I think we will have an even better team tomorrow because we took 15 minutes to talk this through. Maybe if we had taken two days, we could have come to the same place without ruffling any feathers, but we don't have two days. We have 10 minutes, and maybe not that, if all those phones ringing out there are any clue.

"I'll tell you something else, and I don't know if you will understand this, ladies, or not. But if this were a men's team, we would yell at each other and say vile things, and then when it was over we'd go have a beer and forget about it. No recriminations, no hard feelings.

Over is over. That's the way boys are raised, lots of yelling. Coaches yell. Fathers yell. Every boy on every team yells at everybody else on the team. Then after the game, we're all buddies again.

"With the mixed league that we are playing in now, I wonder if that works. I get the idea that girls aren't yelled at enough when they are growing up, so you don't know how to take it. Oh, you can yell well enough yourselves, but I don't know if you can forget about it when the game is over and be buddies again. If you can't, then we don't have a team, we have a bunch of individuals with delicate sensibilities more concerned with remembering every slight than moving the ball down the field.

"So, I worry about that."

Crawford screwed up his face and contemplated something, but he didn't continue on that theme. Nan knew that he had been talking to her more than to Susan or Alice. Nan knew, but she didn't know what to make of it. Maybe Jack could explain it to her later. Having raised two boys and having been at lots of games when they were on various teams, she understood that lots of yelling went on. She also understood that the kids were buddies again after the game. At home, her twin boys had spent a lot of time yelling at each other even though they hardly needed words to communicate. They certainly didn't stay mad at each other very long. Did she, Nan, hang on to every slight? Did she know how to be buddies after a good yelling match? Something more to think about. Meanwhile, it seemed like a good time to keep quiet.

Crawford had finished his contemplation. He looked around the table, put something of a smile on his face, and changed the subject.

"Nan, I don't normally notice when women change their hairdo, something my wife points out to me every so often. But I notice that you are a different you today. Is that part of the television talk show you were on this morning?"

"Yes, Phil," Nan responded, happy to have a change in subject, even if the new subject was herself. "I got made up by professionals with green and orange makeup so that the camera would make me look normal. They also trimmed my hair and added some accents so that the hair would look right on camera. Then they made me up again afterward to get the green and orange off, and what you see is the result. What I'll look like tomorrow is anybody's guess."

Susan Gunn, wanting to keep the new topic going, chimed in. "Nan, you look great. I did some TV when I was in college, and back then they were big with the green and orange makeup. It was like Halloween all year round. But I don't understand how you got the

29

Settling Up
with Number One

Late in the afternoon, Nan asked Marcy if Josey had struck a price with Number One to settle the gift tracksuit question.

"Yes, ma'am. The final price is $68.40. That includes the sales tax."

"Marcy, that's quite a reasonable price for that beautiful track suit."

"Yes, ma'am. It took Josey a little while to get through to Number One that you were not complaining about the gift, you were just trying to conform to the hospital's policy against gifts from vendors. Of course, he said that he gives gifts all the time and gets gifts from his suppliers all the time and if he wants to give a gift, he doesn't want to be getting money for it. It spoils all the fun.

"Then he said you could make out a check for any amount you like, because he would never cash the check. Josey convinced him eventually that wouldn't work because that would still be a gift.

"Finally, he wanted $10 and Josey offered $135. They came together in the middle, plus tax."

"Marcy, she didn't threaten him, did she?"

"Josey doesn't have to threaten anybody who knows her family. Her cousin Crusher Morgenstern has a certain reputation."

"Crusher Morgenstern?"

"He used to be a wrestler. He's pretty big, but he is as sweet as a lamb. Most people don't know that, though. He's got this scar along his cheek that makes his smile go crooked. You don't notice it particularly after you get used to it, but at first sight it catches your eye."

"Crusher Morgenstern?"

"Josey just told Number One that if they couldn't strike a price on the phone that she would have her cousin drive her over and they could settle it in person. She didn't say that she dropped Crusher's name at all. So it got settled pretty easily, considering we were sort of impinging on his honor by refusing to accept his gift to you."

"Well, I hope he doesn't take it out on me if we do another TV show sometime. It wouldn't take too much more of that orange and green makeup to make a lasting impression on an audience."

"No, that would put him out of business. He'll get over it. Josey says that all three of them were really taken by you. The pictures are beautiful. They do Hollywood stars all the time, and they say they are real pills to work with. I suppose you get that way if you are treated like royalty all the time. They said you didn't act that way at all, even though you could hold your own with the lot of them."

Nan took that with a large pinch of salt, but she did not reject the idea out of hand. They were the experts, weren't they?

Marcy continued, "Mrs. Mills, here's the DVD copy of the TV show that Willie did for you from the studio master. I haven't tried it, because the PC at my desk doesn't have a DVD player. I think yours does, if you want to try it here."

"I think I'll take it home and watch it there. How would it look if Mr. Crawford walked into my office and found me watching myself on TV?"

"Mr. Crawford has not been in your office since you moved in."

"Well, there's always the first time, and I think that DVD would draw him like a magnet, and he'd have Alice Newcomb, the chief counsel, in tow. So, I'll do it at home. Thank Josey and Willie for me, if you please."

30

Nan and Susan Talk Policy

Marcy said to Nan, "May I bring you up to date on your managers' responses to your request that anybody interested in a rotational assignment should say so?"

"Yes, please do."

"Okay. Well, it was Monday when you made that request during that little stand-up staff meeting you had. I got some phone calls from people wondering if this was going to be obligatory or if they could pick a new slot, and the usual sorts of questions that anybody would ask. Then, Tuesday, when the word got around that Ms. Lincoln was being transferred, well, the level of interest went up a whole lot.

"We now stand at the following point: All your managers but one have volunteered for a rotational assignment, and they are ready to go wherever you tell them to go. The one who has not come forward is the OR nurse manager.

"All the ones who volunteered have asked that the department organize a Six Sigma Green Belt program for them and for others. Three have actually enrolled in a Green Belt program on their own, using an Internet self-paced program that Sanjar found for them. I don't know if they would actually want to continue with that or join a departmental program if you organize one. They get tuition reimbursement either way. "

"Marcy, let me see if I understand this. Interest in rotational assignments was low until the word got around about Shewan Lincoln transferring out. Interest in Six Sigma training was modest until the same event. Now everybody is enthusiastic.

"I think I scared some people."

"Yes, ma'am. I don't know if that's good or bad, but you did scare some people."

"I don't know what to do, Marcy."

"Mrs. Mills, Susan Gunn, the head of personnel, called to ask me about the level of interest in rotational assignments this afternoon. I guess you and she talked about that subject. I figured since you two had talked about it, you'd want her to know the facts, so I told her."

"Yes, that was the right thing to do. You have a good sense for that sort of thing."

"Thank you. Well, Susan Gunn thought you might want to talk about it some more, so she volunteered to come over and talk about it. Now, if that's convenient."

"That is kind of her, don't you think? She impressed me yesterday with the way she handled the Lincoln matter. I hadn't seen that side of her before."

"Okay, I'll call her office and tell her you'll be available in 10 minutes. That will give you time to freshen up." Marcy wrote notes to herself on her steno pad and left the office.

Nan sat down and rested her eyes, just for a moment. Then she checked her mail log, finding that Marcy had taken care of all the bumf with the same deft hand she always displayed. What would become of Nan if Marcy got run over by a bus on the way home today? Perish the thought.

At the appointed minute, Marcy brought Susan Gunn into the office, Marcy carrying a fresh pot of tea. Marcy waited two seconds to see if any orders would be issued in her direction and, hearing none, left, closing the door silently behind her.

Susan took a chair and presented Nan a smile that seemed to mean many things. Conspirator. Confident. Professional. Friend.

Nan started. "Susan, I am so glad you could see me this afternoon. Marcy told you that interest among my nursing managers in rotational assignments and Six Sigma training program went up nine million percent today, when the Lincoln story got around. By osmosis, you understand. I didn't tell anybody anything and neither did Marcy. Nobody else over here was in the know.

"So now I think I have created a panic response that is likely to make me more enemies than friends. What do I do now?"

Susan waited a few seconds before replying. "Nan, you have proven that the grapevine is alive and well in your department. That's a good thing, because the grapevine is pretty often the right way to get a message out.

"You've also proven that your managers take you seriously. They don't think they can gang up on you and push you around. That's in your favor, probably."

"Susan, I don't want to be Machiavelli, I just want to do a decent job running the nursing service. How do I get myself out of my own snare?"

"The right thing to do is to get everybody together and speak straight from the shoulder. The next right thing to do is to figure out what you are going to say."

"What am I going to say?"

"Nan, you are going to tell them that you want to do a decent job in running the nursing service. I know you want that, because you just told me. Telling me won't do any good; telling your managers might."

"Keep going."

"Let's look at this. The OR manager did not respond and volunteer. What do you make of that, Nan?"

"The OR nurses never, or almost never, bid on other openings. They consider themselves specialists. The supervisors and manager are almost always promoted straight up from that group. So they are an island unto themselves."

"Is OR nursing all that different from other nursing?"

"No. Well, it's specialized, but then a lot of the other services are specialized, too, like the emergency trauma service and the burn unit. All nurses do an OR tour in school and in early training."

"So, maybe it's tradition, and maybe it's that the OR service does a better job of team building than the other services do."

"Susan, I never thought of it that way. Do you mean that that is good or that it's bad?"

"I don't know, Nan. Maybe I could find out by snooping, but I might get caught."

"Somehow, I don't think you would get caught, Susan.

"I'm interrupting myself here, Susan, but I am curious about one thing. You called Marcy to ask about this. That's fine, but would it not have been better protocol to have your secretary call Marcy? Marcy doesn't let me call people directly. She says it would be too big a shock."

"My secretary does fine, and she handles a lot of delicate information all the time, so it's not a matter of trust or lack thereof. I just like to get my information straight from the horse's mouth once in a while so I can get the flavor as well as the facts. Isn't that why you show up during the midnight shift once in while, in addition to reading the shift reports? You want to know more than you can get from a spreadsheet. You also want to make yourself available to anybody who wants to say something to you, without exactly breaking the chain of command."

"So, did Marcy tell you anything with a flavor to it?"

"Marcy can say more by saying nothing than any person I have ever known."

"Susan, you're right about that, but answer my question, if you please."

"Marcy didn't say, but I divined, that things had taken an unexpected turn. That's all."

"Susan, I am more dependent on my secretary than I am on my husband. How many monsters am I creating here?"

"Lots and lots, and blessings on you for it. You know how Marcy operates because you see it every few minutes. You observe how your informal staff operates, including Josey Walberg just this week. You don't observe how your managers behave because they aren't here in your office with you every day or hour. I observe them, at a distance, naturally, and I see some things. I also saw them and how they behaved before you came along. I'll just tell you that they are all responding, after their individual fashions, as best they can. Some of them are surprising themselves. You can't see it yourself, but you need to understand they have never seen anybody like you before in their professional lives. And, while some people like Marcy and Sanjar and now Josey made conscious decisions to get into your orbit and took their own steps to get close to you, your managers were already there. You happened to them."

Nan thought about that for a good while. Then she said, "Of the managers who were here when I was given this job, two have left. Maggie Kelly got a better job, and Shewan Lincoln accepted a transfer. Neither resisted leaving my orbit, as you put it, although Maggie sought my blessing before she left. I don't know what she would have done if I had twisted her arm to stay."

Susan said, "I don't know either. She's a strong woman, and I think she probably would have decided that leaving was the right thing to do, but I can't say for sure. She didn't answer that question for me because I didn't ask it."

"Well, Susan, let's go back to the original quandary. I think, generally speaking, managers and professionals are better prepared for higher rank if they have some variety of management and professional experience. Don't you?"

"Yes, Nan, I do."

"So, when I speak to my managers straight from the shoulder, I should say that?"

"Yes. You believe it. You should say so."

"So, do I mandate that everybody rotate positions every six months, or what?"

"I don't know. Six months is probably too short, but I suppose you were asking the question in a general way."

"I'm not sure what I was asking. What do I do if people don't want to rotate? What do I do if a manager is pretty good in one unit and is a complete dud in another unit? Do I take them off the rotation?"

"I don't know. I seem to be saying that a lot, don't I? Let me put that in a more positive way, speaking of myself. What I can do, and what I want to do, is to help you get those questions out on the table and then help you sort out which ones you really care about and which ones you don't."

Nan felt frustration. "Well, Susan, let's go back to the point of all this. I want better-rounded managers, and I want my eventual replacement to be a well-rounded manager chosen from my managers, not brought in from the outside."

"Okay, Nan. That's progress. You can say it just that way. You can also add one sentence of explanation as to why you want that."

"Yes, I can say that, I think.

"But Susan, I don't want rotation because I see it a certain way. I want my people to want it because they see it that way."

"Okay, Nan. That's good. You want initiative. That's a hallmark of your tenure and your personality. So, tell people you want to see initiative in career management. Say that rotation has been found over the years to be positive for career development."

"Susan, at the professional level, we have enough openings all the time that there are just about always slots for people to transfer to, if they want to. Those jobs are posted, and people can bid on them.

"We also post the management positions, and people can bid on them. Does that mean I don't have to do or say anything?"

"Our bidding process is set up for people to seek promotion. Nothing stops people from bidding on a rotational basis, but not many people do. If people bid on a lateral move, it's usually to get a better shift or some other personal benefit."

"So what do I do?"

"Let's review the bidding, pun intended. You want people to want to prepare themselves for eventual promotion, even if those promotions take the person out of your department."

"Yes, that's what I want."

"Well, Nan, say that."

"How about all the other questions? How many rotations are the right number? How long should any assignment last? I don't know the answers to those questions at all."

"Nan, let's sort out the policy issues from the technical issues, and I put most of that last lot in the technical category. You have a department at your very elbow to deal with the technical issues. I speak ever so modestly of mine own department in case I was too subtle in my phraseology for you to take my meaning.

"You make the policy decisions and the policy proclamations. I'll take care of the technical goop."

"Okay. I think that's progress. Sorting out roles is usually good. Now what is my policy?"

"Your policy, based on what you have said in the past few minutes, is that people are better prepared for promotion if they have a breadth of experience at each level. Your policy will be that breadth of experience will be given weight in the selection of candidates for open positions. Your policy is to leave it up to each individual to decide what to do for their own career management, and the hospital's policy is to provide career counseling through our human resources department."

"Susan, I didn't know that was my policy until you said it for me. Now I understand that that is my policy. Thank you for saying it for me.

"That's only half the agenda, though, for today, Susan. I have not said to anybody in my department that they should get a Green Belt or a Black Belt in Six Sigma. When I heard that Sanjar Subramaniam had gotten a Green Belt, I was pleased. When I heard today that three of my managers are taking Green Belt courses, I was perplexed. Are they doing that because they want to improve themselves, or are they doing it because they think they have to?"

"I don't read minds. Let's work on what your policy is."

"Let me try this one for myself. I think my policy is that Six Sigma is worth knowing, and I think I want people to figure that out for themselves. I don't want to coerce people to acquire rote skills, I want them to think things through and figure it out for themselves."

"Do you put yourself forward as a Black Belt, Nan?"

"I never mention it, but it comes up so often that I presume everybody knows that about me."

"You shouldn't trust others to describe yourself. If you think Black Belts are important, then put it on your business card and your short résumé and your long résumé. That will encourage people who collect credentials to get their belt credentials. Bring it up when you have group meetings, and don't wait for others to bring it up."

"Okay, I can do that. You can see I have my Black Belt certificate here on my wall along with the college degrees and licenses.

"So, now I want to say that my Six Sigma policy is that Six Sigma is good, and I encourage its application in our work. As for promotion or performance evaluation, I will look to see Six Sigma projects undertaken and completed, for good or ill, rather than credentials. That is to say, the credentials are a means to an end and not an end in themselves."

"By Jove, Nan, I think you've got it. You need to get that down to a pithier statement, but that's the nub of it.

"Maybe you can have Josey work on a shorter version for you."

"No, I love Josey, but I will require of myself that I be able to present my own policy statements in meaningful language. I don't want to delegate that."

Nan sat thoughtfully for a moment. Susan sat silently, portraying just a little of her Professor Higgins side. Nan looked at Susan and asked herself if she would have to get herself one of those huge hats that Eliza Doolittle wore in the movie. Was she being shaped by events or hardened by experience? Blooming? Metamorphosing? Not wilting, anyway. Not yet.

"Susan, if we leave it to people to manage their careers for themselves, what happens if somebody occupies a position and just stays there. Doesn't that defeat the whole idea?"

"If you want them out, you move them. You did that with Shewan Lincoln, and you can do it with others, now that you know how. Every position in your department is within your gift, as they used to say. Nobody has a right to a particular job."

"Well, that's clear enough.

"What do we do about Six Sigma training courses?"

"Our personnel development body dug up those online courses that some of your people, and I will add that some people outside your department, too, are taking. If the headcount gets up to the point that we would save money or accelerate the process by bringing in somebody to teach a course here, we'll do that. Let's let nature take its course. We offer all kinds of courses, so we know how to manage that part okay."

"How did you dig up Six Sigma courses?"

"I confess that none of my people had a clue, so somebody finally asked Sanjar, and he figured it out."

Nan enjoyed Susan's frank smile. Nan continued, "So, now, Susan. Do I call a staff meeting and speak this out? Do I call an all-hands meeting? What?"

"Policy, you need to get out in writing so it doesn't get cobbled up in the telling. It's usually good form to draft a policy, then have a staff meeting and read it out, so you can get feedback and correct the wording and that sort of thing. It also gets your staff involved in policy development. It's also less threatening to them to hear it from you than to read it in a policy paper. That's for your managers. For the professionals, they don't expect to hear things from you directly, so their reading it is good enough, especially if their own manager has heard it from the Oracle herself and can speak with some authority on the matter."

"What do I say about Six Sigma training courses?"

"Nan, just say that you are pleased to hear that a number of people are pursuing training in Six Sigma and in other matters, which is also true by the way, and that you look for more Six Sigma projects to be cropping up around the department. Then mention that you will give weight to Six Sigma project completions in evaluating people for performance and promotion, and that you know that formal training is not necessary in every case. You will look for results more than credentials."

Nan sipped her tea and did some deep breathing to promote oxygenation of her blood, figuring that it wouldn't hurt and might help her cogitations.

"Susan, six months ago, when I took this position, there was something almost every day that overwhelmed me, and I felt bouts of inadequacy. I don't feel that any more, or almost never any more, but there are periods when I feel frustration that I can't quite get my hands around something. That's how I have been feeling this afternoon on these topics. I like to think that I would have come to the same place we got to, but I know it would have taken me a long time to get there. Or a lot longer than the half-hour we just spent on it together. So you were a catalyst for me, speeding things along."

"Yes, Nan, a catalytic converter just like on a car exhaust system. Making benign outcomes from acidic components. Or is it acetic components? I never understood that chemical stuff."

"I don't know myself. I'd even forgotten that they put those things on cars.

"Susan, you and your catalyst have helped me a lot. I treasure your help," Nan said. "We have been talking about my issues all this time. What's on your plate that might need some catalysis from me?"

"I love it when you talk Latin to me," Susan responded with something between a laugh and a giggle. She rose and made as if to leave. "I don't have any burning issues that touch your department at this particular instant in time.

"I will say, though, and this is strictly girl talk, I see some change in Rudy Rudolf these past few days. What's with him?"

"Susan, I haven't seen him enough over time to have a good reference plane. I have seen him a lot this week, it seems, but that has been by circumstance, I think. He does seem to be a little more—

what, buoyant?—this week. I talked at his staff meeting this week for a few moments, and I think his staff have more fun in their staff meetings than mine do in ours."

"I'll stay away from Freud, but I will say my experience is that humor hides more than it reveals."

"Susan, that is shockingly profound! What am I to make of that?"

"Oh, Nan, don't make anything of it. Humor lubricates the day, and only those with something to hide do any hiding.

"Enough of that. I still love the way you have decorated this office and your conference room," Susan added, looking around the room.

"But Susan, the painters pyramid up to you. You can have your office done over any time you want."

"No, that wouldn't work at all. Mine will be the last one to get the treatment, or else people would be sticking pins in their Susan dolls all day long."

"Okay; that, I understand. The burdens of leadership."

"'Heavy rests the head that wears the crown.' I think that must be Shakespeare, too. But it's only heavy if you've got it, and it's worse if somebody else has it."

"Susan, we must do this more often, and we should do it when Marcy has a fresh box of chocolate chip cookies on hand."

"Yes, Nan. Cookies are my favorite weakness, out of many."

Nan thought for a moment, and then she said, "Susan, I think that we should complete the task before we break up here. Let's do a policy statement draft. We've been talking about a policy for the nursing service, but it seems to me that a lot of what we have been talking about involves your department. So, let's do a joint policy statement. What do you say?"

Susan said, "Okay. How do we do that?"

Nan replied, "The easy way. I changed my mind on who does the writing. We get a writer to write it for us. You had the answer 10 minutes ago. It took all this while to soak in."

Nan hit the intercom button. "Marcy, please join us for a moment."

Marcy came in, steno pad in one hand and a fresh pot of tea in the other.

Nan took charge. "Marcy, we are going to dictate some bullets. We want Josey Walberg to turn those bullets into a policy statement to be reviewed by lots of people and eventually issued as a joint policy statement by Susan's department and by this department. Get the idea?"

"Yes, ma'am. You give bullets, Josey writes a two-department policy statement."

Nan continued, "I know that Josey could do it if she were here with us and had followed the discussion. Let's see if she can do it blind."

Marcy nodded and said, "Shoot the bullets." She poised her pencil on the steno pad.

Nan: "Rotational assignments are optional. Rotational assignments are good preparation for senior professional responsibility, for promotions to management, and for promotions to higher management."

Susan: "Career planning should include broadening assignments. We have counselors who help people with their career planning."

Nan: "Six Sigma training and practice are good. People who complete Six Sigma projects have something to brag about when evaluations are done."

Susan: "We have outside courses in Six Sigma. We will offer inside courses if and when the demand materializes."

Nan: "Does that cover both topics? That's really compact."

Susan: "Yes, I think so. Did you understand all that, Marcy?"

Marcy replied with a nod, finishing off her shorthand notes. "Yes, ma'am. I have the bullets you fired. I will send this as an e-mail note to Josey. I will also send her a couple of sample policy statements so she will know what her draft should look like.

"What's the due date?"

Nan looked at Susan and thought for a moment. "How about three days hence? I'd like to keep this moving, but I can't say that the world will end if we don't have it tomorrow morning. I'd just as soon give Josey enough time to think it through and maybe talk to somebody if she wants to."

Marcy wrote more notes. "Okay. If Josey can't write something a whole lot clearer than our standard policy statements, she's off my cookie list."

After Marcy left, Nan and Susan looked at each other for a moment, and then they shared a grin.

Susan said, "You have the knack for getting people to do extraordinary things, Nan. How many vice presidents do we have who would invite an intern to write an important policy statement? I'll tell you. One. You. I can see why the more energetic moths buzz around your candle."

Nan closed her eyes and enjoyed a grin. Eyes open again, she said, "Do moths buzz? Well, we'll see what Moth Josey can do with a stuffy policy statement. I hope she doesn't put it up on a website to get advice from the world community on the phraseology. When do you think she will produce the first draft?"

Susan considered that question for five seconds and said, "I'd say about two o'clock tomorrow morning."

More grins.

Susan left, stopping by Marcy's desk to pick out a chocolate chip cookie.

31

Jack's Mad

Nan drove into her half of the family two-car garage, pushed the button on the radio thing on the visor to close the garage door behind her, and headed into the house through the door to the kitchen, eager to review her day with Jack. Highs and lows, highs and lows. TV starlet to loose cannon in two hours. She looked forward to Jack's steadying influence on her emotions.

Nan found Jack in the kitchen. That was not uncommon, since he worked at home and didn't mind helping out by getting supper started if she happened to be running behind schedule, which happened these days about as often as not. She found Jack, and she found a Jack she didn't see very often. This Jack was furious.

"Jack, what's wrong?" Nan tried for a middling level of alarm in her voice.

"Those dummies at El-Cor. I bent over backwards to accommodate their schedule on their new real-time operating system, and about ten minutes ago they called to say they had just been acquired by JQL, and everything would be on hold for several days. I know those JQL guys, and they are going to screw this up. They are going to take all the advice that I gave El-Cor, turn it upside down, make a hash of it, and blame me when it turns to dross.

"Last week I turned down two other jobs that would have paid me more money and would have been less work, but no, I had talked myself into doing this El-Cor deal at a low price because it was going to be the start of a big, long-term relationship.

"'Long term' turned out to be half a day.

"I am really mad about this, and I am mad at me. I haven't screwed up a deal this badly in 10 years. Twenty years. This was really stupid. Now I have to wait until they decide who's in charge and then try to get out of my contract there. Then they aren't going to want to pay, so that's more time down the drain trying to get paid for what I have already delivered.

"This was a rookie mistake, at my age. I am really steamed."

Jack looked really, really mad. But Jack wasn't a person to throw things, so Nan didn't feel at risk of getting a flying dinner plate on the noggin. She just felt a dreadful sinking feeling in her middle. The world picking on her man. She didn't like it.

"We don't need the money, Jack. Just send them an invoice and a good-luck card. If they pay, they pay, If they don't pay, forget about it or turn it over to a collection agency. It's not worth an ulcer or a burst blood vessel."

"Oh, I know that. I know that. That's for tomorrow. Right now, I want to be mad at myself for a while.

"Anyway, I feel like a jerk for telling you about it at all. This was your big TV debut, and here I am talking about petty business come-uppances. I'm sorry, Nan. Tell me all about it. I'll shut up."

"No, you won't. Not until you blow off all that steam. Do a good long shout, and then you'll feel better."

"Aaaahhhh urrrrrrr aaaaaahhhhhh urrrrrrrrr." Jack shouted at the top of his voice and kept it up as long as he could. Then he fell back against the kitchen counter with a goofy half-smile for Nan.

"One more time. I'll help."

This time they both shouted as loud and long as they could. "Aaaahhhh urrrrrrr aaaaaahhhhhh urrrrrrrrr." At the end, they were holding each other and laughing to the point of tears streaming down cheeks.

"Your scream therapy is great, Nan. You ought to write a book."

"Your scream is awful. Tarzan, you ain't," replied Nan. "No tigers and elephants are going to come to the door. Just look. No tigers."

"There are no tigers in Africa, Nan. Tigers live in India."

"That's what I said. No tigers answering your scream."

"I give up. And I'm not mad anymore. It's over. Hell with those dummies. Plenty more fish in the sea. Let's talk about your TV gig. I taped it this morning for you. I watched it live, too, but I want to play it back and have you tell me about how you got that look and that wardrobe and that poise and those snappy answers."

"Jack, Willie did up a DVD from the studio master, which they tell me is a much better recording than anybody can get with a VCR. It's here in my bag."

Jack put the DVD in the player. He came back to take Nan by the arm, ushering her to her easy chair, and bowed. He extended his hand, palm up, using body language to convey that he was waiting for a tip.

Nan gave him a kiss on the cheek. Jack left the hand out.

Nan said, "Why don't you pour me a glass of iced tea while I change? Then we can watch the replay, and I'll give you a blow-by-blow account of what was really going on."

Jack nodded and headed for the kitchen. Nan did a very quick costume change, figuring she wanted to get the replay going before Jack had any opportunity to fall back into that funk.

Jack started the DVD player. Nan saw herself entering, stage left, onto the set, walking at a good pace but not running, extending her hand to the hosts, polite smile evident even in this side view.

Jack clicked the stop-action button. "I thought that was a wig, but now I see you in the flesh with that new hairdo. When did you do that?"

"That was all done on the fly by three characters with numbers for names. I've never met anybody like them. Showbiz types, I guess. Josey turned them up. They came over yesterday to do a fitting and chroma, whatever that is. Then they did me a complete makeover, including a pedicure, before the show. Here, look at my toes." Nan waggled her toes to show Jack her toenails. "They did the hair, they made me the clothes I am wearing there. Wait until I sit down and then look at that shoulder pin."

Jack started the player again. They watched as Nan sat down and the conversation began.

"Nan, that skirt looks longer sitting down than standing up. I am glad it's long enough so you could cover your knees. Not that there is anything wrong with your knees. It's just that women look so awkward when they have short skirts and then cross their legs. Very awkward. So this is good. Short skirt when you are standing up and long skirt when you are sitting down."

"Jack, they do that on purpose, they cut the skirt so it hangs longer in that position. I'll have to take the skirt apart and see how they cut it that way. It is a better design than the cheerleader skirts people wear these days. Number One said it was to keep the cameraman paying attention to the program. Number One was in charge."

"Don't tell me the other guys were Two and Three?"

"Okay, so I won't tell you."

"Well, Numero Uno knows his skirts and his cameramen."

"It's just Number One. That's his name. It's not an affectation."

"Right. No affectation."

They played the whole program through. Since they were watching the studio master, there were no commercials, just idle time while the commercials were patched in by the control room. The microphones were live, but nothing of particular note was said during these breaks. The two hosts were mostly talking to each other to select the next topic to take up with Nan. The hosts found one or two things to say to Nan just before the breaks were over, probably so that she would not have a wooden face when they went back live. The hosts clearly knew their stuff. Even Number One hadn't told Nan about that.

"So, tell me about your slush fund, Nan," Jack said at the end of the second playing.

"There isn't any slush fund, Jack. There may or may not be a development fund when the Mr. Bill estate finally pays into the hospital endowment. I haven't heard about that for quite a while. I was going to go ask the chief counsel about it this afternoon, before we were overtaken by events."

"What events?"

Nan told Jack about the telephones going out, cell phones, too, and her rapid-fire action to protect pacemaker patients. Then she told him that the suits were not all that excited about how she handled the crisis and that she was a long ways from being a team player.

Now it was Nan who had the long face and Jack who was being solicitous.

"You thought lives were at risk, so you took preventive action. Now these suits think you should have consulted the emergency drill manual first or maybe formed a committee to evaluate alternatives? Is that what you are telling me?"

"Yes."

"And if some old lady had kicked off because her pacemaker went wild, what would they have had to say, then?"

"You got it."

"They are dumber than those clucks at El-Cor."

"They aren't dumb, they're just scared. Every little thing that happens at the hospital gets blown way up, and then the ambulance chasers come sniffing around, and then the best intentions get twisted around to being evil. Maybe I'd be scared, too, if I knew more about what I am doing."

"What you are doing is saving lives, Nan. Don't back off from that. You're saving lives. I love you for it. So do all those old ladies with pacemakers who didn't croak this afternoon, or at least they will when they find out what happened.

"I'll put this DVD up on our private web page and send Jake and Bake an e-mail so they can check it out from college. They'll probably be selling tickets in their residence hall and signing autographs.

"That reminds me. I went out to get some supplies before noon, and when I got back, Marcy was in the bedroom stuffing clothes into a suit bag. She told me it was an emergency and that you were going to have to change at the hospital after the TV show. I figured if you had given her your keys, then you trusted her to pick out your clothes. If I had thought about it before, I would have had a set of keys made for her.

"But if you went directly to the TV studio, how did Marcy get your keys?"

"Don't ask."

"Oh."

Jack pushed some buttons to discharge the DVD, the result of which was that the TV wound up on a broadcast channel showing the local news. Nan's eye was caught by the sight of Philip L. Crawford and Dr. Robert Anderson being interviewed by a swarm of reporters. Crawford was talking.

". . . don't have the details on the outage yet. We took precautionary measures inside the hospital. We are set up to anticipate and cope with just about everything. Today it was RFI."

A stentorian voice from the back of the pack asked, "What's RFI?"

"We have a rule against cell phone use in the hospital because the radio frequency energy can interfere with some electronics. Chief among them are heart pacemakers. That's called radio frequency interference, or RFI for short."

"What about the pacemakers?" asked the same voice.

"Dr. Anderson, our chief medical officer, was on the scene. He can tell you about pacemakers. Dr. Robert Anderson." Crawford pulled Dr. Anderson forward a step to get him closer to the bank of microphones.

Dr. Anderson put on his professional face and said, "Pacemakers give voltage impulses to the patient's heart to keep it beating on the right rhythm. They are given instructions by the patient's cardiologist, who can set the rhythm and make other adjustments the patient may require. These instructions are given by radio, with the pacemaker tuned to certain frequencies. It happens that cell phones radiate near these same frequencies. This is well known, so the pacemakers are designed to require a very strong signal, so that a patient using his own cell phone doesn't interfere with his pacemaker. So one cell phone or a few cell phones don't matter, but with the breakdown this morning, a lot of people ignored the hospital rule and tried to make calls with their cell phones. Their cell phones didn't work, so they kept trying. I can understand their behavior, and of course I don't think anyone meant to do any harm, but we needed to put a stop to it."

That voice again. "Mr. Crawford, do you mean to say that you have a written emergency procedure to cover the case where the telephones and the cell phones both fail at the same time?"

Crawford leaned back into the frame to get his face in front of the microphones. "We have specific emergency instructions for some things and general emergency authorizations for others. This fell in the general category."

That voice: "Dr. Anderson, did you jump in and save these pacemaker patients yourself?"

Crawford was out of the frame. Dr. Anderson was a little slow to offer a response, but he clearly felt that the cameras were going to be staring at him until he said something. So, he said, "I did not, myself. This was handled very well by our nursing department, and our head nurse, Mrs. Nan Mills."

That voice: "When did this happen, again?"

Crawford was back in the frame. "It was around 11:30 this morning that the problem occurred. It took some time for word to get around the building, since you don't notice a telephone that doesn't ring, at least not right away. And we didn't even get e-mail messages saying the phones were out because we are still suffering from that manhole fire on Sunday night that knocked out our email and web service. So it was some time after 11:30 this morning."

That voice: "Nan Mills was on that live TV gab show at 11:30 this morning. How did she do this pacemaker thing with no telephones and no email at the hospital?"

Crawford was back in the frame, his professional smile looking a little stiff. "Mrs. Mills returned to the hospital directly after that TV show and took immediate charge. She acted promptly. Every patient, employee, visitor, and contractor who has a pacemaker was identified. Instructions were given personally to everyone in the building to knock off the cell phones. Everyone complied, I am happy to say. I am even happier to say that we have had no repercussions, no medical events, and the whole thing may have been a bit overdramatized. That's okay, we need to be on the safe side on things like this. I am sure you would want it that way if your loved ones were here with pacemakers."

That voice: "So you're saying that you sat on your duff until Nan Mills got back from the TV studio?"

Crawford leaned back into the frame, his smile looking the worse for wear. But, before Crawford could think up an answer, Dr. Anderson leaned forward with a stern face and said, "Mrs. Mills diagnosed this very unusual situation quicker than the rest of us did. She took action. She took the same action I would have taken if I had been on the ball. She did her diagnosis, she notified the executive offices, and she ordered a bed watch on all patients with pacemakers and a put out call for visitors, employees, and contractors with pacemakers. She mobilized the whole place. She went herself to the cardiology ward and conferred with the cardiologist on duty, Dr. Benedetta Parsons, who confirmed the plan. Dr. Parsons personally contacted the intensive care unit, the operating theaters, and the neonatal units because those units in particular have a lot of electronic life support equipment that might be jeopardized by RFI. Then they worked out a plan to notify everybody in the building, quietly, not to use their cell phones within a block of the building. So, that was good thinking and good execution. Everybody cooperated, and a tense situation was taken care of without any theatrics, just good hospital management. As a professional man, I was impressed by how this was done, quickly and effectively.

"You can ask the other hospitals in the area how they are set up to handle RFI."

Crawford jumped into the frame. "Look, now, we are happy to tell you how we handle these things, but we don't want to start a war with the other hospitals. I am confident they would have handled it just the way we did. If they have an even better procedure, I am sure we will be hearing about it shortly, and we'll be happy to learn from them."

That voice: "Where is Nan Mills? Why isn't she out here with you? She's the one who saved your bacon."

Crawford: "This request for a press conference came rather late in the day. Mrs. Mills had gone off shift. She'll be here tomorrow if you want to talk to her then. I invite you all back, if you want to do that."

That voice: "The press conference was set up at 2:30. What kind of hours does Nan Mills work?"

Crawford: "Oh, I guess I got my times mixed up. Mrs. Mills works the usual office hours and is here late more days than not. In any case, come tomorrow and I will arrange for you to talk to Mrs. Mills.

"Any more questions?"

Jack clicked the mute. "That guy Crawford does press conferences all the time. He didn't look like he was on his game today. Is there more to this story? You'd better be ready, tomorrow."

"Jack, that's exactly what has been on my mind this afternoon, and I want to tell you about it so you can give me some advice on how to handle it. But first I need to make a phone call."

Nan picked up a phone and composed the number. She waited, and when the call was answered, Nan said, "Marcy, forgive me for calling you at this hour at home, but I was just watching the local news with Jack, and we saw the press conference. Did you see it? Good. Now tell me, Marcy, did you recognize the voice from the press crowd, the big voice with all the questions? I just thought that might be the case. Thank you for the information. I'll see you in the morning. Goodbye."

Nan put the phone down. She turned to Jack and said, "Crusher Morgenstern."

Jack thought about that for a moment. "Crusher Morgenstern?"

"Crusher Morgenstern is a cousin or something of Marcy's, an ex–pro wrestler. Big man. Big voice, too. Marcy just told me that he works as a stringer for the local sports channel and wound up at this press conference somehow."

"So, you think Marcy fed him those questions?"

"I didn't ask."

"How did Marcy know that the suits were going to try to spin their way out of the RFI thing? Did you tell her?"

"No, but I wouldn't be surprised if somebody else told her. She probably noticed that I was in a snit when I came back from suit-land this afternoon while she was wrapping up my souvenir track suit to send back."

"Souvenir track suit?"

"Oh, Jack. Look at this." Nan ran to the pile of things she had lugged home, threw open the gift box, and drew the upper half of the tracksuit across her chest to model it for Jack. "Isn't this beautiful?"

"You just told me that Marcy sent it back."

"Yes, she was going to send it back because it would violate the vendor gift limit policy. But I arranged to buy it, so it's not a gift any more. Number One was all bent out of shape about my rejecting his gift, and that's where Crusher Morgenstern came into the picture as peacemaker."

"Bent out of shape may be the apt term," surmised Jack. "You have an interesting informal collection of characters at your hospital."

"The Nan Mills Irregulars. Maybe we need T-shirts with this monogram," said Nan, pointing to the Gemini symbol on her tracksuit.

"If those are diamonds, you're going to have a very exclusive club."

"Oh, God, I hope those are rhinestones or cubic zirconia or something. Otherwise, I'll have to send Crusher over to see Number One again with another check."

Nan was back in her easy chair. She clutched the tracksuit to her breast and closed her eyes. "What a day, Jack, what a day."

Then she sat upright, eyes wide open. "Jack, Marcy may have found out about the press conference through her grapevine, which is the best in the world. But one person who would definitely have known about it because she probably set it up is Josey Walberg, our intern press flack. Josey knew about the RFI thing because she was involved, executing tasks as fast as I could dump them on her and very well, too, I might add. Crusher is Josey's cousin, too. I think I know what happened."

Jack leaned forward and said, "You figure Josey doped out that the suits would be out there waving their arms to cover up their own lack of action, and she wanted Crusher there to pull out the real story.

"Nan, you have your own press agent, or maybe your own press activist," he said. "What are you going to do now?"

"Jack, I've created a monster. Or my monsters have created me. I don't know what to do. That's why I wanted to talk to you about it."

Jack leaned back and enjoyed a good belly laugh. Nan was pleased that he was out of his funk, but she wasn't sure what to do next. So, she waited.

Jack eventually sat up straight again and looked at her. "Nan, my love, you have been an executive for six or seven months now, and you have been through the best fast-track executive training program since Harry Truman was installed as president on one day and told the next day he had to decide whether or not to drop A-bombs on Japan. On the Truman scale, your issues are pretty mild.

"You have the liveliest people in your organization working for you, people who seek you out because they think you are the one who can deal with lively people. Marcy, Sanjar, and I'll bet Josey all pulled strings or cut corners so they could work for you. Isn't that right?"

"Yes, That's right. Sanjar has been promoted since. Maggie Kelly is leaving, but what you say is correct. They could all be working someplace else if they wanted to."

"So, you attract lively people, you get lively people. You smile upon initiative, you get initiative. You tell people you trust them, and they take you at your word. They succeed when you succeed, and they want to succeed, so they want very much for you to succeed.

"Don't you tell them that Japanese dictum, that the purpose for going to work every day is to make the boss look smart?"

"I don't tell my own people that, ever. Just others."

"Well, they are out there doing their damnedest to make you look smart, so maybe they got it by osmosis.

"So, Nan, my love, how are you going to keep this together tomorrow?"

Nan thought for a while. "Let's see. I have several choices. One is to keep a low silhouette until the next news story comes along and blows this one off the tube. Another is to deny it all. The third is to give credit to Crawford. The fourth is to blow my own horn. How do you vote?"

"That's easy. You can't be sure some other news story will come soon enough to trump this issue by tomorrow. You don't need to blow your own horn when you have a whole brass band doing it for you, including Dr. Robert Anderson, the chief medical officer, from what he said at that press conference just now. So, do it the way the Japanese do it. Make the boss look smart. That can't hurt you, it might help him, and that takes the edge off the story, so it will go away in one news cycle."

"Jack, you say that so well, which is why I love you, among all the other reasons why I love you. My irregulars look out for me, I look out for the suits, and devil take the hindmost.

"I learned something else this week, Jack. I don't want my irregulars deserting me for somebody else. When I settle bills with a vendor, I want Crusher Morgenstern on my side of the table."

They looked each other in the eye, warm smiles on both faces. Then they both laughed. Nan reached for Jack's hand. "Even with my irregulars looking out for me, Jack, I think I need to learn a few more executive lessons. I acted on impulse today with that RFI stuff. My impulses are pretty good, but the next time, I might be flying off in the wrong direction. What do I do about that?"

"It comes with experience, Nan. In the meanwhile, don't change a thing. If you pull in your horns now, you won't get the experience, and you'll let down the biggest gaggle of admirers since Elvis."

32

Thursday Morning at Nan's Office

N an walked briskly into her office Thursday morning, about 20 minutes before eight. Marcy was at her workstation, so they exchanged "good mornings" as Nan walked by. Marcy followed Nan into Nan's office, two steps behind, steno pad and pencil in one hand, teapot in the other.

"Marcy, before we get started, tell me something more about Crusher Morgenstern."

"Well, Crusher is my cousin once-removed, and of Josey, too, on that side of the family. When he was a kid, he was really, really skinny. You know how boys grow, they don't grow all at once, some parts grow earlier than others, and in his case, his ears sort of got ahead of the rest of him. When he was 11 or 12, the other kids hung a nickname on him: Skate Key."

"Skate Key Morgenstern?"

"Yes, ma'am. And being so skinny he couldn't convince anybody to call him Chester, so that nickname stuck for a while. So he reacted to that by taking up weight lifting. In a couple of years, nobody was calling him Skate Key anymore.

"He stuck with the weight lifting, and then in high school he was the heavyweight wrestler, because by then his body had caught up with the ears. He did pretty well at it, kept in up in college, and then he went on the pro wrestling tour for several years. I guess he's about 30 now."

"That sounds like a positive way of dealing with his preteen troubles. Better than some kids manage. What's he doing as a press stringer?"

"Well, he decided he had had enough of the pro wrestling game, and he is really pretty smart, an A student in college. He thought he would eventually wind up as a television sports commentator, but he has that scar on his face that can't just be covered up with pancake makeup, so he thought he should try to get himself established as a sports writer and then maybe get some cosmetic surgery or something later on to work his way into television."

"Maybe he could wear a mask over half his face."

"Funny you should mention that. For a while on the pro circuit, he actually wore a mask over half his face, but it was the other half."

"So now he's doing sports writing? How did that get him into the press group yesterday afternoon who were harassing Mr. Crawford?"

"He doesn't have enough seniority yet to have a sports byline or anything. He takes whatever assignments he can grab. He isn't exactly an employee; he just gets paid if they use any of his stuff. So, being a little pushy helps him earn a little extra money."

"Marcy, did you pull any strings to get him assigned to that press briefing yesterday?"

"No, ma'am."

"Did Josey?"

"I don't know."

"What's your best guess?"

"My best guess is that Josey called him up after she notified the newspapers and television stations, she read him the press release, and then she told him the whole story."

"That's my best guess, too, and I've never met the gentleman. I do know Josey. I like her. I'm glad she is helping her family member get going in his new career. Not that I approve of playing favorites in the press, you understand. That just makes everybody else mad."

"Yes, ma'am."

Well, so what do we have booked for this morning, Marcy?"

"The first thing, at eight o'clock, is the presentation by the future nurses twins, Lu and Ray Morgani. That's in the training room. After that, the public liaison office would like you to give half an hour to the press so they can follow up on the press conference from yesterday afternoon. Mr. Crawford sort of invited the press to come back to talk to you today."

"Marcy, I've never done a press interview before."

"You did fine on that television gab show yesterday morning."

"They were trying to make me look good. I think the intent of the press is to make me look bad. Or stupid. Or venal. Or grasping. Or evil."

"Yes, ma'am. I think you'll find some of the press to be sympathetic, and maybe the rest will get the idea before the session is over."

"Let me guess. Crusher Morgenstern, heretofore known as Skate Key Morgenstern, is going to be in the press gathering?"

"I don't know a thing about it."

Nan laughed until tears ran down her face. "Marcy, I love you and I love all your cousins and nieces and nephews and adoptees and your chocolate chip cookies. How I would ever function on a level playing surface, I don't know, and I don't want to find out. I want every advantage I can get in this game.

"So, lay out the schedule for me."

"Yes, ma'am. Eight o'clock, half an hour with the Morgani twins. That will take 45 minutes. Then a 15-minute buffer. Then half an hour with the lawyers before the press interview, then the interview. They will cut that off after half an hour. The press interview is in the executive conference room upstairs."

"Okay, Marcy. I'll go see what the future nurses think of our nursing present."

33

The Morgani Twins and Staph Infections

When Nan got to the training room, she found several of the members of her department, two youngsters she took to be the Morgani twins, a woman who looked like she might be a teacher from North High, and Josey Walberg talking to five people who just might be reporters, since they were wearing over-size badges saying PRESS. One of them looked to be rather larger than most people are.

Annie Rostow had been watching for Nan to appear. She came forward with the twins and the teacher to make introductions. The teacher turned out to be Gale Hansen, who was a counselor rather than a classroom teacher. They exchanged pleasantries. Nan sensed flash pictures being taken of the group. Nan asked Annie to get things started.

Annie Rostow went to the lectern, called for attention, and introduced the Morgani twins, saying simply that they have been working in her department as a part of a future nurses project, and they would explain where the project stands at this time.

The twins both went to the front. They were well turned out, being at that age where school clothes are not suitable for a business meeting but too young to look anything but overdressed if they were to wear business attire. They had struck a reasonable balance, and they looked like what they were: earnest high schoolers who were talking, probably for the first time in their lives, to an adult audience.

Being brother and sister, they certainly were not identical. But, they did share a good deal in their looks and size and deportment. They also gave away the fact that they were twins by standing much closer to each other than other siblings would do. They were doing little things in such a coordinated way that Nan, being in the know on such things, knew that they didn't need words to communicate.

Lu and Ray, in unison: "Good morning, ladies and gentlemen."

Lu: "I am Lu Morgani."

Ray: "I am Ray Morgani. We are members of the North High Future Nurses Club, and it has been our honor to be involved in a research project under the supervision of Nurse Anne-Marie Rostow here in the hospital. Our high school club counselor, Ms. Gale Hansen, made the arrangements and is here with us this morning." Ray smiled and nodded in the direction of Ms. Hansen. "Our project has been to observe normal nursing operations and to keep track of adherence to, or deviation from, standard procedures governing staph infection minimization.

"For those of you who are not nursing professionals, I will just say that staph germs are not a problem for healthy people, but they can be lethal for people who are very sick or weak or just getting over an operation or who have another disease already. The particular concern is that a nurse or an aide might pick up staph germs from Patient A and carry them inadvertently to Patient B. Nobody would do that on purpose, of course, but since you can't see germs with your naked eye, anybody might do it by accident.

"So there are things nurses and aides and orderlies are supposed to do. They amount to cleaning the hands and any utensils between beds."

Lu interjected: "I never thought about the need to sterilize a stethoscope between patients before we did this study. Once it was pointed out to me, to us, of course it was obvious."

Ray picked up the story: "We followed people around. The first couple of weeks, everybody was on good behavior, and we didn't observe any departures from standard procedure. Then, I guess the staff got used to seeing us around and thought we were part of the furniture, because they reverted to their normal habits. I think we would have done the same thing if the tables had been reversed."

Lu Morgani: "For the first few days, we just followed people around to see what they do. Then we made a form we could carry around on a clipboard to check off things that looked like departures. We didn't try to count the things that were done correctly, we just looked for departures. The departures were very few in comparison with the correct actions, and anyway we haven't learned any statistics yet."

Ray said, "We were just told this morning that this table is called the frog table because you dissect frogs on it when you do training programs. They don't let us cut up frogs in high school biology anymore."

Ray turned on the projector connected to the PC on the frog table. The large wall screen filled up with a PowerPoint curtain slide with a cartoon of a nurse in traditional cap, a rarity in this hospital, being followed by two kids carrying clipboards and pencils.

Lu continued: "Our point was not to catch people making mistakes. Our point was to find a couple of things that might be improved. I mean, everybody makes mistakes."

Ray took up the presentation and clicked to get the next slide. "Looking at this bar chart, we see that our subjects, nurses, aides, orderlies, and anybody else who touched one patient and then was near to another patient shortly thereafter, we see that our subjects made utensil departures several times. Almost always stethoscopes. They had hand-washing departures less often but still sometimes. They had a few glove-changing departures.

"You will notice that our bar chart has no scale, so the only meaning here is that utensil events are that high, hand events less, and glove events less again."

Lu: "Since we are just high school kids and not even student nurses, there may have been other kinds of departures that we didn't recognize. We are only dealing with those things that were evident to us."

Ray: "My understanding, based on these observations and maybe some common sense, is that our subjects don't always think of a stethoscope as something that might carry germs, even though they know better. They always wash up if they get a patient's blood or saliva or something on their hands but they don't always wash up if they don't have any visible evidence on their hands that they might be carrying germs, even though they know better. The same with gloves. And we see that events happen more often when the subject is hurrying from one bed to another. I guess that's common sense, too."

Lu: "It didn't take us long to find these events. The next question was, what should we do, or what should the hospital management do? Put up yellow stickers? Hire somebody with a police whistle? Hire one nurse per patient?"

Ray: "Here's where we learned something. Nurse Rostow taught us about the three elements of prevention of inadvertent error."

Ray and Lu looked at each other for a few seconds, smiling, then turned to the audience and said in a louder voice, "Poka-yoke!"

Ray advanced the slide show to the next slide, which presented the three poka-yoke guidelines. Make it easier to do a task right than wrong. Make any error evident. Make it easy to correct the error on the spot.

Lu continued: "Let's look at these from the bottom up. The subject can correct the error on the spot by washing hands, say."

Ray: "But the design of the task does not make it easier to do it right. In fact, the design of the task is the opposite, making it easier to rush to the next bed than to stop and decontaminate, if that's the right word." He glanced over to Annie Rostow with a quizzical look. Annie just smiled encouragingly.

Ray advanced the slide. "We thought about a lot of ways to make it easier to do it right than to do it wrong. Here's one." The slide showed a referee's whistle on a cord.

Lu picked up the story: "You probably laughed when we said 'police whistle' a minute ago. We laughed, too, the first time we said it. But think about it, please, for just a minute before we go on to other possibilities. If each subject had a referee following the subject around, and if the referee blew the whistle every time the subject deviated from standard practice, then that would fire Rule Two, making the subject aware of the error. The subject could then correct the error. So, while we are not saying this is a good way to run a hospital, we do respectfully suggest that this would be a solution to the problem."

Ray continued without missing a beat: "We offer this partly as a little high school whimsy and partly to show you that we didn't feel constrained to think only about conventional solutions."

Lu advanced the projector to the next slide and continued: "Here's one that is a little more conventional, because it uses equipment that is already common on the floor where we have been assigned."

The slide showed a medicine cart, the kind used by floor staff to carry medicine orders around the floor, a sort of abbreviated shopping cart.

"Nurse Rostow told us to figure out where somebody else had already solved this problem. That's how we thought of referees, because we see lots of those at our high school games. Then we thought about how operating rooms work, or at least how we think they work from watching television and movies. We've never actually been in an operating room while we were awake. What we see on television is that the surgeon walks in to the room and is met by a nurse who pushes gloves onto the surgeons hands and when the surgeon needs to wipe sweat off his forehead, say, a nurse does it for him." Lu paused. Lu and Ray looked out at the audience to see if anyone might be snickering. They knew they were talking about operating rooms when every adult in the room knew more about them than they did. No snickers.

Ray continued, advancing to a slide with the three poka-yoke rules in one column and remarks in a second column. "Suppose we don't have a referee, but we have a helper with a cart, and suppose that the cart has latex gloves, hand-cleaning goop, and spare stethoscopes, and maybe spare face masks and gowns. Would this address the poka-yoke elements?

Lu and Ray in unison: "Yes to number one."

Lu continued: "It would be easier to do it right than to do it wrong because the helper would be right there with the goods."

Lu and Ray in unison: "Yes to number two."

Ray continued: "The helper is right there to notice even if the subject doesn't."

Lu and Ray in unison: "Yes to number three."

Lu continued: "The gloves and everything are right there, so it's easy to correct a goof if necessary."

Ray advanced the projector to show a slide with a nurse pushing a medicine cart. "We know that hospitals are short on money and are not apt to hire helpers for every nurse and aid and orderly. So we wondered if maybe the cart could be designed so that the gloves and hand goop and so on were all on the cart. Maybe it's the same medicine cart they are already pushing. Maybe it's a second cart. Maybe it's the same cart plus a referee's whistle that blows itself every time the cart is moved. We don't know how to design a cart."

Lu: "But we didn't want to leave this up in the air, so we thought the one thing we could contribute is to put a name on this new cart." Lu advanced the projector to show a Victorian scene with a lady being dressed by her maid. "What every nurse should have is a maid. If the cart is doing the duty of the maid, then we thought the cart should have a name that brings *maid* to mind. But we didn't want to just say 'maid' because that brings housekeeping to mind, and that's not what we are talking about."

Ray: "So we made a quick list of names for servants who are on the order of a maid." Ray advanced the projector to show a slide with a lot of words in various fonts, giving the impression they had been cut out of a newspaper and glued to the background. "Maid. Servant. Batman. Dog's body. I like that one, but I'm not sure it translates very well from the English. Gopher. Stooge. Runner. Grunt. Churl. Valet. Varlet. Boy. Girl."

Ray advanced the projector, the new slide giving another list of words in the same cut-newspaper style. These words were less familiar. In fact, Nan had never seen most of them before at all. "Then we did an Internet search for some equivalents in other languages. I am sure each of the other languages have 10 or 20 terms for 'maid,' just like English does, but we just have a sampling here. Fantesca. Dienstmädchen. Dienstmeisje. Szobalány. Jungfru. Frukin. Дева. Bonne. Μαρίκα. Lots of choices out there."

Lu: "To cut to the chase, we picked one that is Spanish. One of the Spanish terms for maid is 'chacha.' So we propose to call the new cart the Chacha Cart. We mean this to be complimentary, and we picked this one because it has the best sound, to our ears anyway."

Ray advanced the projector to a slide showing a girl in a French maid's costume pushing a medicine cart. The title on the slide was "Chacha and Cart."

Lu continued. "We don't know if our recommendation of a chacha cart is a serious one or not. What we do know, and what we have learned in this project, is that the poka-yoke method of thinking about tasks and how to design them so that people do them right more readily than they do them wrong, and making mistakes obvious, and making it possible to correct errors on the spot if an error gets made, those make up a good way of thinking about problems. We believe that the starting point, that errors are inadvertent and not malicious, is a good place to start so you don't have everybody mad and defensive before you even start."

Ray: "We don't know if chacha carts are going to prove to be practical or not. What we do hope, though, is that our little study will cause people who know a lot more about this than we do to pay attention to this issue and come up with a good solution."

Lu and Ray, in unison: "Ladies and gentlemen, we thank you for your kind attention." Then they smiled, partly in friendship to this friendly audience, and partly in relief at having gotten all the way though without a major gaffe.

Annie Rostow started the applause going, and hearty it was. She walked to the lectern to say, "Lu and Ray, I know I speak for all the nursing service when I tell you that we are pleased with your study and with your contribution to nursing. I hope you can stay with us for the rest of your term and maybe try this idea out. You have my pledge of support."

After more applause, Annie said, "Ladies and gentlemen, our budgeted time is about up, so I am going to end the formal part of this program now and invite you to stay around if your schedule permits and have a cup of coffee and a no-cal doughnut at the refreshment table on your right. I believe our student researchers will be able to stay for a few more minutes to talk to you informally."

But before Annie could get away, the members of the press were waving their hands and shouting for attention. That froze Annie in place. She decided she would have to field at least one question, from the look on her face, so she nodded at the closest reporter.

"I'm Nelson from *Morning News*. Can you please say something about staph infections and why that's an issue in hospitals.

And can you say if it's a particular problem in your hospital and in your ward?"

Annie knew the answers, but she thought for a moment before trying to put the answers into words that would look right in the newspaper. "Staph infections are a problem anywhere there are people who are seriously sick or debilitated. It's not a problem for healthy people. Since seriously sick people are in hospitals, staph infections are an issue for hospitals. My unit, or 'ward,' as you say it, cares for post-operative patients. Some of them, but certainly not all, are debilitated and therefore at risk. Because our caregivers move from patient to patient, we take pains to reduce the risk that we might carry staph from one patient to another. That involves a lot of hand washing, changing of latex gloves, and even changing of gowns and smocks between beds. It also means sterilizing our utensils, including stethoscopes.

"Some studies show that a large number of people die of staph infections, a number on the order of 100,000 American patients a year. There are 6000 hospitals, so you can do the arithmetic. Now a lot of those patients were in poor condition and would likely have died of something else, but not all. Some of them would have had long and productive lives if they hadn't gotten a staph infection. So, we take staph seriously, and so do all hospitals."

Nan thought she had better get up to the front of the room and take the next flurry of arrows in her own chest. She went to the front of the room and introduced herself.

"I am Nan Mills, head nurse. If you want to ask about hospital policy, I will be happy to answer your questions. But first let me add my own expression of thanks to Anne-Marie Rostow for hosting this study, and I do not say 'little study' because I think we have all learned something from it. I want to thank Lu and Ray Morgani, and I want to thank Ms. Hansen from North High for encouraging her students to think of nursing as a career. Your students have certainly shown themselves to be a credit to North High.

"Now, to you members of the press, I believe we are already scheduled to be meeting in just a few moments, so why don't you get a cup of coffee, ask any questions you want of our student researchers about their project and of Ms. Hansen about her work, and I will take any questions when we meet shortly."

Nan gave her best nurse's smile to discourage any argument. The lure of doughnuts turned the tide in her favor, and the Fourth Estate moved in the direction of the refreshment table.

The press photographers had clearly spent the presentation time at the refreshment stand, from the number of doughnut crumbs on their shirt fronts, not to mention powdered sugar, and they seized the opportunity to stage group shots of the twins, the twins with Annie Rostow, with Ms. Hansen, and then with Nan.

Nan took the opportunity to size up Crusher Morgenstern, who was busy asking questions of everybody and making notes in a small notebook, the old-fashioned way. Nan wondered if he took short-hand, and if so, if he was as proficient as Marcy, who could write her shorthand hooks and squiggles faster than Nan could talk. Crusher was a very big man, a thick man. Not at all fat, just thick with layer on layer of muscle. In her student-nursing days, she had seen football players being treated in the trauma unit who had that same muscular thickness. Nan could see muscles rippling under Crusher's sports coat, something she had never seen before. It hardly seemed possible. Jack and their boys were in decent physical condition, but they were not in Crusher's league at all.

Nan found herself free from the photographers, so she moved in the direction of the refreshment table to see if she could get a cup of tea. She found Annie Rostow, the Morgani twins, and Maggie Kelly talking with Gale Hansen.

Annie immediately said to Nan, "Nan, I hope you know that this project was started by Maggie. Maggie has been our contact with the North High Future Nurses Club for years. Maggie asked me if we could put up with a staph study, and I of course jumped at the chance. The Morgani twins have been a delight. I think we learned something, and I hope you two have." Annie gave the twins her biggest mater-nalistic smile.

Nan added her own smile and then turned to Maggie. "Have you lined up someone to take your place as liaison with North High?"

"Yes. In fact, Annie volunteered for that duty even before she knew that I would be leaving the hospital. So this little study has had lots of impact already."

Nan asked Gale Hansen, "Do you take charge of several of the student organizations or just the Future Nurses Club?"

"I have three. The ones that have been organized for many years, like this club, pretty much run themselves, so I can handle three of them without ignoring my regular job as career counselor for the juniors and seniors."

Nan looked at the Morgani twins. "Would you like to see a real operating room in action?"

Lu and Ray answered in unison, "Yes, ma'am." Big smiles.

Nan looked at them in turn, intently. "I don't mean as tourists. I want you to take your clipboards with you and do the same thing there that you have been doing on the third floor. Some studies say that the operating room is the place of highest risk for staph infections. I want you close enough to see what's going on, so you'll have to scrub and wear masks, gowns and gloves. Do you still want to do it?"

Unison response: "Yes, ma'am." Big smiles.

Lu replaced her smile with a straight face and asked Nan, "Mrs. Mills, we understand that you are a twin yourself and that you are named for your twin sister."

"Yes, that's right. My sister is Ann and I am Nan, short for not-Ann."

Lu continued, brow furrowed. "I am named after a woman in the Middle Ages who poisoned her husband so that her brother could advance his career. Isn't that weird? It was all involved in who got to be pope, even though the Borgias were Spanish and not Italian. My brother was named for that woman's brother, and he died wearing a suit of armor."

Ray contributed, "He died like a man, doing what a man did in those days. He didn't poison anybody. Besides, maybe he got a staph infection and that got him. Nobody knows for sure, since they didn't know about germs back in those days."

Nan could see that these young people had the same mixture of the real and the unreal, romance and reality, that her own twin sons exhibited, and there wasn't much difference in age between these twins and her own. Normal, delightful, kids.

"Are you going to be able to continue this project a little longer?"

The twins answered, "Yes, ma'am, we'd like to."

Ray continued. "We don't really know anything about carts, but we have some notions about things to try. If you have an old medicine cart we can hot-rod, we'd like to stay with this until we go off to college."

Nan replied, "We can't recycle old equipment through the floors with at-risk patients, but we can issue you a new one to experiment with."

Lu said, "We saw you on that TV show, and they said you have a slush fund for little development projects. Does this qualify for your slush fund?"

Nan smiled. "The development fund only exists on paper right now. We can pay for what you need out of our regular budget."

Ray said, "That's great. We are going to need a cart, or better yet two carts, laptop computers, GPS positioning systems, some sensors, and maybe some other stuff before we get this figured out. We want the cart to know when it is moved from bed to bed. Maybe we need a referee's whistle, too."

Nan's smile grew to a bona fide grin. "Go easy on the whistle. Tell Ms. Rostow what you need." Nan turned to Annie. "Tell Marcy or Carl Burke what you need. I'll tell them you'll be calling." Nan turned back to the twins. "If you need any help with the computer work, we have some people who can give you a hand."

Ray said, "We have this pretty well worked out already with an old junker computer our dad had at home. We'll probably get stuck, though, so if there is somebody we can ask questions, that'll be great."

Nan asked, "Have you decided where you are going to college and what you are going to study?"

They answered, "Yes, ma'am. State University."

Lu said, "We are both taking computer science for undergrad, and we both think we will take graduate programs in medicine or nursing, we don't know yet. We figure computer science is a good place to start for any of the health professions. I mean, it's too late to get in on the ground floor with computers because they have been around for ages, but maybe it's not too late to get in on the ground floor for computer-assisted medical care."

Nan smiled again. "My twin sons think computers are old hat, too. That seems radical to anyone my age. They are into nanotechnology, whatever that is.

"So, I wish you luck with your continuation of this project. You have done very well, and you say you have learned something. I know you will have caused people around here to think again about how we control contagion. Be sure to document your findings so that others can benefit."

"Yes, ma'am."

Ray said, "We are getting everything on videotape as we go along. We don't shoot any patient faces, we observe your privacy rules. In fact, we don't shoot any faces at all. The videotape goes to your legal department before it will be shown to any other audience, even our Future Nurses club."

Nan thought that to be wise, so she concluded with, "I look forward to seeing your video report." Nan smiled to everybody in the group, shook hands with the twins and with Gale Hansen, and then she tried once more to get to the refreshment table.

Before Nan could get away, Ray Morgani asked her, "Mrs. Mills. Do you mind if we tell you a couple of other things that occurred to us, I mean things that weren't really in our scope of study but still sort of caught our eye."

Nan stopped, looked Ray in the eye, and said, "Shoot."

Ray said, "The first thing is that you have those poles in practically every room that you hang IV bags on, and then if the pouch goes empty, a beeper goes off. The beeper is right there, so the patient hears it but the nurse doesn't unless the nurse happens to be standing right there. So the patient gets terrified. It seems to us that the beeper is a good idea, but it should beep at the unit desk, not right there in the room. Then it would do some good and not scare the patient."

Lu said, "The other thing is that you have these call lights that turn a light on out in the hallway over the room door, so that when the patient wants something, they push a button and the light goes on. The nurse is supposed to see the light when it goes on. From what we saw, some of the lights get quick attention, and some don't, like maybe when everybody is already busy. So we think maybe it would be a good idea to have a standard response time of two minutes or four minutes, and then keep track of whether that is practical or not. I mean, if you aren't committed to answering the call light, then you should take them out, shouldn't you?"

Nan looked at these two youngsters, marveling at their powers of observation and clear thinking. She said to them, "You're definitely right about the IV beeper being better at the unit desk. I'll have to look into that.

"You're also right about the call lights. We should have a service standard and commit ourselves to responding within a set number of minutes. We'd say it a little differently, saying that we would answer within that number of minutes 95 percent of the time, so that if we have a real emergency somewhere that is taking everybody's time, we don't get caught short. And we don't want to give patients any incentive to hit the call button all at the same time just to be ornery.

"You're right on both of these. I like them both. Please include both of these in your report, and make sure you tell Nurse Rostow that you explained these to me."

Nan smiled her best smile, maybe even a maternal smile, and started toward the refreshment table to get a new cup of tea.

It was not to be. Josey Walberg caught her by the elbow and told her politely but firmly that it was time to meet with the lawyers to prepare for her press interview. Nan did a generalized smile in all directions on the way out, with Josey one step behind her and one pace to the left. Nan wondered if there would ever be a Josey-cart and decided that no, the personal touch would always be necessary when it comes to expediting executives.

34

Getting Ready for the Press

Josey stecred Nan to the small conference room of Alice Newcomb, the chief counsel for the hospital. Alice's secretary admitted them, remarking to Nan that her hair still looked very nice. Nan thanked her with a smile, thinking to herself that this was a perceptive woman, and besides, the new hairdo created the day before by Numbers One, Two, and Three was indeed more durable than she had expected.

Alice Newcomb had been on friendly terms with Nan, after something of a rocky start six months before. Today she was friendly and professional, taking control of the meeting from the outset.

Alice began. "Nan and Josey, welcome. I believe you saw the press briefing yesterday on television?"

Nan replied, "Yes, I saw it on the evening news."

Josey said, "I was there in person, and I saw the replay later on."

Alice took charge again. "The newsies have now had an extra half-day to dig into their files to find out about cell phones and pacemakers. They probably found that what we said yesterday was right on the money, so they may ask one question about that and launch off into other directions. Maybe that crazy manhole fire. Maybe the telephone outage from yesterday. By the way, I see that the telephones and cell phones are all working again, so somebody must have fixed that problem.

"Is there any other topic that I don't know about?"

Josey answered before Nan could, impetuous youth that she was. "A couple members of the press attended the study report that the North High Future Nurses Club put on an hour ago in the training room. They might ask about that."

Alice looked puzzled for a few seconds, then asked Josey, "I know that we agreed the press could be there, and maybe I innocently thought that the high school students would be doing something inane. What were they studying?"

Josey answered, beating Nan to the punch again. "Contagion control and staph infections on one of the floors. They followed nurses and aides and orderlies around to see if they were following standard procedures. They found some small number of deviations, and they proposed a better way of doing things so the goof-rate would go down."

Alice thought about that for a moment, holding her pencil very firmly against her pad of yellow legal paper but not actually writing anything. "Did they keep records?"

Nan jumped in this time, even before Josey could answer. "They have made a videotape with no faces. They are holding the video-tape for review by you before it is shown to anybody, even their Future Nurses Club. They say they have no other records."

Alice looked up at Nan and said, "That sounds like it is under control for the moment. We have a better record with staph infec-tions than the average hospital, but we still have a few cases, that we know about, every year. Defensive statistical arguments never get us very far, because everybody knows somebody who got an infection in a hospital, and that anecdote carries more weight with them than a statistic.

"In any case, if the press already knows about this study, that's a genie that's already out of the bottle. We can't get the genie back in the bottle, so let's make friends with the genie.

"Nan, you haven't had any formal training or executive training in press conference handling. Just wait a second before answering any question so I can butt in if I need to. Otherwise, just give short, simple answers to every question. Smile, but be just a little distant so that you maintain your executive aura. You handled that talk show really well yesterday, so this should be just as easy."

With that, Alice stood and started to lead them to the executive conference room where the handful of reporters had gathered. Before Alice could get to the door, Nan said, "Alice, can you tell me what's going on with the bequest from Mr. Bill and the development fund that it was supposed to put money into?"

Hand on doorknob, Alice said rather formally to Nan, "Yes, we need to talk about it soon. Perhaps after this next meeting if your schedule permits."

Nan didn't like the sound of that, although the facts couldn't be any worse than what she was conjuring up in her own mind. That development fund had all seemed so simple when Mr. Bill's estate lawyer proposed that a fraction of the multimillion-dollar bequest be set aside to fund small development projects outside the hospi-tal's formal planning system that takes two years to get anything started, let alone anything done. It was left to Alice Newcomb and the estate lawyer to work out the final language, and Nan hadn't heard anything in more in six months.

No point in brooding about it, but if something sneaky were going on, better that Nan should find out while she *might* still be able to do something about it. The chacha cart project would be a fine first case to run through that small-projects development fund, getting it started while the Morgani kids were still around to work on it. A few thousand dollars ought to cover it. If she went to the formal planning system for that money, the hospital would spend more on shuffling paper than on the project. She could bury it in her own operating budget if necessary, but Nan thought this might just the right occasion to make an issue out of the development fund. Slush fund.

35

Nan's Press Conference

Nan smiled and nodded to Alice. Alice opened the door and led Nan and Josey to the conference room to meet the press. Josey went to the least conspicuous corner of the room. Nan went to the front.

A couple of the newsies had brought along doughnuts from the previous session. Crusher Morgenstern had taken a seat in the back.

The reporter closest to the front, Nelson from the *Morning News*, asked a series of quick questions "just for the record" to get Nan's name, title, years with the hospital, college degrees, and licenses. Then he asked the camera crew in the back of the room if they were ready and got a nod.

He began the interview by asking, "You saw our interview with Mr. Crawford yesterday?" Nan answered in the affirmative. "Does your version of events conform to what Crawford told us yesterday?" Nan again answered in the affirmative. "In that case, I don't have any particular questions on that topic. Does anybody else have a question on that?" Nelson turned to check with the rest of the newsies.

Crusher spoke up. "I figured out the timeline for your morning yesterday. You got off that television show and got to the hospital in record time. You were not able to issue orders to your staff from the car because the telephones weren't working at this end. Were you worried about your people running around without your supervision?"

Nan liked that question. "I never for a moment worried about my staff. We deal with situations every day that others would call emergencies. I was worried about the unknowns, but I was not worried about the nursing service."

Crusher followed up. "You got to the hospital in a hurry, and I guess you were not driving so you were not speeding. The car might have been but you were not. You changed clothes in your office at the hospital, and you jumped on this cell phone thing. Do you always keep a change of clothes in the office?"

"Yes, I often do. Yesterday, as it happens I did not have a change of clothes in the office but my assistant, Marcy Rosen, had gone to my house and gathered up something for me to wear."

Crusher continued. "That's better secretarial work than we see at newspapers these days." Everybody laughed.

Nelson butted in. "One thing I didn't understand about yesterday and the cell phones. You organized volunteers to spread the word to stop using cell phones, and in fact I talked to a couple of non-medical employees who were involved. Why didn't you just use the loudspeaker system? I have heard loudspeaker announcements many times when I have visited people in the hospital."

"We decided not to use the loudspeakers because people were already nervous about the cell phones not working, and we didn't want to add any stress to the situation. Josey Walberg, here, organized the volunteers to get the word out, and she did a magnificent job."

Josey beamed.

Nelson said, "Whom do you mean by 'we?'"

"Dr. Benedetta Parsons and I. Dr. Parsons is the cardiologist who was on duty yesterday when all this happened."

Nelson continued. "So you always check with somebody before you do anything?"

Nan saw a land mine in front of her, and she saw the wisdom in Alice's advice to wait a second before answering. "Yes, circumstances permitting. After putting out the word to attend to pacemaker users yesterday, I went to the cardiology unit and found Dr. Parsons on duty. We reviewed all actions taken to that point and decided what to do next."

Nelson asked, "So you consulted Dr. Parsons after the fact."

Nan waited a second and replied, "I instructed my nursing service to put all known pacemaker users on bed watch as a precaution, then I went immediately to the cardiology unit to consult with the cardiologist on duty. I stand by that."

"Okay. That sounds reasonable to me," Nelson said. "Can we talk about that manhole fire last Sunday night? Do you know what happened?"

Nan replied, "All I know is what I see on the news. We admitted two patients who were caught in that fire. One has since died, and that was reported in the newspapers. I don't have anything to say about the other patient, although you can check with Josey to see if the hospital or the family has issued any statement."

Crusher spoke up. "Can you answer some questions about this future nurses research project we just saw downstairs? To start with, how come you have high school students doing research projects?"

Nan replied, "We maintain contact with future nurses clubs in those high schools that have such a club. North High has one. We want to encourage young people to consider nursing as a career, because we are desperately short of nurses. Sometimes we have little projects that they can do for us here at the hospital. This particular project involved just two students, the Morgani twins. They were given physical exams before they came in just to make sure they weren't carriers of anything. Then our nurse managers worked with them to think up a project that was meaningful but did not actually involve patient contact. In this case, they followed nurses around to see if the nurses were conforming to established rules."

"Were your nurses upset about having these kids following them around, spying on them?"

"The kids were always in plain sight, so I don't call that spying. We commonly follow each other around as part of our quality assurance program. We were not looking for malicious acts; we were looking for inadvertent error. Those happen to the best of us. We were hoping to find some changes in rules or equipment or training that would reduce the incidence of these errors."

"So how many errors did they find?"

"Very few. Statistically insignificant. But every one is a concern, and we don't want any."

Crusher asked, "This kid study apart, what do you do with a nurse who breaks one of these rules, like maybe not washing hands between beds?"

Nan said, "We find that people make errors, inadvertent errors. The way we deal with them is to retrain the person. We don't yell at them, we don't write it up. We just send them back for retraining. For this particular thing, the retraining is a 15-minute video training tape. That just reminds the trainee of what they already know, but it makes it clear to each employee that we take these matters seriously and want people to follow the procedures, and for good reason."

Crusher followed up. "So while the careless nurse is off doing the retraining, the rest of the nurses have to do extra work to make up for that absence."

Nan replied, "I didn't say carelessness. Careless people don't last long here. I said inadvertent error. There's a difference. Yes, the retraining is a burden on the rest of the staff. We don't find any resentment about that. If somebody thinks of a better way, we'll be happy to learn from them."

Crusher asked, "Have you tried a headlock or a full nelson?" That got a laugh from the newsies. Nan let it go.

Nelson asked, "Let's talk about this staph infection stuff. We have heard about that over the years, and I guess we all know a little about it, and we know that people can die from infections they catch while they are in the hospital getting cured for something else. That other nurse said maybe a 100,000 deaths a year. Is that your number?"

Nan counted to one and said, "That might be a little high but it is not entirely wrong."

Nelson asked the obvious follow-up question, "How many of those died here in this hospital?"

Nan decided to duck that one. "I don't know. You might ask Mr. Crawford or Dr. Anderson, our chief medical officer. I will tell you that we have had instances of staph infection here. I think there are some state reports on that sort of thing that list all the hospitals and clinics. That might give you a better perspective."

Nelson tried one more along that line. "Do you presently have any cases in the hospital of staph infections?"

Nan decided to look pensive and gave it a try. "I am not at liberty to answer that question because it involves patient information."

Nelson put on his own pensive look, furrowing his brow and looking closely at Nan's face, trying to figure her out. After a moment he said, "Fair enough. Let's try this from another angle. Do staph infections happen solely as a result of a nurse carrying the germs from patient to patient?"

Nan figured that she must be holding her own so far, and she liked the way all this was going. She had figured Crusher Morgenstern to be on her side, at least so long as she treated him straightforwardly, but she had never set eyes on Nelson of the *Morning News* before. Since the other reporters were letting Nelson take the lead, Nan figured that he must be first in the pecking order of reporters. Pecking orders wouldn't mean much to Crusher, but they would probably mean a lot to the ordinary reporters. Nan then wondered why there was a camera crew here from a television station but none of the glamorous on-screen television reporters were here. She'd have to ask Josey how that worked. If some part of this wound up on television, Nan had visions of flying visits from Numbers One, Two, and Three to tell her not to go on the tube again until they had a chance to paint her orange and green. And do up her pedicure.

Nan tried a medium smile and said, "Human carriage is one path. Staph can also be carried around through the air handling system. So, our maintenance people have regular duct and vent cleaning programs and they have filters built into the pipes or whatever they're called. You can ask that department head for details. I recently heard that they are doing up some charts to explain their systems to civilians, but that's not really my scope, and I don't know any particulars."

Crusher Morgenstern decided it was his turn to ask a question. "Can you tell us something about those design rules the Morgani twins are telling us about. Sounded Japanese. And can you tell us if those are your rules or if that's something they found someplace else?"

Nan warmed her smile up two notches. "We practice poka-yoke here." Nan spelled it out for the print reporters. "This applies to the design of any task, manual, computer, or robotic. Three rules: Make it easier for the worker to do it right than to do it wrong, make it obvious to the worker if and when an error is made, and make it easy for the worker to correct an error. *poka-yoke* is Japanese for prevention of inadvertent error. You can see that these rules wouldn't help stop malicious acts, but we don't have those. We do have inadvertent errors, and we try to apply these little rules to prevent them. Since our tasks change pretty often, we have to keep reapplying these rules."

Crusher followed up. "Is that part of your Six Sigma Black Belt stuff?"

Nan: "Yes, it is." Nan decided that this would be the time to put on a slightly inscrutable face, and she did so.

Nelson was back. "Let's go back to that Mr. Bill business from six months ago. One part of the settlement of that deal was that his estate would put some money into a slush fund for you to run little development projects. I suppose you figure anything less than the Manhattan Project is a 'little development project' that you can run it off your own bat with this slush fund money. Tell us about that, please."

Nan waited two seconds, hoping to hear Alice's voice. No such luck. Nan replied, "The Mr. Bill estate executor did propose that a small development fund be set up. I have not heard that that has been finalized, and I guess you know that it can take years to settle a large estate. So far as I know, no actual cash money has been put into any fund yet. The hospital's legal counsel has been working with the estate lawyer to set up the rules and other things that lawyers do. You can ask her. I mean Alice Newcomb, our chief counsel."

Nelson continued. "So, like this Morgani twins project with their chacha cart—and I want to add that I like bright teenagers with a sense of humor a lot more than the mutts we see in the newspapers more days than not—if that took $500 to do, then the idea is that you would take $500 out of your slush fund and not spend six weeks shuffling paper with committees."

Nan had rather been hoping that "slush fund" would not be the permanent name for her development fund, but she now could see that that cause was hopeless. It was going to be "slush fund." "That's the idea," she said.

Crusher was back. "Do you do research projects with the university and with vendors and pill companies and who-all?"

Nan smiled and said, "Not in any serious way. This is not a research hospital like the ones you find at universities. We do a few small projects now and then. Sometimes we are involved in trying out a new medicine for particular populations under careful controls, but not often. We have an internal review board that passes on anything involving patients. Dr. Anderson runs that board. All hospitals have one."

Crusher said, "I want to follow up on the air duct thing. Who do I see about that?"

Nan let her gaze fall upon Alice Newcomb but did not say anything. After a moment, when it was clear to Alice that she was going to have to answer that one, Alice spoke up to say that she would go out and make a call to see if someone could meet with them on short notice. Alice left.

Josey stepped forward to say that while there was a break in the action, any still photographers who wanted to get any posed shots could get them now. For the others, an urn of fresh coffee was about to be brought in, along with more doughnuts.

Since the photographers had just shot posed shots of Nan in the training room, there wasn't much interest in more of those. The newsies milled around, talked to each other, and headed for the coffee trolley. Josey stayed with them, most apparently to snoop. That left Nan on her own at the front of the room. She didn't figure she could sneak out, so she stayed put.

Alice came back, strode to the front of the room to stand next to Nan's chair, and announced, "Our chief building engineer, Hank Powers, will be available in about five minutes. He will brief you on the HVAC system and take questions. He was about to give the same presentation to some of our other staff people, so the total audience is too large for this room. We will adjourn to the auditorium. You can have the front row of seats if you want. The auditorium has very good taping facilities, so you can do your own videotape or you can have a copy of ours. You can shoot from the auditorium floor, or you can shoot from the video booth. You decide, we will accommodate."

There were no dissents, so Alice led the group from the conference room to the auditorium. There was another delay of about

10 minutes while the video photographers decided where and how to set up their gear, but since yet another urn of coffee and even more doughnuts were supplied in the auditorium, the time went quickly.

Nan noticed that Rudy Rudolf and Susan Gunn were there. Susan was responsible for the buildings, among other things, and Nan guessed that Rudy was there to see how the "civilian-level" HVAC diagrams had come out. The last time Nan had seen him, he was about to expedite the completion of the engineering drawings.

Nan took a seat near the front and off to the side. Alice Newcomb was the last to take a seat, and she took one next to Nan. Nan tried to deduce some great meaning from that, but she could not.

36

The Building Engineer's Press Conference

Hank Powers took the lectern in the middle of the stage. He fiddled with light and microphone controls for a minute. Nan had known Hank since she had joined the hospital's nursing department, way back when. He struck Nan as the embodiment of the practical sort of hands-on, dirt under the fingernails mechanical guy. She supposed he had a college degree, but maybe not. He had steel-rim glasses with protectors on the sides, a steel-gray crew cut, and he actually had a pocket protector holding a half-dozen pencils, measuring rules, and other bric-a-brac. While he was not exactly wearing a maintenance-crew uniform, he managed to convey that look. Anyone would have picked him out of the crowd.

Hank began, "Folks, I don't get much chance to talk to the press, and if I say something the wrong way it's because I'm me and not because I am trying to smoke one past anybody. Mostly I talk to other building engineers, and if you don't follow my lingo, just put up a hand and I will try to say it over in English."

Hank pushed some buttons, the lights went down, and the large screen filled with an engineering drawing, probably of the hospital. It had a dark circle in the lower left quadrant.

"This here is an engineering drawing. You know it's authentic because of the coffee stain." Hank chuckled and waited for everybody else to chuckle, too. Some did. "We keep our drawings on a computer these days, and the computer makes them look like this. This drawing has a wealth of information on it, if you know what solid lines mean and what this kind of dotted line means and that kind of dotted line. We engineers are supposed to know that secret code.

"Now when it comes to the heating, ventilating and air-conditioning system, what we call the HVAC system, you have a three-dimensional set of conduits, you have fans and dampers and shutoffs and all the electrical power supplies and electrical controls and all the thermostats and all the filters and other stuff. We have hand-holes and man-ways and take-down panels and other details. Now this hospital has been built up over the decades by adding a wing here and tearing down a wing over there. Believe me, there was no air-conditioning when the old wings were built. So a lot of this HVAC is like Topsy, it just growed.

"We don't do anything by halves around here, so every time there was any construction, we had architects and engineers design everything and test everything. We use a lot of experts.

"Now if you look again at this drawing, and I tell you that it is a typical drawing and not at all the most complex one I could have pulled out of the drawer, if you look at this you might say to yourself you can't quite make out all that's going on in this drawing. You might ask if an expert drawing reader like I am supposed to be, if an expert ever makes a mistake reading a drawing.

"I'll be the first to tell you that yes, experts can make a mistake drawing the drawing in the first place and in reading the drawing later on. The standard way of dealing with that is to have lots of checkers. Look at this signature block down here in the right-hand corner. I count one, two, three . . . six . . . 10 signatures on this particular drawing. That means 10 competent people looked at this drawing and figured it was correct. Now maybe they weren't all checking every detail, but they were checking their own part. So that amounts to a lot of checking. So, you'd figure that there aren't too many goofs on this drawing.

"Of course, what we really care about is not the drawing, it's the system itself that runs through the building. But we cannot see all of that system at once, so we need some way of dealing with the information, and that's why we have drawings in the first place.

"Any questions so far?" Hank squinted out at the audience, not seeing them very well since the room lights had been turned down when he began to speak. In fact, Hank had turned them down himself.

No questions.

"Okay, well, several weeks ago, somebody told us about the NASA test for complex drawings and displays. NASA deals with stuff a lot more complicated than my HVAC business, and over the years they figured out something about complex drawings. What they figured out is that experts make mistakes reading complex charts and drawings and displays, not very often but sometimes. Human beings make mistakes, even experts. So far, no news there. But NASA did something pretty smart. They figured out that if the drawing is simpler, then the expert is less apt to make a mistake. That stands to reason, too, doesn't it?"

No argument from the floor.

"So when is the drawing simple enough that the expert is just not going to make a mistake? Remember I am talking about helping the expert here, not the man on the street. The expert.

"NASA figured out that the drawing is simple enough when the man on the street, or a *civilian*, as they say it, can understand the drawing. That's simple enough, don't bother to make it any simpler.

"So since we have a lot of engineering work going into the design of our new wing, it seemed like a good idea to put a little bit of the effort into redrawing the HVAC system into drawings a civilian could be expected to understand.

"So, here's one of them."

Hank pushed some buttons, and a new slide appeared. This one had no coffee stains, but more than that, it looked like a cartoon rendering of the air-flow system, in three dimensions. Some parts were in blue, some in a sandy shade of red. The outline edges of the conduits were in three distinct colors: green, yellow, and orange. There were some other lines that ran to what looked like control panels.

"Folks, this is just one wing of the building; in fact, it is this wing that we are in right now. What we are looking at is the summer configuration, with the air conditioning running, and we have the cold air supply in blue and the warmed air return in this color here. Somebody called it ochre, but you can't prove it by me. The edge colors show the three independent air-handling systems we have so that if one of them craps out the other two are still running.

"Now we got our engineering contractor to put a little torque on the computer so that it can generate these cartoons for different configurations of the dampers and vents and fans. Here's an example." The next slide showed the green-edged conduit as before, but the others had been reduced to a gray color. "This shows the Green System up and the Yellow and Orange Systems down. You get the idea."

"I want to call your attention to these thingamabobs here." Hank used a laser pointer to pick out an element that looked sort of like a screen door. "This is a filter. Filters are a big deal here, because we don't want germs flying around through our conduit. So one thing we look for as we go through all the combinations of settings, is whether all the air is getting run through one or more filters. Get the idea?"

Hank must have brought the room lights up a little, because as Nan looked around, she could see a lot of heads nodding in the affirmative.

"So just this morning, I was getting familiar with this, and I tried some different combinations of fans and dampers and what not. Guess what I found? I found a way to push control buttons—now I am talking about pushing them on this drawing computer but the same buttons exist on real control panels in the hospital that control real fans and dampers—I found a way just by fooling with this to bypass a filter. Here, I'll show you."

Hank advanced to the next slide, which had blue conduit with an orange edge, connected in such a way that a filter was clearly bypassed.

"I am not saying that anybody ever actually pushed this combination of buttons in real life, what I am saying is that it might have happened yesterday, and it might happen tomorrow if we don't check this out.

"You see, this is a design error. When the design engineers designed this part of the plant, they were told to make sure that no conduit configuration can ever be punched up that would have no filters in the line. I don't think anybody set out to make this error on purpose, but it happened anyway, and 10 or 12 signatures on the drawing didn't make it right.

"So, folks, you are looking at a new believer in the NASA rule. Everything we engineer around here from now on is going to pass the NASA test. We'll probably still do the traditional drawings, too, since the same computer can generate both kinds, and we will still need someplace to put our coffee mugs. But we are going to have a whole lot of these NASA drawings around here, too."

Hank brought the room lights up some more. Nan found that she could scrunch down in her seat and get a good look at the press row and at Hank Powers at the same time.

"Mr. Powers, I am Nelson of the *Morning News*. Are you telling me that you could have had the HVAC system set up wrong, bypassing a filter, for years and you didn't know it?"

"I don't think I said that. What I will tell you is that I have three maintenance people walking this conduit right now, right this minute, to find out. We also have one of my building engineers on the phone with the architect-engineer who did the design to crank them up and, shall we say, get their fervid attention to this matter."

Nelson followed up. "Let's suppose this is found to be the case. Is the architect liable or is the hospital liable or what?"

Hank replied, "I wouldn't dare answer a lawyer question like that one."

Crusher Morgenstern spoke up, in a way that everybody in the room could hear him. "If these filters are bypassed, does that mean germs could be flying around the hospital and maybe making people sick?"

Hank replied, "You're Crusher Morgenstern, aren't you? I remember seeing you wrestle in high school and again in college."

Crusher, not having gotten anything approaching an answer, tried again, "Thanks. Now what about germs and filters?"

Hank waited a few seconds to see if any of the executives wanted to answer that one for him, and hearing none, he said, "I guess the filters were put in with that in mind. Bypassing the filters can't be very good medicine. Whether it actually puts anybody at risk, I can't say."

Nelson asked, "What else besides filter bypass are you looking for, now that you have these NASA cartoons?"

Hank furrowed his brow and said, "Well, maybe I shouldn't have called them cartoons. They are a little more graphical than the line drawings we started with here, but they are real drawings with engineering information on them. They aren't cartoons like the funny papers.

"I didn't expect to find any filter bypass. What I was looking for, and what my technical guys are looking for right now and will be until they get through every combination, they will be looking to see if there are any cross connects between, say, the green ductwork and the orange ductwork. There aren't supposed to be any. Then they will be looking at the isolation dampers to make sure when we think we are isolating Unit A, we are really isolating Unit A. There are a lot of combinations, so this is going to take a few days."

Crusher asked, "So where did you get this NASA idea?"

"I heard it from somebody in the information technology department, and he heard it from Nan Mills, the head nurse. She is one of those Six Sigma Black Belts, and they know about stuff like this. So I went over to see Nan Mills, and she told me all about it, and it made sense to me, so we gave it a shot. Nan Mills' husband is that Jack Mills you hear about in the paper once in a while, so she knows how to talk to engineers like me."

Crusher turned to the attorney. "Ms. Newcomb, I think you'd better get Crawford down here. This NASA filter story is going to be on the front page of the next edition and on the tube this evening, too, if my hunch is worth anything. If you need a few minutes to consult, I'll wait, and my guess is the rest of the press corps will wait, too, if you don't stall too long. Considering what we already have in the can, I don't think you want us to run just with what we've got now."

Alice had her head down, pencil pressed against her yellow pad. "Yes, I will go to Mr. Crawford's office now and check his availability.

If I am not back in five minutes, just figure that the world is short one lawyer."

Alice left at a good pace. Nan stood, because everybody else was standing. Nelson and Crusher were up close to the lectern talking with Hank. Nan guessed that the reporters wanted to talk about piping goofs and Hank wanted to talk sports.

For the first time, Nan noticed that the Morgani twins and their faculty adviser from the high school, Gale Hansen, were there. They were talking animatedly among themselves. Thinking up a new role for their chacha cart?

Josey was talking to the camera crew. The other reporters were, believe it or not, helping themselves to another round of doughnuts and black coffee.

Alice and Crawford came in. Hank Powers made room for them and took a seat off to the side, in the front row. The newsies returned to their places, the cameras came live, and things were about to resume.

At that moment, Rudy Rudolf stood up and went to the lectern, gently but nonetheless effectively nudging Crawford to the side.

Rudy spoke. "I am Rudy Rudolf, chief information officer for the hospital. I am going to say a few words before Mr. Crawford does, because I have been involved in this, and I want to give you the proper perspective.

"You reporters know about bureaucracies. A lot of what you do is poke around and find stupid things that bureaucracies do in government agencies, in big businesses, and even in hospitals. You may be about ready to jump on Mr. Crawford because something stupid may, or may not, have been going on with that air filter Hank Powers told you about.

"Things can go wrong in any operation as complex as a hospital. You can't figure that that's news. What is news, and that's why I want to tell you about it, is that under Mr. Crawford's leadership, our bureaucracy seeks out and corrects things that are wrong. We try really, really hard to find them before any harm is done. Pretty often, we succeed. Sometimes we don't. But it's not for want of trying. It's not for want of getting the right energetic people into the management slots. It's not for want of encouraging all the people to learn how to find error and prevent future inadvertent error. So, when you talk to Mr. Crawford, see if you can let this little bit of news color your thinking.

"Now, before Mr. Crawford speaks, I would like Ms. Susan Gunn, who is vice president over various departments including the works engineering department, and Mrs. Nan Mills, head nurse, to join me. I know you know Mrs. Mills from earlier this morning and from previous events."

Rudy beckoned to Susan and then to Nan. Both stood and walked to the lectern, winding up on both sides of Rudy Rudolf.

Rudy acted as interlocutor. "Susan, did you understand Mr. Crawford to be encouraging you to use new technology to find out anything that might be suspect in our plant engineering?"

Susan took that soft pitch and gave it a good ride. "Mr. Crawford has been a champion of technology in all aspects of hospital operations."

Rudy nodded. He turned to Nan. "Mrs. Mills, has Mr. Crawford given you to understand that technology is to be applied throughout patient care to reduce error and to improve operations?"

"Yes. Yes, I do. Mr. Crawford has encouraged that at every turn. Mr. Crawford and the board paid for my specialized training in Six Sigma and gave me release time to attend the courses. Yes, Mr. Crawford has been stellar in that regard."

Rudy nodded and addressed the newsies. "That's my experience, too. This NASA complexity business that Hank Powers was talking about is an element of Six Sigma. Mrs. Mills is a trained Six Sigma Black Belt, because of Mr. Crawford's initiative. Now nobody expects a chief operations officer like Mr. Crawford to be doing everything with his own hands, but the public should expect that the COO of an important hospital have the judgment to get people into responsible positions who can take the lead on improving operations. There is no question here but what Mr. Crawford has done his job, and very well, too. In Six Sigma, our senior executive is Mrs. Mills. In other matters, it's somebody else. But there is only one man in charge, and that's Mr. Philip L. Crawford, whom I now present to you."

Rudy stepped back and to the side, and reached out to invite Crawford to come to the lectern.

Philip L. Crawford was well accustomed to public speaking. He was well accustomed to flowery statements being made in favor of the next speaker. He was much less well accustomed to hearing flowery statements about himself from his staff of vice presidents. Just the slightest taint of embarrassment toned his visage as he nodded to Rudy and stepped forward.

He began, "Ladies and gentlemen of the press, I am at your service." There were in fact no ladies of the press present, so this looked to be a cautious beginning. Crawford waited for the first question, profiting from the momentary break to get his face into its standard public look.

"Mr. Crawford, I am Nelson from the *Morning News*. Is this the first you have heard about this filter problem in the air handling system? Are you worried about foul-ups like that? Can this kind of a filter foul-up cause staph infections?"

Crawford smiled intently at Nelson. "Well, my goodness, Mr. Nelson, you pack a lot of punch into one question. Or maybe that was six questions. I'll try to answer them all for you.

"Worrying is normal in my line of work. I am more worried about unknown problems than I am about known ones. This filter thing, if upon further study it is indeed a 'thing,' is no longer an unknown thing. Now that we know about it, we can fix it. Seeking out things like this is something we are pretty good at, and I think we are getting better at it. Mrs. Mills has brought a good deal of benefit to the hospital with her Six Sigma technology. More of our staff are learning from her and in training classes the hospital board sees fit to pay for. I think it's money well spent, and I'll bet you do, too.

"As for one filter causing staph infections, that sounds pretty far-fetched to me. Fixing the error, if indeed there is an error, makes it even less likely, and that's fine with me."

Crusher posed a question. He felt no need to give his name. "Mr. Crawford, how come you invited the press to see two presentations this morning, one by Mr. Powers and earlier one by the Morgani twins, both of which point out errors being made by your people? I'd expect you'd do that kind of thing in private and try to keep it buttoned up. Did you stage these presentations today?"

Mr. Crawford managed to look just a little wounded by that question. "Mr. Morgenstern, I did not stage anything today. I did not even know myself that these sessions were going on. I am happy they are, I am happy we are learning things here and there about our operations that will allow us to do better from this day forward. But nothing here has been staged by the management. As for how much stagecraft went into the individual presentations, I didn't see them, and I can't say.

"I will say that I have known Mr. Powers for a good long while, and stagecraft doesn't come to mind when I visualize Hank." Crawford gave a sort of knowing grin in the general direction of Hank Powers, who seemed to be taking the ribbing in good part.

"I understand the little presentation by the Morgani twins was taped, and I look forward to watching it shortly. I heard the word *chacha* but I don't know the rest of the story. Yet." Crawford beamed in the direction of the Morgani twins.

"Let me be very serious for just a moment." Crawford put on his sternest face. "We serve the community here. We deal with you and your loved ones at the most vulnerable moments of your lives. We try hard to do our job as well as it can be done, and we strive even harder to get better at our job every day. Sometimes that means discovering things we could have been doing better. I don't hide that for a minute. I am as proud as I can be of our staff.

"And I'll tell you something else. We don't have a big R&D budget, so we can't invent our own solutions to every problem that crops up. We try really, really hard to find somebody else who has already solved our problem or one like it, and we steal that solution and make it ours. So we are frugal as we go about our improvement process, and you spend a lot of ink writing about hospital costs, so I want you to know that we are doing what we can to keep costs down, every chance we get.

"Doing everything without error is one way of keeping costs down. If somebody gets a staph infection here, that's discomfort for that person and it's more cost for us, because we have to treat the infection. So, everybody wins when we smoke out a source of error. That's just good management as well as good healthcare."

Nelson spoke up. "Mr. Crawford, I'd expect Six Sigma, from what I know about it, to be something your engineering people would be leading, or maybe Mr. Rudolf, since he has all the computers. How come your head nurse is the leader?"

Crawford nodded to acknowledge the question and said, "Rudy leads on some topics. Hank on others. Nan on some. Susan on others. We have plenty of room for leaders on many topics here. I am happy with Nan Mills and her work here. You know that she finds herself involved in the matters that get in the newspapers, even on the sports page these days, so you'll be getting to know her better. I think you will be as impressed by her as I am, as the Board is, and as the rest of our senior management is. Nan Mills is a really fine person.

"And that's not to slight the rest of our fine staff. Good people doing good jobs, that's what we have for you in our hospital. If you ever happen to get sick, keep that in mind."

Crawford looked around the room, ignored hands being waved by other reporters, and said in conclusion, "Why don't we break up now so the Morgani twins can get back to school and our management can go do their managing. I'll stay around for a few minutes if you want to ask follow-up questions. I'll meet you by the doughnut tray and coffee urn." As good as his word, Crawford headed for trolley.

The audience broke up, some heading for the doors, some heading for more coffee. The junior newsies took the opportunity to ask their own questions to Crawford. The camera crews struck their setups and headed for the coffee urn.

Nan thought to herself that this news conference stuff was all the more mysterious, the closer she got to it. And Rudy Rudolf, he'd become a whole new creature. What had become of the amiable bumbler?

Nan scanned the room to find Rudy Rudolf. She found him staring, in fact, in her direction, with a slight smile that hid more than it revealed. Catching her gaze, Rudy gave Nan a slow wink. His eyes twinkled.

Well, Nan thought, smiling slightly and nodding but not winking because her face could be seen by the entire throng, Rudy learned the Japanese lesson about making the boss look smart, and he learned it quickly. Crawford had probably been in for hammer and tongs before Rudy jumped in to set the tone. Masterful. That's something, Nan thought, that I could never have done. I could throw myself on a hand grenade, maybe, but I could never, ever seize control of a press conference.

37

Josey's Policy Draft

As Nan got back to her office, she found Stan Laurel chatting with Marcy and nibbling on a chocolate chip cookie. Nan smiled and said to Stan, "Stan, we don't see you around anymore, since you were made chief of detectives. We see your replacement once in a while, but I don't know that you have been by to see us in months. It's good to see you."

"Thank you, Mrs. Mills. No, I don't get by here much any more since I have a new assignment. Thanks to you, of course."

"No, Stan, not thanks to me. You earned it, and we are all happy to see that the city administration appreciates you the way we do."

"Yes, well, I had a craving for chocolate chip cookies, so I took a chance that Marcy might let me have one." He took a sizable bite out of his cookie and smiled in Marcy's direction. Marcy beamed appropriately.

"Are you here on business, Stan?"

"We never sleep."

Nan didn't think that sounded like an answer, so she took it to mean that he was indeed here on business and that he wasn't in a position to talk about it.

"If you need anything, just tell me, or tell Marcy. I mean anything other than cookies." Nan smiled and proceeded into her office.

A moment or two later, Marcy came into Nan's office with her steno pad, a pencil, and a pot of tea. She said to Nan, "Are there any action items from your press briefing or your other meetings?"

Nan replied, "The Morgani twins are going to need a little money to build a chacha cart, so please tell Carl Burke to find them some money from my budget someplace. I think it will be less than $5000, but it might go a little higher. I don't mean to give the kids a blank check, but just to identify a source of the money now so they can spend it when they come up with a plan. We'll also need to provide some technical support for them, I think. Tell Annie Rostow that she has the ball there and can call on anybody she wants to help her out.

"I invited the Morgani twins to observe things in a real operating room. I think Annie is handling that, but you could double check.

"Then, the twins also gave me two really good ideas. One is to have the IV pole beep at the unit desk instead of in the patient's ear when a pouch runs dry or the line gets fouled. The other is that we should establish a service level for responding to call light calls from patients, setting a standard of performance for ourselves. I really like that idea, and I should have thought of it myself. If we carry that through, it even gives us an additional basis for justifying the staff level on the floors, something quantitative that we can report on every day and week. That's an important thing, substituting meas-urable performance objectives for mushy good intentions. That is Six Sigma duck soup. That's why I should have thought of it myself.

"Why don't you make a short note on this and feed it to Sanjar. He may have ready answers, or he may be able to write out a short specification for what we would need to create a pilot program for both of those. Don't tell him to run off and build everything in his basement, I just want to get some documentation in place so that interested parties can discuss the matter in an informed way.

"First of all, Marcy, do you understand what I have been saying? I want to do a communications check with you."

"Yes, ma'am. I know about call lights and IV beepers. I don't know what a chacha cart is, but I'll ask Annie Rostow to go through it with me."

Nan nodded and said, "Okay. That takes care of our action items, I think. Rudy Rudolf took charge of the press meeting and turned around what could have been a hostile situation. Your cousin or whatever he is, Crusher Morgenstern, certainly has a presence, and the Morgani twins were delightful. I think all those sessions were taped, so see if you can get copies for us to look at. The camera may have had a different recollection."

"Yes, ma'am," Marcy said. "The next thing here, after you freshen up, is that Josey has a draft policy statement for you to look at. If you want to just read it and mark it up on your word processor, that's fine. If you want Josey here so you can talk about it, I'll get her. She's on call. In fact, she's waiting just around the corner down the hall."

"Okay, give me two minutes and then send her in. Do I have her draft here someplace on the computer?"

"Yes, you do. You also have a hard copy with double spacing and large type and a big blue pencil if you want to do it the old-fashioned way." Marcy put oversized sheets of paper and an oversized blue pencil on the table, glanced at Nan to see if there were any other action items, and seeing none, smiled politely and left.

Josey came in, smiled nervously, put her hand on a chair back and waited a second to see if Nan would tell her to sit down or stand up or leave, and then she sat down. Josey had her own oversized print of the draft.

Nan smiled at Josey, waited for her to sit, and then took up the papers and the blue pencil.

The top half of the first page was the usual boilerplate, policy number, issued by, applies to, updated on, blah, blah, blah. Nan scanned ahead to find the meat.

> *Purpose: To prepare the professional staff for positions of increasing responsibility.*

Well, Nan thought, that must be right. Nothing to argue with there.

> *Policy: It is the policy of the patient care department that qualified personnel should prepare themselves for roles of increasing responsibility at the professional, supervisory, and management levels. A breadth of experience is part of that preparation. The department will therefore facilitate rotational assignments at all levels.*
>
> *It is, furthermore, the policy of the department to give weight to candidates for promotion who have attained a breadth of professional and managerial experience.*
>
> *(end)*

Nan read it through, twice. "Josey, this seems to hit the nail on the head, and you have avoided the noxious way we usually write these things. That's good. In fact, it's remarkable. But you didn't say anything about career counseling, and I think that needs to be mentioned."

"Mrs. Mills, I looked at several other policy statements on various topics, and then I cross-checked the training material on the hospital's internal website, and I came to the conclusion that the way to handle that is a separate mailer later on pointing out all the good things, including career counseling, that are available. That way, if the HR department changes course numbers or something, you don't have to re-issue your policy."

Nan reflected on that for a moment, and decided Josey's way was sound. "Okay, I'll take your advice on the matter.

"Now, let's look at the Six Sigma policy."

Same sort of boilerplate at the top.

> *Purpose: To promote the reduction of inadvertent error in patient services.*

Well, that seems to be on point, Nan thought.

> *Policy: It is the policy of this department that all personnel strive to eliminate inadvertent error. Six Sigma is a management method for eliminating inadvertent error. It is therefore our policy that Six Sigma be understood by all personnel and applied suitably in patient services.*
>
> *Weight will be given in personnel evaluations and in consideration for promotion to those who have completed Six Sigma tasks.*
>
> *(end)*

Nan looked up at Josey and said, "You get right to the point. These are the shortest policy statements I have ever seen. They usually run to six pages and have the most complicated syntax this side of Congress. Tell me what you want to do to make people aware of Six Sigma training courses."

"I think the same as above. We, or better yet the HR department, wait a week and send out a brochure on all the Six Sigma courses that they are going to make available now that there is a ready market. The HR department can send those same brochures to other departments, too, and I think they are going to find some takers in the engineering department and IT department. Maybe even the accounting department and their own HR department.

"I already signed up for a beginners' course on the Internet. I have no background in anything other than journalism, so I am the perfect beginner. No bad habits to erase, no false theories to overcome. Tabula rasa, that's me. "

Nan leaned back a little in her chair, still holding the papers in one hand on the table. Nan looked at her young friend and saw eagerness and twinkling eyes. "Okay, I'll take them both, as is. You'll square them away with Susan Gunn, right?"

"Right. I have a meeting booked with her in 20 minutes. She'll probably have a couple of her staffers in the meeting, so I left extra copies with Ms. Gunn's secretary. Then, come to find out, policy statements are subject to review by the legal department, so I left a copy with Alice Newcomb's secretary, marked DRAFT, just so they can't complain later that nobody ever tells them anything. I don't really expect anybody in the legal department to look at it."

"All right, Josey. Work with Marcy to figure out how to get this out to my managers so they can chew on it before our next staff meeting, and do something so they will know about training brochures, the way you explained it to me.

"Anything else?"

"No, ma'am. I will take care of it. Details 'R' Us. Legwork, too." Josey smiled, gathered up her papers, and left the office at a trot.

What a delightful young woman, Nan thought. A blessing on the hospital and on this department in particular.

38

The Cops!

Nan was occupied with gathering the latest operating statistics for her department to put on her tracking charts, which Marcy would post out in the hallway when Nan had finished with them. It didn't really take much work, and Marcy would have been happy to do it for her, but Nan wanted the word to get around on the grapevine that she paid so much attention to these tracking charts that she updated them herself every week. One way to get everybody else to pay attention to her charts and their own, a better way than hortatory memos.

Marcy came in, abruptly.

"Mrs. Mills. Turn your computer browser to the local TV news channel. Something has happened. The phones are ringing off the hook."

Surprised by Marcy's tone—Marcy, who was always in control—Nan pointed the browser at the local news channel. Marcy came forward to look over her shoulder.

The website was feeding live video, which showed up in a rectangle the size of a bubble-gum card. The voice was garbled, but the image was plain to see. The camera was looking at the front of the hospital. Cops were there in great number. Stan Laurel was there.

Sanjar was there!

Two cops were walking Sanjar to a police car. Sanjar's hands were bound or cuffed, Nan couldn't tell which. Sanjar was not wearing a jacket, which struck Nan as odd for an outdoor shot. Sanjar was going quietly.

Nan then found running text, like a ticker tape, telling the story over and over. "Man arrested in connection with the recent fires. Name withheld temporarily. No official statement from the district attorney yet but one expected in the near future. Rumor of fingerprints having been found."

The video feed showed the police car door closing behind Sanjar and the car moving slowly away from the curb. They must have every television camera in town out on our hospital lawn, Nan thought.

Nan picked up the telephone. She composed the number for Alice Newcomb, the chief counsel. It rang busy. She called Rudy Rudolf. It rang busy.

Well, so much for consulting others, Nan thought. She depressed the plunger to get a new dial tone and called home. Jack answered on the second ring.

"Jack, I don't know what's going on, but the police have just hauled Sanjar off in a police car in handcuffs. What are we going to do?"

"I'm on it. Did you get this on the radio or what?"

"I'm watching it on the TV news website. I'll bet it's on every channel."

"Okay, Nan. I'll take care of things and let you know."

Jack broke the connection. Nan tried Alice and Rudy, but their phones were still busy. She thought about walking to their offices, but she was tantalized by the video images.

A talking head was now in front of the camera. Nan fiddled around with the settings and got a decent voice quality to go with the miniature video picture. ". . . said Chief of Detectives Stan Laurel of the metropolitan police force, who was here on the scene. Now we are going to jump to our reporter at city hall, where the district attorney is coming up to the microphones right now."

The video feed changed to a standard sort of pulpit with a dozen microphones on it and a big city flag hanging behind it. A young woman stepped to the microphone. She didn't look like the district attorney, whose face was known to all who read the newspapers.

"I am the media communications associate for the district attorney," she said. "I am authorized to tell you that the district attorney will have no statement on the arson investigation until after the arraignment of the person arrested this afternoon at General Hospital. We are not releasing the name of that person yet, although we expect to do so shortly after going through some formalities. We are following our standard practices, and those of you who follow police matters will recognize that we are doing so. Those of you who do not follow police procedure closely, I'll just tell you that we are doing things the way we always do them because our standard way conforms to all statutes and regulations.

"Any questions?"

"Yes, I'm Nelson from the *Morning News*. Tell us please when the arraignment will be of this unnamed person whose face has just been on all the television channels."

"That is never certain at this stage, but if the usual schedule works out, arraignment will be at night court this evening. It takes us about that long to get the paperwork ready. It might take until tomorrow morning, but my guess is that it will be this evening. I'll have a handout for you to give you the time once I hear it."

A voice that sounded a lot like Crusher Morgenstern's asked, "What's the story on the fingerprints found at the scene?"

"We never talk about evidence at this stage. So, no comment."

Crusher asked again, "Does no comment mean no fingerprints or does no comment mean yes fingerprints?"

"No comment means no comment."

Nelson asked, "Have you picked up anybody else, or was this a solo crime?"

"This is the only arrest that I am presently aware of. If there are others, I don't know about them. That doesn't mean there are or there aren't, only what I said."

Crusher asked, "You sure know a lot of ways to say 'no comment.' "

That got a laugh, even from the press flack at the microphones.

There were a couple of other questions that seemed to be about other cases or other topics, because Nan couldn't figure out any connection to the fires or to Sanjar.

Nan used the intercom to ask Marcy if she could find a home telephone number for Sanjar. Marcy read it out to Nan. Then Marcy said, "I've been ringing it, but it rings busy."

Nan tried Alice, Rudy, and Susan Gunn. All rang busy.

Nan thought about using e-mail, but she didn't know what to type. She didn't know what she would say to any of her fellow vice presidents if she got through to them by telephone either, but she could wing that. She didn't want to wing the e-mail, because that lived forever.

Nan was transfixed by the video feed. The video was now looping back over the arrest, and Nan watched her protégé being led off in irons once again.

This can't be happening, thought Nan. Of course I don't believe that Sanjar set any fires, but I can't believe that Stan Laurel thinks he did, either. Stan knows Sanjar, I know that for a fact. This is all crazy.

Nan's phone rang. Nan grabbed it before Marcy could. It was Jack.

"Nan, I got through to our lawyer, Ned Williams. Ned will go immediately to the jailhouse and present himself to Sanjar and offer to represent him for free. I mean, free to Sanjar. He'll bill us. Ned will call back once he has talked to Sanjar or when he has anything else to report. Of course, he can't tell us anything that has to do with the case, since that'll all be privileged communications between Sanjar and Ned, even if we're paying the bill. That's the way it should be, and I'd be concerned if he had told me he would call me back and blab the whole thing."

"Jack, I can't believe this is happening. Sanjar!"

"I don't believe Sanjar did anything criminal in a million years. There's something goofy going on here. It'll probably clear itself up in a day or so. They haven't even said what they are charging him with. Maybe it has nothing to do with the fires."

"It must have *something* to do with the fires, from what the television said. Oh, Jack. I'm really worried about this, about Sanjar."

"Okay, I'll call your cell phone if Ned calls me or if I find out anything else. You do the same, will you?"

"Yes, Jack. I'll call you the moment I hear anything."

Nan broke the connection and tried dialing the vice presidents again. Still ringing busy. This must have lit up all the phones in the hospital, thought Nan. Everybody knows Sanjar, and everybody knows about the fires.

Nan sat at her desk, hypnotized by the video feed.

39

Night Court

Nan and Jack found the benches pretty well filled in the public section of the night court room. Nan saw Alice Newcomb sitting next to a man in a thousand-dollar suit, so she nudged Jack into that pew. Nan followed him, nodding with a smile to Alice and introducing Jack. Alice introduced the man next to her as Randall Pinkston, the hospital's new chief outside counsel, whom both Jack and Nan had met six months earlier in the Mr. Bill affair.

No sooner had they shaken hands than Rudy Rudolf arrived and pushed in beside them. Susan Gunn came in a moment later, so they had a full bench of keenly interested observers from the hospital family.

Nan recognized Sarita Subramaniam, sitting in the front with two boys. Sarita was wearing a standard-issue American dress, and the boys looked like all American boys that age.

There were TV cameras set up along the side walls, taking up most of the aisle space. Nan saw Nelson of the *Morning News* and Crusher Morgenstern sitting near the TV equipment. Nan guessed that more newsies were here, too, somewhere in the throng.

A deputy brought Sanjar in by a side door and led him to a table on the left side where four people, who looked like they might be lawyers, stood and took turns shaking his hand. There were more lawyerly-looking people at a separate table to the right, whom Nan took to be the prosecution.

For a few moments, nothing happened. There was a general murmur in the audience, but nothing specific was going on.

Then a crier stood and looked out at the audience. This was an elderly man, showing a scrubbed look that extended to the neatness of his rather ordinary suit and his spit-shined shoes. A man who took pride in himself and his work, Nan guessed. The crier cried out in a very strong voice, "Oyez, oyez, oyez. Municipal Court Section Four is now is session, the Honorable Jonathan Higgins presiding. All ye who have business before this honorable court come forward and ye shall be heard. God save this honorable court, and God save the United States of America."

The crier looked for an extra moment out over the audience and then turned to watch the judge come in from a side door, climb the two steps to the platform, and sit in the large chair behind the beautifully carved desk.

The judge looked out at the audience and TV crews; he looked to be as interested in the goings-on as everybody else.

The judge nodded to the audience and said, "Good evening, ladies and gentlemen." Then he nodded to the clerk and said, "The clerk will call the first case."

Before the clerk could say a word, one of the defense lawyers jumped up to say, "May it please the court, may I approach the bench?"

The judge replied, "We haven't started yet. You're out of order. Please wait until the clerk calls your case, and then I will hear your request."

The defense lawyer stood his ground. "Your Excellency, I make bold to ask you for your grace in this matter because the regular order will serve justice but it will not serve another important principle, and that is fair play."

The judge counted the cameras and decided that the better part of valor would be to show himself to be in favor of fair play, however that might fit into the evening's proceedings.

"Very well, I am in favor of both justice and fair play. If the People do not object to proceeding in this order, you may approach."

The prosecutor did not seem to object. The defense lawyer took one step forward but did not go any closer to the bench. The prosecutor, who had started to walk up to the bench, was caught flatfooted by this, so he took a matching position, closer to his table than to the bench.

"My name, sir, is Rajiv Pankar, I am a licensed attorney, and I have given my card to your worthy clerk. I am appearing before you as lead counsel for the defendant in the first case to be called this evening, Mr. Sanjar Subramaniam. I am joined by co-counsel, as you see. Some of these may be known to you. I will ask them to give their names for the record." Rajiv Pankar nodded to his three co-counselors. They were all on their feet, having risen when Rajiv Pankar arose.

The first said, "William Eastman of Cody-Cromwell, co-counsel." He was a well-turned-out man of about 30, wearing a blue suit that Nan thought looked expensive. He appeared to be quite at home in the courtroom.

The second said, "Xaveria Solana Naredo of Pinkston-Graves, co-counsel." She was clearly the best-dressed person in the courtroom, about the same age as the first co-counsel and just as much a presence in the room as anyone could be. Nan took note.

The third turned out to be the lawyer Nan and Jack used themselves for family business matters, "Ned Williams of Turner-Black, co-counsel." Nan had expected to see him there. He was a few years older than the first two and looked sort of ordinary, dressed in an off-the-rack business suit, neat but not elegant.

The judge nodded politely to each, and when the introductions were finished, he looked, with a clear display of curiosity, to lead counsel Rajiv Pankar to tell him what was going on.

Rajiv Pankar took that to be sufficient permission to proceed, "May it please the Court, the matter of fair play is quite simply stated. The prosecution has placed our client under arrest, which it has the legal power to do. The prosecution has used the Fourth Estate to distribute a story to the public saying that they have fingerprints found at the scene of the telephone company fire, and that those fingerprints are those of Mr. Subramaniam. The prosecution did not see fit to make their statement first in this courtroom, nor did they see fit to stand up and say it outright to the press. Rather, they leaked the story anonymously. That is not fair play."

The judge asked, "Well, we can't very well turn back the hands on the clock. What do you want, specifically?"

Rajiv Pankar bowed to the judge and said, "Excellency, I wish to present a small demonstration that will make clear the value of the prosecution's evidence."

The judge raised his gavel and brought it down sharply on its wooden strike plate, making a sound that reverberated through the courtroom. "Five-minute recess. Counsel will meet with me in my chambers."

"All rise," cried the crier. The TV cameras turned to focus on the faces of their "talent" for the evening, the shining and well-powdered faces familiar to all watchers of the local news. The talent commenced to explain everything to the television audience, filling in gaps with their imaginings.

Nan bent a little so that she could see, and be seen by, Randall Pinkston, the hospital's outside counsel. "Is that young woman a lawyer in your firm?"

"Yes, Xaveria Solana is one of our bright young people who do a lot of courtroom work. Most of the rest of us just fumble around with contracts and tax claims. She is very good on her feet, as I think you'll see if it gets that far."

Rudy Rudolf interjected, "Bill Eastman is my lawyer. I take it that the other guy is yours, Nan."

"Yes, Rudy, Ned Williams is our family lawyer. I don't know how much criminal law he does. He hasn't done any for us, I am happy to say. I thought he might send somebody else from his firm rather than doing this himself, but I see he sent himself."

Jack contributed, "Ned is with a small firm. I think they all do whatever comes in the door."

Nan looked at both Alice Newcomb and Randall Pinkston and asked, "Do either of you know the lead defense lawyer, Rajiv Pankar, I think he said?"

Alice shook her head in the negative. Randall Pinkston said, "I am aware of him, although I have not had any dealings with him directly. Good reputation from what I know."

Nan asked another question. "Is there going to be any problem with our team having so many lawyers at the defense table?"

Randall Pinkston found an opportunity to strut his stuff by saying, "If this gets to trial, the judge will probably put a limit of maybe two at the defense table. At this stage, things are less formal. In any case, the defendant can have as many lawyers as he wants, with the excess being relegated to sitting in the audience."

"Alice," Nan asked, "did you organize all this?"

Alice replied with a smile verging on a grin, "I found out about it after the four of them met this afternoon. By the time your lawyer, Rudy's lawyer, and my lawyer, by whom I mean Randall's lawyer on behalf of the hospital board, discovered each other at the jail, Sarita had already gotten Rajiv Pankar into action. So the three we sent offered to serve as co-counsel under Rajiv Pankar. Rajiv just took charge, told them they were welcome, and that they would sort out who would do what later on. Then the four of them met with Rudy, and I don't know what happened with that."

"Are you going to tell us, Rudy?"

Rudy gave them all a very wide grin and said, "I had some help, that you'll hear about soon enough. And no, I am not going to tell you what's coming next."

Susan Gunn gave Rudy an elbow in the ribs for holding out on them, and the whole bunch of them shared Rudy's infectious smile. Even Alice and Randall caught a bit of a smile. Nan wondered where Rudy had gotten his "help," and she saw that Jack's smile seemed to be holding back a secret or two. Rudy and Jack? Without her knowing?

The recess took longer than five minutes, but not so many as 10. The crier cried, the crowd stood to show respect, and the judge mounted the bench. The lawyers returned to their tables.

The judge rapped his gavel lightly and said, "This court is back in session. Mr. Pankar will continue."

Before Rajiv Pankar could say a word, the prosecutor stood to say, "Your Honor, the People object to this proceeding as being outside established courtroom practice and ask that all the preceding be stricken from the record."

Judge Higgins nodded and said, "I will reserve judgment on your motion and reserve the right to strike everything at the appropriate time. For the moment, I will allow the defense to proceed, subject to later ruling."

The prosecutor sat down, having made his point for the record, and Rajiv Pankar took the floor.

"Excellency, the leaked reports now known to every citizen of our city say that the police found one thumbprint at the telephone office fire and that that thumbprint belongs to Mr. Subramaniam. The leaked reports say that there is no eyewitness and no other tangible evidence. The entirety of the prosecution's case rests on this one thumbprint. Now, the defense is willing to stipulate that there is a good match with Mr. Subramaniam's actual thumb. The question is whether the thumbprint's being at the telephone office, near where the fire happened, means that Mr. Subramaniam himself was there.

"Excellency, I show you now a small computer device known as a palmtop computer. You perhaps use one of these to keep track of your appointments and telephone numbers. This particular one requires a sort of password to be turned on. I am sure you are familiar with passwords and computers.

"The kind of password this device requires is a thumbprint. You put your thumb on the screen, and the computer looks at the thumbprint pattern and checks it against that of the authorized user. This is now common in computer practice and for gated entries and the like.

"I show you how this works to keep unauthorized users out of the computer. I push the button to activate the computer, I put my own thumb on the screen, and I wait for two seconds." He waited. Everybody waited. Nobody breathed.

The computer gave a double beep. Rajiv Pankar stepped closer to the bench and showed the screen message to the judge. "Excellency, the computer has rejected me, and I will read the screen message for the record and show the screen to the clerk." Rajiv

Pankar showed the screen to the stenographer, who read the screen and nodded. "The screen message is 'Access denied.' "

Rajiv showed the screen to the prosecutor and to the closest TV camera, then turned quickly back to face the judge.

"Excellency, I will now ask Mr. Subramaniam to try his luck." Rajiv Pankar pushed the activate button and held the little computer out to Sanjar, who put his thumb on the screen. The computer made a single beep.

Rajiv showed the screen to the judge, the stenographer, and the prosecution. "I will read the message for the record. It says, 'Access permitted.' "

Rajiv showed the screen briefly to the closest TV camera.

The judge said to Rajiv Pankar, "Please address yourself to the Court."

"Thank you, Excellency.

"What we have now seen is that the thumb print device in the little computer can tell the authorized user, in this case Mr. Subramaniam, from an unauthorized user, in this case me. This little computer is in fact one used by Mr. Subramaniam in his work at the hospital. Several others, particularly senior managers at the hospital, have their own."

Rudy, Alice, Susan, and Nan found themselves nodding in agreement. They each had such a palmtop computer with the thumbprint access control scheme.

Rajiv Pankar continued. "I now will try my luck again."

He pushed the activate key and held the little computer out in his left hand so that everybody could see, and then he placed his right thumb on the screen. The computer gave a single beep. The audience said, "Oooh."

The judge rapped his gavel and said, in a medium voice and in a rather routine way, "Order in the court."

"Now, Mr. Pankar, are you going to show the court how you managed to defeat the computer this second time? And will you be telling us what this has to do with fair play and this case?"

"Yes, Excellency. I am not a magician, and I am here to explain, not to baffle. I show you my right thumb."

Rajiv Pankar raised his right hand with the thumb extending upward, showing it first to the judge, then to the prosecutor, and then briefly to the audience. Rajiv Pankar took an extra 10 seconds to show his thumb to the cameras.

The thumb had something sticking to it. It looked like a flattened piece of gummy candy, in a bright orange.

Rajiv Pankar continued, addressing the judge. "For the record, I declare that I have flattened a piece of gummy candy between my fingers and stuck it to my thumb, and after Mr. Subramaniam used the computer, I placed the flattened piece of gummy candy on the screen.

"A fingerprint results from the deposit of the naturally occurring oil, present on the skin, onto a surface. The deposit takes the form of the swirls on the fingertip. A fingerprint kit as used by the police uses a chemical that reacts with the natural oil or simply sticks to it and makes a visible pattern that can be photographed.

"In this case, when I put this flattened gummy candy onto the computer screen, after Mr. Subramaniam had put his thumb there, the sticky surface of the gummy candy just lifted the oil off the screen and kept it on the candy.

"Then, I pressed the button to ask for access and put the candy surface on the screen again. This time, the computer scanned the print and found the oil on the surface of the candy. The oil is in the pattern of swirls found on Mr. Subramaniam's thumb.

"Therefore, Excellency, I assert that fair play calls for the prosecutor to tell the public and this honorable Court that Mr. Subramaniam's thumbprint's being found at the scene of the telephone office fire does not at all nor in any way prove or even hint that Mr. Subramaniam's thumb nor any part of his body was anywhere near that fire at that time nor for that purpose. Lacking any corroboration, the prosecution has no case at all. I invite them to withdraw their case forthwith.

"Excellency, the defense has completed its demonstration."

The judge looked at Rajiv Pankar with a deepened expression of curiosity. "Mr. Pankar, I see how you can fool a computer with your piece of candy, but the matter at hand, as I understand it, is a thumbprint found on a wall or on a pipe, not on a computer. Can you link this up for me?"

"Excellency, I have used the computer device because it is easy to see and comprehend in respect for your precious time. Fingerprints can be transferred from water tumblers with cellophane tape; they can be photographed and printed anywhere. If your time were less valuable, I would have shown all of these things, and more. I trust, however, that you will agree that a print with no corroboration is no evidence at all."

The judge turned to the prosecutor, at which time Nan noticed that the judge had slicked back his hair and maybe powdered his face during that five-minute recess.

"How say you for the People?"

"Your Honor, I repeat my motion to strike."

The judge nodded and said, "I have that noted, and now I ask you what you have to say."

"Your Honor, the People are prepared to drop all charges against Mr. Subramaniam and will make a public statement as soon as a press briefing can be organized saying that we have done so. The People reserve the right to bring new charges in the event that new evidence comes to light."

"Mr. Prosecutor, you are free and indeed you are charged with bringing charges against all persons against whom evidence is found, so I trust you will rephrase your statement when you make it in public so as not to be prejudicial against the defendant in this matter and actionable against yourself. I would consider finding you in contempt myself in such case."

"Yes, your Honor. The People hold no malice and wish to cast no aspersions on Mr. Subramaniam. If I may add, your Honor, Mr. Subramaniam and his several counsel have treated my office and the other authorities with courtesy and cooperation throughout this matter."

The judge rapped his gavel and struck a full-face posture for the cameras. "Very well. All charges are dropped. The defendant is released from custody, and this case is closed." He rapped again and stood.

"All rise."

They stood while the judge exited, courtroom left, robe billowing behind him.

Sanjar was mobbed by wife, sons, and newsies. The TV cameras were close, carrying the manifest relief and joy of the Subramaniam family out to their audiences at home.

Nan, Jack, Susan, Rudy, and Alice were clapping their hands. Randall Pinkston nodded to them in a positive way with a reserved sort of a smile.

Nan turned to Rudy and then to Jack. "Now, you two have to tell us how you cooked this up."

Rudy smiled all the broader and said, "The next time I tell this story, it's going to be a two-martini classic with all the trimmings. I'll just give you the highlights now.

"I knew in a heartbeat that Sanjar didn't set those fires. When the word got out that the police had found a thumbprint, I screwed up my courage and called your home number, Nan, which is in our emergency list, hoping that I would find your husband there. I introduced myself and told Jack the story. Jack said he would check it out. Ten minutes later, he called me back to tell me about sticky, gummy candy and how to do the demonstration.

"I then went to see Alice, so you see this is a major cabal we had going, not just a two-man thing. Alice, Jack, and I got on the phone with our three lawyers, they went and got Rajiv Pankar, I laid out the scheme, and they did the rest."

Nan faced Jack. "Your turn. How did you know about sticky candy and fingerprints?"

Jack went into a slightly defensive crouch and told them his story. "Everybody in the software world knows about fingerprints and voiceprints and handprints and eyeball prints, because people have been trying to get them to work for computer security. Fingerprint devices are pretty good, and they are cheap, so they are now getting some wide use. But they aren't bulletproof. The candy idea came from a press report from Japan, of a guy who wanted to show how easy it is to defeat a fingerprint device by doing exactly what the lawyers did this evening. He got in line behind people, copied their fingerprints onto gummy candy, and then beat the fingerprint test every time."

Randall Pinkston leaned in so that he could be heard in the little group and asked, "Mr. Mills, how then are fingerprint tests of any value in providing security?"

"Well, they are pretty good, they are cheap, and if the security matter is important, other kinds of biometric devices can be used in addition, like a voiceprint or a face print. It's possible to defeat any one of these, but it's pretty hard to defeat two or three of them at the same time in a real-life situation. Or, you can wipe the little screen clean after every use.

"You can add some barriers, and the more barriers, the better the security, but you never get to 100 percent."

Jack smiled his modest smile. Nan thought again that that smile would do better on somebody who had more to be modest about. Nan took Jack by the arm.

After a moment, Rudy said to them, "I am tempted to say we should go across the street to that bar where all the lawyers hang out and have a celebratory toddy. But, I know that you need to get back to the office, Alice and Susan, so that you can hammer out an appropriate statement for Crawford to issue right away to catch the morning papers, and I know that you two," indicating Nan and Jack, "have to get about solving the crime. So, I bid you all a good evening."

The little group broke up. Rudy went forward to congratulate his lawyer, and Jack followed Rudy's lead. Susan, Alice, and Randall Pinkston left together. Nan waited to see if the crowd around Sanjar would let up, but there was no sign of that. Not only was the

Subramaniam family around him, but the newsies were also still at him, the cameras were still on, and a dozen of Sanjar's countrymen who had turned out to lend their support were gathered about him. That caused a tear to well up in Nan's eye, so she decided it was time to leave. She gathered up Jack, who was talking to Xaveria Solana Naredo, and they headed for the door to the parking lot.

Nan, relieved of worry on behalf of Sanjar, started to wonder about the crime.

40

Contretemps in the Parking Lot

As Nan and Jack were walking up to their car, Jack said, "Look here, Nan, that lawyer spells her name with an X instead of a J." Jack held out the business card he had been given by Xaveria Solana Naredo moments before, in exchange for one of his own.

"She's not your type, Jack."

Jack stopped dead in his tracks.

"What's with this 'type' stuff, Nan? She spells her name funny, so she's a type?"

Nan answered just a little more quickly than she should have. "She's an overdressed lawyer, is what she is."

"Who cares what she is? You've been giving me this 'type' stuff all week, and I want to know why. What's going on with you?"

"Nothing is going on with me. There's nothing more to discuss."

"Look, Nan, we've been married for half our lives, and I want to know what's going on. Did I do something to you? Did I say something to you? Did I put salt in the sugar bowl by mistake? What's going on?"

"I don't want to talk about it."

"You start something, and now you don't want to talk about it? What kind of a deal is that?" Jack, not prone to outbursts, was speaking a lot more loudly than circumstances required. He was clearly in a snit.

Nan felt that she was in the wrong, but she didn't know how to get out of the situation. "I don't think this is the place to talk about it. I don't want to talk about it." Nan felt her face flush, and she looked at the ground.

"That's no deal. Tell me what's going on. You mad at me for something?" Jack waited a second and got no response. "You think I have a crush on this lady lawyer I never set eyes on before this evening? What kind of sense does that make?"

Nan had no answer.

"I do software, Nan. Half the people in software are females. They come in long and tall, they come in short and stout. Every one of them is bright. Some of them are knockouts. You know that. You know some of them. If I wanted to make a hobby of collecting girl-friends, I don't think I'd start with a lawyer who can't run a spell checker. But the fact is, I don't want to, and I haven't wanted to, and I don't. What's more, you know that as well as I do.

"I don't like being accused. I don't like getting the needle. I don't like any of this. You've really gotten me upset with this 'type' busi-ness. If this is a joke, it's a pretty sorry one.

"So, what's going on here?"

Nan looked at Jack, briefly, without smiling. She got into the car and sat there, waiting for Jack to get in. After a few moments of fum-ing, Jack got in, started the car, and drove them home in silence.

Nan tried to remember the last time she and Jack had had any-thing close to argument. Nan wondered to herself why she had been giving Jack the "type" treatment, wondering if she had at first meant it as a joke or as something else. She had no reason to complain of Jack's deportment with other women, and in fact he had never shown any sign of a wandering eye. Jack had been right to call her on it, and now she didn't know what to do. If she were to apologize, she would have to explain what had been going on, and she didn't know herself.

They got home, said very few words to each other the rest of the evening, and turned in, in silence.

Nan had gotten herself in a mess and she didn't know how to get out of it. The furthest thing from her mind was to make her husband, her own true love, mad at her, disgusted with her, but that was just exactly what she had done.

Nan lay awake. Jack was asleep, turned away on the far edge of his side of the queen-size bed. There was a lot of distance between them, in more ways that one. Having gotten nowhere in figuring out what to do with her marriage, Nan put her mind to work on the arson episodes. Around three in the morning, Nan eased herself out of bed, went to her computer, typed in an e-mail message to Marcy, and went back to bed. She didn't get much sleep, and she found her-self feeling really blue when dawn came.

Breakfast was funereal.

41

A Professional Visit

As Nan approached her office, Marcy stopped her, saying quietly that Dr. Robert Anderson, the chief medical officer, had been waiting 20 minutes in her office. Neither Nan nor Marcy could think of any time Dr. Anderson had been to Nan's office at all, let alone before office hours. Marcy reported that he had accepted a cup of Marcy's tea, although she had offered to get him coffee if he preferred.

Nan went in, forcing a smile. "Good morning, Dr. Anderson. You are always welcome here, but tell me what brings you over here at this hour?"

"Nan, this is a professional visit." Dr. Anderson reached around Nan to close the office door. Then he sat down again, waiting for Nan to seat herself. "Nan, when I say this is a professional visit, I mean I am here in my professional capacity. I am not your doctor or your priest, and I am meddling in your affairs and I go to great lengths not to meddle in anybody's affairs, certainly not the affairs of friends and coworkers. But here I am, and I am here to meddle."

Nan found she had nothing to say. She looked at Dr. Anderson and wondered what he would say next.

"Nan, I was at night court last evening, as I guess just about everybody in the hospital above the rank of corporal was. I saw you and Rudy and Susan and Alice sitting together, and I was thinking about joining you when the clerk called the court into session. So I sat in the back. Then, after everything was over and people were leaving, I didn't make it across the crowd to speak to you and the others in the courtroom before you broke up. I did happen to wind up in the parking lot just as you and your husband were walking up to your car.

"I couldn't help hearing what I heard.

"I think I know you well enough, and while I can't say I know your husband any more than to speak to, I know both of you well enough to know that you two are not a couple who shout at each other all the time. I know plenty of couples who do, and in my kind of family medicine, I know whereof I speak.

"So if you and your husband are shouting at each other in public, I know there is a reason for it, and I want to get to the bottom of it.

"I know that's meddling. You're younger than I am, and you can probably throw me out of the room with a good judo chop, but until you do, I am here to stay."

Nan was mortified to learn that her encounter with Jack in that parking lot had been observed. If it had been observed by Dr. Anderson, it probably had been seen by half the hospital staff, six newsies, and two television crews.

"I am not going to throw you out, Dr. Anderson. I do think I am going to cry. I hope you brought a large supply of handkerchiefs." While Nan had meant that as levity, she soon realized that she had spoken the truth.

"Let's start at the top. Do you and your husband quarrel?"

"No. We never quarrel. We are the most contented couple I have ever known."

"Did your husband give you cause?"

"No. Not yesterday, not this week, and never at all."

"Did you cause yesterday's quarrel?"

"Yes, and I didn't mean to. It just happened."

"Tell me."

"This past week, I find myself telling Jack 'She's not your type' every time he, or we, encounter a woman. I guess I mean any younger woman. That female lawyer in the court last evening was one. Jack mentioned that she spelled her name with an X instead of with a J. He had gotten her card after the court session, and Jack knows that I make something of a hobby with names. Instead of saying, 'Oh, that's interesting,' or 'Isn't she stupid,' I just said, 'She's not your type, Jack.' Then he wanted to know why I have been giving him the needle about women, and I didn't have an answer."

"So, if it wasn't something Jack said or did, it must have been something with you, yourself. What was it?"

"I don't know. I asked myself that all night."

"How well are you handling the stress of your job, Nan?"

Nan thought about that. "I don't know. There are certainly stressful moments, and I seem to get myself crosswise with Crawford more often than not. I don't have ulcers, yet, that I know of. I don't yell at you or Marcy or anybody, so far I as know. But I've never had a job on this scale before, and I don't have any way to know what to expect or how to act, a good part of the time. Maybe I'm in over my head. I think about that; well, I used to think about that a lot when I first got the job. Maybe I should be thinking more about it now. Maybe I am acting that out by tormenting Jack."

"How old are you, Nan?"

"I think that's an illegal question, but I'll answer it anyway. I'll be 40 in the near future. Jack and I were born in the same month, under the same sign of the Zodiac."

"Nan, when you were a lot younger, did you at any time have a morbid fear that you were going to die, some day? That you were not going to live forever?"

"Yes. A long time ago, but yes."

"I'll tell you, when you get to my age, it's the other way around. You'll have a morbid fear that you *might* live forever, strapped to a chair in a fetid nursing home, drooling on a soiled bib, and waiting for somebody to change your diaper.

"Do you have morbid fears now?" he asked.

"No. I never get morbid."

"Yes, you do. Everybody does. The morbid fear most common to married women of your age is that your husband is going to trade you in for a new model.

"If you read the society pages, you know that it does happen. Your boys have gone off to college, as I understand it. I'll tell you if you don't already know, that that's a point in married life when a lot of couples look at each other and decide that with the kids out of the house, there is nothing left to be married about.

"In your case, if you pay attention to yourself, you'll see that it is a very remote possibility, hardly a probability, and that if you give it any thought you'll see it's a foolish thing to worry about."

"You mean I am trying to control Jack's behavior because of a morbid fear that I am not even conscious of having?"

"It doesn't have to be conscious. It just has to be happening to you at some level."

"So, doctor, what do I do?"

Dr. Anderson waited a minute before he answered. He fiddled with his teacup and took a sip, rather obviously playing for time. Nan waited and wondered. Her eyes were more than moist by this time. Dr. Anderson's eyes looked a little moist, too.

"Nan, would you say that your husband is an honorable man?"

Nan was struck by that question out of the blue. "Yes. Jack Mills is an honorable man. He is honorable himself, and he spent time and effort to make sure our twin sons knew what honor means and how they should live their own lives in an honorable way. So, yes, Jack Mills is an honorable man."

"I thought so. Now, when you two got married, did you say that you would love, honor, and obey your husband?"

"Even that many years ago, I think the vows were to love, honor, and cherish. If the vow had been to obey, I would have accepted that vow, so, yes, you're close enough."

"When you say something to Jack on the order of 'She's not your type,' he will naturally take that as a challenge to his honor. You don't mean it that way, exactly, but do you see what I mean?"

Nan waited. "Yes, I can see that. I am casting aspersions on Jack's honor by hinting that he might be doing or thinking of doing something dishonorable."

"Is that what you mean to do?"

"Certainly not. Surely not."

"Well, then, you see that you can't say that any more, and you can't say anything else like it that casts aspersions, as you put it, on Jack's honor."

"Okay, so I won't say it. But is that enough? Am I stuck with morbid anxiety that Jack will trade me in for a trophy wife and leave me on my lonesome in my declining years?"

"Some fears and anxieties are normal for people at each age. You surely studied enough psychology in college to know that. Right now, one anxiety has gotten hold of you. It's up to you to recognize it for what it is and conquer it, just as you did your earlier morbid fear of death. When you feel anxiety coming on, just change the subject. Some people stamp their feet. Anything to distract the brain and get it on a new subject."

"What do I do about Jack?"

"That's the easiest part. Tell him you love him."

Nan dug into her pocketbook for a handkerchief to wipe her eyes. And her cheeks. Then she gave up, put her head in her hands, and cried.

Dr. Anderson sat in his chair, stirring his tea absently, watching Nan closely, more as a friend than a counselor.

Some moments later, Nan raised her head, sniffled, wiped her eyes again, batted her eyelids, and picked up the phone. When her call was answered, she said into the phone, "Jack, remember when we promised to love, honor, and obey? I meant it then and I mean it today. I love you, Jack Mills, today, tomorrow, and always. I've been a little nutty recently, and it was about me, not about you. But I am over that now, and it's behind me and will never come between us again."

Nan waited. Jack answered her, "Nan, I don't know what's going on, but if it's behind us, that's fine with me. I want to go back to the way things were, and besides, it wasn't love, honor, and obey, it was love, honor, and cherish."

"Whatever it was, I meant it then and I meant it now.

"Jack, we also said in sickness and in health. I don't mean to say that I have been sick, because I haven't been sick and I am not sick and I am not going to be sick. I just mean that sickness and health are part of life, and what's happened to me recently is part of life, too, and I didn't understand that until this morning. I have been talking to Dr. Anderson. You remember him?"

"Yes, of course, I remember him. A nice old doc of a guy. A big fan of yours, too, from what I can see."

"Maybe. Anyway, he and I have been talking, and I learned something about what happens at various stages of a lifetime, and all that caused me to want to call you up and tell you I love you, because I do."

"You can call me anytime to tell me you love me. I wish more people would."

Nan churned through several possible retorts to that and settled on, "Everybody loves you, Jack, and I love you the most.

"Goodbye, Jack. I love you."

"Goodbye, Nan. I'm glad you love me, because I can't even imagine life any other way."

Nan was pleased with herself for not letting her voice break while talking to Jack. Now she was smiling, although tears were still in her eyes.

"Dr. Anderson, I don't know if you make a practice of causing middle-aged women to cry, but I think your therapy may be working."

"I've seen a lot of people cry, Nan, men as much as women, and I've done some crying myself. It's nature's way, and there's no point in fighting it. Sometimes a good cry is the best therapy."

Nan slid her chair forward and put her hand on top of the back of Dr. Anderson's hand on the table. "You're a dear man, Dr. Bob. A dear man."

Dr. Anderson looked a little uncomfortable, but he made no move to draw his hand away from Nan's.

"Let's talk about stress. You're a nurse, so you know about job stress. Every nurse does. Those who can't handle it, they don't last long, and they certainly don't last as long as you have.

"But now that you have this executive position, you're in for a different kind of stress, one that you don't have any training for.

There's a big difference between the kind of unit manager's job you had before and what you're doing now.

"You've probably found yourself in a lot of situations where there is no rule book to follow, or where the rule book says something that you figure to be wrong or counterproductive.

"That's true. That's as true as can be."

"You probably find yourself doing things that seem perfectly logical to you, and then you find out that the suits think you did it all wrong, for reasons that baffle you."

"Right again."

"So, how do you handle it?"

Nan drew her hand back, and then she sat and looked at the good doctor for a full minute. "Dr. Bob, do you worry about all the staff around here as much as you worry about me?"

Dr. Anderson looked down at his hands, then he looked up to say, "Maybe I do, maybe I don't. I worry about the hospital. I guess you know I rode in on the first load of bricks when they were building the modern part of the hospital here, and that was a good many years ago. I've been here ever since, and I have seen the hospital go through good times and bad. I've been on the management staff here since about the time you started to kindergarten, or thereabouts.

"Medicine has changed for the better over the years, and the hospital has learned to manage itself better. We've got a pretty good group here, now. That wasn't always the case, but I think it's true now.

"But we've never had anything like you before, Nan. You bring electricity to everything you do around here. You started with a bang, when was that, six or seven months ago? You've attracted the best people into your orbit, you've done wonders with the nursing service, and you've had a big influence on how all of us medical types, there's that word again, go about curing the halt and the lame.

"Six months ago, you were sort of a one-woman band, getting heroic things done, as much in spite of the organization as because of it. That was impressive, almost beyond comprehension, but it was worrying, too, because no mortal can do everything solo around here. You have certainly given Crawford more than a few gray hairs.

"Then just in the past few days, I've been seeing a change, not so much in you but in others on the hospital staff. Rudy Rudolf, for one. Ever since he took that job he has, he's been kidding around and making jokes to avoid serious participation in management. That's a common enough defense, and so I am not complaining about Rudy at all. But just this week, we have a new Rudy, a take-charge, stand-up guy. I've been hoping to see that ever since I first met him, because he ought to be pretty high on the replacement list for Crawford as the next chief operating officer. So, being an old codger, I just went up to him and asked him what had happened to him. He told me. He told me that you had told him what his job is. He put it a different way. He said you had told him his purpose for coming to work every day. I don't know if it was as simple as that, but he thinks it was.

"And Susan Gunn. She was always the super bureaucrat, always going by the book and thinking of reasons not to do anything or change anything and protecting her turf. Now she's a new person, too. She's discovered that there's more to senior management than memorizing the rulebook. I see initiative. I see responsibility. I see a new Susan Gunn.

"We've had a lot of head nurses in my time, here, Nan, but we've never had one who impacted the place like you do.

"So, when I meddle in your business, it's for the most selfish of reasons. I love this old hospital and all that goes with it. It's been my professional life and a lot of my personal life too."

Now it was Dr. Anderson who had the moist eyes and a loopy sort of a grin.

Nan waited, and then she said, "I've seen a new Rudy, too. And I have seen a side of Susan Gunn I didn't know existed. She knows a lot more about how to manage people than I knew, and a lot more than I would have guessed she knew. She's been a big help to me, just this week."

"You've just said something important, Nan. You know, it's necessarily true that people who get middle management positions have to do a lot of on-the-job learning, because there isn't any movie to watch or book to read. A lot of people never figure it out and just settle into a paper-shuffling mode. Some go off on a tangent. I guess some people are born with the right instincts. I mean you."

"No, Dr. Anderson, you don't mean me. I have been as baffled and frustrated in this job as anybody else could ever have been. I don't think I have any instincts at all. I do have a lot of people around me who bail me out, and I need bailing a lot more than most people do."

"Nan, I've watched the bright people around here, like Marcy and Sanjar and Carl Burke and others, they hitched themselves to your wagon the first day you had this job. Others like Maggie Kelly were already here, but they have blossomed since you've been here. Not everybody has your gift, Nan."

"I have been lucky with the people who have decided to work with me. I know they all have had other choices." Nan reflected for a moment. "Dr. Bob, did you know that Marcy was second in seniority when my secretarial position opened up, and so she touted the more senior candidate off this job so she could have it herself? That's the strangest thing I've ever run across in this organization."

"I just told you that the high-energy ones are the ones who think of ways to be here with you. I hadn't heard that story, but I've known Marcy longer than you have, I guess, and while I am not sure I could handle having her as my own secretary, I can see that she shines working for you. That's what I was talking about. You get people to blossom, just by being yourself.

"They figure that being with you is bound to be lively, and that they'll have their chance to shine. So it's good for their careers as well as a lot more fun than shuffling paper, even if they get thrown in jail now and then."

At this point, they were both laughing, maybe a little more than they needed to.

"What's more, Nan, they know if they get thrown in jail, you are going to be there to bail them out."

"Everybody was there to bail Sanjar out. Rudy sent his lawyer, Alice got a lawyer from the firm that represents the board. I'm surprised you didn't send a lawyer," Nan said, thinking that that would not be taken as a dig.

"Well, now, as it happens, I did send a lawyer. I called my lawyer, but he just does malpractice, so he called his brother, who does this kind of law. By the time the brother got down to the jail, he was told there were four lawyers in with Sanjar already. So he called back for instructions. I told him to wait in the back of the courtroom to see what would happen. I was sitting by him. So, I tried, but without much effect."

"Dr. Bob, that was wonderful of you! That was above and beyond the call of duty."

"No, it was my duty, it just took my a little longer to figure that out, and I am glad I gave it a try, anyway. You see, you even have an impact on an old codger like me.

"People want to help, Nan. People don't always know how to help, but they generally want to help. That's certainly true of the managers here with rare exception, and the professionals, too. Maybe that's your magic, Nan. You let people help."

"Well, if being in great need of help is all that it takes, I am secure for all time," Nan answered with a little laugh.

Dr. Anderson looked intently at Nan. "You didn't answer my question about stress."

Nan sat back and returned Dr. Anderson's look. "I know what I used to do, when this job was new, and I was on the hot seat with Crawford all the time. As I walked to his office to defend something

I'd done, I would say to myself, 'Jack loves me, my sons love me, my twin sister Ann loves me, Jack makes plenty of money for both of us, so I don't need this job.' "

"That's a better attitude than the opposite, saying to yourself that you want to keep onto the job so much you'll do anything just to hang on. It gives you a certain independence. It might cause you to overdo it, sometimes, making you too independent. I don't know how to get the right balance."

Nan shook her head. "I don't either. And I don't find myself saying that little speech to myself any more, so maybe I've outgrown it, or maybe I should be saying it. What do you think?"

"Beats me. If I had a cure for occupational stress, I'd bottle it and make a million. Maybe a billion."

Dr. Anderson arose, took Nan's hand, and said, "You're cured, Nan. You're as good as new. If I were your doctor, I'd send you a big bill.

"I guess you know, we doctors try not to get involved treating our own family and our own friends, because there's too much emotion involved. So, I am not going to think of you as a patient, because I want to think of you as a friend."

"Friends, friends for life, Dr. Bob," Nan said, holding the elderly doctor's hands warmly. "And no more morbid anxieties about things I can't do anything about anyway."

When Dr. Anderson had gone, Nan closed the door and called Jack again. She said, "Jack, it's me. I meant every word. I'll be home for lunch. Don't bother to fix anything."

42

The Morgani Twins Report

Nan sat at her desk and stared at her computer screen without actually seeing it, her mind a blank. Then she caught her reflection in the screen and decided she needed to fix her face and hair. She rose and turned to the door, just as Marcy came in.

Marcy was carrying the customary pot of tea, which looked pretty good to Nan just then, and she was carrying a cafeteria plate with a washcloth and hand towel.

Marcy wasn't exactly looking at Nan, casting her gaze on the table and the things she was placing there. Marcy said, "When I see a doctor, I always need a complete makeup do-over, so I brought you a warm washcloth and towel. If you turn on your computer camera, you can see yourself just like with a vanity mirror."

"Marcy, I have to ask you something. Dr. Anderson was just here because he overheard Jack and me having a loud argument in the parking lot near the courthouse last evening. Did you hear about that?"

"Well, a couple of people called me this morning to get the low-down, after they saw the item in the gossip column this morning. They didn't give your name, but it wasn't too hard to guess who was being talked about."

"I'm in the gossip column?" Nan was mortified.

"It's in your mail file on the computer. It's pretty tame."

Nan called up her mail folder, picked out the file titled "gossip column.html." She sighed deeply and opened the file.

> *Local nursing executive goes Hollywood after one session on local gab-TV show. No lamps were flying, but tempers were hot in the courthouse parking lot last night as nurse and hubby explained things to each other.*

257

Oh, great, thought Nan. I've gone Hollywood. Sports page to gossip column in one week. How am I going to live this down? Should I send it to Jake and Bake at college, or will they have seen it already? What will Jack say? What will Crawford say? I don't need the job, but it would be nice to have my good name back.

Nan reached for the phone and called Jack. When he answered, she said to him, "Don't read the gossip column today."

"Nan, I haven't read the gossip column since Congressman Whatsisname was found wading in the fountain on the Mall in Washington. And anyway, I didn't have to read it because about 40 people sent it to me by e-mail from all over the country. People are getting a big laugh out of it."

"A big laugh at my expense."

"No, Nan, just a big laugh. Nobody who knows you at all will think you've gone Hollywood, whatever that means. They got a laugh when you were on the sports page, and they got a laugh out of the gossip column. Why don't you give it a laugh, too, and forget about it?"

Nan did another deep sigh. "Jack, I know you're right, and I hope I can do it.

"I love you, Jack. I'll see you at lunchtime."

"I love you, too, Nan. I look forward to seeing you. You haven't come home for lunch since you took that executive position all those months ago."

They hung up. Nan told Marcy, "Jack says to have a good laugh and forget about it. How does that sound?"

"Yes, ma'am."

Marcy continued. "Now, I took care of the day's bumf, but there's one item you may want to look at. The Morgani twins did a video report for you after their session in surgery this morning. They seem like such nice, excited, active, energetic kids. People used to say the same about ours, although all that energy used to wear me out."

"I know that feeling, Marcy."

"There's one other item. Tanya Hunt from the burn unit called to say that that Mr. Carlson died yesterday around suppertime. He's the one from that manhole fire last Sunday."

Nan nodded several times, acknowledging that the message was received and that she had expected the news to be bad.

Nan turned to her computer, found the Morgani report, and launched the video application so she could see what they had to say. Or show. Marcy watched over Nan's shoulder.

The twins came into view, dressed in green surgical scrubs with caps and gloves, their surgical masks hanging down their chests from the tie-strings. Big beaming smiles. They started in unison, "Hi, Mrs. Mills." Then Lu took over.

"We are giving a quick oral report because we have to go to school now.

"We were invited to witness a gallbladder operation this morning, and we scrubbed up and dressed up, and you see us with our surgical outfits still on. Early morning stuff isn't too big with our age group, but we were here before dawn because that's what we were told to do.

"We were close enough to see a lot of the action with the two surgeons, a bunch of nurses, and the anesthesiologist. Or course, we don't really know anything, so we were just there with our mouths open, covered by our masks of course, and taking notes.

"Maybe we'll have something more to say after we think about it and go over our notes, but we wanted to give you the first reactions right away."

Ray spoke up. "First of all, we were surprised to find that the whole room was not sterile, but only the part of the room near the action. There's a tape circle on the floor. I don't know if that's so hot for keeping staph germs from getting into the wound or whatever. I know you like to hear solutions and not just gripes, so we talked to each other about how this is done in the semiconductor factories, because we had a tour of one last month. They have a lot of sterile rooms, and they use air curtains around the doors. That's a blast of air that shoots down from the ceiling along a dividing line. You can walk through it, but dirt in the air can't get from one side of the air curtain to the other. I think that would work better for germs than a tape stripe on the floor."

Lu spoke again. "We noticed that the surgeon and the others go through a lot of steps, and I suppose they have all done the same operation lots of times and know the drill, but we remarked to each other that nobody is working down a checklist. Our cousin is an airline pilot, and he tells us that they work through a checklist before every takeoff and every landing, even though they fly the same plane every day and do takeoffs and landings six times a day. Maybe somebody ought to ask why it's a good idea for pilots and why maybe it's a good idea for surgeons."

Ray spoke again, nodding for emphasis. "Our cousin told us that when he was in the Air Force flying fighter planes, they even had a checklist to go through before they bailed out in a parachute or fired the ejection seat. They had checklists for everything."

Lu and Ray in unison, again. "End of oral report. Written report soon. Bye now." They waved to the camera and offered toothy smiles.

Well, thought Nan, I wonder why pilots have checklists and surgeons don't. Maybe that's one for Dr. Bob. The air curtain sounded like a good idea, too, what with the constant worry about staph infections, particularly during surgery. That's one for Hank Powers and Susan Gunn, since Hank pyramided to Susan. No action items for me.

Putting first things first, Nan used the warm washcloth and towel to bathe her face, then she used the camera and PC screen as a vanity mirror, taking advantage of the key lights that came up around the screen to light her face. Repair work done, she used the camera and microphone to dictate a thank-you note to the Morgani twins with copies to the future-nurse sponsors on her staff. Then she forwarded the Morgani report to various people on the staff, with video notes added, customized for each one. Crawford. Susan Gunn and Hank Powers. Dr. Anderson. The chief surgeon and her nurse manager for surgery. Then she did a more general note and forwarded the Morgani report to all of her staff. Then another one for Alice Newcomb, who was worried the previous day about liabilities arising from high school kids finding fault with the hospital operations, even though that was exactly what Nan had hoped they would do.

Then Nan sent the Morgani report to Josey Walberg with a video note saying that the newsies who had seen the first Morgani report might want to follow up.

That had taken a lot of time to do, Nan found. Simple-text e-mail would have been faster, maybe. But then, maybe showing her face around the place was one way to get people to forget about the gossip column. Maybe.

If not, well, Jack loved her, her twin boys loved her, her sister Ann loved her, and she didn't need the job anyway.

Was she being too independent?

Marcy had left Nan's office while Nan was doing her video messages. Nan used the intercom to ask Marcy back in. Nan said, "I am going to go home for lunch. Cancel anything that was booked for me during the lunch hour, please."

Marcy's pencil flew across her steno pad. "You were booked for the managers' luncheon for Maggie Kelly. It's going to be right here in your conference room."

"Oh, I guess I knew that a luncheon was in the offing, and I figured you were taking care of the schedule, so I didn't bother to ask which day. Well, I am going home for lunch, so cancel me out with apologies all around. Did I pay for my lunch? Let me say that the other way around. I hope I paid for my lunch, because I don't want to stick anybody else with my tab."

"Yes, ma'am, you paid $8 for the lunch and $15 toward a gift for Maggie. You paid by bank transfer. The department is paying for the dessert, since that is below the level that catches anybody's eye."

"Okay, that's fine. Maybe I'll be back in time for dessert. Those luncheons usually run over."

"Yes, ma'am. That would be nice if you get back for dessert. People don't really expect you to attend these things because they know you have a million obligations. They will probably have a better time if you aren't there anyway."

Nan laughed a little. "Yes, I know what you mean. So maybe this will work out best for everybody. They can read the gossip column to each other if I am not there.

"All right, Marcy. The warm washcloth, the energy level of the Morgani twins, I'm back on track now. Let's go to work."

Marcy consulted her steno pad and said, "You are planning to attend that neighborhood block party for Maggie this evening aren't you? I think it was planned that you and your husband would attend this one. They've been going on all week, from what I read in the papers, in different neighborhoods around Maggie's clinics."

Nan figured that Marcy was asking if she and Jack would be appearing in public together anytime soon. "Yes, thank you, Marcy. Jack and I will be there with bells on."

Marcy wrote more notes on her steno pad. "You sent me an e-mail and asked that I invite that list of people to meet with you this afternoon. That's all set for two o'clock. Everybody you asked for has confirmed."

Nan thanked Marcy for the report. Marcy looked up to see if Nan had anything else to bring up, and seeing no sign, she smiled and left, leaving Nan to her own devices.

43

Alice Newcomb and the Slush Funds

Marcy came into Nan's office to say that Alice Newcomb, the chief counsel, had called to ask if she could see Nan. Time was available, so Marcy had told Alice to come over. Nan said, "Okay. I wonder what she's up to?"

Alice Newcomb came in, looking a little more professional than friendly. Nan figured this to be a business call.

Nan said, "Alice. Nice to see you. You're always welcome. What's on your mind?"

"Well, after the excitement of night court and drama for television cameras, I suppose it is boring to be dealing with old topics, but I am here on old business. Well, old business with a new wrinkle."

Nan didn't know what to say to that, so she nodded politely and sat with her hands in her lap, waiting for Alice to say her piece.

"Nan, you asked the other day about the development fund that was to be a part of the bequest made by Mr. Bill six or seven months ago."

"*Was* to be? I don't remember it quite that way."

"Everybody agreed in principle back then, and Mr. Bill's lawyer and our own outside counsel have worked up three or four different ways to handle it. There is no disagreement about the idea or the money, since it is part of the bequest anyway. They did three or four different ways of handling the financial controls at this end.

"You see, the hospital board has established limits of authority for each officer, writing down who gets to authorize what kinds of outlays and commitments and up to what dollar figure. You, as head of the largest department, are authorized to spend all the money that is specifically budgeted for the various categories of expense. You are allowed to obligate the hospital up to $20,000 on your own signature, with or without a budget item. Other department heads and the suits each have an assigned level of authority, and I will tell you that most of them are a lot less than yours, which goes with the fact that you have the biggest department and handle the biggest budgetary amounts. I think you understand all that."

Nan nodded. "Yes, I understand the idea of limits of authority established by the board so that if somebody shows up at the cashier's cage with a letter signed by the mail clerk for $10 million, the board doesn't have to pay the money out. I haven't paid much attention to my authorization level, because I always ask Carl Burke to handle that kind of thing, and he takes care of it."

Alice Newcomb nodded in turn, her face now looking a little stern. "Yes, that's the point of it all.

"Now, when the board agreed to the development fund idea, what they were agreeing to is that there may well be a time and place when some development money should be put to use without waiting for the annual budgetary cycle. They even like the idea.

"What they haven't yet decided is whether to raise your unrestricted authorization level up to the total value of that development bequest, which they now figure will be $5 million.

"You're telling me that they are willing to take the money and put it in a development fund under my control, but they won't let me spend the money."

"I don't think they would say it quite that way. They would say they like the idea in principle, and they like you, but they don't know what to do about the limits of authority. You see, they have to figure for the long term, and when you have gone on to some higher position, the new head nurse will wind up with this fund, and they can't imagine giving unlimited authorization to somebody they don't even have a name for yet."

Nan kept her best poker face in place, wondering how much of what Alice was telling her had arisen first with some worrywart on the board and how much had arisen in the fertile mind of Alice Newcomb. It probably didn't matter, since the effect was the same. Somebody was worried that Nan or some future head nurse would take the money, blow it on something stupid, and leave the board with a black eye.

Nan then wondered if the gossip column had been read by Board members. Or by the legal staff.

Nan found herself sighing deeply.

"Okay, Alice. Tell me how this gets resolved in a workable way."

"I think the board would like to see a compromise. They give you a higher level of unquestioned authorization, say double what you have now. Then they put in place some checks and balances, probably a small review board, for higher amounts beyond that new level."

"Alice, that would re-invent the review process we already have, and the whole point of the special bequest was to avoid all that red tape."

"I know, Nan. I remember it very clearly, and I have been in a dozen meetings to try to work this out. I am on your side here."

Nan took that with a grain of salt. Nan was sure that Alice Newcomb was on Alice Newcomb's side, which meant in practice that Alice was on the side of the most recent board member or executive who had spoken to her. Staff positions were too political, Nan found herself thinking. Not for her. She liked concrete line responsibility and the authority that went with it. So now she would have responsibility for the new development fund, but not much authority.

Alice Newcomb was looking down at her yellow legal pad, sharp pencil poised but not writing anything. Nan smiled, inwardly, at the posing or posturing that Alice Newcomb did, at least when dealing with Nan. Nan almost felt sorry for her, for half a second.

Nan decided to outwait her.

Alice Newcomb waited a long while, then she continued.

"Nan, I need to tell you that board members have asked if they will be getting development progress reports, like the ones they get on other major projects around the hospital." Alice Newcomb did not look up while she waited for Nan to say something.

Nan took that in. So, she would have the responsibility and a tiny amount of discretion over the money, and she would need to write reports every month or maybe every week, on every little project. Red tape seemed to grow like staph germs.

Nan found herself wondering why today happened to be the day for Alice to tell her all this. Nan had asked before and had never gotten a response at all. So, why today?

"Alice, what triggered your visit here today?"

"Why, you've been asking about this, so I wanted to bring you up to date."

"What else triggered your visit here today?"

"There is one other thing. Young Mr. Collins stopped by my office yesterday to say that it looked like his father was not going to make it through the day. In fact, he died last evening."

"Yes, Alice, I got that report this morning. A real tragedy for that family, losing both mother and father the same week."

"Yes, a tragedy. Well, young Mr. Collins said it was his intention to sign over the life insurance policies on the father and mother to the hospital. He said his lawyer would call in the next few days to take care of the paperwork. He said he wants to stipulate that the money goes toward the cost of the new wing, and that the money be spent in particular to make the new wing more hospitable to visitors and patients who are in for longer stays. He said that he had talked to you about this, and that you would know what he means. Do you?"

"He mentioned that to me when I visited the room his father and mother were in, earlier in the week. He and his wife were here for five days straight, so I suppose they have a better view of what long-stay visitors and perhaps long-stay patients might like to have. I suppose our architects know that, too, but I think that's what he was talking about. I can't say that we discussed it at length. I only saw him a few times and never for more than a few minutes."

"Nan, he wants to stipulate that *you* decide how to spend the life insurance money."

"Me? That's something for the architects, not for the head nurse. I know about beds and patients, not about visitors' lounges."

"He says that's not negotiable. He says that the nursing department acted like it cared about his folks, and he never saw anybody else from the hospital except the cleaning lady, so he wants you to manage the money."

"What if I say no?"

"The insurance policy is for $1 million with double indemnity for accidental death. So, it's $2 million each. If you say no, the board is going to have a conniption."

"So, tell me, Alice, what am I to do? I can't take responsibility for something I don't know anything about."

"I suggest that you agree, and that you form a small advisory panel to advise you on how to spend the money. The architect can be an adviser to the panel. You could get some of your nursing managers, and we could probably dig up some visitors or family members who have been here for extended periods. I think the burn unit probably has more of those than other departments, but you could ask around.

"It's a one-shot deal, as I see it, Nan. The money gets committed to the new wing, and then it's over with. Maybe you do a follow-up report six months after the wing opens to see how it came out."

"Yes, an advisory panel would certainly be necessary. I'd want to go check out some other new hospital wings to see what they are doing, maybe some of the other hospitals that have burn units and extended patient stays. Our unit managers, and particularly Tanya Hunt in the burn unit, could get up some names of people who have hung around here for extended periods.

"I guess I haven't heard if the new wing is going to have a burn unit or not."

"The latest I heard, Nan, is that the burn unit would be moved to the new wing and expanded quite a bit to meet the demand. The board thinks we can get more grant money to supplement the burn unit revenue."

"Well, all the more reason to get Tanya's input and some of her visitors' input."

Alice seemed to relax, no longer pressing quite so hard on her pencil, which had yet to write the first word.

"Nan, I think the board will be thrilled to hear that you will accept these terms for the Collins bequest. It's more than just the money, you know. It's the better job we can do if we have the money."

"I think I read that in a fortune cookie, Alice."

"Let me reflect on what I have just been saying," Nan said. "I have just been saying that in the Collins matter, I don't have enough confidence in myself to just tell the architect how to design the new wing, but I am willing to do so if I can have an advisory panel. Is that what you heard me say?"

"Yes, Nan. That's what I heard you say."

"And in the slush fund matter, I am saying that I don't like the idea of a committee looking over my shoulder because I am entirely confident that I can put the slush fund to good use all by myself. Is that what you heard me say?"

"You didn't say that, but I could sort of get the idea from your body language."

"Well, I never learned to play poker. Okay, I can hear the clash in my own ideas, so let's come down somewhere that doesn't clash so much.

"I'll agree to an executive board for the slush fund that will be briefed on projects that will go over $100,000, provided that the executive board is Susan Gunn and Rudy Rudolf, and that Josey Walberg is assigned to do project reports from time to time. The executive board can complain to the suits if they don't like something I plan to do, but they can't say no.

"Is that good enough." That might have been a question in other circumstances, but here it was declarative, pretty much take it or leave it.

Alice couldn't play poker either, from the look of her. "Yes, Nan, that will be a big relief to the board. I think they will go along with the higher authority limit for this fund, and having an executive board will broaden support for your projects. Josey is an intern, so I don't know how long she will be here. We could make it Josey for now and do something about her replacement when the time comes.

I guess the same is true for Susan Gunn and Rudy Rudolf, too. We can't figure that any one person will be here forever. Not even you and me."

Nan brightened her smile a few watts. "Alice, now that I think about it, I am sure I would have wanted Susan and Rudy to know about the slush fund projects anyway, because some of the projects will surely involve computer stuff and some will involve the buildings, so I am not giving anything away."

Nan thought some more. "I think I'll want Dr. Anderson, too, plus one outsider, the dean of the nursing school at the university, Dean Freddy. I don't suppose you know her. She can be a source of ideas from the outside, and she may know of places where things that looked like good ideas turned out not to be so hot in practice.

"Since I am dreaming up this executive panel all by myself and for my own reasons, I don't think this will be adding red tape at all. Funny how that works."

Alice Newcomb was definitely up to a smile by now. "Yes, Nan. Red tape is in the eye of the beholder.

"I'll get everything fixed up the way you just said it.

"Thanks, Nan. I am happy to have all this ironed out."

Nan thought she should test one other subject, just to see what would happen. "Alice, did you see my write-up in the gossip column this morning?"

Alice Newcomb, heading for the door, turned back to face Nan with a bit of a grin. "Yes, I saw that item. Going Hollywood. Are you going Hollywood, Nan?"

Nan thought that was a friendly rejoinder, and she could handle a little ribbing, maybe. "Yes. Hollywood, here I come."

Alice took that in good part, turned, and left. Nan wondered if Marcy could make her a Hollywood T-shirt over the lunch hour. No, better not to ask, because she might do it. She probably had a cousin someplace in town who did specialty items. No, better not to ask.

44

Friday Lunch Break

Nan got away 20 minutes before her normal lunch break and headed home to make up with Jack. Nan was back to the hospital a quarter of an hour after her usual lunch break would have been over, richer for the experience, renewed in her marriage, restored in her self-confidence, and reassured that Jack knew he already had his trophy wife.

45

Maggie's Luncheon

Nan got back to her office in time to have dessert with her managers, who had gathered in Nan's conference room for a farewell luncheon in honor of Maggie Kelly.

Nan breezed by Marcy's workstation with a wave, dropped off her handbag on her desk and went through the connecting door to her conference room.

Nan found the ambience light and frothy, the right sort of a thing for a happy/sad occasion. People noticed when Nan came in, but they didn't clam up. Nan took that as a good sign that she didn't look to be frightening to her managers this day.

Most of the managers hadn't bothered to eat much of their lunch, either because the servings were too large, the conversation too entrancing, or the need to feign dietary control was too strong. The dessert dish, which looked to be a peach melba, was set out but nobody had yet dived in. Maybe the salad had been too big.

Nan, not having had any lunch at all, did not feign. They had saved her a chair, or perhaps Marcy had made sure there were more chairs than people. Either way, Nan took the remaining chair, seized a dessert and dug in, giving something of a wave to her troops with her free hand.

Nan's action was enough to trigger the lifting of dessert spoons all around the table, and people turned to see what Nan might have to say. Not exactly a lull in the conversation, just a change of focus. Nan did not oblige them, smiling but giving priority to her spoon. She also managed to convey an interest in a cup of tea without actually saying so, and her cup was soon filled.

Maggie spoke. "Nan, it was so good of you to drop in. We've all been talking about Sanjar and the cops. We have not been talking about the gossip column." (Twitters around the room made that a little hard to believe.)

"Are you going to solve the mystery?"

Having polished off her first serving of dessert and sipped her coffee, Nan let her gaze float around the room, seeing that all eyes were on her and that all the faces were offering friendly smiles. "Yes, of course. That's what I do around here while you are not reading the gossip column!"

That got a laugh, the gossip column was laid to rest, and everybody was obviously relieved.

Nan laughed, too. "Okay, I admit I don't have any more idea than anybody else does about the fires. If you have any ideas, call the cops or tell Alice Newcomb. I'm going to be busy doing my Hollywood antics."

People weren't quite sure how to take that, and Nan thought she might have stumbled by harking back to the contents of the gossip column, so she changed the subject.

"Maggie, Jack and I will be at the block party for you this evening. I understand the first one was last night, so tell us all about it."

"Oh, Nan, I didn't think Cash and I were ever going to get home last night. If it hadn't been for this luncheon, I might have called off today. Oh, you know I wouldn't have, but it crossed my mind.

"Last night was the party over by the clinic in the Latino neighborhood, so we had too much spicy food, too much mariachi music, too many babies to kiss, and too much time on my feet. They do a kind of square dance that's more of a mob scene, and I never did figure out if there was a dance step we were supposed to be doing or what. Anyway, it's a good thing I have had 20 years of being on my feet all day, or I'd be in traction today."

Maggie looked around the room. "I saw some of you there last night, which grabbed me right here," said Maggie, thumping herself on the chest, well north of her heart. Nan didn't know if that meant Maggie should touch up on her anatomy or if Maggie was having a little indigestion. Latino food, maybe the latter.

"There were some others from the staff, too. Well, any occasion for a party, I always say. That was great, this luncheon is great, the gift is touching. . . . Nan, we opened the gift first because some people had to leave right after lunch."

Everybody was still there, well after the usual lunch hour would have been over, but Nan let that one pass. If Maggie wanted to open her gift first, well, why not?

There appeared to be two gifts. One was a nice velour robe. The other was a large picture frame holding about 40 photographs of different sizes and shapes and images. They all included Maggie, and they were a trip down memory lane. Her first employee badge photo.

Some award ceremony. Lots of shots of Maggie and patients. A thoughtful and bittersweet gift, Nan thought.

Nan asked, "Did Willie do this?"

"Yes," Annie Rostow answered. "He has a gift for the visual."

"It's great. I wish I could have a copy for my own scrapbook."

"Willie made us all electronic copies. There's one for you in your e-mail."

Nan looked at Maggie, seated at the far end of the table and looking with a friendly smile at Nan. "I got here last, so I get to say something, don't I?"

No one there was going to contradict her, and the group quieted down.

Nan checked each face for an instant, and then said, "I got some news from Alice Newcomb, our chief counsel. The family of Mr. and Mrs. Collins, who were in that awful manhole fire last Sunday evening, have told Alice that they intend to direct some insurance proceeds to the hospital to use for the new wing. The family wants two things. One, that the money goes to facilities for long-term patients and for family visitors of long-term patients. Two, that I decide how that money is to be spent. I suppose that's because the family never got a chance to meet anybody else besides the nursing corps, but in any case that's part of their deal.

"I know about beds and nursing stations, just like each of you do. I don't know much about visitors' facilities. You each may have ideas, but more to the point, some of you, at least, know some patients who are now or who have been with us long term, even though our average bed stay is hardly more than three days now. Some of you know families who have been long-term visitors.

"So, I am now asking you to think about this issue and tell me at the next staff meeting whether you can contribute your own ideas, and all ideas will be welcome, and whether you can contribute some names of patients and families who might have something useful to say.

"The responsibility rests with me, but I am going to rely heavily on you and on the architect. If I can find a research project or expert on this subject at the university nursing school, I'll tap them. I don't want a mob scene, just a few interested people.

"In particular, I am looking for a deputy from among you to put a little time into this on my behalf. To work with me, do some leg-work, coordinate with other parties, maybe go visit some hospitals that have a good name in this particular specialty.

"The first time we talk about this, at the next staff meeting, let's just talk about your direct ideas and patients and families we might tap. The second time we talk about this, I'd like your thinking on what this deputy should do. For instance, should it be a full-time assignment for four months or six months, or should it be an extra duty loaded on one of you to do in your spare time.

"If I were you, any one of you, I would be thinking to myself, 'If I take the deputy thing for six months, what happens to me then? Can I have my old job back?'

"So, I'll tell you the answer to that one. We have a meeting next week to talk about rotational assignments as part of career planning. I am going to tell you then that rotational assignments should include a staff assignment or two, too.

"Working as my deputy on an assignment like this one would fit nicely into that mold. A person taking a job as my deputy would not be dumped at the end of that assignment, I can guarantee you that.

"Also, the deputy doesn't have to be one of you. Maybe it should be a nurse who shows some upside potential and could use a little exposure to something other than hepatitis and measles.

"So, think about that. We'll be talking about it soon."

Nan had not included Maggie in her eye contact around the table as she had talked about the deputy assignment. It wasn't going to be Maggie, that's for sure. Now Nan looked Maggie in the eye and said, "Maggie, the sports page got it right the other day when it wrote that I should be thrilled that you are moving up with another team. I should be, and I am. It hurts me to lose you, but I am smiling through those tears because you're doing the right thing for yourself and even for our hospital. It helps us recruit, and these days, most of nursing is recruiting."

"So, Maggie, tell us. If last night was the Latino party, what do we have to look forward to this evening?"

"Tonight the party is out in the street in front of the clinic over where the immigrants from Eastern Europe live. Cash took a vacation day so he could sleep and get in shape for tonight. I'll tell you, the first time I ever saw anybody do a polka was at our wedding. I had thought polkas were for Germans, but I found out that there are polka freaks from Germany on east for thousands of miles. So bring your polka shoes when you come tonight.

"Oh, I said we were doing some kind of square dance last night, and we were. We also did the tango around midnight. You know what they say, 'Close only counts in horseshoes and tango!' "

That was a good break point. The others got up to leave, lining up to hug Maggie on the way out, so Nan followed suit, exiting back to her office through the connecting door.

46

Crusher Interviews Nan

Marcy detected that Nan was back in her office, so she brought in a fresh pot of tea, her steno pad, and her pencil. She asked Nan, "Are there any action items from the luncheon?"

Nan thought for a moment and then said, "Write a memo or something for me to Susan Gunn to say that I am thinking about adding a special projects person to my staff to be paid for out of the slush fund, and that this would be a short-term assignment for a nurse or a manager, part of our rotational assignment program. Tell her this is just in the thinking stage, and I welcome her thinking to add to the mix."

"Yes, ma'am. Special assistant, paid for by the slush fund, short-term rotational assignments."

"Right."

"I'll call her secretary, tell her the whole thing, and find out if this will resonate best if it shows up as your idea or their idea. If they want to, they could write you a memo proposing this, would that be all right?"

Nan smiled and chuckled to herself. "I think it was President Truman who said that it's easy to get things done in a bureaucracy if you don't care who gets the credit. So, yes, if they want to flash this idea as their very own, that's fine with me. It might even work better that way."

Marcy scribbled on her steno pad. "Maybe I'll walk over there and handle this without leaving any tracks."

She looked up to say, "Your two o'clock meeting is set up. Crusher Morgenstern got here a little early and is out by my desk eating all my chocolate chip cookies. He asked if he could ask you a few questions, one on one, before the meeting. You'll have a few minutes to squeeze him in, you should pardon the expression."

Nan tried to read Marcy's face to divine what Crusher Morgenstern might want, but she found no clues. She had the time, so why not? "Okay, send him in. Then interrupt us if we aren't done by two o'clock."

"Yes, ma'am."

Marcy came back immediately with Crusher Morgenstern, who seemed to be even bigger than he had before. A very big man. Tall, broad in the neck and shoulders, thick through the chest. A real specimen.

Crusher inhaled so Marcy could get by him and out the door. Then he nodded politely to Nan and asked if he could take a seat. Crusher took a chair by the little table and eased himself down into it. He looked to have had experience with chairs collapsing under him.

"Mrs. Mills, I am Chester Morgenstern. You know by now that everybody calls me Crusher, even my wife. So please, you call me Crusher, too.

"I am an independent reporter. I have been following the developments here this week, and there are a few questions I would like to put to you to bring my reporting up to date. Will that be all right?"

Nan felt butterflies, but she convinced herself that she should face Crusher rather than another news conference. "Okay. I reserve the right to refuse to answer any particular question, and in any case we will have to stop in time for the two o'clock meeting. Go ahead."

"Yes, ma'am. I'll start with this. I was leaving night court about the same time you were, and I saw the argument you were having with your husband. I don't care if you argue with your husband or not, but that got written up in the gossip column, and if you want to have a chance to put your own version of the story out there, tell me."

Nan hadn't expected that question from a sports reporter, and she didn't want to say anything at all. Should she duck that question, or was this going to be the best chance she would have to reply? Tricky matter. "Crusher, I am a happily married woman." Nan looked him intently in the eye. "Do I look like a happily married woman?"

Crusher Morgenstern met her gaze and fixed his own gaze upon Nan for 30 seconds. "Yes, ma'am. You do."

"Let that be my answer. People will believe you before they believe me."

"Yes, ma'am. Now let's talk about that night court case from last evening. There were four lawyers for the defense. I talked to two of them, and they say they had been put on the case by Mr. Rudolf in one case, by the hospital in another, and by you and your husband in the third. That's in addition to the lawyer that the family hired. Then

I heard that at least one other lawyer was there but never got to the defense table by the time the case was called. Why did all you people send lawyers?"

"I can only speak for myself and for my husband. This all happened so quickly we didn't have time to find out if Sanjar had his own family lawyer, and we didn't want to take a chance, so we sent our lawyer. The others did the same thing. So we don't look very coordinated, I'm afraid."

Crusher took some notes in his little notebook, looked up, and said to Nan, "Reporters get thrown in the can all the time, so there is a standing procedure for the union and for the newspaper or TV station to get a lawyer organized. I don't suppose that happens very often with hospital staffers."

"No, I am happy to say it does not. We get sued all the time for malpractice, so we know how to defend against that, but we don't get into many criminal cases. Happily."

"Okay, another subject. What happened with Hank Powers and the air filters?"

"You should talk to Hank or Susan Gunn. What I hear is that when his people looked at the actual filters and piping or whatever they call it, they decided that it was physically impossible to do what Hank had done on paper, or on his PC. So it was a false alarm. That's fine. Better those than a real alarm. They are working through all the other combinations with Hank's staff and their architect engineer contractor. But don't take my word for it."

"Does it bother you that you have been responsible for some false alarms this week? The air filter thing and the cell phone thing come to mind."

Nan thought about that. It was a good question, one she had been trying to formulate in her own mind. Crusher had gotten right to the point.

"No, Crusher, I am not bothered by it. We deal in life and death here. Things that might be minor or negligible in another kind of business might kill somebody here. So we have to react quickly and decisively to minor things. What I am saying is there are no minor things around here, because even a little thing like an air filter is a life-and-death matter.

"As for the cell phone flap, I don't know that that was a false alarm. I know that nobody died. That's good. Nobody had a cardiac episode, and that's good, too. Maybe our actions prevented something untoward from happening, maybe not. I couldn't just hope for the best, I had to act. So did the medical staff and the administrative staff. I stand by our collective decisions."

"Okay, I'll buy that. A lot of people my size have heart problems, so it might have been me walking around with a pacemaker that day. So, I see merit in what you did.

"Now, tell me something about Sanjar Subramaniam. He works for Rudy Rudolf, but you seem to have some connection or attachment to him."

Nan nodded to gain a little time, and then she said, "Yes. Sanjar was assigned to my department until recently, when he was promoted. He is a gifted young man, and I was happy to see him promoted.

"If you are wondering if my husband and I would have sent our own lawyer into a case involving some nurse or manager in my department or some person in another department who is assigned to me, I am looking you in the eye and telling you we would have done the same thing. I will say something else. Sanjar can look out for himself, He's an educated person with a good salary and, I suppose, some financial resources. If he had been an orderly in my department or a nurse trainee, I would have done the same thing. That's my line and I am sticking to it."

Crusher looked at Nan. Then he wrote in his little notebook. "Yes, I think you would. Not just because you're you, but that's the way it is with junior reporters, too. Any reporter tossed in jail gets the same support, whether we'd drink a beer with him after work or not.

"There's one other thing that makes me believe you. I know Marcy, and I know you would never see another chocolate chip cookie the rest of your life."

They both laughed.

Nan said to him, "Crusher, I wouldn't want to have to do battle with you, and I would surrender in a second before I would ever do battle with Marcy."

They both laughed again.

Crusher said, "Tell me one last thing. How are the suits handling things this week? It's been hectic for me, and I am just a spectator."

"Mr. Crawford is the hospital's chief operating officer. I am sure this week has been more than hectic for him. I think he does a fine job. He puts a lot of trust in his department heads, and we try to respond by doing things in ways that are a credit to him and to the hospital and the board. Look at it this way. Mr. Crawford is not a medical doctor or a nurse, so he cannot have any more insight into our patient care than any other concerned civilian. Those of us who are specialists have to accept that nobody is going to be able to get us out of a jam if we get ourselves into one. So, we avoid jams. That's how we repay Mr. Crawford and the board for the trust they place in us."

Crusher looked at Nan for a full minute, tapping himself on the lip with his pencil, a pencil that looked extra tiny in his powerful hand.

47

The Dénouement

At the stroke of two, Marcy knocked lightly and opened the door. Marcy ushered Jerry Miller into Nan's office. Crusher rose and introduced himself. Crusher indicated a chair to Jerry, who accepted the chair and seated himself. Jerry Miller was on the side of the small table away from the door, Crusher was on the door-side of the table. Nan was between her desk and the table.

Crusher began: "Mr. Miller, I would like to ask you some questions about the week's developments. Is that all right?"

Jerry nodded after looking at both Crusher and then Nan.

Crusher continued. "If you give me your business card, I'll be sure to spell your name right." Jerry dug his wallet from his hip pocket and produced a business card to give to Crusher. He gave a second card to Nan, who thanked him.

Crusher stuck the business card into his small notebook and started again. "Let's start with recent events. Were you at the court proceedings last evening?"

Jerry said, "No."

Crusher scribbled something in his notebook and said, "That surprises me. There was a pretty good crowd, and you were working with Sanjar Subramaniam, weren't you?"

"I was working with him because my company is the outside consultant to the hospital, yes. I was as surprised as anybody that Sanjar was arrested yesterday. It didn't occur to me to go to the court last evening, although I was as interested as anybody else in what was going on."

Crusher asked, "Did you believe that Sanjar had committed arson?"

"No, that never occurred to me. I was shocked when I heard it."

Crusher continued, "Let's go back another day or two. You went to that telephone company building earlier in the week with Sanjar and some other people, did you not?"

"Yes, I was there along with three or four other people."

"You saw where the cables all came into the building in one spot, the spot that was to be set afire the next day?"

"Yes, I saw that. So did everybody else who was there and maybe a lot of other people, since it was in plain sight once you knew where to look."

"Do you know where the thumbprint was found?"

"No, not exactly. I gather it was someplace near the cable bundles."

"When you were there with the others, did you see any way that an arsonist could get at those bundles and set a fire?"

"I wasn't thinking about fire."

"Well, you certainly knew about the fire in the manhole Sunday night, and you knew that the purpose of the trip to the telephone office was to check for vulnerability of that network, didn't you? How could you not be thinking about fire?"

Jerry Miller was looking at the table, then at Crusher, then back at the table. His hands were on the table, closed and flexing nervously. Jerry was a normal-sized adult, but Crusher had an enormous presence. "When you put it that way, yes, I was thinking about fire in general, but I wasn't thinking about how to set a fire there."

Crusher leaned forward a little. "You weren't? I would have thought everybody in the group would be thinking exactly that, how somebody might set another fire.

"But let me put it differently so that we don't just repeat ourselves here. Did you notice anybody paying particular attention to how a fire might be started there?"

Jerry Miller nodded. "Sanjar. He was pointing out to the others in the group how vulnerable the cables were in one particular section and how easy it would be for a bad guy to get at them. I did not take that to mean he was planning on setting a fire but rather he was trying to get the telephone engineer to admit that something ought to be done to improve the protection of the cables right there.

"After all, if Sanjar was going to set a fire there, he wouldn't have been calling attention to it, would he?"

Crusher did not answer Jerry's question but instead posed another of his own. "Let's jump all the way back to the beginning, say a month ago. Sanjar asked you or your company to help with checking the external infrastructure, is that right? Were you assigned to the task or did you volunteer or what?"

"I was assigned. I am the junior man in our group, so the clunky stuff tends to come my way. It looked like a dead waste of time to me, then. I told my boss so. He said something to the effect that he thought so, too, but since we bill on an hourly basis, he didn't much care what we were asked to do, he just wanted the meter running. I can see that from a business perspective, but I thought there were more worthwhile things to be doing than that."

Crusher continued, "But you didn't refuse, you just groused for a while and then did as you were asked?"

"Yes, that's right. I could see I wasn't getting anywhere with my boss, and Sanjar seemed to have his mind made up. Maybe he knew something I didn't know then."

"Did he tell you he knew something?"

"No, he just stuck to his position that we should check this stuff out because the consequences of a multiple outage could have been severe. So I went along for the ride."

"When you found those data networks running through that single manhole and tunnel, did you change your mind?"

Jerry brightened up, for the first time. "You bet. I was shocked to find that two contractors had insisted they were independent from one another but had actually subcontracted in such a way that they were both running in the same tunnel and conduit. They were surprised, too, but they were just surprised. I was shocked."

"How did Sanjar take it?"

"He is sort of inscrutable, so I don't know that I can say. He was animated, I guess I would say. He didn't make a fuss. He just made sure we all agreed that we had found a common link where there should have been none, thanked everybody, and said he would call the attention of his management to the issue."

Crusher made some notes and continued. "What did you do yourself?"

"I went back to my office and told my boss about it. I was quite upset about the shoddy work and wanted to get us on the side of righteousness. So I told my boss and I followed it up with a memo to him with times and places and even some snapshots I had taken with my digital camera."

"Tell me what your boss had to say."

Jerry remained excited, getting a little red in the face. "He sort of blew it off. Check the Internet for other manhole fires, he said. Write a paper. I don't know what his problem was, but he sure didn't pick up on the significance of what we found. You'd think particularly for a manager in a consultancy like ours, he would have at least seen that we could scare all our other clients into hiring us to do surveys of their networks. But he didn't seem very interested. I guess he figured it was small potatoes, not a hazard by itself but only if a fire or flood came along to wipe out both circuits at the same time. That was before the fire, of course."

Have you seen your boss since the manhole fire?"

"Yes, I saw him the next day, Monday that would be. He was all upset, worrying about liability. The first thing he told me was to erase my memo about the common link from my computer files and to burn any paper copies. I thought that was stupid, because others had been there to see the same things I had seen, and erasing files smacked of guilt, and I hadn't done anything. I didn't have anything to hide. Maybe he did, my boss, but not me."

"So, did you erase your computer files?"

"No, that's a fool's errand. The computer system keeps backups of everything anyway, so it is impossible for any user like me to get everything erased. So I just ignored him."

"Did you talk to anybody else at your company?"

"That's another thing. Yes, I had talked to all the other engineers in my group before the fire, telling them about the commonality, so it would have been extra stupid to erase files and pretend that it hadn't happened."

"After the fire, did you talk to other managers of your company?"

"Sort of, The big boss saw me across the room and nodded in my direction on Monday as he was going into my boss's office, closing the door behind him. Then there was a memo from the big boss saying that there would be an internal investigation and everybody should preserve all files and documents. That would really have put me in the meat grinder if I had followed my boss's instructions an hour before that. So I just sat on my hands and waited for the axe to fall or the mill wheel to grind or whatever."

Crusher changed subjects. "Tell me about thermite."

Jerry had cooled off again. "Thermite is a mixture of chemicals that burns rapidly when ignited. Anybody can make it from household chemicals. We did it in high school chemistry class. I don't remember the formula exactly but it must be in lots of chemistry books. It burns hot. It doesn't explode, it just burns hot. It flashes and burns. I mean millions of boys and I suppose that many girls know that much about thermite. It is very common stuff. Let me say it differently. There are 10,000 high school chemistry teachers who know how to make it, and I suppose there are industrial companies making it for commercial uses. That's a guess; I am not a chemical engineer. Well, you asked, and that's what I know about thermite."

Crusher continued on the same line. "So somebody with a little bit of chemistry awareness could make it up or buy it commercially?"

"Yes, make it up. I suppose it could be bought commercially but I don't know that for sure. There may be military applications, too, but I don't know anything about that. I am just speculating about that."

Crusher changed tacks. "Tell me about the engineers from the networking companies who were with you and Sanjar when you all discovered this common manhole. How did they take the discovery?"

"They thought it was a joke. Big laugh. Ah, shucks, we got that messed up. Heck of a funny story. They didn't even bother to blame each other, they just laughed about it."

"How did that strike Sanjar?"

"I don't know. He's sort of formal and standoffish. He didn't yell at anybody the way I would have."

"Did you yell at them?"

"Well, no, I figured it wasn't my place. I was plenty burned up about their attitude, though, and I said a few things about professional responsibility, but I don't think it sunk in. "

"Tell me, Mr. Miller, about faking fingerprints. Would you know how to go about that?"

"I guess everybody who watches television spy shows or murder mysteries knows something about that. You get the pigeon to hold a Coke can or a water glass, and then you use cellophane tape to lift off the print and put it down somewhere else. No secret in that. I am speaking theoretically, of course. This is just common knowledge. Anybody can do that with a little practice, I'd guess."

"Let's suppose you had wanted to steal Sanjar's thumbprint. Would you have had occasion to do what you just said?"

"Sure. We were together quite a bit over several days, and we had lunch together and had hit the soft drink machine together more than once. The same is true the other way around, if Sanjar had wanted to steal my prints. The same for the network engineers, we were all thrown together for several days. Or my boss could have stolen my prints if he had gotten up enough initiative to do that. "

"I used to wrestle, Mr. Miller, as you may already know. I'm used to being around angry men, and while professional wrestling is mostly showmanship, if somebody gets mad, a wrestler can get hurt, big time. So I learned to pay attention when the other guy was starting to get angry. I'm pretty big, but I've wrestled men a lot bigger than I am, guys who could pick me up and throw me against the ring post if they felt like it. So in my line, I developed a certain sensitivity to anger in other men just to stay alive.

"I'm telling you that because I see anger in you."

Crusher went silent. He had not exactly asked a question, so Jerry Miller did not offer an answer. Not right away. Instead, he sat there and stared at the table and flexed his hands.

Nan sat absolutely still, not wanting to be noticed by either of the men. She willed herself to be invisible.

Silence. Thirty seconds. A minute. Another minute. Crusher sat quietly, looking at Jerry Miller. Jerry stared at the table and flexed his fists. He was working his jaw, too.

48

Lights Out

The lights went out.

The room went dark but not exactly black. There was a blue glow from the PC screen on Nan's desk that provided a little illumination to the room, enough to see by, once eyes became adjusted.

Nan listened carefully. There was no sound of panic in the outer office or hallway. No phones were ringing. It was very quiet. No rush of air in the air conditioning. Still.

Then there was light under the door. The battery-backed hallway lamps had come on. Nan could feel that the power backup systems were coming alive.

Her PC was on its own battery backup thing under the desk, so it never lost power. The hall emergency lighting had its own battery right with the lamps themselves.

Had the vital circuits come up with diesel power?

Yes! Nan could tell because the little lights on her telephone desk set had come back on. Her desk was on the vital bus, mostly so that her PC would not lose power, even though the PC also had a battery backup. Right then, Nan was in favor of all the belts and suspenders anyone could think of.

If her desk had vital power, at least one of the diesel generators had started up. Thank God, Nan thought. Life and death depended on those diesels and all those switches and controls and other things.

It was over in less than five minutes. The room lights came back on, and Nan could hear fans starting in the air conditioning system and air rushing into the room.

Nan wanted to call Hank Powers to get an instant report from the field, but she knew better than to do it. Hank would take care of it, and whatever Hank learned from this experience would be plowed into the design of the new diesels and switches and cables and things to make the hospital even more immune to accidents in the electrical grid.

Nan decided to wait 10 minutes and then call every unit to get a report. She could hold out for 10 minutes, she thought, clenching her fists.

Back to the immediate. With the room lights back on, Nan could see that Jerry Miller was now pinned to the wall. Crusher, perhaps inadvertently, had shoved the table into Jerry during the lights-out emergency. Jerry was not crushed, just pinned. Had Crusher made sure Jerry didn't leave while the lights were out?

Crusher was staring intently at Jerry Miller. Jerry was returning the stare, a little bug-eyed.

After a long while, Crusher said to Jerry, fixing him with his gaze, "Mr. Miller, I believe you set that manhole fire to get people and particularly your boss to pay attention to the hazard that that common link posed. I don't think you meant to catch a car in the fire because you set the fire in the middle of the night when there should have been no traffic. So I don't say you hurt those people on purpose, you just set the manhole fire on purpose. Then when you discovered that people had been hurt, you set the second fire and faked Sanjar's thumbprint at the telephone office to deflect attention away from yourself. I don't know if you thought Sanjar would beat the rap or not, but I think you figured you had to do something to lay a false trail for the police."

Jerry Miller said nothing.

Crusher continued: "I don't think you meant any harm. I don't think you set out to be a criminal. I don't think you hold any malice toward Sanjar. You got angry and things got out of hand.

"I don't think you make a very good criminal. You're never going to hold out under police interrogation, and you know you want to come clean and get it over with. If I figured this out, the police certainly have, or will shortly.

"So here's what we are going to do. You and I are going to walk outside. My camera crew is out there on the front lawn. We're going to turn the cameras on, and you are going to make a statement to the cameras. Then I will ask you a few questions if things need to be clarified, but I will just be there to help you tell your story. No hassle, no cross-examination. Just your story.

"After that, I'll drive you down to the police station, where you can put it all in writing. The police won't hassle you. They'll help you get a public defender if you don't have a family lawyer. You can make a phone call, and if you give me a list of people to call, I'll call them for you.

"Let's go."

Crusher stood up, pulling the table a little in his own direction so that Jerry could stand. Jerry pushed the table a little more and walked around the table to stand by Crusher.

Jerry said, "Yes, let's go."

Crusher and Jerry left. Nan stood and followed them out the door, staying a few steps behind. Nan stopped by Marcy's desk. Marcy was there, typing something on her computer keyboard, or more likely faking it. Seated on the other side of Marcy's desk on a visitor's chair, and eating a chocolate chip cookie, was the chief of detectives, Stan Laurel. Stan nodded to Nan.

Nothing was said. Nan did not ask if the intercom had been open during Crusher's interview of Jerry Miller, and she certainly didn't want to know if the intercom had been open when Crusher was interviewing her. So, no questions.

After a few minutes, and after Crusher and Jerry Miller had gone a good distance down the hallway, heading for the main door, Stan Laurel rose, nodded to both women, finished off his cookie, and started down the hall. After two or three steps, he turned around and said, "I'll just make sure he gets downtown okay. No hassle. We'll just ask him to write down whatever he says to the television cameras so that we'll have a record. We'll get him a lawyer if his company doesn't have one lined up.

"This time, Mrs. Mills, there won't be any question about who solved the crime. Crusher may get the credit, and that's important in his line of work, but my guess is that he will be telling the whole story, including your part.

"We would have gotten Jerry Miller in another day or so. You and Crusher saved us a little time, and that's fine. We're always glad to have the help.

"And I am glad to have a reason to stop by for a chocolate chip cookie."

Stan Laurel smiled, gave a little salute to Nan and Marcy, and continued on his way.

49

The Soirée

Nan and Jack took their time about getting ready for the block party for Maggie Kelly, being more comfortable in each other's presence than had been the case the previous evening. More than comfortable.

No information had been provided about the style of the block party, so Nan figured that informal clothes would be the right choice. She selected a midcalf full skirt in a dark blue with a subdued pattern and a lighter blue blouse with long sleeves. Minimum jewelry. Jack went for black denim trousers and a western-cut light blue shirt.

Jack drove. When they got near the clinic, they found a man waving a flashlight to direct them to a parking slot in a strip shopping mall. The block party organizers had seized one block, hung festive lanterns over the street, and roped off a dance floor in the street. There was a little platform for a band, which was already playing polka music. The band members were six in number, with that many very large beer tankards at hand. They had a tuba, a clarinet, an accordion, and two trumpets. The other musician didn't seem to have an instrument but was clapping and marking time with one booted foot. They were festive, setting the mood for the entire throng.

Susan Gunn waved to them as they approached, signaling them to go to an area where a few folding tables had been set up, close enough to the dance floor but not encroaching on the festivities. Susan shook hands with Jack and seated them at one of the tables.

Susan explained, "Hank Powers did a nose count and decided that there would be about this many hospital people here this evening. He is in charge of safety, among other things, so he decided it would be safer for you if he brought folding tables from the hospital. And I mean safer for you, Nan. He doesn't care about me or anybody else. He figures you're vital."

Nan happily discovered that Hank had provided padded folding chairs, too, which figured to be a blessing if the evening ran on, as it showed every sign of doing.

Just as Nan and Jack were getting to the table, Rudy Rudolf and his wife were being steered to the same table. Nan had shaken hands with Mrs. Rudolf once at some hospital function, but Jack had not met her before, so Rudy made introductions. "Jack and Nan Mills, I present to you my wife, Ruby. Ruby, here are Nan and Jack Mills." Smiles and handshakes.

As near as Nan could figure it, Ruby and Rudy were dressed in the style of Parisian Apache dancers. Rudy was in black from head to toe, wearing a long-sleeved black sweater with a turtleneck collar and a small-billed cap in black leather that looked like something out of a 1930s movie. He had a blue bandana around his neck. Ruby wore a black sweater, black tights, a crimson leather skirt that hardly reached to midthigh, a wide belt, and a crimson bandana to match the skirt. Ruby's outfit and makeup accented her dark eyes and hair.

At the table there was one other person, who introduced herself as Maggie Kelly's mother-in-law, Wanda Szyvczyk. She seemed to be a pleasant person of middle years, dressed in black. Nan knew vaguely that lots of women of European traditions dressed in black if they were widows, and some dressed in black from the day they were married. That seemed like a question not to ask.

They all found small water glasses in front of them, along with sturdy plates and flatware. Nan wondered if they had come from the hospital too, and she decided she would be no richer if she knew.

No sooner were they seated than a man of substantial girth and not much hair, wearing a green apron, was there to fill their glasses from an unlabeled bottle. Better be careful with this home-brew stuff, thought Nan, although if that man had been drinking the same stuff, it had certainly put him in a good mood.

Somebody hollered "Skål!" and all glasses were raised. Nan faked drinking from the glass, and she looked out the side of her eye to see if Jack was doing the same. He was. So, Nan figured since she wasn't driving, she could at least taste the stuff to see what the locals found drinkable. She took a sip from the glass. Just that tiny sip filled her entire mouth and then her entire head with sensation. One sip was going to be enough of that stuff. It had a good flavor, something between licorice and caraway, maybe. Well, she was not going to do any more sipping just to get a fix on the flavor.

The band stopped, at which point Nan realized how loud the music had been. She saw Cash and Maggie working their way from the dance floor. Cash was dressed in sort of a western style, more or less the way Jack was. Maggie was something to see. She had her strikingly red hair done up in braids, with the braids wrapped up and over the crown of her head like a Swiss milkmaid, and she was wearing a white peasant blouse and a white full skirt that was heavily embroidered with flowers in bright colors. Nan knew that Maggie's braids were an added attraction, since Maggie cut her hair above the collar, which caused Nan to wonder if Maggie had actually found artificial braids to match her red hair, or if she had tinted her own hair just a little to match the braids. Either way, it worked. Do Swiss milkmaids have red hair? If not, they should.

Maggie was clearly excited and pleased to see them all at her table. "Oh, look at me!" Maggie cried with delight. She did a twirl to give everyone the full effect of her outfit. "Isn't this beautiful? Cash's mother made this for herself when she was a teenager, and she spent all this afternoon pinning it up for me." Maggie beamed at her mother-in-law.

Wanda Szyvczyk blushed a little and said to them, "In my day in the Old Country, if a girl wanted a party dress, she made it herself. And a man wanted to see a little meat on the bones of any prospective wife. We were not so skinny as American girls are today." She found that to be all the funnier in her telling of it, so she had a good laugh, which infected everyone else at the table so that they all joined in.

Rudy introduced Ruby to Maggie and Cash.

Maggie continued at a high level of enthusiasm, "I've danced five polkas already, with about 30 different men. They formed a line to cut in on each other after about five seconds. I wore my nurse's shoes." Maggie held up one foot for all to see. "I didn't think I'd last another evening with ballet slippers."

Cash spoke up. "Jack, I know you do software. Since we are moving to Maggie's new headquarters city, I'll be looking for work. I sort of had it in mind to ask you this evening, if we saw each other, for any contacts you might have there. But as it happens, Rudy got my résumé from Maggie on Wednesday, made a couple of phone calls, and got me interviews there already. One of the companies called and did a telephone interview, and they offered me a good job, sight unseen."

Cash told Rudy, "Thanks, buddy. Prost!" Cash tipped up his glass, but Nan noticed that the glass was just as full when he put it down as when he had picked it up.

Rudy replied with a smile and tipped up his own glass. "Glad to be of service to the nursing corps, because your success is ours and mine as well. Let me know when you're hiring up there, because I'm in a line of work that has a lot of turnover."

That got an appropriate laugh from all quarters.

The polka band had left the stage, and another group had ascended to it. This was a different bunch entirely, made up with pirate-style bandanas and open-necked shirts. They were armed with a zither, a violin, a concertina, and one other instrument that Nan couldn't make out. They launched into a haunting melody.

Ruby Rudolf, who was seated next to Jack, put her hand on his and said, "Jack, you must try Gypsy dancing." She lowered her head just a little so that she was looking at him with her large dark eyes from under her dark brows, Nan could see that Ruby had captivating eyes. "Come, I'll teach you," which sounded like "Come, Eye veel titch ewe." Ruby took a rose from the vase on the table, put the long stem between her teeth, and looked at Jack with sparkling eyes.

Ruby led Jack off to the dance floor, where a few others were assembling in something like a ring, joining hands and telling each other how to proceed. Ruby took charge and had everybody following her orders.

Nan spoke to Rudy, "Rudy, I didn't know your wife is an immigrant."

"She's not. She was born about six blocks from here. She turns that accent off and on like a faucet. She is a Gypsy though, at least her great-grandparents were Gypsies. That's where she gets that dark coloring. I don't know if she knows any more than those other yard birds up there about Gypsy dancing, but she has an authoritative approach to such matters. If they believe it's Gypsy dancing, then it's Gypsy dancing."

Nan found that hilarious. "Does Ruby have a crystal ball to tell fortunes? Does she steal babies? Does she keep goats?"

"She has a crystal ball but she makes up the fortunes out of whole cloth. I don't think she steals babies, and the first goat she brings home will be the last."

Wanda Szyvczyk joined in the conversation, looking a little more serious at this moment, "You Americans can laugh about Gypsies, but it was different in the old country. The Gypsies were treated very badly in many countries. Hitler tried to kill them all with his gas ovens. So you should be happy that your wife's family got away from all that. Otherwise, no wife."

That put a damper on things, so Cash interjected, "Hey, Mamma, we are all in America now. Leave that old-country stuff alone. Here we all try to get along, and let's just enjoy the evening while we have it. We'll all be Gypsies for a while, and then we can go dance the polka again. You're going to dance a polka with me, aren't you, Mamma?" Cash picked up two spoons and tapped them on the table to augment the music from the Gypsy ensemble.

Two teenage girls brought two big dishes of food. One was clearly potato salad; the other one not so easy to categorize. Maybe a casserole. Plates were passed to Wanda Szyvczyk, who piled helpings on each and passed them along. Not much chance of being skinny in this neighborhood, Nan thought. Well, there's comfort in food, and this is a good evening to be comfortable.

The Gypsy band finished playing, and Ruby and Jack returned to the table.

Jack gave his report: "I think I came out ahead. I stepped on other people's feet more often than they stepped on mine. And I only fell down once, if you don't count the other times."

Ruby laughed along with him. "As a dancer, Jack, you should maybe stick to your software."

The evening moved along. A steady parade of gentlemen came along to invite Wanda and Maggie to dance. Some of them seemed to wonder if they could, or should, ask Ruby or Nan to dance, but in the end none of them did.

After about an hour, the bands took a break, and someone played phonograph records, not polkas but regular ballroom dance music and popular music. Nan thought about dragging Jack out onto the floor for a waltz or a foxtrot, but in the end she decided not to. Jack would have gone willingly, but will wasn't the issue. Jack, who had a gigantic mind and a fantastic memory, was incapable of remembering a dance step for even a minute. Over the years, Nan had given up. Nan did dance once with Rudy, and that was enough for an evening.

Then the deejay put on a western tune and called for people to come forward to do a line dance. Ruby was on her feet, pulling on Jack's arm and exhorting everybody at the table to get up and dance. Nan, Rudy, Jack, Ruby, Cash, and Maggie joined in. Wanda begged off. Ruby asserted that she knew all the steps and would provide instruction on the fly. She certainly provided instruction, and she may have known the steps. She soon had everybody on the dance floor following her lead. Calamity was avoided, and after the song had ended, the group returned to their table in even higher spirits. Ruby was an animateuse of the first water.

Back at the table, Nan refused more helpings of food and faked her way through several more toasts, enjoying the warm and pleasant evening.

Eventually, Rudy and Jack went off to find some place where they could make a contribution to the cost of the shindig, which the locals appeared to be reluctant to accept. The locals were more interested in making sure that their guests had had ample opportunities to sample the homemade refreshments.

The polka band came back and struck up a tune. Dancers gathered on the dance floor. Nan noticed Crusher Morgenstern, easy to pick out in any crowd. He was dancing with a woman, but the difference in their sizes was so great that Crusher was actually carrying his partner on his right arm. Nan pointed that out to Ruby Rudolph, who had taken Jack's seat when Jack and Rudy had gone off.

Ruby explained. "That's Crusher's wife. She used to be big in gymnastics. You know how tiny girl gymnasts are; she's about 4-foot-9. She took a nasty fall from the parallel bars and smashed her lower back on one of the stanchions. That was maybe a year ago. She's been in therapy ever since, and it's not clear if she is ever going to walk again. I know the story because I am a physical therapist myself, and everybody in the PT field around here is following her progress. For us it's a famous case."

That brought a frown of concern and sympathy to every brow. Nan looked around and found Josey Walberg sitting at one of the tables. Next to her was a sports-model wheelchair.

As the number ended, the whole table watched as Crusher carried his wife back to their table and seated her gently. Then, as the band struck up another polka, Crusher escorted Josey to the dance floor, where they made a sprightly couple. Josey was tiny beside Crusher, so she was well up on her toes. Crusher proved to be quite light on his feet, which Nan figured to be the result of his years in wrestling.

Nan wondered if the gym accident was the real reason for Crusher changing careers, looking for something that didn't require travel away from home the way pro wrestling must. Tough break for the young couple. Maybe she should ask Josey or Marcy. Or maybe she should leave it alone.

Jack and Rudy came back, The evening wore on, and the tone of the music changed again from polka to popular. The crowd had changed, too, with younger people making up the population. That seemed to be a good time to go, so Nan and Jack hugged Maggie and Cash, shook hands with everybody in sight, and headed for the parking lot. Jack drove them home.

While they were making the short trek, Nan thought about the week, which had gone by like a kaleidoscope. Fires. Television. Rudy coming out of his shell. Susan Gunn, too. New friends in Josey and Crusher. New management policies to get going next week. Maybe even summer jobs for the twins. Her slush fund; no, her two slush funds. Nan rested her eyes. I can't complain of boredom, she thought to herself. What's more, I know what's important in life. She leaned over against her seat belt and put her head on Jack's shoulder, grasping his arm in both of hers.

50

Voice Mail

When they got into the house, Nan saw the little light on the telephone flashing. In her line of work, and with two kids off at college, voice messages had to be attended to. She hadn't taken her pager with her to the soirée, which was a departure from her normal mode of operations, so this might be something important, even life or death.

Hoping for the best, Nan hit the playback button. There was only one message.

It was the voice of Philip L. Crawford, the hospital's chief operating officer and Nan's boss. Nan couldn't remember any other time that Crawford had called her at home.

The message was brief. "Nan, this is Phil Crawford. Something has come up. Please come to my office first thing Monday morning. No, wait. If you can fit it in, come over to my house Sunday afternoon. Bring Jack along. We can watch the ball game, and then you and I can talk. I need your help."

Well, Nan thought. What can that mean?

Nan hurried to their bedroom, realizing that Jack had gone that way as soon as they got home. Nan thought the red nightgown would be right—demure, but not overly so. As she entered the bedroom, she heard Jack humming in the shower. She kicked off her shoes and yanked her blouse open, sending buttons flying. The red nightgown could wait.

An Afterword on Six Sigma

The Nan series takes a building block approach to Six Sigma because individual readers and small groups of readers can apply Nan's lessons themselves to good effect. Sound task design, robust communications, training, and retraining are solid building blocks that can stand on their own, contributing to better healthcare delivery.

Getting to the middle level requires support of middle management. What medical protocols should this institution adopt to the exclusion of others? What should it do with physicians who decline to conform to the institution's standards? What hospital practices, often called clinical pathways, are to be followed? What happens if they are not followed? How are these practices to be made robust with double checks, buffer states, and conformance tracking? How are patients to be scheduled through capital-intensive scanners with an eye not only to best use of assets but also of consideration of the patient's time? What problem-solving techniques work in situations as complex as healthcare, particularly when the incidence of adverse events is rare but the consequences can be severe?

The top level requires commitment from the top management. How is the organization to conform to the patient's objectives? Indeed, what are the patient's objectives? How is the organization's performance to be measured against the patient's objectives?

The Nan series gets to all of these.

The best known cases of Six Sigma application in industry and now in healthcare start at the top. Starting at the top is the best way to get everybody's attention, and there is much to be said for this approach. Starting at the top does not remove the need to address all the building blocks eventually, and so it is not clear yet that starting at the top gets to the finish line any sooner. It provides a faster start, certainly.

Six Sigma has something useful to say at the bottom level, the middle level, and the top level. Six Sigma even has something useful to contribute to the next major phase of healthcare evolution, which is getting the patient with a chronic condition to do a more robust job of self-care.*

Fundamentally, Six Sigma is a management attitude, an attitude asserting that much better performance can be achieved, starting right now, and that mediocre peformance is over with. Six Sigma reinforces that attitude by providing visibility into operations, by transforming the patient's external objectives into the organization's internal performance requirements and measures, with visibility provided to all levels of management.

It's not that healthcare organizations don't know how to treat a patient. They do. But, they do fail to perform well at each task for each patient. The job at hand is to reinforce the right things being done and to eliminate the incidence and consequences of things that are not right. Consistency is doing the right thing, rightly.

That's a journey of many steps, whether started at the top or at the bottom or maybe even in the middle. Six Sigma makes a contribution.

For readers who want to plunge in, there are a number of useful texts on Six Sigma, some of which are cited in the bibliography. The principal author of the first book listed is the author of this present book.

---

*Laura Landro. "Dose of Prevention: Six Prescriptions to Ease Rationing in U.S. Health Care." *Wall Street Journal,* December 22, 2003.

Bibliography

Barry, R. F., A. C. Murcko, and C. E. Brubaker, *The Six Sigma Book for Healthcare: Improving Outcomes by Reducing Error.* Milwaukee: ASQ Quality Press,* 2002. ISBN 1-56793-191-X.
This is a textbook written for a nonspecialist audience, focusing entirely on healthcare applications and covering a range of topics from task design to workflow, tracking charts, and statistical methods. Suitable for Six Sigma Green Belt and Black Belt training classes.

Chowdhury, Subir. *The Power of Six Sigma.* Detroit: Dearborn Trade Publishing, 2001. ISBN 0-7931-4434-5.
This is an introductory conversational book for a nontechnical audience. The author has written extensively on Six Sigma, particularly for the automotive industry.

Barry, Robert. *Nan: A Six Sigma Mystery.* Milwaukee: ASQ Quality Press, 2004. ISBN 0-87389-612-2.
The first book in the Nan series. Nan becomes head nurse and finds two mysterious deaths in her hospital. Nan teaches Six Sigma and solves the mysteries.

Blazey, Mark L., Paul Grizzell, Linda Janczak, and Joel Ettinger. *Insights to Performance Excellence in Health Care 2003: An Inside Look at the 2003 Baldrige Award Criteria for Health Care.* Milwaukee: ASQ Quality Press, 2003. ISBN 0-87389-580-0.
One of a series of books by these authors on the prestigious Baldrige awards in health care and in other fields, reporting on what the winners are doing right.

---

*Copublished by the Health Administration Press, which is an activity of the American College of Healthcare Executives.

Index